Plum Blossoms in a Golden Vase

Revised Second Edition

Volume 1 of 5

The Brawn Brothers

Author: Lanling Xiaoxiao Sheng
Translator: Eugene Ying
Editor: Victor Ying

ISBN 978-1-944545-53-6

Contents

Preface

The Chinese have always considered the number four a complete number since time immemorial. According to Chinese folklore, the universe contains the Four Symbols, and the sky is guarded by four celestial kings. Within the four corners of the world are the four continents and four oceans, and China was historically surrounded by four barbarian tribes. It would be difficult, if not impossible, for any ladies to be prettier than the Four Beauties, and all scholars should study the Four Books throughout all four seasons. The Four Great Classic Novels of China are universally considered timeless literary treasures, and we have translated them, as well as three other critically acclaimed classic Chinese novels, into English. The following are brief descriptions of our translations of those seven masterpieces of Chinese historical fiction:

- *Marsh Warrior Legend* 水浒传 *(Shuǐ Hǔ Zhuàn)* by Shi Nai'an 施耐庵 (1296-1372)

  The most famous novel on Chinese martial arts and brotherhood ever published, *Shui Hu Zhuan* has previously been translated by others under different titles, including *Outlaws of the Marsh* and *Water Margin*. Set in feudal China, its plot is based on 108 virtuous warriors who join forces to save their country from corruption and injustice. Unlike many other fictional martial arts sagas, this 700-year-old historical novel is based on real-life characters and describes battles and other events that actually took place. However, the author spices up the story by depicting the 108 warriors as reincarnations of the former inhabitants of 36 stars and 72 planets of the Little Dipper, and their leader as a native of Polaris. The first 80 chapters of *Marsh Warrior Legend* describe the exciting adventures and battles of the 36 stellar warriors and 72 planetary warriors, while the final 40 chapters describe the four military campaigns those warriors launch as a 108-membered team.

- *Three Kingdom Epic* 三国演义 *(Sānguó Yǎnyì)* by Luo Guanzhong 罗贯中 (1330-1400)

  This is the most famous Chinese novel on military strategy and loyalty that has ever been published, and it has previously been translated by others under different titles, including

Three Kingdoms and *Romance of the Three Kingdoms*. Set between the years 180 C.E. and 280 C.E. during the collapse of the Han dynasty, its plot is based on true historical events embellished with interesting folklore. Many warlords of that period tried to take over the country by recruiting intelligent advisors and fierce warriors who came out of the woodwork. Since history repeats itself, many battles of wits described in *Three Kingdom Epic* apply to the modern business world, as well as to the daily struggles of people from all walks of life.

- *Journey to the Western Sky* 西游记 *(Xī Yóu Jì)* by Wu Cheng'en 吴承恩 (1500-1580)

The most famous Chinese adventure and fantasy novel ever published, *Xi You Ji* is based on a historical event that took place in the year 629 C.E. when a Buddhist Monk named Xuanzang went on a 17-year journey to India to obtain 657 Buddhist scrolls written in Sanskrit. The Silk Road he traveled took him through Kyrgyzstan, Uzbekistan, Afghanistan, Bengal, and countries under the jurisdiction of Persia. Xuanzang was an exceptionally intelligent and educated man who could communicate with and impress foreign rulers, enabling him to receive their protection as he traversed numerous treacherous terrains. 900 years after his passing, a scholar named Wu Cheng'en added many fictional characters to this famous story, including the famous, staff-wielding Monkey King and two other humorous and animal-like characters who all became disciples of Xuanzang, protecting him from numerous demons and goblins they encountered throughout the journey.

Journey to the Western Sky was our bestseller at both the Frankfurt Book Fair and BookCon in 2019. Its action-packed adventures, sorcery, light-hearted humor, and fascinating poetry appeal to adults and youths of almost any age, and we usually recommend our abridged version of this novel to readers who have trouble deciding which of the seven great classic novels of China they would like to read first.

- *Plum Blossoms in a Golden Vase* 金瓶梅 *(Jīn Píng Méi)* by Lanling Xiaoxiao Sheng 兰陵笑笑生 (~1500-~1600)

This is the most famous erotic novel that has ever been published in China, and it has previously been translated by others under different titles, including *The Plum in the Golden Vase*. Its plot is based on scandalous events that take place in Chapter

23 of *Marsh Warrior Legend*, but that is about all these two novels have in common. Even though virtually all Chinese people know about this highly entertaining novel, very few of them have read it due to its 300-year ban by the conservative Chinese government; and those who have managed to get ahold of the original Chinese text usually have great difficulty comprehending it because it was written in an ancient northern dialect that is very different from Mandarin, Shanghainese, or Cantonese. The controversy surrounding *Jin Ping Mei's* lewd content has caused it to lose its status as one of the Four Great Classic Novels of China, a status later taken over by the novel *Red Tower Dream* as soon as it came out two centuries later.

- *Red Tower Dream* 红楼梦 *(Hóng Lóu Mèng)* by Cao Xueqin 曹雪芹 (1715-1763)

The most famous novel ever published about interpersonal relationships, romance, and the aristocracy of China, *Hong Lou Meng* has previously been translated by others under different titles, including *A Dream of Red Mansions* and *Red Chamber Dream*. It is the story of Crystal Steward, a being residing in the sky, whose earthly desires cause him to be reincarnated into the human world with a celestial piece of jade hidden in his mouth. Although he behaves like a carefree tourist on Earth, his bookish father wants him to study diligently in school to increase his chances of someday landing a good job in a respectable career, and those expectations cause a major conflict between him and his father. Twelve beautiful fairies also descend upon Earth, reincarnating as his sisters, cousins, and sisters-in-law as a group of women known as the "Twelve Barrettes of Capital South". As the boy grows up, the piece of jade he wears as a pendant acts as a camera that captures everything that happens inside the mansion of his wealthy family, transmitting vivid and sentimental snapshots of ancient China during its last dynasty.

- *Scholarly Journal* 儒林外史 *(Rúlín Wàishǐ)* by Wu Jingzi 吴敬梓 (1701-1754)

This is the least fictional of the seven great classic Chinese novels we have translated; and like *Three Kingdom Epic*, it is one of the more difficult novels to read because of its technical historical, and political terminology. It has previously been translated by others under different titles, including *Unofficial His-*

tory of the Scholars and *The Scholars*. Based on numerous historical events, *Scholarly Journal* pokes fun at the trials and tribulations of attempting to succeed as an academic in an era heavily influenced by Confucianism.

- *Journey of the Lamer* 老残游记 *(Lǎo Cán Yóujì)* by Liu E 刘鹗 (1857-1909)

There is no novel better than *Journey of the Lamer* when it comes to describing the interactions among officials, civilians, and foreigners during the last dynasty of China. Written from the perspective of an astute man who self-deprecatingly refers to himself as a lamer, its rich and picturesque descriptions of numerous historic sites are elegantly woven into a web of stories that leads to an intriguing mystery. *Lao Can Youji* has previously been translated by others under different titles, including *The Travels of Lao Can*.

To facilitate the reading process, the family tree, list of characters, and other background information of the novels are summarized in the appendices of each volume of each novel. Some readers may find it useful to read the appendices of the first volume of each novel before reading the entire novel.

We have translated these classic novels into common, everyday English for two reasons, the first being our desire to make these novels more accessible to recreational readers, students, and teachers all over the world. As long as our readers have at least an intermediate level of proficiency in the English language, they should be able to read our translations with relative ease, even if they know little to nothing about Chinese culture, history, or geography beforehand. For example, the names of all the characters and geographical locations mentioned in the novels have been translated into simple English words that can be found in any standard English dictionary, making it exponentially easier to recognize and remember the hundreds of names contained within each novel. Secondly, it is actually more realistic for most of the characters of these novels to speak colloquially, especially because many of them are blue-collar characters such as servants or soldiers, although we do occasionally employ more formal, yet still easily understandable, English whenever the circumstances warrant it. Unlike many other translations that contain little to none of the original poems, our translations contain most of the poems in each of the seven novels. The few poems we omitted were either redundant or too loosely related to the plots of the novels.

Due to popular demand, we have created single-volume, abridged versions of all of our novels except *Journey of the Lamer*, already a concise, single-volume novel to begin with. We highly recommend these abridged versions to the vast majority of our readers because they are free of the less important events and digressions present in their corresponding unabridged versions. Also, not every reader has the time to read our unabridged versions, most of which are well over 1,000 pages. Our abridged versions, on the other hand, are all fewer than 300 pages, typical of novels assigned to t high school students.

Please visit our website www.TranslatedClassics.com which will direct you to the exact Amazon.com webpages where you can learn more about, or buy, any of our books. With our revolutionary translation methodologies, we believe all our translations are the most readable and accurate versions that have ever been made.

Eugene Ying, Translator,
M. Engr., Cornell University '73
B.S., Cornell University '72

Victor Ying, Editor,
M.S. Ed., Long Island University '11
B.A., Cornell University '03

Chapter 1. Sawn Brawn, the Warrior

During the reign of Emperor Badge 徽宗 of the Song Dynasty, the four lords surnamed Tall 高, Birch 杨, Child 童, and Weed 蔡, abuse their power to such an extent the entire country falls into a state of chaos. Bandits from everywhere come out of the woodwork, and the Polar Star warriors descend upon Earth at a time when the four top bandit chiefs, Stream Song 宋江 of Mount-East 山东, Chin Rex 王庆 of Peace-Badge 淮西, Tiger Field 田虎 of River-North 河北, and Lard Square 方腊 of Long-River-South 江南, have seized control of the nation. Three of those bandit chiefs raid villages, commit arson and murder, and call themselves the kings of the country. Stream Song is the only one of those four chiefs who acts on behalf of the Sky, helps those suffering from injustice, and exterminates the corrupt officials and other criminals.

A man named Dally Brawn 武大郎 resides in Sunvale Town 阳谷县 of Mount-East. His brother, Sawn Brawn 武松, is a six-foot-tall, broad-shouldered, and strong-armed man who is an expert in spear and staff combat. Dally Brawn, despite being the elder brother, is less than four feet tall. He is a timid, simple-minded, and law-abiding citizen who avoids disputes and confrontations of any kind. Affected by the famine that has swept over the country, Dally Brawn sells off the house that has housed generations of his ancestors and moves away from his young brother to Clearstream Town 清河县.

One day when Sawn Brawn has had one too many, he offends Gag Child 童贯, chairman of the Joint Chiefs of Staff. Fearing retribution, he flees to the manor of Little-Cyclone 小旋风 Gin Splint 柴进 of Darkshire 沧州.

Gin Splint, an altruistic warrior, welcomes Sawn Brawn because is always eager to lend a helping hand to any of his heroic fellow countrymen. Known as Tycoon Splint, he is the direct descendant of the last emperor of the previous dynasty.

Unexpectedly, Sawn Brawn is afflicted with malaria, but he recovers quickly. He lives in the manor for over a year before he is overcome by a nostalgic desire to go to his hometown to pay his elder brother, Dally Brawn, a visit. After a few days of traveling, he arrives in Sunvale Town. Along the boundary of Mount-East prefecture is Viewsunridge 景阳冈, a ridge in which an enormous tiger has been terrifying and devouring residents no end. The mayor has given the local hunters a deadline for capturing that tiger. Posted along both sides of the path that lead to the ridge are notices ordering all travelers to travel in groups within a six-hour window from 9 a.m. to 3 p.m.

Sawn laughs off the warning, thinking it is a load of nonsense. He enters a tavern on the roadside, drinks several bowls of wine, and becomes intoxicated. He then staggers drunkenly out of the tavern and drags his staff up the ridge towards Viewsunridge. After walking more than a mile, he reaches the bottom of the ridge. The red sun is about to dip below the ridge at 5 p.m. Despite his drunkenness, he continues to walk along the ridge for 300 yards until he sees an officially stamped notice posted on the door of a mountain-deva temple, and it reads:

A huge tiger has been terrorizing the citizens of Viewsunridge. Any hunter who captures it will receive a reward of 30 oz of silver. Anyone wishing to cross this area must travel in a group, and do so sometime between 9 a.m. and 3 p.m. No group of travelers may cross this area during other hours, and no single traveler may cross this area at any hours. This is to prevent any further loss of lives. All must obey this decree.

Sawn says, “Who cares! I’ll just keep moving along and see for myself if there are any huge tigers around here!” With his staff tucked under his armpit, he makes his way up the ridge, one step at a time, as the sun slowly sets below the ridge. It is the month of November, the time of year when days are short, and evenings arrive early. The effect of the alcohol flowing through his veins intensifies as he continues to stagger along. He walks towards the woods and sees a smooth and large green rock he can lay down his staff. Just when he is about to lie down to take a nap, he feels a gust of wind shooting up to the azure sky. Legend has it that dragons are followed by trails of clouds, and tigers bring along gusts of wind. He suddenly hears the rustling of leaves, and a fierce huge tiger leaps out towards him.

Sawn exclaims, “Whoa!” He springs to his feet in the blink of an eye, grabs his staff, and leaps behind the rock.

With jaws agape, the hungry and thirsty tiger presses its paws into the ground, lashes its tail, and lets out a thunderous roar that shakes the entire ridge.

Sawn is so terrified the alcohol in his body begins to vaporize, causing him to break out in a cold sweat. He dodges and slips behind the massive tiger as soon as it lunges at him.

The shortness of the tiger's neck makes it difficult for it to turn its head around to see its prey. With its front paws digging into the ground, it twists its back and kicks backward.

Sawn steps to the side and avoids the kick.

After the tiger's kick missed its target, its thunderous roar once again shakes the entire ridge. It then lashes its iron-rod tail at its prey.

Sawn deftly dodges the lash.

The tiger attacks its prey by executing a leap, a kick, and a lash of its tail. If those three moves fail, it loses half of its fighting spirit.

When Sawn sees the tiger lose its momentum, he raises his staff with both hands, strikes down with all his might, but all he hears is the rustling of leaves and the crash of a falling tree branch he struck with so much force his staff is snapped in half. After he missed the tiger, only half of his staff remains in his hands, and he fears for his life.

With a deafening roar, the tiger swings its tail and lunges at Sawn who leaps back ten paces. Unable to pounce upon Sawn, the tiger swipes its front paws at Sawn who then drops his staff, grabs the tiger's head, and pushes it down onto the ground.

The tiger tries to wriggle itself free, but Sawn is so strong its head is pinned to the ground. He kicks the tiger in the head and eyes repeatedly, causing it to let out many roars of pain. All four of its legs flail about with such fury and desperation they dig up a pit surrounded by two mounds of soil.

Sawn keeps pushing the tiger's head into the pit. He then frees his right hand and unleashes a barrage of full-power blows. The tiger is as motionless as a large stuffed animal. Panting from exhaustion, Sawn releases its head and goes to the pine tree to pick up a piece of his broken staff. To make sure the tiger is killed, he strikes it a dozen times with the broken staff until it breathes its last. He then thinks, "I might as well drag this tiger's carcass down the ridge." He tries to lift the carcass from the bloody pit, but to no avail because he has used up all his energy! As he sits on the green rock to catch his breath, he hears the rustling of grass on the slope. He is at a loss for words as he thinks, "It's getting dark now. If another tiger leaps out at me, how will I have the energy to subdue it?" He then sees what appears to be two tigers coming out from behind the slope, and exclaims, "Whoa! I'm going to be snuffed out of this world!" The two tigers approach him on their hind legs, and lo and behold, they are none other than men wearing tiger-pelt jackets and headscarves tied in such a way they resemble the heads of tigers.

The two men bow down to Sawn, and the leader asks, “Warrior, are you a human or are you a deva? You must’ve eaten a gorilla’s heart, a leopard’s liver, and a lion’s leg, to be so brave! Otherwise, how could you be alone at dusk and kill this huge tiger without any weapons? We’ve been watching you from a distance for quite a while. May I have your name?

Sawn replies, “I don’t have an alias. I’m Sawn Brawn of Sunvale Town, and I’m the second son of my parents.” He then asks, “Who are you?”

The man replies, “We’re local hunters. This tiger on this ridge came out every night and had killed many people. Even among us hunters, we’ve lost seven of us, and the travelers killed are too many to count. The mayor has set a deadline for us to capture it. If we capture it, we can claim a reward of 30 oz of silver. Otherwise, we’ll be spanked. But this beast is too powerful for anyone to get near it! It’s our turn to do the hunting tonight, and dozens of villagers have set up traps, and have bows and arrows ready to fight the tiger. We were hiding in ambush when we saw you coming up the ridge casually. You later killed the tiger by punching and kicking it. It’s hard to believe you have such supernatural strength. Let’s carry the tiger for you and bring you to the mayor to claim the reward.”

Around 80 villagers and hunters carry the tiger in front, while Sawn is carried in a palanquin to the headsman’s manor where the tiger is put on the lawn, while the local elders all come to greet Sawn. He tells them how he beat up the tiger, and they all exclaim, “You’re such a hero!”

The hunters bring out dishes of game meat, and everyone gives Sawn a toast until they are drunk. The headman orders his servants to prepare a guest room for Sawn to sleep in. He dispatches a messenger the next morning to notify the mayor and prepares a special carriage for the tiger to be carried to town. Sawn rides on a palanquin decorated with red flowers and satin. The mayor dispatches officers to lead the procession to the lounge when they arrive at the town hall.

The Sunvale Town citizens, on hearing a hero has killed the huge tiger of Viewsunridge, all come out to welcome the hero. It is such a big event for the town.

The mayor looks at the warrior-like figure of Sawn and thinks, "This tiger surely couldn't be killed by anyone except this majestic warrior!" He requests Sawn to come to the lounge.

After Sawn pays homage to the mayor, he describes how he killed the tiger with his bare hands, and the officers there all drop their jaws.

The mayor gives Sawn a toast, withdraws from his vault 30 oz of silver contributed by various families, and hands the silver to Sawn as the reward.

Sawn says, "Your Highness, I couldn't have killed this tiger without your blessing. Since I'm being given more credit than I deserve, I dare not accept this 30 oz silver. Please distribute the silver among the hunters who've suffered so much because of that beast. This will display your benevolence and my loyalty to them."

The mayor says, "I'll act according to your wish."

Sawn then distributes the silver among all the hunters in the lounge.

Highly appreciative of the kindness and loyalty of the hero, the mayor says, "Although you're from Sunvale Town, you're not far from our Clearstream Town. I'll appoint you sergeant of this town today. You'll oversee the arrest of bandits causing trouble around our stream. How does that sound?"

Sawn falls to his knees and replies gratefully, "If I'm appointed this position, I shall be eternally indebted to you."

The mayor then asks the bailiff to prepare the necessary paperwork and appoints Sawn sergeant the very same day.

The headman and elders all come over to congratulate and give Sawn a toast, and the celebration goes on for three days. He came to Sunvale Town to look for his elder brother, but unexpectedly, he becomes the sergeant of Clearstream Town. He strolls on the street happily, and the residents of both towns in Eastpeaceshire 东平府 all know him.

Let's flash back to when Dally Brawn began living apart from Sawn Brawn.

The famine prompts Dally to move away and he rents an apartment on Purplestone Street 紫石街 in Clearstream Town. Timid and unpleasant to look at, he is dubbed "Dinky Deadwood" by people around him. Despite being bullied regularly due to his frail physique and overly modest disposition, he maintains his composure and avoids any kind of confrontation.

Dally sells pancakes on the street to earn a living. But just when things seem to be getting better, tragedy strikes, and his wife passes away, leaving behind Eva 迎儿, their 12-year old daughter. He packs up when he is nearly broke half a year later, moves to a shed that belongs to a mansion owned by a man named Honcho Pull 张大户. Honcho Pull's servants, moved by Dally's friendliness, help him out by frequently patronizing his business. Dally treats them well whenever they come and chat with him at his pancake stand. Since the servants put in a good word for him, Honcho Pull does not bother to collect rent from him.

Honcho Pull is a millionaire who owns 100 houses. Despite being over 60 years old, he is childless. And to add to his frustration, his wife, Lady Mine 余氏, is an austere housewife who does not want him to hire any pretty maids to work in their mansion. Honcho Pull beats his chest and heaves a sigh one day.

Lady Mine asks, "You have a bountiful harvest and own large properties, so what are you sighing about?"

Honcho replies, "I'm well into my golden years, yet I still don't have children. Although I own plenty of properties, at the end of the day, money means nothing to me."

Lady Mine says, "OK, fair enough. I'll ask a matchmaker to acquire two maids for you. They'll sing every day to entertain you."

Honcho thanks his wife from the bottom of his heart, and sure enough, she soon asks a matchmaker to acquire two maids for Honcho. They are named Goldie Rinse 潘金莲 and Quartzie White 白玉莲.

Goldie Rinse is the sixth daughter of Tailor Rinse 潘裁 who lived outside the South Gate. She has always been a pretty girl, and her parents have bound her feet since her childhood, hoping her smaller feet would make her strut about in a highly seductive manner. Her father passed away when she was nine years old. Her mother, in need of extra income to support the family, sold her to Pacifier Rex 王招宣's mansion where she learned how to sing. She also learned how to paint her eyebrows, put on makeup, comb her hair, don tight-fitting clothes, and behave seductively. She is so gifted and dexterous by the time she was 15, she was already proficient in sewing, knitting, and playing wind and string instruments including her specialty, the pipa. After Pacifier Rex passed away, Mrs. Rinse 潘妈妈 redeemed her and then sold her to Honcho Pull for 30 oz of silver.

Goldie and Quartzie are brought into the mansion at the same time. Goldie continues to study the pipa, Quartzie, a cute 16-year-old who comes from a musical family, learns how to play the zither, and the two of them share a bedroom.

Since Lady Mine appreciates the musical talent of both maids, they are exempt from housekeeping chores like cooking or sweeping floors, and they receive jewelry and nice clothes from her. But one unfortunate day, Quartzie unexpectedly passes away, leaving Goldie behind.

Goldie, 18 years old, has a face as sweet as a peach, eyebrows curved like the new moon, and a very curvy and voluptuous body. Honcho Pull wants to sleep with her but is afraid his stern wife may find out about such an affair. He secretly summons Goldie to his bedroom one day while his wife is attending a neighbor's banquet, and he does what comes naturally. It's a shame that:

An unblemished piece of jade is stained in a day.
How can a perfect pearl be restored again?

Honcho continues to go all the way with Goldie from then on, and he is gradually afflicted with five different ailments, viz. kidney pain, tearful eyes, significant hearing loss, runny nose, and incontinence. There is one additional ailment too embarrassing to be mentioned. With his health seriously compromised, he takes numerous naps during the daytime and sneezes uncontrollably during the nighttime.

When Honcho's wife later learns of the affair, she scolds Honcho for several days and beats Goldie up mercilessly.

Knowing he can no longer hold onto Goldie, Honcho is so upset he decides to marry off Goldie free of charge. While searching for a suitable husband for Goldie, the consensus among his servants is that Dally, a loyal and honest man, has lost his wife and is living in the servants' quarters, so Honcho should marry Goldie to Dally."

Honcho, still covetous of that girl, heeds their advice and marries Goldie to Dally without asking for a single coin.

After Dally and Goldie tied the knot, Honcho takes Dally under his wing. He gives Dally 5 oz of silver when Dally does not have enough money to make pancakes. He also sneaks into the shed and has a quickie with Goldie when Dally goes out to sell pancakes. Dally accidentally catches them in the act one day, but he dares not say anything. It goes on for quite a while until one day Honcho dies of exhaustion.

When Honcho's wife finds out what has happened, she angrily orders her valet to expel Goldie and Dally from the mansion. Dally then returns with Goldie to Purplestone Street where he rents a two-room apartment from Royalty Rex 王皇亲 and continues to sell pancakes.

Ever since Goldie married Dally, she has despised him for his ugliness and excessive modesty. She once complained, "Honcho, I wouldn't touch Dally with a ten-foot pole even if all the men in the world have died. He doesn't know how to conduct himself but only knows how to drink. Asking him to do anything is like beating a dead horse. I must've been born under an unlucky star to marry such a man!"

Dally bakes pancakes every day, sells them outside, and returns home late. His wife, who has nothing better to do than to eat her three meals a day, puts on makeup, stands in front of the portiere, and ogles every man who passes by. A few of the neighborhood's womanizers are envious of Dally's seductive wife, and they all joke around, gossip, and ask, "How can a nice piece of mutton fall into a dog's mouth?" People all wonder how the scrawny and effeminate Dally managed to get such a wonderful wife who is so talented, especially when it comes to having trysts.

Goldie sits under the portiere to crack pumpkin seeds as soon as Dally leaves the house in the morning. She flashes her dainty bare feet and flirts with every man who walks by. Dally finds it unbearable to continue living in the apartment on Purplestone Street. He wants to move elsewhere, so he consults his wife.

His wife responds, "Listen up, dummy, you've been renting this dinky apartment with rooms so tiny people look down on you. Why don't you scrape together some money to make the down payment to rent a house so people won't keep looking down on you? A stingy man like you sure knows how to make his wife suffer!"

"Where can I get the money for the down payment?"

"Just take my barrettes and bracelets and pawn them, Dummy! How difficult can it be? You can redeem them later."

In compliance with her request, Dally manages to pawn their valuables for 20 oz of silver for the down payment to rent a two-building house with four rooms. He moves into the house to the west of the town hall and continues to sell pancakes.

Dally is strolling on the street one day when he sees a parade of townspeople—displaying tasseled spears, striking gongs, and beating drums—escorting a man sitting on a floral palanquin, and the man is none other than his brother Sawn!

As mentioned earlier, after Sawn slew the massive tiger on Viewsunridge, the mayor appointed him sergeant to express his deep gratitude. To congratulate Sawn on his appointment, the town elders escort him to his new office, and along the way, they happen to bump into Dally who ecstatically exclaims, "Now you're the sergeant, Brother, when will you pay me a visit?"

Sawn turns his head, sees his brother, and excitedly rejoiced at their reunion.

Dally invites Sawn into his house, takes him to the second floor, and asks Goldie to come out and meet Sawn. He says, "It was this man, your brother-in-law, who has killed a huge tiger on Viewsunridge, and we're brothers born from the same mother."

Goldie puts her hands together and exclaims, "Brother-in-law, nice to meet you!"

When Sawn falls to his knees to bow back, Goldie immediately tries to help him up and exclaims, "Please don't do that!"

Sawn responds, "I pay you my respects, Sister-in-law!"

After they bow down to each other, they get back to their feet.

Dally's daughter Eva quickly serves them tea. Afraid of falling under Goldie's seductive spell, Sawn avoids making eye contact with her.

Dally wants to treat Sawn to dinner, so he goes downstairs to buy wine and meat. He leaves Goldie behind to entertain Sawn.

Goldie admires Sawn's brawny physique and handsomeness, and wonders: "How could he subdue a tiger unless he had the strength to lift 1000 lb?" She then thinks, "He was born from Dally's mother, but he's so tall and strong. I couldn't be happier if I married him. Look at the midget I've married who's only 30% human, and 70% ghost. What have I done in my past life to deserve such bad karma? Now I meet this charismatic man, why not invite him to move to my house? Perhaps this is an opportunity for me to upgrade to a better marriage!"

Goldie asks smilingly, "Brother-in-law, where do you live? Who prepares your meals?"

"I just got my job, and I need to report promptly to my boss. Since it's not convenient to live elsewhere, I'm staying at an inn near the town hall, and two soldiers cook meals for me."

"Brother-in-law, why don't you move into my house? The food prepared by the soldiers must be dirty. If you live here, it'll be so easy for me to serve you tea and soup. The meals I prepare for you will be much cleaner." She then adds, "If there's a sister-in-law, please invite her to come here too."

"I'm single."

"How old are you?"

"I've blown away 28 years of my life."

"You're three years older than me. Where did you just come from?"

"I lived in Darkshire for a year. I thought my brother was still living in his old place, so I didn't expect him to move here."

"It's a long story. After I married your brother, he's been so nice everyone takes advantage of his kindness and bullies him, forcing us to move here. Of course, if he were as strong as you, nobody could bully him."

"My brother's a law-abiding citizen, not a vagabond like me."

"I beg to differ. I believe in the survival of the fittest, I'm an action-hero fan who looks down on those who choose flight over fight."

Goldie is a woman who speaks her mind, and Sawn responds, "My brother stays out of trouble so Sister-in-law has nothing to worry about."

While they are talking, Dally returns with meat, vegetables, and fruit. He puts them in the kitchen, goes upstairs, and says, "Wife, please come down to do the cooking."

"You're so inconsiderate! My brother-in-law is here and needs someone to keep him company, and yet you want me to leave him alone, all by himself!"

Sawn says, "Please go ahead, Sister-in-law!"

Goldie asks, "Dally, why don't you just ask our neighbor Mrs. Rex 王婆 to do the cooking?"

Dally obligingly goes next door to ask Mrs. Rex to prepare food for them. He later brings dishes of fish, meat, fruit, and vegetables, as well as some wine, upstairs. He asks Goldie to take the host's seat, and Sawn to sit opposite her, whereupon he sits at the side and serves them wine.

Goldie asks smilingly, "Brother-in-law, why don't you help yourself to a meatball?" She picks up a large meatball and offers it to him.

A straight shooter like Sawn is under the impression that Goldie's behavior is nothing more than a display of sisterly affection. He has no idea it is the beginning of Goldie's attempt to gradually seduce him.

The effeminate Dally is also completely oblivious to Goldie's intentions due to his social ineptitude.

After a few drinks, Goldie continues to ogle Sawn, causing him to lower his head in discomfort.

A few drinks later, Sawn rises from his seat and intends to leave the house.

Dally asks, "Since you're free right now, why don't you have a few more drinks?"

Sawn replies, "I've bothered you too much already. I'll visit both of you another time."

They see Sawn off, and when he is outside the gate, Goldie says, "Brother-in-law, don't forget to move in here. If you don't live with us, people will continue to give us a tough time. Blood is thicker than water and we need your support."

Sawn responds, "Since you're very much in earnest on this matter, I'll bring my baggage here tonight."

Goldie says, "We eagerly await your return."

Sawn packs up when he arrives at the inn near the town hall and asks a soldier to carry them to his brother's house.

Goldie feels as if she has struck gold. She prepares a room for Sawn to stay in, and Sawn dismisses the soldier upon their arrival.

Sawn sleeps in his brother's house, and Goldie hurriedly prepares a basin of warm water for him to wash his face when he gets up in the morning. After grooming himself, he is about to head out to work when Goldie says, "Come back here for dinner, Brother-in-law. Don't eat anywhere else."

Sawn promises to comply with her request. Goldie has dinner ready for him when he returns home from work. Goldie holds a cup of tea in both hands and offers it to Sawn after dinner.

Sawn says, "I don't deserve to be served by Sister-in-law. I'll request the service of a soldier from the town hall tomorrow."

Goldie responds in a heartbeat, "Brother-in-law, how can you treat me like an outsider? We're close relatives. Although we have Eva to help us out, she's quite a clumsy worker. If you send a soldier here, he won't prepare and cook food in a sanitary manner. I don't think too highly of those types of people."

Sawn responds, "Well, despite everything you've just said, I still don't think I deserve such nice treatment from Sister-in-law."

Sawn moves into his brother's house, gives Dally some pieces of silver to treat their neighbors to some refreshments, and the neighbors return the favor soon afterward. He buys a roll of colorful satin a few days later for Goldie to make new clothes.

Goldie beams and exclaims, "Brother-in-law is too kind to me. Thank you very much for your gift!"

Goldie always has dinner ready for Sawn from then on, regardless of how early or late he returns home. However, the overzealous way she serves Sawn makes him feel uneasy. Being a man of few words, he answers all her attempts at seduction in a terse manner.

Time goes by quickly, and a month later, it is December, a time of year when northerly winds howl through the cloudy sky. It snows until 7 p.m. that day, creating a marble-covered winter wonderland.

Sawn reports to work at the town hall the next day, and Dally is goaded out of the house before noon by Goldie to sell pancakes.

Goldie asks her neighbor Mrs. Rex to buy some meat and wine, while she ignites a bowl of charcoal in Sawn's room and thinks, "If I really try hard today to seduce him, how can he not be turned on?" As she stands lonelily under the portiere, she sees Sawn trudging back home along the snowy road. She raises the portiere, and asks smilingly, "Does Brother-in-law feel cold?"

Sawn replies, "Thank you for being concerned about my wellbeing." As he enters the house, Goldie offers to hang up his hat which he has taken off.

Sawn responds, "Don't mind me, Sister-in-law!" He dusts the snow off his hat and hangs it on the wall. He then takes off his green cotton coat and enters his room.

Goldie says, "Why didn't you come back for lunch?"

Sawn replies, "An acquaintance invited me to lunch at noon. I later declined another friend's invitation for a drink and came home instead."

Goldie says, "Please warm yourself up by the fire."

Sawn responds, "Sounds good to me." He takes off his boots, changes into another pair of socks, pulls up a stool for himself near the fire bowl.

Goldie has already asked Eva to lock the front and back doors. She orders Eva to bring food and wine into the room and put them on the table.

Sawn asks, "Where's my brother?"

Goldie replies, "Your brother has gone out selling pancakes, but let's first have a drink together, shall we?"

Sawn replies, "Let's wait for him to join us."

Goldie asks, "Why wait for him?"

As they continue their conversation, Eva brings over a kettle of warm wine. Sawn then says, "If you don't mind, I'd prefer to drink alone, Sister-in-law!"

Ignoring his request, Goldie also pulls up a stool for herself near the fire. She fills the cup on the table to the brim with wine and says, "Brother-in-law, please finish this cup of wine."

After Sawn guzzles down the wine, Goldie fills another cup and says, "You should drink twice as much to stave off the chilly weather."

Sawn responds, "You should have some wine, too!" He guzzles down the second cup and then fills a cup and offers it to Goldie.

Goldie accepts and drinks it. She refills the cup with more wine and places it in front of Sawn. She then partially exposes her breasts, lets her hair loose, and whispers with a seductive smile, "I heard through the grapevine you've had an affair with a singer who lives near the town hall. Is it true?"

Sawn replies, "Sister-in-law shouldn't be swayed by false rumor. I'm not that kind of man."

"I don't believe you. You seem to be the kind of man who talks the talk but doesn't walk the walk."

"If you don't believe me, you can ask my brother."

"The heck with him! Don't even bring up his name...What does he know? He's like a zombie. If he had any business sense, he'd be doing something else other than selling pancakes. Anyway, please have a few more drinks." Like Sawn, she has already had three cups of wine, and as she urges him to have three more, she feels all her inhibitions gradually melt away and starts talking gibberish.

Aware of her intentions, Sawn lowers his head uneasily and refuses to fall victim to her desire.

Goldie gets up and goes to the kitchen to warm up more wine, while Sawn uses a poker to stir up the embers in the fire bowl. Goldie brings back another kettle of warm wine after a while. She holds the kettle in one hand while she squeezes Sawn's shoulder with the other, and asks, "Don't you feel cold wearing only these clothes?"

Growing more and more unsettled by Goldie's behavior, Sawn continues to ignore her advances.

Unable to elicit any responses from Sawn, Goldie snatches the poker from him and says, "Brother-in-law, you're not doing a decent job of stoking the embers; let me stir up the fire for you. A good bowl of fire will keep us warm."

Sawn remains anxiously silent.

Goldie is completely oblivious to Sawn's anxiety. She drinks a mouthful of wine from the kettle, casts a lustful glance at him, and whispers, "If you want to have a quickie, finish the rest of the wine in this kettle."

Sawn snatches the kettle from Goldie, splashes the wine onto the floor, and bellows, "Don't you have any shame, Sister-in-law?" He pushes her away and almost knocks her over. Glaring at her with disgust, he shouts, "I'm a decent man, not like those men who act like pigs and dogs. Have some decency, for crying out loud! If you make any more advances toward me, my fists will have no mercy, even though you're my sister-in-law! Don't ever try to seduce me again!"

Blushing with embarrassment, Goldie summons Eva and asks her to clear the table as she grumbles, "I was just kidding around, but he took it all so seriously! He's so disrespectful!" She then slips away into the kitchen.

Goldie embarrassedly received nothing more than a scolding for her failed attempt at seduction, while Sawn, still fuming with anger in his room, broods over what has just happened.

Dally comes home at 5 p.m. with his carrying pole which he puts away before he enters his room. Noticing his wife's eyes red from crying, he asks, "With whom did you quarrel?"

Goldie replies, "I'm bullied so much by others because of your fault!"

"Who would have the nerve to bully you?"

"Of course you know who he was! He was none other than Sawn. After he trudged his way back through the deep snow, I offered him food and wine. When nobody else was around, he tried to verbally seduce me. Eva witnessed the whole thing. I'm not making it up!"

"My brother would never behave like that. He has always been a man of integrity. Don't talk in such a loud voice or else our neighbors will laugh at us." No longer paying heed to his wife, Dally goes to his brother's room and says, "You haven't had any appetizers yet, why not have some together?"

Sawn remains silent. After brooding for a while, he takes off his silk slippers, puts on his boots, jacket, and hat, and heads for the door, fastening his belt as he walks.

Dally asks, "Where are you going?"

Still refusing to respond, Sawn continues to walk away.

Dally returns to his room and says, "I tried talking to him, but he didn't respond. Instead, he just got up and left, heading toward the town hall. I don't know what's going on!"

"Come on, you moron, it can't be too hard to figure out! Your brother took off running because he's too ashamed of what he's done. He can't even look you in the eye. I guess he'll dispatch someone here to fetch his baggage, and he won't live here with us anymore."

"If he moves out, everyone will laugh at us."

"Hey, blockhead, what people will laugh at you for is how you let him fondle me. If you sign a divorce document, I'll let you keep him in this house."

Not daring to say anything else, Dally falls silent as his wife continues to berate him. During her tirade, they see Sawn arrive with a soldier and a carrying pole.

Sawn enters his room, packs up, and heads out the door.

Dally rushes out and asks, "Why are you leaving?"

Sawn replies, "It's better if you don't know. Delving into this matter will only open a can of worms. Just let me leave."

Dally dares not ask any further. He looks on with resignation as Sawn walks away with the baggage.

Goldie, who has not yet stopped whining, exclaims from inside her room, "Good riddance! People think his brother uses his sergeant's salary to help us make ends meet. Little do they know he's not at all what he seems! You can't judge a book by its cover. I'm so glad he's moving out! It's as if a thorn had been removed from my side."

Dally is at a loss for words as he continues to endure his wife's incessant harping. After Sawn moves back into the inn next to the town hall, Dally continues to make a living selling pancakes. He wants to talk to his brother, but Goldie manages to dissuade him from doing so.

Chapter 2. Chic Westgate Meets Goldie Rinse

Time goes by quickly and in just two weeks, the snow on the ground has already thawed.

For his more than two years in office, the mayor has accumulated a rather substantial amount of money. He wants to find a trusted officer who will deliver some of his money to his relatives in the capital 开封 so that they can bribe the higher officials to help him get a promotion at the end of his three-year term. However, he is afraid the money may be intercepted by bandits. As he considers the possibility of assigning the task to a high-ranking officer, it suddenly dawns on him Sawn is the right man for the job, and he says, "I need a hero like him to help me on this one!" He then summons Sawn to his office and says, "A relative of mine, Marshal Red 朱勔, is currently stationed at the imperial court of the capital, and I'd like to pay him my respects by sending him a present accompanied by a letter. Since the roads leading to the capital are treacherous, I need a tough guy like you to take on this assignment. I hope you don't mind the traveling and the hardship that may come your way. I'll reward you handsomely for your trouble when you return."

Sawn responds, "Your Highness, I'm so grateful for the position you've appointed me I could never refuse any assignments from you. Since I've never been to the capital before, this wonderful assignment will allow me to do some sightseeing there."

The mayor is overjoyed. He treats Sawn to three drinks and awards Sawn 10 oz of silver for the travel expenses.

After receiving the details of the assignment from the mayor, Sawn leaves the town hall. He asks a soldier to accompany him to the market to buy a bottle of wine, and some meat and vegetables. He then heads straight for Dally's house.

Dally is just returning home when he finds Sawn sitting outside the door whereupon he invites Sawn in. Sawn then directs the soldier to bring the food and wine into the kitchen.

Goldie, still head over heels in love with Sawn, looks at the food and wine he bought and thinks, "Is he still thinking about me? Otherwise, why would he come back here? He probably can't resist my beauty! I'm going to take my time to seduce him this time." She goes upstairs, puts on some makeup, adjusts her hair, and changes into a pretty outfit. She then goes downstairs to the door, greets Sawn, bows down courteously, and says,

"Brother-in-law, you haven't visited us for many days because of some misunderstandings, and your long absence has filled my heart with great anxiety. I asked your brother every day to go to the town hall to speak to you, but he always came back and said he couldn't find you. I'm so thrilled you visit us today."

Sawn responds, "I've come here because I have something to tell my brother."

Goldie says, "Alright, please have a seat upstairs."

The soldier goes inside and places the food and wine on the table. Sawn has a cup of wine and averts Goldie's ogling gaze.

Sawn asks Eva to bring him a goblet a few drinks later. After pouring wine into it, he raises the goblet and says, "Dally, the mayor decided today to send me to the capital on a special assignment. I'll depart tomorrow, and the trip may last anywhere from six to ten weeks. Since you're so frail, I'm afraid people may take advantage of you during my absence, so I'd like to make some suggestions for you to consider. Let's say you've been selling ten trays of pancakes per day lately. Then starting tomorrow, you should only bake five trays of pancakes. You must leave home late and come home early. Do not go out for a drink with anyone. Close the portiere and shut the doors as soon as you come back home to avoid other people's gossip. If someone mistreats you in any way, don't confront him, just wait for me to come back and take care of him. If you agree to these suggestions, drink this goblet of wine as a token of your commitment to following them."

Dally responds, "Alright. I'll drink to that!" and downs the goblet of wine

Sawn refills the goblet and says, "Since Sister-in-law is so bright, I don't need to give her much parting advice. But I'll say this: My brother is so meek he needs your help. As the saying goes, 'Charity begins at home.' If you take good care of the house, there'll be nothing for my brother to worry about, right? Remember an ounce of prevention is worth a pound of cure."

Goldie blushes, points at Dally, and snaps, "You're such a moron! You bad-mouth me so much in front of others they all come back here to lecture me! Little do they know I'm actually a tomboy who can take on anyone! Not even an ant dare break into our house ever since I married you. Talk about an ounce of prevention! Every rumor spread about me is nothing but utter nonsense!"

"Sister-in-law, I like your assertiveness, but don't talk the talk if you can't walk the walk. Anyway, I've taken note of what you just said. Here's a toast to your words."

Goldie pushes the goblet away, and storms downstairs as she mumbles, "You think you're so smart, but has it ever occurred to you your elder brother's wife has more seniority than you? I never even knew you existed when I married Dally. I had no idea he had a younger brother who crawled out of the woodwork. And now I have you lecture me as if you were my father-in-law—just my luck!" She then cries buckets as she mumbles away.

Goldie is acting up while Sawn has a few more drinks with Dally before they go downstairs.

With tears in his eyes, Dally says, "Come back as soon as you can, Brother."

Sawn responds, "I'll try my best. By the way, since I'll have someone to deliver money to you so you're taken care of, it's also fine if you don't sell any more pancakes and just stay home." As he turns around to leave, he says, "Don't forget what I told you, and never let your guard down at home."

Dally says, "Don't worry, I'll do as you say."

Sawn returns to the town hall with the soldier, and he has his bags all packed and ready to go the next morning before he heads off to see the mayor.

The mayor has prepared a carriage containing trunks of money and other valuables for Sawn to deliver to the capital.

Goldie continues to berate Dally for several days after Sawn's departure, but Dally just grins and bears it and never strays from his brother's advice. After making and selling only half his usual number of pancakes every day, he comes home early, puts down his carrying pole, lowers the portiere, and shuts the doors before he does anything else.

Goldie observes Dally's daily routine and says disdainfully, "I've never seen anyone who shuts his doors in the daytime as if he were in a prison cell, dumb critter! Our neighbors, who already look down on us, will think our house is haunted if you keep this up. They'll think your brother is a freaking jerk to make you behave this way!"

Dally responds, "I don't care whether other people laugh at me. What matters most is the good advice my brother has given me to keeps me out of trouble."

Goldie retorts, “What a moron you are! Why can’t you make your own decisions like a real man, instead of being manipulated by others?”

Dally shakes his head and replies, “My brother’s advice is worth a pot of gold. Nothing will change this fact.”

Goldie continues to verbally abuse Dally for the next few days until she gives up on changing his ways. She is so used to see the portiere closed and the door shut that whenever Dally is home she decides to follow the routine herself.

Dally thinks happily, “Now isn’t it nice!”

Time goes by quickly, and soon after the plums begin to blossom, and the weather takes a turn for the better. After Dally left the house on a pleasant day in April, Goldie, dressed in elegant attire, stands by the portiere. At the very moment when Goldie is lowering the portiere with a forked pole, a passerby walks up beside the portiere by pure coincidence. Per Murphy’s Law, if anything can go wrong, it will. It is an adage that always holds. A gust of wind suddenly blows past them, causing the forked pole to slip from her grasp and strike the man’s headscarf. Goldie quickly forces an apologetic smile as she glances at the dashing, well-dressed man who is about 26 years old.

When he turns around and is about to unleash a string of expletives, he is surprised to see an attractive woman. He stands still and smiles because her beauty instantly smooths his ruffled feathers.

Seeing the anger immediately melt from his face, Goldie bows and says apologetically, “Sorry for being so careless! I hope I didn’t accidentally hurt you!”

The man adjusts his headscarf as he bows back and responds, “Don’t worry about it! It just slipped out of your hand...”

Meanwhile, Mrs. Rex watches the entire incident through the curtained window of her teahouse next door and chuckles, “It was right on target!”

Still responding to Goldie’s apology, the man says with a grin, “Please forgive me for intruding upon my lady’s property.

“Tycoon, I should be the one asking for forgiveness.”

The man smiles again, makes a deep, chivalrous bow, and says, “No, the fault is mine, and I sincerely apologize.” His eyes study Goldie from head to toe, and as he continues his way, he keeps turning his head to steal another glance at her.

Feeling drawn to the romantic sweet-talking man, Goldie thinks, “I wonder what his name is, and where he lives. If he wasn't interested in me, he wouldn't look over his shoulder so many times to check me out when he left. Perhaps this is the beginning of a budding romance between us!" She sneaks a few more glances at the man before she lowers the portiere, closes the door, and returns to her room.

And who might that mystery man be? He is a nouveau riche of Clearstream Town and the owner of the drugstore near the town hall. He has been a prodigal son since his youth and is good in martial arts, gambling, chess, and solving riddles. He has been earning a lot of money lately by working as a lobbyist in the town hall, where he manipulates lawsuits and accepts bribes to settle disputes, instilling fear in all the townspeople. He is named Chic Westgate 西门庆, and his recent significant increase in income has earned him the moniker "Tycoon Westgate". His parents have passed away, and he does not have any siblings. His first wife has also passed away, leaving behind their daughter. Although he recently married the daughter of Colonel Call 吴千戶 of Clearstream Town, he continues to sleep with several concubines and maids in his mansion. After falling in love with a prostitute named Cutie Plum 李娇儿, he married her as one of his concubines. He hooked up with another prostitute from South Street named Dior Bright 卓丟儿 shortly afterward and married her as an additional concubine. Whenever he gets tired of a woman he has acquired, he orders his matchmaker to sell her. He visits the matchmaker sometimes as often as 20 times a month, and nobody dares question his lifestyle or offend him.

Westgate returns to his mansion and thinks more deeply about his encounter with Goldie at the portiere: "What a nice gal she is! But how can I hook up with her?" It suddenly occurs to him Mrs. Rex, the owner of a teahouse, lives next door to her, so he thinks, "I'll do...this and that...and she'll be all mine. Even if I must spend a little extra money, it'll be well worth it." Eager to put his plan into action, he gets up without touching his meal and heads straight for Mrs. Rex's teahouse where he takes a seat near the curtained window.

When Mrs. Rex sees Westgate, she teases, "I saw how courteously you bowed to her, Tycoon!"

Westgate asks inquisitively, "What family does this next-door lady belong to?"

Mrs. Rex replies, “She’s the sister of the Underworld king and the daughter of a general deva. Why do you ask?”

Westgate replies, “I asked you a serious question, but you replied in such a facetious manner.”

Mrs. Rex responds, “Tycoon, how could you not know her husband sells food outside the town hall?”

Westgate asks, “Is she the wife of Sam Stroll 徐三, the date cake peddler?”

Mrs. Rex shakes her head as she replies, “No, if he were the husband, they could be a compatible couple. Guess again!”

Westgate asks, “Is she the wife of Sam Plum 李三, the pastry peddler?”

Mrs. Rex shakes her head as she replies, “No, if he were the husband, they could still be quite compatible.”

Westgate asks, “Is she the wife of Shawn Slay 刘小二?”

Mrs. Rex replies laughingly, “No, if he were the husband, they could still be compatible. Guess again, Tycoon.”

Westgate says, “I’ve run out of guesses.”

Mrs. Rex says with a grin, “Her husband is Dally Brawn, the pancake peddler.”

Westgate stamps his foot and asks laughingly, “Isn’t he the guy known as ‘Dinky Deadwood Dally Brawn’?”

Mrs. Rex replies, “That’s him alright!”

Stamping his foot again, Westgate cries foul: “How could such a nice piece of mutton fall into a dog’s mouth?”

Mrs. Rex replies, “That’s why people say, ‘Every dog has its day.’ Cupid occasionally makes this kind of mismatch!”

Westgate asks, “How much do I owe you for the tea?”

Mrs. Rex replies, “Not much. Don’t worry about it. You can pay me later.”

Westgate asks, “Your son Charles Rex 王潮 working for whom?”

Mrs. Rex replies, “He went on a business trip with a salesman and hasn’t returned. I don’t know his whereabouts.”

Westgate says, “He can work for me if he wants to. He’s a pretty smart guy after all.”

Mrs. Rex says, “It would be great if you could employ him.”

Westgate says, “Rest assured I’ll take care of him when he gets back.”

Mrs. Rex thanks Westgate for his offer before he leaves.

Westgate returns in less than two hours and sits next to the portiere of Mrs. Rex's teahouse, with his body facing Dally's front door.

Mrs. Rex comes out and asks, "Tycoon, would you like to have some date soup?"

"Yes, make it a little sweeter than usual, please."

Mrs. Rex reappears soon afterward with a bowl of date soup in both hands and sets it before Westgate.

Westgate savors the soup and says, "The dates in your soup taste good. Have you cooked a lot of them here?"

Mrs. Rex replies slyly, "I've been providing dating services for many years, and every date has been cooked up here."

"I asked about the dates in the soup, and here you're talking about dating services. That's quite a different subject!"

"Tycoon, I heard you say my dates are good, which made me think you were interested in getting a date."

"Since you're a matchmaker, please get me another concubine, and I'll reward you handsomely."

"Tycoon, you've got to be kidding. If your wife finds out about this, she'll slap me silly."

"My wife is easygoing. She currently lets me keep several concubines at home, but unfortunately, none of them can satisfy my needs and desires. If you know of a good gal, please send her my way. I don't mind getting a second-hand one, as long as she can satisfy me."

"I spotted a good one yesterday, but I'm afraid you may not like her."

"Just tell me if she's right for me, and I'll reward you handsomely."

"She's very beautiful, but probably a bit too old for you."

"Many beauties are middle-aged. It doesn't matter if she's one or two years older than me. How old is she, anyway?"

"She's 93 years old."

"You must be crazy to come up with a joke like that!" He continues to laugh as he gets up and leaves.

It is getting dark, and Mrs. Rex lights a lamp. Just as she is about to close the door, Westgate returns and sits on the bench beside the portiere, staring at the door of Dally's house.

"Tycoon, would you like to have some consummate soup?"

"Sure, why not? Make it extra sweet."

Mrs. Rex quickly serves him a bowl of soup, and he consumes it. He gets up at nightfall and says, "Please put everything on my bill, and I'll pay you tomorrow."

"Good night! We can continue our discussion tomorrow."

Westgate has trouble sleeping when he returns home because he cannot stop thinking about Goldie.

Mrs. Rex opens her door the next morning, looks outside, and sees Westgate pacing back and forth on the street. She then thinks, "This playboy is so impatient. All I need to do is dangle a carrot in front of him. He's been extorting money from everyone in town, and now it's my turn to make him pay through the nose for his lustful ways."

As it so happens, Mrs. Rex is not a very law-abiding citizen. Not only is she a matchmaker, but she is also a cougar and a bawd especially adept at ensnaring unsuspecting clients by playing hard to get.

After pacing back and forth on the street for quite some time, Westgate enters the teahouse and sits near the portiere with his eyes glued to Dally's door. Mrs. Rex fans the stove fire, pretending not to see him.

"I'd like two cups of tea, please."

"Long time no see, Tycoon! Please have a seat." Mrs. Rex then sets two cups of hot tea on the table.

"Have a cup of tea with me."

Mrs. Rex responds laughingly, "I'm not your lover, so why are you asking me to have tea with you?"

Westgate laughs, and then asks, "By the way, what do they sell next door?"

"They sell pancakes filled with spicy mustard and lots of jalapeño peppers, stuff that's way too hot for you."

"You must've lost your marbles!"

"No, I haven't lost my marbles. Don't forget she already has a husband."

"But in all seriousness, if they can make good pancakes, I'll buy 50 of them and bring them home."

"If you want to buy their pancakes, just wait for Dally to come home and buy them from him outside their house. Why enter their house to buy them?"

"Can't argue with that." Westgate finishes his tea, then gets up and leaves.

Mrs. Rex is still working in the teahouse when she sees Westgate pacing east and west along the street about seven or eight times. He enters the teahouse shortly afterward.

"Tycoon, I haven't seen you for many days."

Westgate laughs, takes an oz of silver out of his pocket, hands it to Mrs. Rex, and says, "This is for the tea."

"It's too much."

"It's alright, keep the change."

Mrs. Rex thinks, "I have this sucker in the palm of my hand. This is just the down payment." She then says, "Tycoon is in heat. I suggest that you try my heat-relieving tea."

"What a clairvoyant you are!"

"That's nothing. I can tell what's on people's minds, and nothing can escape my notice."

"Well, something's been on my mind lately. If you can guess what it is, I'll give you 5 oz of silver."

"Since I already know what it is, I don't need to take a wild guess. You see, I haven't shared this with anyone, but after watching you pacing anxiously around for the past two days, it's obvious to me you can't stop thinking about the next-door lady. How's that for a guess?"

"You're smarter than Archimedes and more logical than Aristotle! Frankly, ever since I was struck by a forked pole that day, I seemed to have fallen under a hypnotic spell, and I can't stop thinking about her for reasons unbeknownst to me. Worse still, I've lost my appetite and energy. Do you know of a cure for my lovesickness?"

"Tycoon this teahouse isn't just for selling tea. It's also known as the 'Shady House'! I opened this teahouse three years ago during a November blizzard, but the business has always been slow, so I've been engaged in some shady dealings to make ends meet."

"What do you mean by shady dealings?"

"Ever since my husband passed away when I was 36 years old, I've worked several jobs to support my son. At first, I worked as a peddler, later as a bawd, and sometimes as a midwife. My sticky fingers came in handy when I was strapped for cash."

Impressed by Mrs. Rex's résumé, Westgate exclaims in admiration, "I never knew you're so talented! If you can hook me up with the next-door lady, I'll give you 10 oz of silver you can put into your retirement fund."

Chapter 3. Mrs. Rex, the Matchmaker

Mrs. Rex says, "Tycoon, listen carefully to me. Seducing someone is no easy task; there are five traits you must have to pull it off. Firstly, you must be as handsome as Apollo. Secondly, you must be hung like a donkey. Thirdly, you must be as rich as Croesus. Fourthly, you must display tender love with a heart as soft as velvet. Fifthly, you must be as free as a bird. If you have these five traits, which can be abbreviated as ApDonCroVelBird, seduction will be as easy as 123."

Westgate responds, "As a matter of fact, I do possess all five of these traits to some degree. Firstly, I'm somewhat good-looking, though not as handsome as Apollo. Secondly, I used to have a pet turtle, and a hard man is good to find. Thirdly, I have a good amount of dough, though not as much as Croesus. Fourthly, I'm extremely lenient, so much so that even if a woman slaps me 400 times, I won't hit back even once. Fifthly, I'm the idlest man in town, otherwise, how could I be hanging around here so much? So just go ahead and do it! I'll reward you for your effort as soon as the mission's accomplished."

Westgate is done tooting his own horn when Mrs. Rex says, "Tycoon, although you possess all five traits, there's still one potential problem."

"Just tell me what it is."

"Tycoon, it should come as no surprise to you the biggest hurdle in the art of seduction is money. If you need to spend 100 coins to hook up with a girl, but you only spend 99 coins, you won't succeed. You've always been pretty frugal, which could be a potential problem!"

"That's very easy to remedy. I'll do anything you say."

"Tycoon, if you're willing to spend the money, I have a plan for you to hook up with that girl. Would you like to hear it?"

"Of course. What's your plan?"

"Why don't you go back home now? Let's discuss the plan six months from now."

"C'mon, stop kidding around! I really need your help."

Mrs. Rex, grinning like a Cheshire cat, responds, "Relax, Tycoon! My ability to formulate plans is legendary. Although I may not be the best planner in the world, I'm a master planner whose plans succeed nine out of ten times! You might also be interested to know although that girl came from a poor family, she's very talented. Not only is she a good musician and singer, but she is also an expert tailor and chess player. Her name is Goldie Rinse, and she was sold to Honcho Pull in the past. She learned how to sing and play musical instruments at Honcho's home, and Honcho was well into his golden years when he married her off to Dally Brawn who didn't have to pay him a single coin. Dally is a wimp who leaves home early in the morning to sell pancakes and comes home late. This girl doesn't step out of their house very often. I often go over there to chat with her in my spare time. Since she considers me her guardienne, she comes here to consult me whenever she runs into trouble. Dally's still leaving home early these past two days, which will make it easier for us to set our plan in motion. The first thing you need to do is to buy me one roll of blue silk, one roll of white silk, one roll of white satin, and 10 oz of high-quality cotton. I'll go over to her place, borrow an almanac from her, and ask her to select an auspicious day for me to hire a tailor.

"If she selects a day, but doesn't offer to do the tailoring herself, all bets are off. But if she gladly offers to do the tailoring, you'll have a 10 percent chance to get lucky.

"If the latter possibility occurs, I'll ask her to do the tailoring in my house, and if she agrees, you'll have a 20 percent chance to get lucky.

"I'll then prepare lunch and wine for her. If she insists on having lunch at home, all bets are off. But if she has lunch here, you'll have a 30 percent chance to get lucky. However, you must not show up that day.

"You'll spruce yourself up the third day around noon, give a cough by the door and ask out loud, 'How come I haven't seen Mrs. Rex in several days? I've come here to buy a cup of tea.' I'll then invite you into the room. If she gets up and leaves as soon as she sees you, all bets are off. But if she stays put when she sees you, you'll have a 40 percent chance to get lucky.

"After you sit down, I'll say, 'This is the tycoon who gave me the fabrics. I'm so indebted to him!' I'll talk about all your good qualities, and you'll praise her tailoring skills. If she doesn't join in the conversation, all bets are off. But if she speaks to you, you'll have a 50 percent chance to get lucky.

"I'll then say: 'It wasn't easy for Goldie to do tailoring for me. I'm so fortunate to have two benefactors: One helps me with finance, while the other helps me with labor! Goldie wouldn't be here if I didn't ask her to come. Tycoon, would you be so kind as to offer her some refreshments?' You then take out some money and beg me to go shopping for some food and drinks. If she leaves, all bets are off. But if she stays put, you'll have a 60 percent chance to get lucky.

"I'll take the money, and I'll say to her before I leave the teahouse, 'Please keep Tycoon company, Goldie!' If she leaves, all bets are off. But if she doesn't go away, you'll have a 70 percent chance to get lucky.

"When I return from my shopping trip and place refreshments on the table, I'll say, 'Goldie, take a break and have a drink with us. It wasn't easy convincing Tycoon to pay for these refreshments.' If she doesn't want to eat with you at the same table, all bets are off. But if she stays put, it'll be great because it means you'll have an 80 percent chance to get lucky.

"I'll find an excuse to leave by saying I've run out of wine while she's enjoying herself drinking and chatting. You'll then beg me to go out to buy more wine and refreshments. I'll close the door, and lock both of you inside the room. If she anxiously heads back home before I can lock the door, all bets are off. But if she lets me lock the door and remains calm, you'll have a 90 percent chance to get lucky.

"You need to increase your chance by a final 10 percent to guarantee the success of the mission, but it'll be quite difficult to do that. Tycoon, you should use your charm to sweet-talk her, but don't be rash and touch her too early. If you spoil the plan, then I won't be held responsible for your failure. In the last step of the plan, you'll sweep your chopsticks off the table with your sleeve accidentally on purpose, bend down to pick them up, and then pinch her foot in a seemingly unintentional manner. If she cries foul, then I'll come to your rescue, in which case the mission will be aborted. But if she doesn't utter a sound, then she's all yours!"

After listening to Mrs. Rex's elaborate plan, Westgate responds laughingly, "This plan makes me feel as if I were on Cloud Nine! It's simply marvelous!"

Mrs. Rex says, "Don't forget the 10 oz of silver you promised me!"

Westgate responds, "Since you know I'd never shortchange anyone, when will we begin putting this plan into action?"

Mrs. Rex replies, "You'll hear back from me tonight. I'll first visit her to borrow the almanac and feel her out before Dally

Brawn comes home, while you ask your servant to bring over the silk, satin, and cotton."

Westgate says, "With you managing this matter, how can I not do my part?" He says goodbye to Mrs. Rex, leaves the teahouse, and shop for three rolls of silk, satin, and high-quality cotton altogether worth about 10 oz of silver. He orders his trusted valet Deon 玳安 to pack and deliver them to Mrs. Rex's house.

After receiving the package with open arms, Mrs. Rex heads out the back door to Dally's house where Goldie offers her a seat upstairs.

Mrs. Rex asks, "Goldie, why haven't you come over for a cup of tea for the past two days?"

Goldie replies, "I haven't gone out much because I haven't been feeling well the past couple of days."

Mrs. Rex says, "By the way, I remember you have an almanac here, Goldie. May I borrow it to select a date for some clothes to be tailored?"

Goldie asks, "What clothes need to be tailored?"

Mrs. Rex replies, "I've been constantly sick and in pain. Since my son is away from home, I need to prepare for the day I'll leave this world."

Goldie asks, "Why has it been so long since I last saw Charles?"

Mrs. Rex replies, "He's been following a traveling salesman around, and he's never written any letters back to me. I'm quite worried about him."

Goldie asks, "How old is Charles?"

Mrs. Rex replies, "He's 17 years old."

Goldie asks, "Why don't you find a wife for him? Then you'd have an extra set of helping hands."

Mrs. Rex replies, "You took the words right out of my mouth. Since I have no one to help me at home, I've been pinching pennies to help him get a wife, but he won't get married until he comes back. I've been wheezing and coughing day and night lately, and I've been in so much pain I haven't been able to sleep for quite some time and therefore need to prepare for my funeral. I'm so fortunate to have a rich tycoon who often drops by my teahouse for tea. He always patronizes me whenever his mansion needs someone to help hire doctors, acquire maids, or act as a matchmaker. And he's given me rolls of silk, satin, and cotton for my funeral clothes. The fabrics have been sitting at home for over a year because I haven't had the time to do the tailoring. I feel my health has been deteriorating this past year, and since it's leap month now, I want to make use of the extra days to get the tailoring done, but the tailor keeps saying he's too busy to work on it. The waiting has been unbearable!"

Goldie responds sympathetically, "I'm afraid I'm not the most skilled when it comes to tailoring clothes, but if you don't mind, I can do it for you."

Mrs. Rex says excitedly, "If you're willing to do it, then I can die in peace. I've heard for a long time you're good at needle-work, but I never wanted to trouble you."

Goldie responds, "Since I've given you my word, you can rest assured I'll do it. Please take the almanac and ask someone to select an auspicious date for me to start tailoring."

Mrs. Rex says, "I know you're good at reciting poetry and singing librettos, Goldie. You're the perfect person to read the almanac, because, after all, there can't be anyone more literate than you."

Goldie responds humbly, "But I stopped attending school at an early age."

Mrs. Rex exclaims, "You're being too modest!" She then picks up the almanac and passes it to Goldie.

Goldie scans through the almanac and says, "Tomorrow will be a mournful day, and the day after tomorrow won't be good either. It's not until two days after tomorrow that the tailoring can be done under auspicious conditions."

Mrs. Rex snatches the almanac, hangs it on the wall, and responds, "It's auspicious enough for you to be willing to do the tailoring for me! Another person I've asked to check the almanac also told me tomorrow will be a mournful day. But isn't dealing with funeral clothes already a mournful matter? I won't mind at all if you begin working on them tomorrow."

"You've got a point. The tailoring of funeral clothes should begin on a mournful day."

"Well, you're more than welcome to come over tomorrow to start the tailoring."

"That won't be necessary. Why don't you bring the fabrics here instead?"

"I'd like to watch you do the tailoring, but I don't have anyone to look after the teahouse."

"Alright, I'll go to your place tomorrow after breakfast."

Mrs. Rex thanks Goldie repeatedly as she heads back downstairs. She informs Westgate of her progress in the evening and asks him to come over two days later. The next morning, she tidies her room, takes out some needles and thread, and prepares a pot of tea as she awaits the arrival of her guest.

Meanwhile, Dally fastens his trays of pancakes to his carrying pole and leaves his house after breakfast.

Goldie closes the portiere and asks Eva to take care of the house before she leaves and heads over to Mrs. Rex's place where she enters through the back door.

Mrs. Rex excitedly invites Goldie to her room and serves a cup of walnut and pine-seed tea. She clears the table and brings out the three rolls of silk and satin.

Goldie measures and cuts the fabrics into pieces of correctly sized pieces and begins to sew them together.

Mrs. Rex showers Goldie with compliments: "What incredible dexterity! I've never seen such a great tailor in the 60 years of my life!"

Goldie tailors the clothes until noon, at which time Mrs. Rex prepares and serves her lunch. She continues the work late into the afternoon and then packs up her tools and returns home. As usual, after Dally returns home with his carrying pole, she lowers the portiere and closes the door.

Noticing a slight flush on his wife's face, Dally asks, "Where did you go today?"

Goldie replies, "Mrs. Rex from next door asked me to tailor some funeral clothes for her. She was kind enough to offer me lunch and a cup of wine."

Dally says, "Since we've also asked for her help in various matters, you shouldn't accept her lunch invitations. If she continues to ask you to do the tailoring, you should come back home for lunch to not trouble her further. If you work on it again tomorrow, bring some money with you, and buy her lunch to return the favor. As the saying goes, 'A relative afar is less helpful than a neighbor.' We don't want to lose her as our friend. If she refuses to let you return the favor, then bring the fabrics home to do the tailoring."

Goldie listens quietly to Dally's little lecture and does not bother to talk back. Mrs. Rex arrives at Goldie's home the next day after breakfast to invite her over. Upon entering the teahouse, Goldie takes out her tools and continues the tailoring as Mrs. Rex eagerly serves her tea. Goldie takes 300 coins out of her pocket at noontime and says, "Mrs. Rex, here's some money for you to buy drinks."

Mrs. Rex exclaims, "Whoa! You've got it all wrong! You're here because I asked you to do some tailoring for me. Why should you be the one paying for things?"

Goldie replies, "My husband insists that it be this way. If you don't let me pay this time, then I'll have no choice but to take the fabrics home and do the tailoring there."

Mrs. Rex exclaims, "Oh my gosh, Dally is so mentally challenged! But since you insist, I'll take the coins."

Mrs. Rex chips in some of her own money lest her plan fall apart. She goes out and buys quality food, wine, and expensive fruit. Since the way to a woman's heart is through her stomach. Mrs. Rex eagerly serves appetizers and wine while Goldie continues to sew until evening. She expresses her heartfelt gratitude to Goldie who then returns home.

In the morning of the third day, as soon as Dally leaves his house after breakfast, Mrs. Rex enters through the back door and asks, "Goldie, may I ask—"

Goldie quickly comes downstairs and responds, "I'm coming!" The two of them head over to the teahouse and enter Mrs. Rex's room where Goldie takes a seat and continues the tailoring, and Mrs. Rex serves her tea.

Westgate dons a new headscarf and suit that day. He swaggers along Purplestone Street with a few oz of silver in his pocket and a handheld fan in his hand. He clears his throat at the door of the teahouse and asks, "Where have you been these past few days, Mrs. Rex?"

Mrs. Rex pretends to be caught off guard and asks, "Who's calling me?"

Westgate replies, "It's me!"

Mrs. Rex rushes outside and exclaims delightedly, "Tycoon, what a surprise to see you! You've come at the right time. Please come in and have a seat." She tugs on Westgate's sleeve as she leads him into her room, looks at Goldie, and says, "This is the tycoon and benefactor who has been kind enough to provide the fabrics for my funeral clothes."

Westgate's eyes fix onto Goldie, who appears extraordinarily beautiful in her elegant attire as she continues to sew the clothes.

Goldie lowers her head respectfully when she sees Westgate enter the room.

Westgate quickly bows and greets Goldie whereupon Goldie puts down her sewing tools and returns the greeting.

Mrs. Rex then says, “I’m so grateful to Tycoon for giving several rolls of silk and satin which I’ve stored in my house for over a year. I’m also very grateful to this neighbor of mine, who sews as well as a sewing machine. The rolls of fabric would still be collecting dust right now if she didn’t volunteer to tailor my funeral clothes. Her stitching is so firm and precise, it’ll blow you away! Tycoon, come over and look.”

Westgate picks up a piece of stitched satin, examines it, and exclaims, “How can she be such a good tailor? What fairylike skill she possesses!”

Goldie responds modestly, “Tycoon, you’ve gotta be kidding. I don’t deserve such praise!”

Westgate asks, “Mrs. Rex, may I ask which family she is from?”

Mrs. Rex replies, “Tycoon, why don’t you take a guess?”

Westgate replies, “I haven’t got a clue.”

Mrs. Rex says laughingly, “Tycoon, please have a seat, and I’ll tell you.”

Westgate takes a seat opposite Goldie, and Mrs. Rex asks, “Tycoon, weren’t you struck by a forked pole not too long ago? It whacked you pretty good!”

Westgate replies, “Yes, I remember the day a forked pole struck my headscarf. I never did figure out who was responsible for that though.”

Goldie says with a sheepish smile, “I accidentally offended Tycoon that day. Please forgive me.” She then stands up and bows.

Westgate immediately bows back and responds, “Don’t worry about it; it was nothing!”

Mrs. Rex says, “She’s the wife of my neighbor, Dally Brawn.”

Westgate says, “So she’s the wife of Dally Brawn! He’s a friendly businessman who never offends anyone in any way when he sells his pancakes on the street. Not only is he good at earning money, but he’s also an affable man. A good man is hard to find!”

Mrs. Rex responds, “It’s no wonder she’s been attentively attending to Dally’s needs ever since they tied the knot. They’re so compatible with each other!”

Goldie says, "This has got to be a joke! My husband is a useless man."

Westgate says, "You're mistaken. A sage once said, 'A reed before the wind lives on, while mighty oaks do fall.' You might consider your husband a cockroach, but cockroaches will still be around long after humans become extinct."

Mrs. Rex looks at Goldie and asks, "Do you know this tycoon?"

Goldie replies, "No, I don't."

Mrs. Rex says, "This tycoon is the millionaire of the town and the mayor has befriended him. He's known as Tycoon Westgate, and he's the owner of the drugstore near the town hall. He's richer than Croesus, his cornucopia of grain overflows his barn, his gold is so brilliant, his silver is so shiny, his pearls are so round, and his treasures are so magnificent. He even possesses rhinoceros horns and elephant tusks. I acted as a matchmaker for his wife, a stunningly beautiful maiden from the Call mansion." She then asks, "Tycoon, why has it been so long since you last dropped by my teahouse for tea?"

Westgate replies, "I've been tied up because my daughter has recently gotten engaged."

Mrs. Rex asks, "To whom did Lassie get engaged? Why didn't you ask me to be the matchmaker?"

Westgate replies, "Her fiancé is a 17-year-old man named Jimmy Show 陈经济, still attending school, whose father is an in-law of Commander Birch 楊提督 of the 800,000-strong imperial army stationed in the capital. Not that I didn't want to have you as the matchmaker, but Mrs. Script, an employee of the Show mansion, has already initiated the engagement, and Mrs. Reed, the florist who frequently visits our mansion, wanted to help Mrs. Script with the engagement party preparations. If you'd like to help them out, I'll send a servant with an invitation to invite you to the wedding ceremony which will take place tomorrow."

Mrs. Rex says laughingly, "I was just kidding. Matchmakers like me are a dime a dozen. If I wasn't hired before the matchmaking process began, then why should I attend the engagement party where I'd run into my competitors who hate my guts? There ain't no such thing as a free lunch!" She continues to chew the fat with Westgate for a while and praises his wealth with wild abandon.

Goldie lowers her head and continues with her sewing as Westgate, captivated by her otherworldly beauty, grows more and more desperate to hook up with her.

Mrs. Rex brings over two cups of tea, one for Westgate and one for Goldie. She looks at Goldie and says, "Please have tea with Tycoon."

Goldie begins to cast flirtatious glances at Westgate after tea.

Mrs. Rex surreptitiously glances at Westgate and touches her face with all five fingers of one hand.

Westgate knows it means he has a 50 percent chance to get lucky.

Mrs. Rex says, "Tycoon, I've never had the nerve to go to your mansion to invite you here. Thanks to my good karma, you've visited me, but as they say, 'No person can serve two masters.' Since Tycoon is my financial master while she is my master tailor, I feel awkward serving both masters here. A better arrangement would be to have Tycoon act as the host and treat her as his guest."

Westgate responds, "If I'm going to replace you as the host, then I should cover your shopping expenses." He takes an oz of silver out of his pocket for Mrs. Rex to buy food and drinks with.

Goldie says, "I don't deserve to be treated as a guest." Despite being polite, she makes no attempt to leave the room.

Mrs. Rex takes the silver and heads toward the door as Goldie continues to stay put in her seat. As she steps out the door, she says, "Please keep Tycoon company. I'll be back soon."

Goldie says, "Mrs. Rex, please don't worry about food and drinks." She is still sitting there.

Mrs. Rex then takes off, leaving Westgate and Goldie alone in the house by themselves.

Westgate continuously stares at Goldie, who in turn steals a glance at the handsome tycoon out of the corner of her eye as she continues with her needlework.

Mrs. Rex soon returns with a tray containing a plump goose and plates of roast duck, fried meat, fresh fish, and delicious fruit. She sets the tray on the table and says, "Please take a break from the sewing and have some food and drinks."

Goldie responds, "Why don't you keep Tycoon company instead? I don't deserve to have such a nice meal."

Mrs. Rex replies, “How can you say that? This meal has been specially prepared for you.” She then arranges the plates on the table, and when everyone is seated, she fills up the cups with wine.

Westgate raises his cup of wine and says, “Let’s have a drink.”

Goldie responds politely, “Tycoon, thank you for your kind invitation, but I’m not much of a drinker.”

Mrs. Rex says, “She’s being too modest, she’s actually a heavy drinker. Goldie, please help yourself to two cups of wine.”

Goldie then toasts the two of them whereupon Westgate says, “Mrs. Rex, please coax her into having some food as well.”

Mrs. Rex picks out a few good pieces of meat for Goldie. After she had three cups of wine, she leaves the room to warm up the rest of the wine.

Westgate asks, “May I ask your age?”

Goldie replies, “I’ve squandered all 25 years of my life. I was born on February 9th, in the year of the dragon.”

Westgate says, “You’re the same age as my wife who was also born in the year of the dragon, but since she was born on September 15th, you’re seven months older than she.”

Goldie responds, “You shouldn’t compare your fairy with a mere human like me!”

Mrs. Rex interjects, “But you’re such a nice lady, and you’re so good-looking and intelligent! Not only are you a master tailor, but you’re also well versed in literature, and skilled at playing backgammon and chess, solving riddles, and calligraphy!”

Westgate exclaims, “Where can one find a wife like that? Lady Luck was clearly on Dally Brawn’s side—how else could he have married this woman?”

Mrs. Rex replies, “I’m in no way exaggerating when I say the numerous concubines in Tycoon’s mansion are no match for this single woman.”

Westgate says, “I couldn’t have said it better myself. To make a long story short, I haven’t been able to get a good wife because I was born under an unlucky star.”

Mrs. Rex says, “Tycoon, your first wife was quite a catch.”

Westgate says, “If my first wife were around, everything would be fine. Now I no longer have a good housewife, my house is at sixes and sevens. Although I’m supporting several concubines, they’re all useless.”

Goldie asks, “Tycoon, when did your first wife pass away?”

“Although my late wife Lady Show 陈氏 came from a poor family, she was pretty and smart, and very considerate. Unfortunately, she passed away three years ago. My second wife is nothing more than a burden on me. Since she often falls ill and is completely useless, the household is at sixes and sevens. I always stay away from home because it’s too depressing over there.”

“To be frank with you, Tycoon, neither your first nor your second wife can match Mrs. Brawn when it comes to tailoring. She so incredibly talented!”

“And may I mention my late wife certainly wasn’t as attractive as Mrs. Brawn!”

“Tycoon, why haven’t you let me see that girlfriend of yours who resides on East Street?”

“You mean the opera singer Citric Pull 张惜春? She’s just a singer, and I don’t like her.”

“How long have you been with Cutie Plum, the prostitute?”

“I’ve already married her as an in-house concubine, but she doesn’t know how to take care of the household. Otherwise, I’d promote her to be my wife.”

“Well, how long have you been seeing Dior Bright?”

“I’ve also married her as my third spouse. But she’s contracted tuberculosis lately, an incurable disease.

“Will there be a problem if you married a woman like Mrs. Brawn who knows how to please you?”

“My parents have both passed away, so I can do whatever I want. Who dares to stand in my way?”

“It’s going to take quite some time to find a woman who can satisfy Tycoon!”

“I haven’t been lucky enough to find the right one yet!”

Westgate and Mrs. Rex continue to converse on that subject for quite a while until Mrs. Rex finally says, “We’re about to run out of this wonderful wine. I hope you don’t mind if I go out and buy another bottle.”

Westgate still has 4 oz of silver in his pocket. He hands them all to Mrs. Rex and says, “Use this money to buy some wine and keep the change.”

Mrs. Rex thanks Westgate, gets up, and glances at Goldie who, after several cups of wine, begins to feel aroused.

Chapter 4. Yorky Exposes the Adulterous Affair

Before Mrs. Rex heads out the door with the silver, she says slyly, "I'm going to the store to buy a bottle of wine, Goldie. Please keep Tycoon company for a while. There's still enough wine left in the kettle to fill two more cups. I'm going to head over to East Street where they sell high-quality wine, and I won't be back for quite some time."

Goldie responds, "You don't need to go there. I've had enough wine already, thanks."

Mrs. Rex whispers, "Psst! Tycoon isn't an outsider. So, what's wrong with drinking with him?"

Goldie remains silent, not budging from her seat.

Mrs. Rex closes the door and hooks a lock through the hasp, locking both guests inside the house before she leaves.

Westgate glances at Goldie, with hair partly let down, bosom partially revealed by her décolletage, and powdered face slightly reddish in color. After filling a cup with wine and offering it to her, he comments on how warm the room is, takes off his coat, and asks, "Would you mind putting it on the radiator for me?"

Goldie quickly accommodates his request.

Westgate swipes his sleeve across the table, knocking his chopsticks onto the floor accidentally on purpose. As luck would have it, the chopsticks land beside Goldie's dainty feet. He quickly bends down, but instead of picking the chopsticks up, he pinches the toe of one of her embroidered shoes.

Goldie says amusedly, "Tycoon, don't play games. We seem to be made for each other. Would you like to hook up with me?"

Westgate falls to his knees at that big moment and exclaims, "Thank you for fulfilling my dream!"

Goldie helps Westgate back to his feet, hugs him, and says, "I'm afraid Mrs. Rex might walk in on us at any moment."

Westgate responds, "Don't worry, she knows."

They both take off their clothes in Mrs. Rex's room and do what comes naturally. One is groaning orgasmically, while the other is in a state of complete euphoria.

Having satisfied their pent-up desires, they are just about to put their clothes back on when Mrs. Rex bursts through the door and cries, "Holy smoke, you're having an affair!"

Westgate and Goldie are both completely caught off guard by her sudden arrival. Mrs. Rex looks at Goldie and exclaims, “My, oh my! I asked you to do tailoring for me. I didn’t ask you to have a tryst. I’ll be in trouble if Dally finds out about this. I’d better be the first one to spill the beans!” She then turns around to leave.

Goldie holds onto Mrs. Rex’s skirt, falls to her knees, and pleads, “Please spare my life, Mrs. Rex!”

Mrs. Rex responds, “If you want me to keep my mouth shut, you must agree to one condition!”

Goldie exclaims, “I’ll agree to ten conditions, not just a single condition!”

Mrs. Rex responds, “If from now on, you’ll have trysts with Tycoon each time he so desires, I’ll leave you alone without letting Dally catch you red-handed. Otherwise, I’ll divulge your secret.”

Goldie says, “Rest assured I’ll comply with this condition.”

Mrs. Rex says, “Tycoon, since I’ve made your wish come true, don’t forget your promise. Otherwise, I’ll spill the beans.”

Westgate responds, “Don’t worry, I won’t break my promise.”

Mrs. Rex says, “Promises are like pie crust, made to be broken. I need both of you to exchange mementos as a token of your sincerity.”

Westgate then removes a golden hair clip from his hair and puts it in one of Goldie’s sideburns.

Since Goldie worries the hair clip might arouse Dally’s suspicion, she decides to hide it in her pocket when she returns home. She then takes a handkerchief out of her pocket and gives it to Westgate. By the time they have had a few more drinks, it is already afternoon. Goldie says, “Dally will be back home soon, so I’d better head back now.” She then returns home through the back door and draws the portiere aside just when Dally arrives at the front door.

Mrs. Rex looks at Westgate and asks, “So, how do you like my plan so far?”

“You’re smarter than Archimedes and more logical than Aristotle!”

“How good is she in bed?”

“She’s absolutely incredible!”

"She's not just talented in playing musical instruments and singing, she can do just about anything. It wasn't easy for me to hook you two up, so don't forget what you've promised me."

"Don't worry. I'll deliver the money to you when I get back home. How could I renege on my promise?" After peeking around to make sure the street is empty, Westgate leaves the teahouse blissfully.

Westgate returns to the teahouse the next day. As Mrs. Rex quickly serves him tea, he takes a 10-oz silver nugget out of his pocket and hands it to her. After all, money talks in this world. Her eyes lock onto the silver nugget, which appears as white as snow, and she is so delighted she bows twice and exclaims, "Thanks for your generosity, Tycoon!" She continues, "Dally has not yet left the house, so let me go over there and pretend I need to borrow a ladle, just so I can see what's going on." She then goes through the back door to visit Goldie.

Goldie is serving Dally breakfast when she hears someone knock on the door, and she asks, "Eva, who's there?"

Eva replies, "It's Mrs. Rex; she's here to borrow a ladle."

Goldie quickly goes to the door and says, "Of course we can lend you our ladle. Please come in and have a seat."

Mrs. Rex gestures with her hand and responds, "But there's no one watching my teahouse right now."

Goldie understands the gesture means Westgate has arrived at the teahouse. After handing the ladle to Mrs. Rex, she goads Dally into quickly finishing his breakfast and leaving the house with his trays of pancakes. She then puts on her makeup, changes into a beautiful new set of clothes, and says, "Eva, take care of this place! I'm going to Mrs. Rex's house now, and I won't be back for quite a while. As soon as your father returns home, you must notify me of his arrival, or else I'll beat you to a pulp!" After Eva promises to do so, Goldie heads over to the teahouse to see Westgate.

Westgate is ecstatic to sees Goldie, and they sit side by side before long.

Mrs. Rex asks, "Did Dally ask you any questions when you returned home yesterday?"

Goldie replies, "He asked me if I'd finished tailoring your clothes. I said I'd already finished making the clothes, but I still need to make your shoes and socks."

As Mrs. Rex hurriedly serves them wine, Westgate notices Goldie is even prettier than the first time he saw her. After a few drinks, her powdered face begins to flush slightly, and with her sideburns hanging down over her cheeks like pretty paintings, she appears even fairer than the Moon Fairy. Captivated by her beauty, he cuddles her and lifts her skirt to admire her dainty feet tucked inside a pair of black satin shoes.

Goldie asks, “May I ask your age?”

“I’m 27 years old. I was born on August 28th, in the year of the tiger.”

“How many wives and concubines are living with you?”

“Other than my wife, I have three concubines, but none of them can satisfy me.”

“How many children do you have?”

“I have only one daughter I’ll soon marry off. I don’t have any other children.” After shooting the breeze with Goldie a little longer, Westgate takes a small silver box out of his pocket. He opens the box, takes out a tea biscuit, balances it on his tongue, and transfer it to Goldie’s mouth. They cuddle each other tightly, and their slick tongues, like those of hissing snakes, slither lovingly against each other.

Meanwhile, Mrs. Rex has only been paying attention to the dishes she has been preparing and couldn’t care less what the two lovebirds are doing.

Goldie goes to Mrs. Rex’s house every day from then on to see Westgate, and they become as close as two coats of paint. But bad news travels fast, and in less than two weeks, everyone in the neighborhood knows about their affair except Dally.

There is a rather astute lad in town named Yorky High 乔郓哥, about 15 years old. Named after Yorkshire 郓州 where he was born, he lives with his father, earns his living by selling fruit and candy at the taverns near the town hall. One day he walks along the street carrying a basket of pears, looking for Westgate, a customer of his who regularly tips him.

A man with a big mouth bumps into Yorky, and when Yorky asks him if he knows Westgate’s whereabouts, he replies, “I know where he is, Yorky.”

Yorky says, “Please tell me because I’d like to earn a little money to help out my father.”

The man responds, “Westgate has recently been having an affair with the wife of Dally Brawn, the pancake peddler. He’s been going to Mrs. Rex’s teahouse on Purplestone Street every day, so he must be there right now. A young kid like you should be able to barge in without any problems."

After thanking the man, Yorky picks up his fruit basket and scurries off to Purplestone Street like a monkey. He walks straight into the teahouse, where he sees Mrs. Rex sitting on a stool tying up some loose ends. He puts down his basket and greets her.

Mrs. Rex asks, "What brings you here, Yorky?"

Yorky replies, "I'm looking for Tycoon. I'd like to do a little business with him to earn some money to help out my father."

Mrs. Rex asks, "Which tycoon are you referring to?"

Yorky replies, "C'mon, you know whom I'm talking about!"

Mrs. Rex says, "No, I don't. The last time I checked, even tycoons have names."

Yorky responds, "Let me give you a hint: he has a two-syllable surname."

Mrs. Rex asks, "Huh? Which two syllables?"

Yorky replies, "Stop playing dumb. I'd like to have a word with Tycoon Westgate." He then heads straight for the bedroom.

Mrs. Rex holds onto Yorky and shouts, "Just where do you think you're going, you little monkey? My bedroom is private—you can't just barge in there like that!"

Yorky replies, "Say what you want, but I know he's in there somewhere."

Mrs. Rex snaps, "Read my lips, you filthy little monkey. This so-called Tycoon Westgate is *not* at my house!"

Yorky responds, "Don't be so selfish! You've already squeezed almost every penny out of him, and I just want to get a little piece of the pie. You can stop playing games now—I know everything that's going on!"

Mrs. Rex shouts, "What exactly *do* you know, you little chimp?"

Yorky replies, "Must you have a finger in every pie? You're depriving others of an opportunity to make some money. If I divulge your dirty little secrets, my pancake-peddling pal will most certainly blow his top!"

His words hit a raw nerve, prompting Mrs. Rex to shout, "Why, you despicable little chimp! What makes you think you can just barge into my house and stink up the place with your nasty flatulence?"

Yorky retorts, "Well, if I'm a chimp, then you're a pimp!"

Fuming with rage, Mrs. Rex grabs Yorky and punches him twice in the head.

Yorky yells, "Why did you hit me?"

Mrs. Rex snarls, "Shut up, you incestuous chimp, or I'll slap you out of here!"

Yorky snaps, "You're nothing but a washed-up old flesh-peddler, and you hit people for no good reason!"

Without warning, Mrs. Rex puts Yorky in a headlock, drags him out into the street, and punches him in the head again. She then tosses his fruit basket out the door, causing the pears to roll down the street.

Unable to fight back, Yorky cries as he scrambles to pick up the pears. He points at Mrs. Rex's teahouse and yells, "Now you listen to me, you flesh-peddling hag! I'm going to tell on you, and once your dirty little secrets are out, you'll never be able to earn another coin from him" With fruit basket in hand, he rushes off to find a particular man. After all, chickens come home to roost.

Chapter 5. The Adultery Leads to Murder

After turning two street corners, the distraught Yorky sees Dally walking along the street with baskets of pancakes suspended from his carrying pole.

Yorky walks over to him and says, "I haven't seen you in quite a while. Have you been fattened up by someone?"

"I still look the same. Why do you think I've been fattened up?"

"I wanted to buy some chicken feed yesterday, but I couldn't find it anywhere. However, everyone said you have some in your house."

"I don't raise chickens or ducks at my house, so why would I have any chicken feed?"

"You say you don't have any chicken feed, but how have you been fed so well? How can you not be upset when you're like a fat cuckold held upside down by its legs, soaking in the pot?"

"How dare you insult me, you little monkey! How can I be a cuckold if my wife isn't having an extramarital affair?"

"Well, your wife may not be having an extramarital affair, but she's certainly having an extra affair-marital!"

Dally grabs Yorky and exclaims, "Tell me who that guy is!"

"All you can do is grab me. We both know you wouldn't have the guts to bite off that guy's pecker."

"My dear brother, tell me who he is, and I'll give you ten pancakes."

"Pancakes are cheap. I need something better than that. You've got to treat me to three drinks before I tell you more."

"You want a drink? Then follow me." With his carrying pole on his shoulder, Dally leads Yorky into a small tavern where he puts down his carrying pole, takes out a few pancakes, and orders some meat and a bottle of wine.

Yorky indulges himself for a while and says, "I don't need more wine. Just get some more slices of meat for me."

"First tell me who that man is."

"Don't be so impatient. Let me finish eating before I tell you. After all, the husband is always the last to know. But don't you worry, I'll help you catch them in the act."

When the naughty boy finishes his meal, Dally says, "You should tell me now."

"Take a look at the bruises on my head before I tell you."

"Why do you have these bruises?"

"I brought along this fruit basket when I went off looking for Tycoon Westgate today to sell him some pears. Although I couldn't find him, someone on the street told me: 'He's in Mrs. Rex's teahouse having an affair with Dally's wife. They do it every day over there.' I was hoping to earn a few coins selling pears, but I didn't expect old hag Rex to stop me from looking for him in her bedroom. She even beat me up and kicked me out of her house. I've come here to look for you, and I made a few snide remarks to rile you up, to provoke you into asking me certain questions."

"Are you telling me the truth?"

"There you go again! You're such a fool! They have a joyous rendezvous in Mrs. Rex's bedroom every day as soon as you leave your house. And you're asking me if I'm telling you the truth?"

After a moment of reflection, Dally says, "To tell you the truth, my wife goes to Mrs. Rex's house every day, but it's supposedly for some tailoring job. However, her face is often red when she comes back home. Further fueling my suspicions, she's been beating and scolding the daughter of my late wife daily, and my daughter's been exceptionally miserable these past few days. Since you've provided the missing piece of the puzzle, I'll put away my pancakes and catch them red-handed."

"How can anyone your age still be so dumb? Mrs. Rex alone is too tough an adversary for you to tackle. And as soon as she sees you, she'll secretly signal your wife to hide. Worse still, Westgate is a skilled martial artist who could take on 20 of you. So, if you can't catch him in the act, he'll accuse you of slander and beat you to a pulp! He could also take you to court, and with his money and power, no one would dare help you out in any way, and it'd be the end of you."

"I couldn't agree more, Brother, but how can I get my revenge?"

"I also haven't taken my revenge against the old hag who beat me up. Anyway, here's my plan: Just act your normal self when you return home this evening. You'll bake fewer than usual pancakes to sell tomorrow, and I'll wait for you in the alley off Purplestone Street. If I see Westgate enter the teahouse, I'll call you over. You then wait nearby with your baskets of pancakes. I'll first go inside to provoke the old hag who will surely attempt to beat me up again. You then barge in as soon as I toss my fruit basket out into the street. You can just run into the bedroom and cry foul, while I pin the old hag against the wall with my head. What do you think?"

"Sounds like a plan. I owe you one! Let me repay you by giving you several strings of coins. Come early tomorrow to the alley and wait for me there!"

Yorky takes the strings of coins and some pancakes and then leaves.

Dally pays for the meal, picks up his carrying pole, and sells more pancakes on his way back home. Although his wife has had the habit of constantly scolding and disparaging him, she has been more accommodating lately due to her recent transgressions. After carrying his pancakes back home in the evening, Dally acts his normal self and does not say anything out of the ordinary.

Goldie asks, "Did you have a drink while you went out?"

Dally replies, "I ran into an agent and had three drinks with him."

Goldie then prepares dinner for the family.

Dally only bakes two trays of pancakes the next day after breakfast.

Goldie, who has only Westgate on her mind, couldn't care less how many pancakes Dally has baked. As soon as Dally carries his pancakes outside, she wastes no time going over to Mrs. Rex's teahouse to await Westgate's arrival.

Meanwhile, Dally walks to the alley off Purplestone Street, sees Yorky looking around carrying a basket, and asks, "What's cooking?"

Yorky replies, "It's too early right now. You may sell a tray of pancakes before you come back here. He'll probably show up pretty soon, so don't wander too far."

Dally sells his first tray of pancakes in a short while and then returns.

Yorky says, "Barge in as soon as I toss my basket out the door."

Dally then puts down his baskets of pancakes.

With his basket of fruit in hand, Yorky storms into the teahouse and scolds, "Hey, why did you beat me up yesterday, you old tramp?"

Mrs. Rex, in her usual obnoxious manner, springs to her feet and retorts, "I don't want to have anything to do with you, you little chimp! Why have you come here to berate me?"

Yorky replies, "What's wrong with berating a hag like you who's no different from a bawd. Who cares about you anyway?"

Infuriated beyond belief, Mrs. Rex grabs Yorky and swings at him.

Yorky cries, "You hit me!" and tosses his basket out into the street.

Before Mrs. Rex has the chance to dish out a beating, Yorky grabs ahold of her belt and headbutts her in the stomach with so much force he almost knocks her to the ground. Luckily for her, the wall behind her stops her from falling, while the naughty boy pins her against the wall with all his strength.

Meanwhile, Dally storms into the teahouse with his sleeves rolled up.

Mrs. Rex desperately wants to stop Dally from advancing any further. But how can she move an inch when she is pinned against the wall by a tenacious naughty boy? She can only scream, "Dally's coming!"

Goldie, in the heat of an affair, scrambles to the bedroom door and pushes all her weight against it, while Westgate dives under the bed.

Dally dashes to the bedroom door and tries to open it. But how can he push it open with his wimpy arms? He can only shout, "I know you're having an affair!"

Still desperately pushing against the door to keep it shut, Goldie grumbles, "You boast about your martial arts when nothing happens, but you're all mouth and no trousers when push comes to shove! Even a paper tiger can scare the pants off you!"

Goldie is hoping her remarks will provoke Westgate into giving Dally enough of a beating to enable them to escape from the teahouse. Sure enough, Westgate comes out from under the bed and says, "I wasn't my usual self...I just had a momentary lapse of judgment." He then swings open the door and shouts, "Stay out of this room!" Just when Dally attempts to grab hold of him, he delivers an exceptionally powerful kick.

The kick hits Dally right in the heart because of his short stature and knocks him over.

When Westgate sees the force of his kick has knocked Dally unconscious, he simply walks away.

As soon as Yorky sees Westgate turn the tables on Dally, he releases his hold on Mrs. Rex and darts out of the teahouse.

The neighbors all know Westgate is a formidable martial artist, and nobody dares intervene.

Mrs. Rex helps Dally up. He is spitting out blood and his face is terribly pale. She calls Goldie over and fetches a bowl of water to revive and hydrate him. They carry him out through the back door, then up the stairs, and let him rest in his bed.

Westgate, not having yet faced any consequences for his actions, continues his affair with Goldie the next day expecting Dally to soon kick the bucket.

Dally feels like death warmed up and cannot get out of bed for the next five days. Goldie does not take care of him at all, but just puts on makeup, leaves the house, and returns home with a rosy glow on her cheeks. She even says, "Eva, listen to me, you little vamp. Don't you dare take care of your father or else I'll beat you up?"

Eva is too scared to ask outsiders for help.

Dally is so angry at what has happened to him he almost faints, but nobody seems to care. He later bellows, "I caught your affair red-handed. You urged your lover to kick me in the heart, and now I'm more dead than alive while you continue enjoying your life as if nothing went wrong! I know I'm going to die soon because I can't put up a fight against you! But no matter what, you're going to deal with my brother Sawn. He'll be back sooner or later, and he'll never let you off the hook for what you've done! If you take pity on me and attend to my needs, I won't mention anything when he returns. But if you don't help me out, I'll tell on you when he gets back!"

Without responding, Goldie heads over to Mrs. Rex's teahouse and repeats Dally's threat word for word.

Those words send shivers down Westgate's spine. He exclaims, "Holy smoke! I've heard Sergeant Brawn killed a tiger with his bare hands in Viewsunridge. He's the best martial artist in Clearstream Town! I've been in love with Goldie for so many days we're now inseparable! Now she brings this matter to our attention, what am I going to do? What a terrible predicament this is!"

Mrs. Rex scoffs, "I've never seen this type of situation before where you, the captain who steers the boat, are more frightened than me, the passenger!"

Westgate responds, "I feel bad a tough guy like me can't come up with a solution to this dilemma on his own! Do you have any ideas how we can hide from him?"

Mrs. Rex says, "I've already hatched a plan on how to hide you from him, but I need to know whether you'd like to have a long-term or a short-term relationship with Goldie."

Westgate says, "Please explain to me what you mean by long-term and short-term relationships."

Mrs. Rex explains, "A short-term relationship means you'll be separated from her today. You'll wait until Dally recovers and apologize to him so there'll be nothing for him to complain about. when Sawn returns, You may resume your relationship with Goldie when Sawn has another business trip.

"A long-term relationship means you'll be able to stay with Goldie every day with no worries, but it'll require you to follow my crafty plan which I think will be too difficult for you to do."

Westgate says, "Please take care of us! We want to have a long-term relationship!"

"My plan requires a certain item. Other people don't have it at home. As it so happens, you already have it in your possession, Tycoon!"

"Even if the item were my eye, I'd gouge it out for you. What item is it?"

"There are more ways to kill a dog than choking it with butter. Tycoon, since that wimp looks like death warmed up, just get some arsenic from your drugstore. Let Goldie buy some heart pain medication, add the arsenic to it to put that dwarf out of his misery, and then cremate him so thoroughly not a single trace is left behind. What can Sawn Brawn do when he comes home? We all know as soon as a widowed sister-in-law marries again, the previous in-law relationship ends. So how can this former brother-in-law intervene? After Goldie observes the mourning period, she can then marry Tycoon. Won't that be a long-term relationship for you to live happily ever after? Any objections?"

Westgate replies, "It couldn't be better! People say that 'When the going gets tough, the tough get going!' Since I'm at the point of no return, so be it!"

Mrs. Rex says, "You said it. This is what we call 'Nipping it in the bud.' Go ahead and get some arsenic, and I'll teach Goldie how to apply it. You'll have to give me a handsome reward when the mission is accomplished."

Westgate says, "Certainly," and he soon comes back with a package of arsenic and gives it to Mrs. Rex.

Mrs. Rex takes the arsenic and says, "Goldie, let me teach you how to use this poison. Just pretend to be nice to Dally. Put this arsenic in the heart-pain potion when he asks you for the medication. Wait for him to get into a sitting position, help him swallow the entire bowl of potion, and then walk away. His stomach and guts will burst when the poison takes effect, and he'll scream in agony. Smother his face with a blanket so other people can't hear his screaming. Prepare a bowl of water and a towel ahead of time. This poison will make him bleed through his mouth, nose, ears, eyes, and all other orifices, and there'll be bite marks on his lips. Remove the blanket as soon as he breathes his last. Use the towel to wipe away all the bloodstains before putting him cleanly into a coffin. After he's cremated, what can go wrong?"

Goldie replies, "It's easier said than done. I'll be too scared to do anything, let alone perform the task of an undertaker."

Mrs. Rex says, "It'll be a piece of cake. If you need any help, just knock on the wall, and I'll come over."

Westgate says, "Go ahead with your plan. I'll come at 5 a.m. to get your progress report." He then leaves.

Mrs. Rex pounds the arsenic into a fine powder, after which she hands it to Goldie who then hides it.

Goldie returns home. She sheds her crocodile tears when she sees Dally short of breath and waiting to die.

Dally asks, "Why are you crying?"

Goldie replies, "My momentary lapse of reason caused me to be cheated by Chic Westgate. I didn't expect him to kick you in the heart! I've heard of a good medication and I'd like to buy it to cure your illness, but I'm afraid you may be suspicious of me, so I dare not buy it."

Dally says, "If you can cure my illness, t I'll let bygones be bygones, won't bear a grudge against you, and won't mention it when Sawn returns home. Hurry up and buy the medication to save my life!"

Goldie takes some coins, goes straight to Mrs. Rex's house, and asks Mrs. Rex to buy heart-pain medication. She then takes the medication upstairs, gives it to Dally, and says, "This is the heart-pain medication. The licensed doctor said you should take it at midnight and then sleep with a blanket covering your head. After you sweat, you can get out of bed tomorrow."

Dally says, “That’s great! Thanks. Stay awake tonight so you can prepare it for me.”

Goldie says, “You can sleep without worry. I’ll take care of you.”

In the evening, Goldie lights the lamp in the room and then goes downstairs to boil a large pot of water and get a towel.

The drum tower strikes midnight. Goldie first puts the arsenic in a cup, scoops up a bowl of hot water, goes upstairs, and asks, “Where’s the medication, Dally?”

Dally replies, “I’ve put it under the mat, near my pillow. Hurry up and prepare it for me to drink!”

Goldie lifts the mat, gets the medication, pours it into the cup, mixes it with the poison, pours hot water from the bowl into the cup, and stirs the mixture evenly with her hair clip. With her left hand supporting Dally upright, she uses her right hand to pour the potion into his mouth.

Dally takes a sip, and exclaims, “Wife, this potion is hard to swallow!”

Goldie responds, “Desperate diseases must have desperate remedies.” When Dally takes a second sip, she pours the entire cup of potion down his throat, lays him down, and quickly jumps off the bed.

Dally cries cringingly, “Wife, this potion gives me a stomachache. Oh no! It’s unbearable!”

Goldie grabs a blanket in a split second and smothers Dally’s face with it.

Dally yells, “I can’t breathe!”

Goldie says, “Sweating will make you recover quicker. That’s just what the doctor ordered!”

Dally wants to make another statement, but before he can utter a word, Goldie, fearing he may put up a struggle, leaps onto the bed, mounts him, and presses the blanket firmly into his face.

Dally feels as if his lungs had been sautéed, his liver and guts fried, his heart stabbed, and his stomach chopped up. With his body stiffening up and blood oozing out of his orifices, he gnashes his teeth as his spirit descends to the Underworld’s City of Wrongful Death.

Goldie lifts the blanket, and she is so horrified by what she sees she leaps off the bed and knocks on the wall.

Mrs. Rex hears the knocking. She goes to the back door and gives a cough.

Goldie then goes downstairs and opens the back door.

Mrs. Rex asks, “Has he given up the ghost?”

Goldie replies, “Yes, that’s for sure. As for me, the spirit is willing, but the flesh is weak. I don’t know what to do now!”

Mrs. Rex says, “There’s nothing to it. I’ll help you out.” She rolls up her sleeves, scoops a bucket of water, puts a towel in it, and carries it upstairs. After rolling up the blanket, she first wipes away the bloodstains from Dally’s lips and orifices.

After carrying the corpse downstairs one step at a time, they lay an old door on the floor and place the corpse on top of it. They comb his hair, change his clothes, and dress him in his scarf, socks, and shoes before they cover his face with a white cloth and put a clean blanket over him. They then go upstairs to do more cleaning before Mrs. Rex returns home.

Goldie then pretends to cry her heart out to appear to mourn the death of the head of household.

Dear reader, you should know a woman like Goldie can cry in three different ways:

She is crying when she sheds tears and makes a racket.

She is weeping when she sheds tears but does not make a racket.

She is wailing when she does not shed tears but makes a racket.

Goldie wails for quite a while at night.

At 5 a.m., before dawn, Westgate rushes over to get a progress report, and Mrs. Rex gives him a detailed account of what has transpired. He gives her some money to pay for a coffin and other funeral expenses.

Goldie says, “Now Dally’s dead, I have to depend on you.”

“Don’t worry your pretty little head about it.”

“What’ll happen if you dump me?”

“If I dump you, I’ll end up like Dally Brawn!”

Mrs. Rex says, “Tycoon, don’t talk nonsense. We now have a more critical issue to deal with. I’m afraid the coroner may cry foul when he performs an autopsy on the corpse tomorrow! Jupe Quest 何九, the coroner, is a rather shrewd man. I’m afraid he may refuse to sign the death certificate.”

“It shouldn’t be a problem. I’ll talk to him. He won’t have the guts to act against me.”

“Tycoon, take care of him quickly. There’s no time to lose.”

Chapter 6. Chic Westgate Bribes Jupe Quest

Mrs. Rex goes out to buy a coffin, incense, candles, and joss paper. She and Goldie set up an altar soon afterward.

Goldie puts a lantern on the altar. She sheds crocodile tears when the neighbors visit her.

A neighbor asks, "What did Dally die from?"

Still pretending to be heartbroken, Goldie replies, "My husband had a heartache I worsened about every day. Unfortunately, he passed away at midnight. Oh, pity me!"

The neighbors know Dally died in mysterious circumstances, but they dare not be too inquisitive.

A neighbor says consolingly, "No matter how bad things seem, life goes on. Don't be so depressed in this hot weather."

Goldie pretends to be thankful for the consolation as the neighbors leave the house.

After Mrs. Rex brings a coffin into the house, she sends for Coroner Jupe Quest. She also hires two Zen monks from Grateful Monastery 報恩寺 to pray for the departed.

Jupe sends his undertakers over to prepare for the autopsy before he leaves his office at 10 a.m. and heads to Purplestone Street where he bumps into Westgate at the street corner.

Westgate asks, "Where are you going, Jupe?"

Jupe replies, "I'm going to examine the body of Dally Brawn, the pancake peddler."

Westgate says, "I'd like to have a little talk with you."

Westgate takes Jupe to a small tavern at the street corner, walks over to a corner table, and says, "Jupe, please have a seat."

Jupe says, "I'm a peon not worthy of sitting with Tycoon."

Westgate says, "Jupe, don't be so modest. Please have a seat."

After they both sit down, Westgate orders, "Waiter, give me a bottle of good wine."

After the waiter serves them food and wine, Jupe thinks, "Westgate never drinks with me. There must be a special reason for all this."

After a few drinks, Westgate takes out a shiny silver nugget, puts it on the table, and says, "I hope this isn't too little for you, Jupe. I'll reward you more tomorrow."

Jupe shakes his head and says, "Tycoon, since I haven't provided you with any services, how can I accept your gift of silver? If you have any assignments for me, I won't decline it."

"Jupe, don't treat me like an outsider. Please accept it."

"Tycoon, just tell me what's on your mind."

"It's nothing special. Just take it easy when you examine Dally Brawn's corpse. Sweep everything under the rug and don't say anything."

"This is such a minor issue. Why should I accept Tycoon's silver for something so small?"

"Jupe, not accepting it means you're refusing to work for me."

Jupe is quite intimidated by Westgate who has a lot of influence in court, so he accepts the silver.

After a few more drinks, Westgate says, "Waiter, come to my store tomorrow to receive the payment for the bill."

As Westgate leaves the tavern with Jupe, he repeats, "Jupe, remember what I just told you, and don't tell anyone else what I said. I'll reward you in the future." He then walks away.

Jupe thinks, "My job is to examine Dally Brawn's corpse. Why did he give me 10 oz of silver? There must be some monkey business..." When he arrives at Dally's house, he sees several undertakers waiting for him. Mrs. Rex is also awaiting his arrival. He asks an undertaker what Dally die from, and the undertaker replies, "His wife said he died from heartache."

Jupe lifts the portiere and enters the house.

Mrs. Rex says, "We've been waiting for you for a long time. The monks have also been here for half a day. Why have you arrived so late?"

"Sorry, I had a few little things to take care of."

Goldie comes out in her mourning clothes and once again sheds crocodile tears.

Jupe says consolingly, "Don't be sad. Dally has already returned to the Sky!"

Goldie covers her face full of fake tears and says, "I don't know what to say! Who would've thought my husband's heart condition would make him meet his maker in just a few days?"

Jupe looks at Goldie from head to toe and thinks, "I've heard people gossip about Dally's wife, but I've never had the chance to see her until now. I'm surprised he was able to marry this kind of woman! There must be some story behind Westgate's 10-oz silver nugget." He then goes over to examine Dally's body.

The monks say some prayers, wave banners, remove the white satin from the corpse, and splash around some holy water.

During his examination, Jupe notices Dally's azure fingernails, purple lips, and bulging eyes, and knows it was a case of murder by poison.

An undertaker standing nearby asks, "Why is his face purplish, his lips bitten by his teeth, and his mouth bloody?"

Jupe replies, "Don't talk nonsense! The body has decomposed a great deal over the past two days because of the hot weather!" He casually orders that the corpse be placed in the coffin tightly hammered shut with long nails.

Mrs. Rex takes out a bunch of coins to tip Jupe and the undertakers.

Jupe asks, "When will the coffin be taken outside?"

Mrs. Rex replies, "Goldie said the funeral will be three days from now, and there'll be a cremation."

Goldie treats the neighbors to dinner in the evening. She hires four monks on the second day to pray for the departed. The undertakers arrive on the third day at 5 a.m. to carry the coffin. Several neighbors also join the funeral procession.

Goldie dons mourning clothes, rides a palanquin, and sheds crocodile tears on her way to the crematorium outside the city. The coffin and corpse, burned to ashes, are thrown into a pond. The mourners' complimentary meals are all paid for by Westgate. Goldie moves the altar upstairs when she returns home. The tablet has words, "In memory of my husband, Dally Brawn". Atop the altar is a lit glass lamp pasted with golden paper money.

Goldie and Westgate can do whatever they want in Dally's house from then on, unlike their surreptitious tryst in Mrs. Rex's teahouse in the past. Dally's demise allows them to freely express their love for each other without the fear of being scrutinized by others.

Westgate at first does not want to be seen openly by the neighbors when he visits Goldie, so he first goes to Mrs. Rex's teahouse to sit for a while. He later openly brings his valets along and enters Goldie's house through the back door. He often stays over for three to five nights without returning home, and his wife and concubines all complain when his own house is at sixes and sevens.

Time flies like an arrow, and before long Westgate has openly had an affair with Goldie for over two months. Dragon Boat Festival is just around the corner. One day, Westgate visits

Mrs. Rex's teahouse again when he comes back from a trip to Mount Temple 岳庙.

Mrs. Rex serves a cup of tea and asks, "Tycoon, where did you go? Why haven't you visited Goldie?"

Westgate replies, "I decided to visit the temple to make an offering of incense for this upcoming large festival before I visit Goldie today."

Mrs. Rex says, "Her mother, Granny Rinse, is here today, and I don't think Granny has left yet. Let me go over there to see what's she's up to, and then report back to you."

Mrs. Rex sees Goldie drinking with Granny Rinse in the room as she enters through Goldie's backdoor.

Goldie quickly offers Mrs. Rex a seat and says cheerfully, "You've come at the right time! Please have a drink with my mother and by tomorrow, you'll have already given birth to a nice baby."

Mrs. Rex says laughingly, "After my husband passed away, how can a baby be born from me? In contrast, you're young and ready to have one!"

Goldie says, "A young blossom doesn't bear fruit. It's the old blossom that bears fruit."

Mrs. Rex says, "Mrs. Rinse, see how your daughter makes fun of me, saying I'm an old blossom? But she'll still need help from an old blossom tomorrow."

Granny Rinse says, "She's been talking through her hat since her youth. You shouldn't stoop to her level."

Ever since Mrs. Rex hooked Westgate up with Goldie, she has been eagerly serving Goldie to earn tips from Westgate. She then says, "Your daughter's so cute and smart. I wonder which man will be lucky enough to hook up with her in the future."

Granny Rinse says, "Mrs. Rex, you're an excellent matchmaker. She'll depend on your guidance."

After Mrs. Rex has a few more drinks, she begins to worry Westgate may be restless from having to wait quite a long time at the teahouse, so she winks at Goldie before she leaves.

Goldie understands the signal means "Westgate has arrived," so she urges her mother to leave. She cleans up the room, burns exotic incense, clears her mother's leftover dishes from the table, and places new dishes on the table to serve the new guest. She receives Westgate in the room and bows down to him when he sits down.

Not long after Dally's passing Goldie stops wearing mourning clothes. She has already pushed Dally's altar tablet aside and covered it with a piece of white cloth, and has never bothered to make any offerings. She puts on makeup and colorful clothes and presents herself in the most seductive manner possible whenever she keeps Westgate company. One day, when Westgate visits her after a two-day absence, she scolds, "You heartless thug! Why have you neglected me and hooked up with another woman? You left me out in the cold and don't care about me anymore!"

Westgate replies, "A concubine in my house has passed away, so I was tied up with the funeral for the past two days. I went to the temple today and bought some jewelry and clothes for you."

Westgate orders his valet Deon to come over and take the gift out of his baggage one at a time. Goldie receives them gratefully.

Goldie has been beating Dally's daughter Eva every day. To show Eva Westgate has taken over Dally's place in the family, she openly displays her relationship with Westgate. She orders Eva to serve Westgate tea, while she sets up a table to serve Westgate appetizers.

Westgate says, "There's no need to serve me appetizers. I've already given Mrs. Rex some money to buy food and fruit. Let's spend some time together during this important festival."

Goldie says cheerfully, "This appetizer was originally prepared for my mother. It's going to take a while for Mrs. Rex to buy some more food. Let's enjoy this appetizer for the time being." She sits shoulder to shoulder with Westgate, their cheeks making contact.

Meanwhile, Mrs. Rex takes a basket and a scale with her as she heads out into the street to buy meat and wine. It showers frequently in June and a rain cloud suddenly appears before the red shining sun. She has just bought a bottle of wine and a basket of fish, red meat, chicken, goose, vegetables, and fruit when the rain begins to pour down heavily. Although she manages to quickly take shelter from the downpour under an eave and tie up her hair with a handkerchief, her clothes are already wet. She rushes back home when the rain begins to taper off. She enters the house, puts the meat and wine in the kitchen, and enters the room where she sees Goldie and Westgate drinking. She then says slyly, "Tycoon and Goldie are happily enjoying their drinks while I'm standing here soaking wet. Tycoon should compensate me for my suffering."

Westgate exclaims, "Just look at her. She's such a vamp!"

Goldie says, "Mrs. Rex, come over here and have some hot wine."

Mrs. Rex drinks three cups and says, "I'll go to the kitchen to bake my clothes dry." The chicken, goose, and vegetables, all sliced and prepared nicely, are placed on the table in the room. Westgate and Goldie continue to indulge themselves with food when she serves them hot wine.

While Westgate is drinking, he notices a pipa hanging on the wall of Goldie's room and says, "I've heard you're good at pipa. You should play a song today while I drink."

Goldie responds meekly, "I learned how to play a few pieces when I was young. I hope you don't mind my rustiness."

Westgate takes the pipa from the wall, gives it to Goldie who places it on her lap, and starts playing *Two Southern Tunes*. After listening to the wonderful music, he is so excited he cuddles and kisses her, and says admiringly, "I never knew you're so talented. I've heard this piece performed by courtesans in the brothels, but they're no match for you."

Goldie says happily, "Tycoon, I'm so glad you appreciate me. I'll always do whatever you want me to do. I hope you won't forget about me in the future."

Westgate holds her chin up and asks, "How can I forget about you?" He continues to chat with Goldie for a while, takes off one of her embroidered shoes places a small wine cup in it, and then drinks the wine from the cup in the shoe.

Goldie says, "I hope you don't mind I have small feet."

When they are somewhat drunk, they lock the door of the bedroom, take off their clothes, and fool around on the bed.

Mrs. Rex locks the main door and eats with Eva in the kitchen.

Since Goldie is better in bed than any prostitute in town, the couple is like a pair of entwined phoenixes in a state of euphoria. The way Westgate performs in bed resembles the way he skillfully thrusts his spear in a martial arts tournament. The woman is gorgeous, the man is talented, and they are both young.

Westgate stays in Goldie's house until evening. Before he returns home, he gives some silver pieces to Goldie to help subsidize her living expenses. Unable to make him stay any longer, after he leaves, she lowers the portiere, shuts the door, and has a drink with Mrs. Rex.

Chapter 7. Towie Prime, the Third Spouse

Mrs. Reed 薛嫂, the florist, is carrying a basket of flowers and looking for Westgate. She asks, "Deon, where's Tycoon?"

Deon replies, "My boss is in the store checking the ledger with Jason Aide 傅自新."

Jason is the clerk of Westgate's drugstore.

Mrs. Reed heads straight for the drugstore, looks through the portiere, and sees Westgate doing bookkeeping with the clerk. She then greets Westgate.

Westgate leaves Jason behind when he sees Mrs. Reed. He goes to a quiet place and asks, "What's up?"

Mrs. Reed replies, "Tycoon, I've come here to do matchmaking. I found someone I guarantee will satisfy you as the replacement of your third spouse who's passed away. I was at your mansion a while ago selling flowers to your wife who invited me for tea. I dare not mention the matchmaking to her, so I looked for you to directly speak to you. The lady I'm talking about is someone you also know. She's the wife of Clothier Birch 贩布杨家 outside the south gate and is very rich. She has two Capital-South loft beds, clothes for four seasons, and her fur coats are too many to count. She also has four or five trunks of pearls, bracelets, and jewelry. She has over 1000 oz of silver in her treasure chest. Unfortunately, her husband died while selling fabrics, and she's been a widow for over a year. She's childless, with only a young brother-in-law who's just ten years old. Why should she remain a widow when she's still so young? Her husband's aunt suggested that she marry again. She's 25 years old, has a beautiful figure, and looks like a romantic and cute model when she dresses up. Not only is she good at housekeeping, but she also does needlework, plays chess and banjo. She's the third daughter of the Prime 孟 family. I guarantee it'll be love at first sight when you see her. None but the brave deserve the fair!"

Westgate is excited to know Lady Prime can play banjo. He then asks, "Mrs. Reed, when can I meet with her?"

Mrs. Reed replies, "There's no problem meeting her. The most senior person in her household right now is Aunt Birch 杨姑娘. her late husband's paternal aunt. Although her late husband has a maternal uncle named Sid Pull 张四, maternal relationships are not as strong as paternal relationships. Aunt Birch was married to Walter Heir 孙歪頭 who lived in the house of Eunuch Stroll 徐公公. After Walter died, she remains a widow and childless for over 30 years and depends on her nephew and niece to support her. I'll go with you tomorrow to see Aunt Birch who only cares about benefiting from the wealth of her late nephew's wife and doesn't care about anything else. Just give her a few oz of silver. Since you have so many rolls of satin at home, take one roll, buy a big gift, visit her in person, talk to her, and the marriage proposal will be a piece of cake. With her support, who else can object?"

Westgate grins like a Cheshire cat while listening to Mrs. Reed.

Dear reader, in this world, a matchmaker only cares about earning money and is economical with the truth. A jobless man will be described by her as having a good career. Concubinage will be described by her as a regular marriage. Ask no questions and hear no lies. Caveat emptor.

Westgate makes an appointment with Mrs. Reed: "I can visit Aunt Birch tomorrow, and I'll bring along a big gift." He then goes back to his drugstore to continue the bookkeeping with Jason Aide while Mrs. Reed carries her flower basket and leaves.

Westgate gets up early the next day, spruces himself up, buys four trays of appetizers and fruit, and hires a porter to carry them. He rides his horse, followed by his valet, and they are led by Mrs. Reed to Eunuch Stroll's house to visit Aunt Birch.

Mrs. Reed first enters the house and says, "Aunt Birch, a millionaire at your door wants to propose to your niece-in-law. I told him Aunt Birch has the most seniority in the household, so he's come to first visit you. I'll lead him to see the lady afterward."

Aunt Birch exclaims, "Whoa! Why didn't you tell me about it in advance?" She then asks her maid to clean up the room and prepare tea before she invites Westgate in.

Mrs. Reed, eager to flatter the senior lady, first brings the gift boxes in and takes the contents out. She then leads Westgate into the room.

Westgate bows down four times to Aunt Birch who quickly bows back. They then exchange greetings and sit down.

Aunt Birch asks, "What's Tycoon's name?"

Mrs. Reed replies, "He is Chic Westgate, one of the very rich men of Clearstream Town. He owns a drugstore near the town hall and lends money to the officials. He has more money than he knows what to do with, and his grains overflow the largest barn in the world, but he has no wife to take care of his household. When he heard your niece-in-law is ready to get married, he made a special trip here to propose." She then adds, "You can both have a heart-to-heart talk so a matchmaker like me doesn't have to fabricate lies. If he doesn't speak frankly to you, whom else can he speak to?"

Aunt Birch says, "If Tycoon wants to talk about my nephew's wife, then a simple visit should be enough. There's no need to spend money on a gift I don't deserve!"

Westgate says, "Aunt Birch, if you accept the present, I'll feel much better."

Aunt Birch receives and puts away the gift thankfully and says, "My nephew worked hard to earn some money when he was alive. Unfortunately, he died young and left behind more than 1000 oz of silver. As his paternal aunt, I've always been close to him. If you marry his widow, I need you to provide for my funeral expenses in the future, and the money won't come out of your pocket anyway. I'll confront the old scoundrel Sam Pull, to make sure your proposal will be successful. After the marriage, let her come back to my birthday party every year. It's my only request if you accept me as your new but poor relative."

"Aunt Birch, don't worry. I already knew all the issues you just said. Not to mention paying for your funeral expenses, even paying for ten funeral expenses is OK with me." Westgate then takes out of his pocket six shiny nuggets worth 30 oz of silver, puts them on the table, and says, "This is just for you to buy tea. I'll give you 70 more oz of silver and two rolls of satin on the wedding day, enough for your funeral expenses. She can always visit you during the eight festivals of the four seasons."

Since money talks, Aunt Birch looks at the 30 oz of shiny silver nuggets and says smilingly, "Tycoon, I hope you won't forget to support me in the future—"

Mrs. Reed interrupts, "Aunt Birch, you worry too much! Tycoon is a man who always takes care of his relatives. The sheriff and mayor are his friends, and he's generous to his friends around the world. So how could you be a burden on him?"

Aunt Birch is so satisfied she can't help releasing her gas while drinking her tea.

When Westgate decides to leave, Mrs. Reed says, "Aunt Birch, since we've talked to you, we'll visit your nephew's wife tomorrow."

Aunt Birch says, "Tycoon, you don't have to visit my nephew's wife. Mrs. Reed, tell her this is what I said, 'If you don't marry this kind of man, whom else can you marry?' "

Westgate says goodbye to Aunt Birch who then says, "Tycoon, I didn't know you'd condescend to visit me, so please forgive me for not making enough preparation to welcome you." She walks with a cane to see him off.

Westgate is riding on his horse when Mrs. Reed asks, "Haven't I done a decent job? It's so much better to convince the senior lady first than to convince her other relatives."

Westgate then tips Mrs. Reed an oz of silver.

Westgate spruces himself up the next day, rides a white horse, followed by his valets Deon and Peon 平安, while Mrs. Reed rides a donkey, and they get out the south gate via Hog Street to the Birch mansion. The front building has four rooms, and there are five buildings. Mrs. Reed enters the mansion first. Westgate dismounts and sees a brightly painted building facing north. As he walks through the inner gate, he sees bonsais planted in the yard. When Mrs. Reed opens the red door, he then sees statues of Bodhisattva Compassion 观音菩萨 and Prosperous Boy 善财童子. Hung on all four walls are landscape paintings of famous artists. The tables and chairs are all shiny and clean.

Mrs. Reed offers Westgate a seat while she goes inside. After a while, she comes out and whispers, "The lady is still grooming herself, please sit for a while."

A valet serves Westgate a cup of tea.

Mrs. Reed is a typical matchmaker who loves to talk, and she says excitedly, "Tycoon, in this household, besides the senior lady, this lady is the second in seniority. She has a younger brother-in-law not grown up yet. In addition to silver pieces, the copper coins earned by her late husband filled up two barrels every day when he oversaw the business. The daily meals of the 30 employees were all managed by her at that time. She has two maids and one valet. The 15-year-old maid who combs her hair is named Orchie 兰香. The 12-year-old junior maid is named Phoenie 小鸾. They'll follow the lady when she marries you. I work on this matchmaking for you and hope I can move to a two-room apartment better than the remote apartment in the north which is so inconvenient for me to travel around. When I bought your maid Plumie for you last year, you promised to give me several rolls of fabrics, but you haven't given them to me yet. You can give them to me tomorrow. When Salsa Birch 杨宗锡 was alive, he spent so much money on this street. This mansion worth 800 oz of silver, with five buildings that span up to the street in the back, will belong to her young brother-in-law."

While Mrs. Reed is speaking, a maid beckons her over, and after a while, a lady comes out.

The lady looks like a marble statue, and her body is perfectly proportional: not too fat, not too skinny, not too tall, and not too short. She has natural beauty with a few freckles on her face and attractively walks on her two small feet. The jade jewelry over her chest jingles when she walks. The orchid fragrance comes out of her body when she sits. She is like the moon fairy who has left the moon palace and descended on Earth.

Westgate is excited to see her. She comes out gracefully, bows to him, and sits opposite him. Since he keeps staring at her, she lowers her head. He then says, "My wife has died, and I'd like to marry you as my wife to manage my household. What's your take on that?"

Lady Prime asks, "Tycoon, how old are you? When did your wife die?"

"I've squandered 28 years of my life. I was born on August 28th. Unfortunately, my wife died over a year ago. May I know how old Lady is?"

"I'm 30 years old."

"So you're two years older than me—"

Mrs. Reed, sitting on the side, interrupts, "If a wife is two years older, the husband earns gold every day. If a wife is three years older, the husband gets a pile of gold."

A young maid serves orange-flavored tea in three silver cups with silver spoons while they are talking.

Lady Prime stands up, picks up the first cup, wipes the water stain with her slender finger, and hands it over to Westgate who quickly and thankfully receives it.

Mrs. Reed moves over to lift the lady's skirt to reveal the lady's tiny feet, which are tucked inside a pair of red shoes. Westgate is pleased to look at them.

Lady Prime picks up the second cup and gives it to Mrs. Reed. She then picks up the third cup for herself and sits down with her guests.

After tea, Westgate asks Deon to offer a gift of two brocade handkerchiefs, one pair of jeweled barrettes, and six golden rings.

Lady Prime graciously accepts the gift, asks Westgate the wedding date, and says, "I need to be prepared."

"Since you've accepted my proposal, I'll send another gift to you on the 24th of this month. We'll get married on July 2nd."

"Well, I'll dispatch a messenger tomorrow to inform my aunt-in-law in the north suburb."

Mrs. Reed says, "Tycoon already visited and spoke to her yesterday."

"What did she say?"

"When Tycoon mentioned this proposal, she was overjoyed and asked me to bring Tycoon here to visit you. She said, 'If you don't marry this kind of man, whom else can you marry?' I then volunteered to be the matchmaker."

"I'm glad my aunt-in-law agreed!"

"Dear lady, I'm a matchmaker who dares not lie!"

When Westgate takes leave of Lady Prime, Mrs. Reed sees him off and asks, "How do you feel about the lady?"

"I made you work too hard."

Westgate rides back to town while Mrs. Reed visits Lady Prime again and says, "It's good for you to marry this man."

"Does Westgate's mansion have other spouses? What kind of business is he in?"

"Dear lady, even though he has other spouses in his mansion, they're all like dummies! When you go there and look around, you'll understand I'm not lying. He's so famous; how can anyone not know him? He's one of the extremely wealthy men in Clearstream Town. The mayor and sheriff all make friends with him. He'll soon have an in-law who's an in-law of Commander Birch of the capital. Who dares to offend him?"

A valet dispatched from Aunt Birch's house arrives while Lady Prime treats Mrs. Reed to dinner. He offers a box of flour-date cakes, two pieces of candy, and several sweet rice balls.

The valet asks, "Lady, have you received the tycoon's engagement gift? Aunt Birch said, 'If you don't marry this man, whom else can you marry?' "

Lady Prime replies, "Thanks for Aunt Birch's concern. I've accepted the engagement gift." She receives and takes out the desserts, then fills the box with appetizers and sausage, and gives the box together with 50 coins to the valet, and says, "Give my best regards to Aunt Birch when you return home. Tell her the engagement is on the 24th of this month, and the wedding is on the 2nd of next month."

After the valet leaves, Mrs. Reed asks, "What did Aunt Birch give you? May I bring some home for my kids to eat?"

The lady gives one piece of candy and ten rice balls to Mrs. Reed who pleasantly leaves.

Meanwhile, Sid Pull, the maternal uncle of Lady Prime's late husband Salsa Birch, wants to control his nephew Salvo Birch 杨宗保 to swindle Lady Prime's properties. He is very eager to have Savant Still 尚举人, Magistrate Still 尚推官's son, marry Lady Prime. If the competitor were from a small family, it would be quite possible, but he does not expect the competitor to be Chic Westgate, owner of the drugstore next to the town hall, and the government lobbyist too tough to fight against. He thinks for a long time and decides it is best to dissuade Lady Prime first. He then comes over and says, "Lady, you shouldn't marry Chic Westgate. You should follow my advice and marry Savant Still, a gentleman who owns a big farm and is quite rich. Savant is much better than Westgate who nastily manipulates the town hall and already has the daughter of Colonel Call as his wife. Do you want to go over there as a concubine and not a wife? Won't you be disappointed? Moreover, he already has three concubines and many seductive maids. You'll be upset to enter his mansion that has so many competitors!"

Lady Prime replies, "There's always enough space to fit another ship in the ocean. If his mansion already has an official wife, I'm willing to have her as my superior. Although there are many concubines, it's up to him to decide whom he loves. Nobody can force him to love the one he doesn't love. I'm not worried even if he had 100 concubines. Even a beggar on the street can have several girlfriends, let alone a wealthy man like him. You worry too much! I know what to do when I marry into his mansion. No problem!"

Sid says, "Lady, I heard he's a human trafficker and a wife beater. Any concubine who doesn't satisfy him will be sold by his matchmaker. Are you willing to endure the injustice?"

Lady Prime replies, "Uncle Sid, you're mistaken! No matter how dumb a man is, he won't beat his wife who saves money and is hardworking. If I manage the household well and don't gossip about other people so other people don't gossip about me, why will he beat me? Of course, a husband is justified to beat a wife who lives to eat and gossip and gets him into trouble."

Sid says, "I heard he has a 14-year old daughter. If you marry into his mansion, you may not get along with her."

Lady Prime responds, "Uncle Sid, with all due respect, after I marry into his mansion, I'll treat the old and the young equally well. If I treat my husband's daughter well, I don't worry he won't love me, and I don't worry his daughter won't express her filial piety. I don't even worry about ten daughters, not just one daughter!"

Sid says, "I heard he doesn't behave properly. He sleeps with other women outside his mansion. He may not be wealthy and may have a lot of debts. I'm afraid he may hurt you emotionally and financially."

Lady Prime responds, "Uncle Sid, you're mistaken! Since I can only take care of issues inside the mansion, I don't care what he does outside the mansion. Do you want me to follow him around every day? As the saying goes, 'There is nothing permanent except change.' How can anyone be rich or poor forever? When the going gets tough, the tough get going. You shouldn't worry too much."

Sid feels bad to be refuted by Lady Prime so many times. He gets up after tea and returns home dejectedly. He consults his wife and decides to use his nephew Salvo Birch as an excuse to snatch Lady Prime's trunks of valuables before she moves out.

Westgate brings along Lady Call on the 24th of the month, which is the day for the engagement ceremony. They ride on palanquins, followed by porters who carry a gift of 20 trunks of clothes, robes, fruit, desserts, and silk and satin rolls.

Lady Prime invites her aunt-in-law and her elder sister to keep the guests company.

They invite 12 monks to say prayers and to make offerings of incense on the 26th. These are all managed by Aunt Birch.

Sid Pull comes with several neighbors to speak to Lady Prime on the day she is ready to leave her mansion.

Mrs. Reed leads Westgate's servants and a few porters to move the lady's bed, furniture, and trunks of valuables, all on the same day. The movers include 20 soldiers borrowed from Protector Fringe 周守備.

Sid stops the movers and says, "Matchmaker, don't move anything out! Listen to me." He then invites the neighbors in, and they sit down.

Sid Pull says, "My dear neighbors, please listen. Lady, I'd like to emphasize your late husband Salsa Birch and your young brother-in-law Salvo Birch are my elder sister's sons. After my first nephew's untimely demise, the way you manipulate the inheritance is difficult for me to intervene. However, I'm responsible for the well-being of my second nephew who's so young. He and your late husband were born from the same mother, so shouldn't he have his share of the inheritance? Since I don't know what items belong to you, I want you to open your trunks and let everyone inspect the contents so you can carry away the items that belong to you. Any objections?"

Lady Prime replies tearfully, "Everyone please listen. Uncle's dead wrong! I didn't murder my husband, and I shamefully marry again today. You all know whether my late husband was rich. The money he earned has all been spent on this mansion. I'm not taking away this mansion left behind for my young brother-in-law. The kitchen sink and stove are still here. For the 300 oz of silver he's loaned to the outside, the ledger has been handed over to you, and you can keep collecting them to pay for the family expenses. So, what other silver are you talking about?"

Sid replies "I don't care what you said. Just open the trunks and let everyone inspect them."

Lady Prime asks, "Do you also want to inspect my shoes?"

Aunt Birch walks in with a cane during the argument. She exchanges greetings with everyone, sits down, and says, "Dear neighbors, I'm the paternal aunt of her late husband. Not to mention Lady Prime has no money, even if she has 100,000 oz of silver, it's none of your business. She's childless and is such a gentle lady. Why do you stop her from getting married?"

The neighbors all say, "Aunt Birch, you've got a point!"

Aunt Birch asks, "Do you want to hijack the dowry she's brought to this mansion? Since she's never privately given me anything, you can't say I'm biased and try to protect her. To tell you the truth, my nephew was so loyal and faithful I always miss his gentle character. Otherwise, I wouldn't come out to intervene in this matter."

Sid Pull, standing nearby, sneers, "It's such a farce. You're a vulture, and vultures are circling!"

Those words hit a raw nerve. Aunt Birch stands up and scolds, "Enough with your nonsense! I belong to the Birch family, no matter what. With which Birch master did your mother copulate to give birth to you?"

Sid replies, "Although I have a different surname, the two nephews were brought up by my elder sister. You're a bloodsucker who betrays the Birch family; you're an arsonist who pretends to be a firefighter!"

Aunt Birch says, "You shameless old fart! What do you have in your mind to keep a young lady in this mansion? Do you want to rape her or rob her to satisfy yourself?"

Sid replies, "I don't covet money. I fight on behalf of my elder sister who'd brought up my nephews. If something bad happens, I'll be responsible while you wash your hands of it."

Aunt Birch says, "Sid Pull, you old slave who can only sweet talk! Nobody will put you in a coffin when you die tomorrow."

Sid says, "You gossiping old slut! I'm not surprised you have no son and no daughter."

Aunt Birch anxiously responds, "Thievish Sid Pull, you old hog! My not having a son or daughter is better than your mother who went to the temples to seduce the monks and sleep with the priests! And you still don't know about it!"

They quarrel so fiercely they almost get into a fistfight. Fortunately, the neighbors intervene and say, "Uncle, leave Aunt Birch alone."

Mrs. Reed leads Westgate's valets and the soldiers to quickly carry away the lady's belongings during the commotion, while Sid Pull stares at them and dares not protest. The neighbors console him for a while and then disperse.

Westgate hires a big palanquin with four pairs of red gauze lanterns on June 2, and the lady's elder sister sees her off.

Salvo Birch, the lady's young brother-in-law, ties up his hair, puts on azure gauze clothes, and rides a horse to marry her off. Westgate gives him a roll of satin as a gift.

Orchie and Phoenie, the two maids, and Xylo 琴童, the 15-year old valet, are brought along to continue to serve Lady Prime.

The two sisters-in-law of Lady Prime and Aunt Birch throw a birthday party for Lady prime on the third day.

Westgate gives Aunt Birch 70 oz of silver and two rolls of fabric. He frequently communicates with his new relatives from then on. He cleans up the three rooms in the west suite for his third spouse. He calls her Towie 玉楼 and spends three nights with her.

Chapter 8. Goldie Awaits Westgate's Return

Westgate marries Towie, and they are as close as two coats of paint. It so happens the Show mansion 陈宅 dispatches Mrs. Script 文嫂 to notify him his daughter Lassie Westgate 西门大姐 will marry into the Show family on July 12.

Towie brought with her a colorful Capital-South loft bed as part of her dowry when she married Westgate. Since Westgate cannot build a bed in a rush, he borrows that loft bed as part of the dowry of his daughter. Those activities keep him busy for a month and prevent him from visiting Goldie.

Goldie leans at the door every day and waits despairingly for Westgate. She sends Mrs. Rex to his mansion twice.

The valet at the gate, acquainted with Mrs. Rex, knows she is dispatched by Goldie. He ignores Mrs. Rex and responds nonchalantly, "Tycoon is not free!" Since Mrs. Rex cannot provide any good news, Goldie becomes so desperate she beats and scolds Dally's daughter Eva.

Eva is forced to look for Westgate on the streets. But how can any young girl have the nerve to enter the big mansion? She just peeps at the gate twice, and unable to see Westgate, she returns, only to be spit in the face by Goldie who slaps her and complains she is useless. She is punished to kneel and have no lunch.

Feeling very hot in her room on the dog days of summer, Goldie orders Eva to boil water for her to take a bath. She also steams a cage of dumplings to serve Westgate. She puts on a thin blouse, sits on a stool, and hopes Westgate will show up while puckering her lips and complaining he is a heartless thief. She takes off her two embroidered shoes, taps a tambourine, and hopes it will induce him to come. She taps for a while, but Westgate still does not show up. She feels tired, lies on the bed, and falls asleep.

She wakes up two hours later, and while still feeling upset, Eva asks, "Mom, the water is hot, do you want to take a bath?"

Goldie asks, "Are the dumplings hot? Bring them over here."

Eva promptly brings them to the room.

Goldie uses her slender finger to count. She originally put 30 dumplings in the cage, but after counting back and forth, she can only count 29 of them with 1 missing. She then asks, "Where did it go?"

Eva replies, "I haven't seen it. I'm afraid Mom miscounted."

Goldie says, "I counted twice. There should be 30 dumplings waiting for your dad to come and eat them. Why did you steal one? You're such a slut! You're a glutton who only covet my dumplings! You think I made these dumplings for you to show my filial piety to you!" She gets a horsewhip, and unceremoniously strips and lashes Eva who squeals like a stuck pig while being lashed 20 times. She then says, "If you don't confess, I'll give you 100 lashes!"

Eva responds desperately, "Mom, don't whip me, I was so hungry I stole and ate one."

Goldie says, "If you stole it, why did you accuse me of miscounting? You're such a slut! When that son of a bitch was around, you could depend on him to put in a good word for you. After he kicked the bucket, you still want to make a scene! I'll beat you to a pulp!" She then puts on a light blouse and orders, "Eva, fan me." Eva fans her for a while, and she says, "Move your face over here so I can scratch you, slut!"

Eva submissively lets Goldie's fingernails make two scratches on her face.

Goldie finally lets Eva off. She later goes before the mirror, spruces herself up, and stands near the portiere.

As it so happens, Westgate's valet Deon, carrying his baggage on horseback, passes by Goldie's door. Goldie calls, "Where are you going?"

That valet is a smart kid. He often accompanied Westgate to visit Goldie, and Goldie treated him nicely. Since she put in a good word for him whenever he made a mistake, he gets along quite well with her. He dismounts and replies, "My boss asked me to deliver a present to Protector Fringe."

Goldie invites Deon in and asks, "What happened in your boss' mansion that prevented him from coming to see me? He must've found a better woman and left me out of the picture."

"My boss doesn't have a new woman. He's been so busy at home these few days he couldn't find the time to see you."

"Even if he's busy at home, how could he ignore me for a month without telling me anything? He just doesn't have me in his mind. Please tell me what makes him so busy?"

"It's just a simple issue. Why do you want to know?"

"You're as sly as a fox. If you don't tell me, I'll be annoyed at you for the rest of my life!"

"If I tell you, please don't tell my boss I told you."

"I won't tell him."

Deon then describes how Westgate married Towie.

Goldie bursts into tears as she listens to the news.

Deon says anxiously, "You're so narrow-minded, Goldie! If I'd known your reaction, I wouldn't have told you the news."

Goldie leans against the door, heaves a deep sigh, and says, "Deon, his love for me in the past was so deep it was in big contrast to how he dumped me so unceremoniously now!" She cannot stop her tears from streaming down her face.

"Don't act like this, Goldie. Not even his wife can control him."

"Deon, since that evil rotten egg hasn't come for a month, I had no choice but to sleep alone, a total of 30 sleepless nights. He enjoys his life elsewhere, while I idiotically remain in love with him. As the saying goes, 'Easy come, easy go!' "

"Don't cry, Goldie. He may be missing for a few more days, but he'll visit you on his birthday. Just write a few words for me to deliver your letter to him, and he'll surely come."

"If you can invite him to see me, I'll sew a pair of good shoes for you to wear. I'll also throw a birthday party for him here! If he doesn't come, it's all your fault. Anyway, if he asks you why you came here, how will you respond?"

"If he asks me, I'll just say while my horse was drinking water on the street, you asked Mrs. Rex to give me the letter of invitation to deliver to him."

"You cunning little lad, I hope you're the Cupid to reignite the romance!" She then orders Eva to put a plate of the steamed dumplings on the table and serve Deon tea. She goes to her room, gets a flowery piece of paper, and writes a letter. She folds the paper, hands it over to Deon, and says, "Please deliver it to him, and make sure he comes here on his birthday when I'll eagerly wait for him."

After Deon finishes the appetizers, Goldie also gives him 30 coins and before he rides his horse, she says, "Tell your master I'm mad at him when you see him. And if he doesn't show up tomorrow, I'll ride a palanquin to fetch him in person."

Deon says, "There ain't no such thing as a free lunch, Goldie. After I ate your dumplings, I'd better deliver your letter promptly." He then trots away.

Goldie waits every day for Westgate to come, but it seems like a pipe dream. Westgate's birthday occurs seven days later. She waits an entire day and feels as if she had waited for half a summer, but Westgate never shows up. Unable to hold back her tears, she gnashes her teeth until evening when she invites Mrs. Rex for dinner. She pulls out a golden hair clip from her hair, gives it to Mrs. Rex, and asks Mrs. Rex to go to Westgate's mansion to invite him over.

Mrs. Rex says, "It's too late to invite him. Let me go to his mansion tomorrow morning."

Goldie says, "Don't forget about it."

Mrs. Rex says, "You can rest assured I'll bring him here." The way to Mrs. Rex's heart is through her stomach. She returns home after being wined and dined and bribed by a golden hair clip.

Unable to sleep in her bedroom, Goldie keeps tossing and turning. She then picks up her pipa and sings a sad love song.

In the morning, Goldie orders, "Eva, go next door and see if Mrs. Rex has invited Westgate."

Eva returns after a while and says, "Mrs. Rex has left very early."

Mrs. Rex grooms herself early in the morning. She arrives at Westgate's mansion and asks, "Is Tycoon home?"

The servants all say no.

She waits at the wall across the street. When Jason walks by to open the store, she goes over, greets him, and asks, "Is Tycoon home?"

Jason asks, "Why are you looking for him? You ask me so early in the morning. Nobody here knows his whereabouts." He then adds, "Tycoon threw a party for his birthday for an entire day yesterday. He went with his friends to the brothel at night. Since he hasn't come back yet, where can you find him?"

Mrs. Rex leaves the town hall area, walks along East Street, and heads for the lane where a brothel is situated. It so happens Westgate is trotting on horseback from the east, followed by two valets. He looks quite drunk and is sitting unsteadily. She shouts, "Tycoon, you had one too many!" She goes over and grabs the horse's bridle.

Westgate says drunkenly, "My valet returned home and told me Goldie was mad at me. I'll go now." He follows Mrs. Rex, and they chat along the way.

When they arrive at Goldie's house, Mrs. Rex first enters and reports, "You're lucky I went there, Goldie. I managed to invite Tycoon here in less than an hour!"

Goldie wastes no time asking Eva to clean up the room, while she goes out to meet Westgate.

Westgate holds his handheld fan, enters the room half-drunk, and greets Goldie.

Goldie greets back and says, "Tycoon, your time is too valuable to see me. You've dumped me and don't show up anymore. You and your newlywed concubine are so hot and heavy you don't have me in your mind. To think you don't have a change of heart!"

"Don't listen to other people's gossip. What concubine are you talking about? I had no spare time to see you because I marred off my daughter, and the activities kept me busy for a few days."

"Don't fool me! If you haven't switched your love to another woman outside, you'd better take an oath that bodes ill to your health to make me believe you."

"If I dump you, may I have a bowl-sized tumor, have yellow fever for three years, and have large cockroaches fill up my pocket."

"That's bull! What do large cockroaches have to do with our issue?" Goldie snatches Westgate's hat and throws it onto the floor.

Mrs. Rex nervously picks up the brand-new from the floor, puts it on the table, and says, "It wasn't easy for me to invite him here, Goldie, and this is how you treat him! Why don't you put it back on his head so he won't catch a cold?"

"I couldn't care less if this heartless man dies of a cold!" She then pulls a hair clip from his head and inspects it. It is a shiny golden hair clip inscribed with two clauses, "Horsy neighing on the lawn, Towie drunk in the floral sky." It is one of the dowry items brought over by Towie. Goldie guesses it must be an item given to Westgate by another girlfriend, so she puts it in her pocket and refuses to return it to him. She then says, "And you told me you didn't have a change of heart! Where's the hair clip I gave you? Why wear another hair clip?"

"As regards your hair clip, I fell off the horse and dropped my hat when I was drunk yesterday. With hair hanging loose, I couldn't find it."

"Not even a three-year-old kid would believe the hair clip fallen onto the ground when you were drunk would vanish into thin air."

Mrs. Rex says, "Goldie, don't blame Tycoon. He watched a bumblebee taking a dump when he was 15 miles away from the city, and an elephant wrestled him to the ground during his momentary lapse of reason. He should've known better than to be so careless."

Westgate says, "Mrs. Rex, you joined in the game and made fun of me just when she started the inquisition!"

Goldie snatches the fanciful fan held in Westgate's hand and looks at it carefully. It is a red fan bound by golden pins. She has been a paramour long enough to know the fan with so many toothmarks must be a gift from a lover. Without waiting for an explanation, she breaks it in half.

It is too late for Westgate to come to that fan's rescue. He then says, "A friend of mine gave this fan to me. I have it for only three days, and you destroyed it."

Goldie responds sneeringly while Eva comes to serve tea. She asks Eva to put down the tea tray and bow down to Westgate.

Mrs. Rex says, "You both have been fooling around for half a day. Let me go to the kitchen to work on more important business."

Goldie orders Eva to set up a table in the bedroom to prepare dinner to celebrate Westgate's birthday. As usual, the food served consists of fried chicken, roast goose, fresh fish, braised meat, and fruit. The dishes are soon all on the table. She goes to a chest, takes out the birthday present she has prepared for Westgate, and places the items on a tray for Westgate can look at. They consist of a pair of black satin shoes, a pair of leg warmers, knee pads adorned with drawings of pine, bamboo, and plum trees, a purple sash, a floral dudou, and a hair clip that has both the image of a lotus and a poem imprinted on it.

Westgate is so excited to see the birthday present he cuddles and kisses Goldie, and says, "A girl with your intelligence is hard to find!"

Goldie asks Eva to pour a cup of wine for Westgate. Like a flower in the wind, Goldie bows down four times to Westgate.

Westgate quickly helps her up, sits with her shoulder to shoulder, and they give each other a toast.

Mrs. Rex has a few drinks with them and then returns home.

After seeing Mrs. Rex off, Eva closes the door and sits in the kitchen.

Goldie keeps Westgate company until evening when he orders his valet to bring his horse home while he stays overnight at Goldie's house. As lustful as a cat in heat, she makes love to Westgate with abandon at night.

Time goes by fast while Goldie and Westgate are enjoying the calm before the storm.

Let's flash back to when Sawn Brawn was assigned to deliver the mayor's present and letter:

Sawn leaves Clearstream Town, travels to the capital where he delivers the letter and the present to Marshal Red, then strolls on the street for a few days for sightseeing. He then receives the reply letter and leads his team back home via the major roads of Mount-East. He left home in May, and he returns at the beginning of autumn. The continuous rainfall delays his trip, so his roundtrip takes more than three months. He feels uneasy while traveling in the rain and wants to quickly return home to see his elder brother. He first dispatches a soldier to report to the mayor ahead of time. He also writes a letter to his brother about his return in September.

The soldier reports to the mayor before he rushes to Dally's house. When he sees the door locked, he wants someone to open it. As it so happens, Mrs. Rex is near the door.

Mrs. Rex asks, "You look for whom?"

"I've been dispatched by Sergeant Brawn to deliver a letter to his elder brother."

"Dally Brawn is not home. He has gone to the cemetery. If you have a letter for him, give it to me and I'll deliver it to him when he returns home."

The soldier thanks Mrs. Rex, takes out the letter, and gives it to her. He then gallops away.

Mrs. Rex, with the letter in her hand, gets out her back door to Goldie's house and Eva opens the door for her. It turns out Goldie and Westgate had a sensually arousing night and consequently oversleep for breakfast. Mrs. Rex calls, "Tycoon, Goldie, get up! I need to speak to you. Sawn Brawn has dispatched a soldier to deliver a letter to tell his brother he'll soon arrive. I received the letter on Dally's behalf and sent off the soldier. Get up fast so we can discuss this matter."

Westgate feels as if someone were pouring cold water on his head and sending shivers down his spine. He and Goldie get up, quickly put on their clothes, and invite Mrs. Rex into the room.

Mrs. Rex takes out the letter for Westgate to read, and the letter says Sawn Brawn will be back before mid-autumn. He asks nervously, "What should I do? Please cover up for me, and I'll return the favor. I'm now deeply in love with Goldie and can't be separated from her. If Sawn Brawn returns and separates us, what should I do?"

Mrs. Rex replies, "Tycoon, there's nothing to it. As I said in the past, a girl's marriage is arranged by her parents and a woman's marriage is arranged by herself. The brother- and sister-in-law relationship terminates when the marriage terminates. After Goldie observed the 100-day mourning period, she should invite a few monks to remove the altar. Goldie will be carried in a palanquin and married into Tycoon's mansion before Sawn arrives home. I'll speak to Sawn at that time. What can he do afterward? You can both live happily ever after."

Westgate says, "It couldn't be better." After breakfast, he decides with Goldie to invite monks to pray and remove Dally's altar on September 6, which will be the 100th day of Dally's passing. Goldie will then be married into Westgate's mansion.

Deon brings a horse to pick up Westgate before long.

Time flies like an arrow. Westgate brings along two bunches of coins, 20 liters of rice, and arrives at Goldie's house on September 6. He asks Mrs. Rex to hire six monks from Grateful Monastery to organize a water-and-land memorial service to redeem Dally's soul and remove Dally's altar in the evening.

The apprentices arrive with Scriptures at 5 a.m. to do the setup, while Mrs. Rex helps the chef prepare vegetarian meals at the stove, and Westgate rests in Goldie's house.

The monks who arrive shake rings on the scepters, strike drums and cymbals and say prayers.

Goldie, unwilling to participate in the ceremony, continues to sleep with Westgate when the sun is already high up in the sky. When the monks request t the head of the household to make an offering of incense, she gets up, grooms herself, puts on casual clothes, and bows at the altar. The monks' Zen practice goes out the window when they see Dally's seductive widow. The novice burning incense accidentally pushes down a vase, and the friar who should hold a candle holds an incense box instead. The monk absentmindedly declares the Song dynasty as the Tang dynasty while making declarations. The monk who prays for

Dally Brawn confusedly calls him Dairy Brawn. The elder monk is so mesmerized when he hits the drum, he hits his disciple's hand. The novice is so aroused his drumstick hits the old monk's head. Not even 10,000 Diamond Guards can bring those seduced minds back from Cloud Nine.

Goldie makes an offering of incense, signs her name, bows down, returns to her bedroom, and enjoys a meal of meat with Westgate.

Westgate says, "Mrs. Rex, if there are any issues, you resolve them. Don't let them disturb Goldie."

Mrs. Rex responds laughingly, "Tycoon, don't worry. I'll take care of those bald donkeys so you can both make love with abandon."

Dear reader, in this world, virtuous priests and monks are hard to find. Since they do not need to work hard to earn their living, many are too idle, and an idle mind is the devil's playground. In contrast, the office worker, or farmer, or tradesman, or merchant, regardless of his wealth or age, is so preoccupied with his career and income even if he gets aroused—if it ever happens—the thought of losing his job, not getting a raise or a promotion, would wipe out his sexual desire in no time despite having a pretty wife or girlfriend sleeping next to him.

The monks pay special attention to Goldie who behaves so seductively. They go back to the monastery for vegetarian lunch and return at the time when Goldie and Westgate are fooling around in the bedroom. It turns out Goldie's bedroom and the room where the religious service is performed are separated by a wall only.

A monk who arrives early goes to the basin next to Goldie's window to wash his hands when he suddenly hears someone exclaiming in a soft and trembling voice, "Ooh, ah, hoowee!" as if someone in the room were in orgasm. He stops washing his hands, stands still, and listens for some time. He then hears a woman say, "You keep thinking with the wrong head, darling! Aren't you afraid the monks can hear us? Spare me!"

Westgate responds, "Well, you ain't seen nothin' yet!"

The couple does not expect their pillow talk can be joyfully heard by the monk. The news about the woman performing another service in the bedroom next door spreads fast to the other monks who arrive later, and they all get excited.

At the end of the religious service, Goldie takes off her mourning clothes, changes into a beautiful dress, and stands shoulder to shoulder with Westgate to watch the removal of the altar. The monk who earlier eavesdropped on the couple can vaguely see them standing behind the portiere, which reminds him of the conversation he has overheard. He gets so distracted he forgets to stop beating the drum.

Mrs. Rex asks, "The joss paper has been burnt, so why are you still beating the drum?"

The monk replies, "You ain't seen nothin' yet!"

When Westgate hears the embarrassing reply, he asks Mrs. Rex to tip the monks and send them away.

The monk says, "Thank you."

Goldie says, "You're welcome."

The monk then says, "Spare me!" And they leave cheerfully.

Chapter 9. Sawn Brawn Kills the Wrong Guy

After they remove Dally's altar, Goldie treats Mrs. Rex to dinner and asks Mrs. Rex to continue to take care of Eva.

Westgate says, "Mrs. Rex, when Sawn Brawn returns home, just say since Goldie couldn't live by herself, her mother asked her to marry another man in the capital."

Goldie's luggage has been moved to Westgate's mansion ahead of time. The broken furniture and old clothes are all given to Mrs. Rex. Westgate also tips Mrs. Rex an oz of silver.

A palanquin with four lanterns arrives the next day, and Mrs. Rex sees them off. Goldie is carried to Westgate's mansion, escorted by Deon. Every man and his dog on the street know about the affair, but since Westgate is nasty, wealthy, and powerful, nobody dares say a word.

Westgate prepares three rooms on the first floor of the building in the garden for Goldie to live in, and the door leading to the rooms is at the secluded corner of the yard where there are bonsai and other types of plants. Since few people are there during the daytime, it is a quiet place with an access room and a bedroom. Westgate spends 16 oz of silver to buy a black-painted canopy bed with a red bed curtain. The dresser, table, and chairs are neatly arranged. His wife Moonie Call 吴月娘 has two maids; one is named Plumie 春梅, another is named Flutie 玉箫. Westgate assigns Plumie to serve Goldie. He then spends 5 oz of silver to buy a junior maid named Jadie 小玉 to serve Lady Call. He also spends 6 oz of silver to buy a stove maid named Chrysie 秋菊 to serve Goldie.

Lady Show was the late wife of Westgate. She brought with her a dowry maid named Snowie Heir 孙雪娥, about 20 years old. She is short but pretty. Since Westgate has promoted Snowie to be his fourth spouse, Goldie is assigned as his fifth spouse.

Westgate sleeps in Goldie's room that night, and they are on Cloud Nine. Goldie grooms herself the next day, puts on a beautiful dress, and after Plumie serves her tea, she goes to Lady Moonie Call's room to pay her respects to the lady and the other concubines.

Moonie looks at Goldie from head to toe and notices the attractive 25-year old woman has willow-leaf-like eyebrows, peach-like face, slender figure, and thinks, "Every time the valet returned home, he mentioned Dally Brawn had a gorgeous wife

I'd never seen. I now see she's indeed cute. No wonder my husband loves her so much."

Goldie first bows down to Lady Moonie Call and then offers the traditional present of a pair of embroidered shoes. She pays her respects to Cutie Plum, Towie Prime, and Snowie Heir who are the more senior concubines. Moonie orders her maid to pull up a chair for Goldie.

Moonie Call, about 25 years old, is Westgate's first spouse and the official wife. Since she was born on Mid-Autumn Festival, the day people celebrate the day of a full moon, she was named Moonie. She has a silver-plate-like face, almond-like eyes, and a gentle and taciturn character.

Cutie Plum, Westgate's second spouse, was a singer in a brothel. She is quite chubby and often coughs in front of people. She is good at making love but not as seductive as Goldie.

Towie Prime, Westgate's newlywed third spouse, has the natural beauty with a pumpkin-seed-like face, a few freckles, a willow-like waist, a long and slender body, and small feet.

Snowie Heir, Westgate's fourth spouse, used to be his maid. She is short, graceful, a good cook, and a good dancer.

Goldie goes to Moonie's room three days later. She stitches clothes and repairs shoes every morning. She presents herself as a self-starter who knows what tasks need to be done for Moonie and commands Moonie's maids skillfully.

Moonie is so pleased with Goldie she treats Goldie as her sister, gives Goldie good clothes and jewelry, and eats and drinks with Goldie at the same table.

Cutie Plum and the other concubines do not like the special nice treatment Goldie receives from Moonie. Cutie complains, "Lady Call doesn't care about our seniority. Goldie arrived only a few days ago and is already spoiled rotten by her!"

Meanwhile, Sawn arrives at Clearstream Town in early September and hands in the reply letter to the town hall.

The mayor is greatly pleased with the safe delivery of the gold, silver, and jewelry. He rewards Sawn with 10 oz of silver and treats Sawn to dinner.

Sawn goes to his apartment, changes his clothes and shoes, puts on a new headscarf, locks his room, and heads straight for Purplestone Street. The neighbors who see Sawn return all break out in a cold sweat. One neighbor comments, "This is the day of reckoning for the adulterers! How could this superhero let them off easy? We'll wait for the other shoe to drop!"

Sawn arrives at his brother's house, lifts the portiere, enters the foyer, and sees his niece Eva knitting. Since nobody else is in the house, he asks, "Where's your father and mother?"

Eva just cries and dares not answer.

Mrs. Rex is working next door when she hears Sawn's arrival. Lest the murder plot be exposed, she quickly comes over to help Eva answer questions.

Sawn greets Mrs. Rex and asks, "Where's my brother? Why don't I see my sister-in-law?"

"Please have a seat. Let me tell you. After you left, your brother fell ill and died in May."

"On which day in May did my brother die? What illness was it? Whose medication did he take?"

"Your brother suddenly had a heartache on May 20th. He was ill for eight days. He then succumbed to his illness which could neither be cured by prayer nor by medication."

"My brother never had heartache. How could he die of that illness?"

"Sergeant, you shouldn't say that. Nothing is certain but the unforeseen. Who could guarantee he would never have any illnesses?"

"Where's my brother buried?"

"Your brother was penniless when he kicked the bucket. His wife, like a legless crab, couldn't find a cemetery for him. Luckily, he had a rich acquaintance who donated a coffin. He was cremated three days later."

"Where's my sister-in-law?"

"She's a young woman who doesn't have any means to support herself. After she observed the 100-day mourning period, her mother persuaded her to marry again last month. Since the man she married lives in the capital, she left behind Eva, the orphan, she asked me to take care of until you return. I can now hand Eva over to you to fulfill my duty."

Sawn hesitates for a while. He takes leave of Mrs. Rex and heads straight for the inn near the town hall. He rents a room, changes into simple clothes, and asks a soldier to buy from the stores a hemp rope, a pair of brocade shoes, and a mourning hat to wear. He also buys fruit, appetizers, incense, candles, and joss paper, then goes to his brother's house and sets up a brand-new altar where he lights a lantern and candles. Everything is set up properly after four hours, and he bows down and prays at 9 p.m., "My brother, whose spirit is nearby, although you were timid when you were alive, you should feel free to speak up after death! If you've been murdered, please appear in my dream, and I'll avenge you!" He libates wine, burns joss paper, and cries his heart out.

Sawn's cry moves the neighbors deeply. He then gives the offering of food to the soldier and Eva to consume. He gets two sleeping bags and asks the soldier to sleep at the side of the room. He asks Eva to sleep in her bedroom, while he puts a sleeping bag in front of the altar and sleeps there.

Unable to fall asleep, Sawn tosses and turns around midnight and heaves deep sighs. The soldier is sound asleep snoring. He gets up and looks at the altar where the candle in the glass lantern is half burned out. He sits on the sleeping bag, and mumbles, "Although you were timid when you were alive, Brother, you should feel free to speak up after death—" A gust of chilly air blows out from under the altar before he can finish his statement. It swirls around in the darkness as it dims the lantern. The objects hung on the walls all begin to swing. The cold air makes Sawn's hair stand on end. He focuses his eyesight and sees a man coming out from under the altar. The man says, "Brother! I died a horrible death!" Since he cannot see too clearly, he goes over to investigate, but the cold air and the man both disappear. He then sits on the sleeping bag and thinks deeply, "It's weird! It seemed to be a dream, but it wasn't a dream. He wanted to tell me something, but my positive earthly energy was so strong it dispersed his negative Underworld energy. He obviously died a wrongful death." The drum tower strikes 1 a.m. While the soldier behind him is still sleeping, he thinks, "I'll wait until dawn before I work on it." He then falls asleep.

The soldier gets up before dawn at 5 a.m. to boil water. Sawn grooms himself, asks Eva to take care of the house, then leads the soldier out the door to visit his neighbors and asks, "How did my brother die? Whom did my sister-in-law marry?"

Although the neighbors all know the answer, they are too afraid of Westgate to get involved. One neighbor replies, "Sergeant, you don't need to interview us. Mrs. Rex is his next-door neighbor. Just ask her to get the answer."

However, another neighbor with a big mouth says, "Yorky who sells pears, and Jupe Quest the coroner, know the details."

Sawn walks on the street to look for Yorky, and he manages to see the naughty boy carrying a willow-weaved basket of rice. He then says, "Long time no see, Yorky!"

Yorky says, "Sergeant Brawn, you've come too late to join in the fight. My 60-year-old father has nobody else to take care of him right now, so it'll be difficult for me to go to court with you to sue the murderer."

Sawn says, "Dear comrade, follow me." He leads Yorky to a restaurant and says, "Waiter, give us two servings!" He then says, "Yorky, although you're young, you express filial piety to your father. I don't have much to give you now." He takes 5 oz of silver pieces out of his pocket, gives them to Yorky, and says, "Take these to pay for the living expenses of your old father. I'll need you in the future, and I'll give you 15 oz of silver when the job is done so you can start your own business. Please tell me in detail: With whom did my brother quarrel? Who murdered him? Who married my sister-in-law? Please tell me without hiding any facts."

Yorky receives the silver and thinks, "These 5 oz of silver are enough to support my father for three to five months. I'll help Sawn in court." He then replies, "Sergeant Brawn, I'll tell you, but don't be upset." He describes how he tried to sell pears to Westgate and was then kicked out by Mrs. Rex, how he helped Dally catch the adulterers in the act, how Westgate kicked the heart of Dally who then fell ill for a few days and then died in mysterious circumstances.

Sawn asks, "Did you tell the truth?" He also asks, "Whom did my sister-in-law marry?"

Yorky replies, "Westgate carried your sister-in-law all the way to his mansion, and you're asking me if I told the truth!"

Sawn says, "Don't tell lies!"

Yorky responds, "I'll say the same thing even in court!"

Sawn says, "OK, comrade, let's finish our meal."

After they fill up their stomachs, Sawn pays the bill, and they leave the restaurant.

Sawn orders, "Yorky, give the money to your old father when you go home. Come to the town hall early tomorrow and be the witness." He then asks, "Where does Jupe Quest live?"

Yorky asks, "You wait until now to look for Jupe Quest? He moved to some unknown location three days before you arrived."

Sawn lets Yorky return home. He gets up early the next morning and goes to Mr. Show 陳先生's house to have the complaint written up. Yorky is already waiting for him when he arrives at the town hall. He brings Yorky inside the hall, kneels, and cries foul.

The mayor knows Sawn and asks, "Whom do you want to accuse? Why did you cry foul?"

Sawn replies, "The mobster Chic Westgate kicked my brother Dally Brawn in the heart when my brother confronted Westgate who was having an affair with my sister-in-law Goldie Rinse. Mrs. Rex was the accomplice who murdered my brother. Jupe Quest covered up for the murder by cremating my brother to eliminate all evidence. Westgate has snatched my sister-in-law and had her as his concubine. This young man Yorky is the witness. I hope Your Highness will administer justice." He then submits the complaint.

The mayor receives the complaint and asks, "Why don't I see Jupe Quest?"

Sawn replies, "Jupe Quest was afraid of his involvement and has disappeared."

The mayor takes Yorky's statements, adjourns the court session, and discusses the problem with his assistants. It turns out the mayor, the deputies, and the registrar, are all friends of Westgate, so it is difficult to get an unbiased decision during the discussion. He comes out and says, "As the sergeant of this town, don't you know the laws? Everyone knows for adultery, catch the pair; for theft, show the loot; for murder, show the body. Your brother's body is gone, and you haven't caught the adulterers in their act. You now claim a murder case based on the words of this lad, how can the accusation stand? Don't be so rash. Think twice before accusing anyone and be reasonable."

Sawn responds, "Your Honor, it's all true. I didn't make it up."

The mayor says, "You may get up. Let me think about it. If it's feasible, I'll arrest him."

Sawn gets up, goes outside, and keeps Yorky in his inn.

Someone has already reported to Westgate who then knows Sawn has returned and led Yorky to court to submit a complaint.

Westgate is so scared he sends his trusted servants Lebron 来保 and Leroy 来旺 to bribe the officials.

Sawn goes to the town hall the next morning and urges the mayor to arrest the murderers. However, the mayor who has accepted Westgate's bribe refuses to file the complaint and says, "Sawn, don't listen to other people's gossip and fight against Chic Westgate. This case is too unclear for us to make any judgment. As the saying goes, 'Believe nothing of what you hear, and only half of what you see.' Don't be rash!"

The penal officer puts his two cents in, "Sergeant, since you work in the town court, you should know the law. Every murder case requires the corpse, wounds, ailments, weapons, and an alibi before you can work on it. Your brother's corpse has disappeared. What can we do?"

Sawn says, "Your honor, if you don't let me sue them in court, I'll take matters into my own hands." He takes back the complaint, returns to his inn, and lets Yorky return home. He heaves a deep sigh, gnashes his teeth, and keeps scolding the slut. Unable to vent his anger, he runs straight to Westgate's drugstore to look for Westgate. He sees Jason, who has just opened the store, sitting at the counter. He angrily approaches the clerk and asks, "Is Tycoon in his mansion?"

Jason recognizes Sawn and replies, "He's not home, Sergeant. Do you have anything to tell him?"

Sawn replies, "Please come out, I have a word with you."

Jason dares not say no.

Sawn leads Jason to a quiet alley and suddenly grabs the clerk's collar. He stares at Jason and threatens, "Do you want to die, or want to live?"

Jason replies, "Sergeant, I haven't offended you. Why are you angry with me?"

Sawn replies, "If you want to die, don't tell me anything. If you want to live, you'd better tell me honestly where Chic Westgate is. How many days has he married my sister-in-law? Tell me everything, and I'll leave you alone."

Jason is a timid man. When he sees Sawn explode, he replies, "Sergeant, don't be upset. Tycoon pays me 2 oz of silver a month to manage his store. I don't know his other businesses. He just went with an acquaintance to the restaurant on Lion Street 獅子街 for a drink. I dare not lie."

Sawn releases his hold and runs to Lion Street. Jason is so scared he is frozen to the spot for some time.

There is a policeman named Gossip Plum 李外传 who eavesdrops on everyone in the town hall to earn money. He is very eager to help anyone who greases his palm whenever two parties are involved in a lawsuit. Thus, people in town call him Gossip Plum. After he saw the mayor refute Sawn's complaint, he reports Sawn's failure to Westgate that day.

Westgate then treats Gossip Plum to lunch on the second floor of the restaurant and gives Gossip Plum 5 oz of silver. While they are happily drinking, Westgate glances downstairs through the window and sees Sawn running towards the restaurant. Knowing Sawn is coming for revenge and since there is not enough time to go downstairs to escape, he says he needs to go to the restroom at the back of the building, then leaps through the back window onto the roof of another building.

Sawn rushes to the restaurant, and asks, "Is Chic Westgate here?"

The restaurateur replies, "Tycoon Westgate and his friend are drinking upstairs."

Sawn runs upstairs and sees a man sitting there with two courtesans. Knowing Gossip Plum must have alerted Westgate of the latest event, he growls, "Where has Chic Westgate gone?"

Gossip Plum is too scared to speak at all when he sees Sawn.

With one kick, Sawn knocks down the table and breaks all the bowls and cups. The two courtesans are scared stiff. He then punches Gossip Plum's face.

Gossip Plum endures the pain, jumps onto a bench, and wants to escape through a window. Sawn helps him out by lifting and throwing him out the window onto the middle of the street.

The restaurateur downstairs is too terrified to intervene when he sees Sawn explode.

The pedestrians on the street all stop and stare at Gossip Plum who cannot move any parts of his body except his eyeballs, and he is more dead than alive.

Sawn is still fuming as he runs downstairs, and again kicks Gossip Plum who then bites the dust.

A pedestrian says, "Sergeant, he's not Westgate, you beat up the wrong guy."

"I beat him up because he didn't answer when I asked him a question. It turned out he couldn't withstand any beatings."

The headman sees a dead man, but he dares not arrest Sawn, so he approaches Sawn slowly. Anyway, Sawn surrenders.

Luan Rex 王鸾, the restaurateur, and Ms. Bag 包氏 and Ms. Bull 牛氏, the two courtesans, are also arrested. They are then brought to the town hall to see the mayor.

Chapter 10. Sawn Brawn Exiled to Firstshire

Meanwhile, Westgate jumps out the window, crawls on the roof of another building, leaps to someone else's yard, and hides there.

It turns out the house belongs to Elder Wild 胡老人 who practices medicine. A big fat maid who works for him goes to the outhouse to answer the call of nature. Just when she crouches, she sees a man hiding at the yard's wall. She runs away at once and screams, "Burglar!"

Elder Wild rushes to the yard. He recognizes Westgate and says, "Tycoon, you're lucky Sawn Brawn couldn't find you. He killed another man, and he was arrested and brought to the town hall. They'll most probably sentence him to death. You can go home with no problem."

Westgate bows and thanks Elder Wild, swaggers home and tells Goldie his adventure. Since their major threat is gone, they feel very relieved.

Goldie says, "Bribe the high- and low-ranking officers. We must kill him. Don't let him come out."

Westgate dispatches his trusted servant Leroy to deliver to the mayor a gift of golden goblets and 50 oz of shiny silver. He also bribes various officers in the town hall to plot against Sawn.

The headman brings Sawn to court the next day, together with the restaurateur and the courtesans.

The mayor, who has accepted Westgate's bribe, grumbles, "Sawn Brawn, why did you break the law by submitting a false complaint yesterday? You then beat someone to death. Why?"

Sawn bows down and explains, "Your Honor, I originally wanted to fight my enemy Chic Westgate, but I unexpectedly bumped into Gossip Plum in the restaurant. He refused to answer when I asked him, 'Where has Westgate gone?' I was so angry I accidentally punched him to death."

"What kind of nonsense is that? Don't you know he's a policeman in this town hall? There must be another reason, and you lied!" The mayor then orders, "Guards, beat him up. Otherwise, he won't confess!"

Several guards come over, push Sawn onto the floor, and spank him.

After being spanked 20 times, Sawn pleads, "Your Honor, I've provided a lot of good service for you. Can't you take pity on me?"

The mayor becomes angrier on hearing the plea and says, "You killed a man, and you still try to sweet-talk me?" He then orders, "Knock him hard!"

The torturers knock Sawn's fingers 50 times. They then put a heavy-weight pillory on him and put him in jail.

Many deputies and officers are friends of Sawn. They admire his loyalty and courage and want to help him out but are unable to do so because Westgate has bribed so many people in the town hall. To help Sawn, the coroner makes up a false report when he and the witnesses go to Lion Street to do the autopsy: "Sawn Brawn couldn't get back the money Gossip Plum owed him. Since they were drunk, there was a fistfight, and Gossip Plum fell to his death." When they finish all the paperwork, they send Sawn to Eastpeaceshire for sentencing.

Venture Show 陈文昭 of River-South 河南, the sheriff of Eastpeaceshire, is a virtuous official. He starts a court session and looks at the complaint filed by the mayor:

Murder report from Clearstream Town: The suspect Sawn Brawn of Sunvale Town is 28 years old. Since he is strong, he works as a sergeant of Clearstream Town. He made an offering to his late brother when he returned from a business trip. Since his sister-in-law Goldie Rinse married again before she finished observing the mourning period, he went out for more fact-finding. It so happened he bumped into Gossip Plum in Luan Rex's restaurant on Lion Street. He was drunk when he asked Gossip Plum to pay back the 300 coins owed him. They had a fight when Gossip Plum refused to pay. Gossip Plum was seriously wounded and died. The courtesans Ms. Bull and Ms. Bag were the eyewitnesses. He was arrested by the headman, and the mayor dispatched the coroner and the neighbors to the crime scene to perform an autopsy. The report they filled in is submitted here. It is our opinion the suspect Sawn Brawn be hanged; the restaurateur Luan Rex, and the courtesans Ms. Bull and Ms. Bag who were witnesses, be released.

September 9, 1113

Signed by: Town Mayor Data Plum 李达天, Town Counselor Howard Tune 乐和安, Registrar Holly Fame 华荷禄, Penal Officer Gorge Fab 夏恭基, and Deputy Lou Cash 钱劳

After reading the complaint, the sheriff requests that Sawn be brought over, and he asks, "Why did you beat Gossip Plum to death?"

Sawn bows down and pleads, "Your Highness from the azure sky, I hope you'll spare my life! I originally wanted to avenge my brother. I accidentally killed that man while I was hunting down Chic Westgate." He then describes the events in detail and says, "My brother's murder was an albatross on my neck. Chic Westgate is so rich nobody can accuse him. It's a pity my brother Dally Brawn died a wrongful death."

The sheriff says, "Alright, I understand." He then summons and spanks Deputy Lou Cash 20 times and says, "Your mayor is so corrupt. How could he accept a bribe and abuse his power?" He then uses his pen to rewrite Sawn's confession, and says, "Deputy, this man wants to avenge his brother and accidentally killed Gossip Plum. He's a loyal warrior, different from an ordinary murderer."

The sheriff replaces Sawn's heavyweight pillory with a lightweight pillory before he puts Sawn in jail. He then sends a document to Clearstream Town to request that the bully Chic Westgate, Sawn's sister-in-law Goldie Rinse, Mrs. Rex, the lad Yorky, and the coroner Jupe Quest, be questioned for a retrial.

Since everyone in Eastpeaceshire jail knows Sawn has been framed, the jailers do not ask him for money but feed him well instead.

Someone reports the sheriff's request to Clearstream Town. Westgate is scared by the news. He dares not bribe Venture Show, a virtuous official, so he asks a trusted servant of his in-law Honk Show 陈洪 to accompany his servant Leroy to deliver a letter to Commander Birch of the capital to plead with Preceptor Weed 蔡太師.

Preceptor Weed worries Mayor Plum's reputation may be damaged. He then quickly writes an urgent confidential letter to Venture Show in Eastpeaceshire and specifies that Chic Westgate and Goldie Rinse be exempt from interrogation.

Venture Show used to work at the Supreme Court 大理寺 before he was promoted to prefect. Since he used to be the student of Preceptor Weed, and Commander Birch is an influential officer of the imperial court, the best he can do is spare Sawn of capital punishment.

Sawn is spanked 40 times and is exiled 600 miles away.

Since Dally has been cremated, it is not possible to investigate his death under suspicious circumstances.

After the verdict is approved by the higher court, Sawn is released from prison, and an 8-lb iron-leafed pillory is put on him. He has two rows of golden words tattooed on his face, and two correctional officers will lead him to the prison camp in Firstshire 孟州.

After Sawn leaves Eastpeaceshire, he returns home, sells his furniture, and uses the money to pay for the travel expenses of the two correctional officers. He asks his neighbor Elon Grace 姚二郎 to take care of Eva and says, "If I get the amnesty from the imperial court and return home, I'll repay your kindness."

The neighbors and wealthy families know Sawn is a loyal warrior who unfortunately got the punishment, and they all chip in money and food to help him.

Sawn asks a soldier to get his baggage, leaves Clearstream Town on the same day, and heads for Firstshire in mid-autumn.

Sawn's exile takes a heavy load off Westgate's mind. With the thorn in his side removed, he joyfully orders his servants Leroy, Lebron, and Lesing 来兴 to clean up the Hibiscus Pavilion 芙蓉亭 in the back garden. He throws a party and asks musicians and dancers to perform for his family that consists of his first spouse Moonie Call, second spouse Cutie Plum, third spouse Towie Prime, fourth spouse Snowie Heir, and fifth spouse Goldie Rinse, for a happy family gathering. The housekeepers and maids stand on both sides to serve them. They are enjoying themselves when Deon brings along a valet and a junior maid who carry two boxes.

The junior maid says, "We're from your neighbor Eunuch Bloom's mansion, and we bring blossoms for Lady Call to wear." She goes in front of Westgate and Moonie, bows down, stands aside, and says, "Our lady asks us to deliver a box of desserts and a box of flowers for Lady Call." She opens a box of hair clips with fresh blossoms.

The valet opens a box of dumplings and cookies made by the imperial chefs.

Moonie says cheerfully, "Your lady is so kind!" She tips them by giving the junior maid a face towel and the valet 100 coins, treats both to lunch, and says, "Tell your lady I thank her very much." She then asks, "Junior maid, what's your name?"

The junior maid replies, "I'm Stitchie 绣春, and my valet companion is Taffy 天福."

After the visitors are gone, Moonie says, "The lady of the Bloom mansion next to us is quite nice. She often sends her valet and maid to deliver presents to me, but I haven't sent her any presents."

Westgate says, "Comrade Bloom married that lady two years ago and often says she has a good personality. Otherwise, how can she have two nice maids in her room?"

Moonie says, "Her uncle-in-law died in July. I met her at the funeral on the hill. She's short, has nice skin, curved eye-brows, and her white skin displays her warm personality! She's still young, around 24 to 25 years old."

Westgate says, "She was the concubine of Regent Beam 梁中書 of Famed City 大名 before she married Jesse Bloom 花子虛, and she brought along a huge dowry."

Moonie says, "She's our next-door neighbor who sends us presents to make friends with us. We should return the favor and send her a present tomorrow."

Jesse Bloom's wife's name is Vasie Plum 李瓶兒. She was born on February 15, and she was named Vasie because someone gave her a gift of a pair of fish vases that day. She first married Regent Beam of Famed City as a concubine. Regent Beam, the son-in-law of Preceptor Weed of the capital, has a very jealous wife who beat many maids and concubines to death and then buried them in the back garden. Vasie lived in the outer studio and was protected by her nanny. When Quake Plum 李逵 massa-cred the Beam's family on February 15, 1113, Regent Beam and his wife were on Aqua-Cloud Tower 翠雲樓. After Regent Beam ran for his life, Vasie fled with her nanny to the capital to stay with her relatives. She brought with her 100 large western pearls and a pair of 2-oz emeralds.

Eunuch Bloom, who worked in the imperial court at that time, was promoted to commander of Wide-South 廣南. Since his nephew Jesse Bloom was single, he acted as a matchmaker and married Vasie to Jesse as the official wife. Eunuch Bloom also brought along Jesse for half a year when he went to Wide-South. He then fell ill and retired. Since he was from Clearstream Town, he moved to that town. After he died, Jesse inherited all his properties.

Jesse Bloom visits brothels every day, and his friends are all members of the Westgate Club led by Chic Westgate.

The club has a monthly meeting that hires two songbirds to entertain them. Seeing the Jesse is the nephew of the imperial eunuch with lots of money to spend, the members all encourage him to hold the meetings in brothels for several days and nights.

Westgate enjoys the entire day at Hibiscus Pavilion with his spouses until evening. He is half-drunk and aroused when he returns to Goldie's room, and he wants to make love to Goldie.

Goldie quickly lights incense, makes the bed, takes off her clothes, and lies in bed.

Westgate changes his mind and does not sleep with Goldie. He sits next to the azure-gauze bed curtain and calls Plumie in to serve tea.

Goldie, embarrassed to be seen by the maid, quickly lowers the bed curtain.

Westgate exclaims, "What are you afraid of!" He then says, "Our neighbor Comrade Bloom has two good maids in his room. The one who delivered blossoms here is the junior maid. There's another one, same age as Plumie, Comrade Bloom has slept with. When her lady stood at the door last time, she also came out, and she looked so pretty. Who'd have thought Comrade Bloom at his youthful age knew how to have gorgeous girls to sleep with him in his room."

Goldie glances at Westgate and exclaims, "Big deal! If you want to sleep with my maid, go ahead. Why did you say it in a roundabout way, and use someone else to compare with me? I'm not that kind of woman. I'll go to the living quarters tomorrow to give you the chance to ask Plumie to come to my room to sleep with you." She then sleeps while cuddling Westgate.

Goldie indeed goes and sits in Towie's room in the living quarters the next day.

Westgate asks Plumie to come into the room and makes love to her.

Plumie is promoted by Goldie from then on. She does not need to do kitchen work, but only makes the bed and serves tea.

Goldie selects her favorite clothes and jewelry and gives them to Plumie.

It so happens Chrysie is very different from Plumie who is intelligent, eloquent, pretty, and with a good sense of humor.

Westgate likes Plumie very much. Since Chrysie is dumb and cannot provide good service, Goldie beats her up. It is different strokes for different folks.

Chapter 11. Snowie Heir Confronts Goldie Rinse

Goldie is spoiled because she is Westgate's favorite concubine, and she acts whimsically. With her cynical personality, she eavesdrops on other people to find fault with them and causes a lot of trouble.

Plumie is also not easy to deal with. One day when she is scolded by Goldie for a minor issue, she goes to the kitchen in the back to vent her frustration by banging the counter and plates randomly.

Snowie finds Plumie annoying and teases, "If you're lovesick, go somewhere else to think about him. Why vent your frustration here?"

Plumie snaps, "This vamp claims I'm a seductress!"

Snowie falls silent when she sees Plumie's wild character.

Plumie has a fit as she walks back to Goldie's room and reports to Goldie with exaggeration what Snowie has said, and adds, "She claimed we're seductresses accepted by Master."

Goldie is very upset to hear the report.

When Moonie needs to attend a funeral, Goldie gets up early to see her off. She then feels tired and takes a nap. She later goes to the pavilion and sees Towie approaching her.

Towie asks smilingly, "Why do you look upset and not say anything, Goldie?"

Goldie replies, "I was very tired this morning. Where did you come from?

Towie replies, "I was in the kitchen for a while."

"What did Snowie say to you?"

"She didn't say anything to me."

Although Goldie does not say anything, she is at odds with Snowie from then on.

Goldie and Towie are doing needlework when Plumie carries a pot of soup, and Chrysie carries two cups of tea to serve them. They set up a table to play a game of Go after tea. Just when the game becomes exciting, the valet Xylo comes in from the garden gate and reports, "Master is coming."

The two concubines quickly put away the board and stones. Westgate comes in, sees both concubines beautifully dressed, and teases, "My two darlings are worth over 100 oz of silver."

Goldie responds, "I'm not your darling. Your darling is in the kitchen."

When Towie wants to leave, Westgate holds onto her and asks, "Where are you going? You want to escape when I come. Honestly tell me what both of you were doing while I wasn't home."

Goldie replies, "We were so bored we played two games of Go. We didn't steal anything. Who would've thought you arrived?" She then takes off his coat and asks, "You returned early from the funeral today?"

Westgate replies, "The reception hall was full of imperial officials today. The weather was hot, and I was impatient, so I came home first."

Towie asks, "Why hasn't Lady Call returned home?"

Westgate replies, "Her palanquin is waiting to enter the city. I'll dispatch two valets to receive her." He sits down and asks, "What did you bet when you played the Go game?"

Goldie replies, "We played without betting anything."

Westgate says, "I'll play a game with you, and the loser will spend an oz of silver to treat the winner to dinner."

Goldie says, "I don't have any silver."

Westgate says, "Since you don't have silver, you can use your hair clip as collateral." He sets up the game board, and the three of them play the game.

Goldie loses, and while Westgate is counting the stones, she wipes the stones away from the board and walks to a flower patch to pick flowers.

Westgate finds Goldie and says, "You hide in here after you lost the game, chatty!"

Goldie responds laughingly, "You didn't harass Towie when she lost to you, but you harassed me, bozo!" She separates the petals of the flowers in her hand and throws them at Westgate who then hugs and kisses her.

Towie walks over and says, "Lady Call has arrived, Goldie. Let's go and meet her."

Goldie leaves Westgate alone and says, "I'll speak to you when I return, darling!" She goes with Towie to greet Moonie.

Moonie asks, "Why are you laughing?"

Towie replies, "Goldie played a game of Go with Master today and lost an oz of silver. She'll treat you to dinner tomorrow."

Moonie laughs.

Goldie just says a few words with Moonie. She then goes to her room to keep Westgate company. She orders Plumie to light incense in the room and filled the bathtub with water so that she can sleep with Westgate at night.

Dear reader, although Moonie Call is the lady of the family and lives in the main bedroom, she frequently has ailments and does not take care of the household. She goes outside the mansion only when she needs to socialize with relatives or friends. The ledger is taken care of by the songbird Cutie Plum. Snowie Heir oversees the housekeepers in the kitchen to take care of everyone's meals. Snowie prepares the food and wine when Westgate stays in one of the concubine's room, and the maid of that room will go to the kitchen to pick up the food and wine.

Westgate drinks with Goldie in her room and takes a bath, and they then go to sleep.

Westgate promises Goldie to buy pearls at the temple the next day. He gets up early and wants to have lotus pancakes and fish soup for breakfast. He dispatches Plumie to the kitchen to order his breakfast.

Plumie does not move, and Goldie says, "Don't dispatch her. A woman over there said I've spoiled Plumie and let you sleep with Plumie, and she claimed the two of us team up like a gang of seductresses. That woman jumped down my throat, bullied Plumie and me, and you dispatch Plumie to the kitchen?"

Westgate asks, "Who said those words to bully Plumie? Tell me."

Goldie replies, "Walls have ears. Instead of asking Plumie to go to the kitchen, ask Chrysie to go."

Westgate then orders Chrysie to go to the kitchen to ask Snowie to prepare his breakfast.

Although Goldie has set up the dining table, after half an hour, the breakfast has not arrived, and Westgate is jumping up and down.

Goldie says, "Plumie, go to the kitchen and look around. My maid Chrysie has taken root over there."

Plumie goes to the kitchen unwillingly, and when she sees Chrysie waiting there, she scolds, "Madam Rinse will beat you up, dummy! She asked why you haven't returned. Master is waiting to have pancakes for breakfast before he goes to the temple. He was anxiously jumping up and down and asked me to find your whereabouts!"

Snowie hears those words and snaps, "The frying pan is made of iron, slut! It takes time to heat it. I've prepared porridge for him, but he doesn't want it. He suddenly came up with the idea of pancakes and soup. Does he think I'm a clairvoyant?"

Plumie, upset by the scolding, replies, "It's all bull! If Master didn't have the clout to decide what he wants for breakfast, who has the clout? I'll go back and tell on you and see what will happen." She then twists Chrysie's ear and before they return, Snowie scolds, "It's a shame a slave like you behaves so badly!"

Plumie retorts, "A leopard can't change her spots!" She then returns in disgust.

Goldie sees Plumie angrily dragging Chrysie back, and asks, "What happened?"

Plumie replies, "Go ask Snowie. She was still slowly making the dough when I went there. I told Chrysie, 'Master is waiting for his breakfast, and Madam Rinse asked why you haven't returned and dispatched me to find you.' Madam Heir then lashed out at me and kept calling me slave, as if I'd convinced Master not to have porridge for breakfast and changed to pancakes and soup for no good reason. She kept scolding everyone in the kitchen and refused to make the pancakes."

Goldie says, "I didn't want Plumie to go to the kitchen so Snowie couldn't get a chance to accuse Plumie and me of manipulating Master in this mansion."

Westgate explodes. He walks to the kitchen, and without waiting for Snowie to give any explanations, he kicks her a few times and scolds, "I asked Plumie to come here to get pancakes, hussy! Why did you scold her? You called her a slave, but why don't you look yourself in the mirror?"

Snowie dares not talk back as Westgate kicks and scolds her before he goes out the kitchen door. Barrette 一丈青, the wife of steward Lejon 来昭, is nearby, and she says, "Barrette, see how jinxed I was today. You were here earlier and didn't hear me say much. Plumie angrily came here, shouted at me, and dragged Chrysie away. She then exaggerated minor issues to Master as if they were big deals and provoked him to come here and beat me up for no good reason. This master will spoil his slave rotten. I'd better watch my steps."

Surprisingly, Westgate overhears Snowie's complaint. He comes back, punches her a few times, and scolds, "Slave! You claimed you didn't bully her, but I heard you scold her with my own ears!"

Snowie is painfully beaten by Westgate who then returns to Goldie's room. Snowie is so upset she cries bitterly in the kitchen.

Moonie, grooming herself in her bedroom, asks, "Jadie, why is there a commotion in the kitchen?"

"Master wants to eat pancakes before he goes to the temple, but Snowie scolded Plumie who was dispatched by Master to rush Snowie. After Plumie told on Snowie, he went to the kitchen, kicked Snowie a few times, and Snowie's crying."

"If Master wants to eat pancakes, Snowie should quickly make them. There's no reason to scold his maid!" Moonie dispatches Jadie to the kitchen to urge Snowie and a few housekeepers to quickly prepare breakfast for Westgate to send him off.

Westgate then rides his horse to the temple, followed by his valet.

Snowie is so upset she goes to Moonie's room and tells Moonie what has happened.

Unexpectedly, Goldie comes and stands outside the window to eavesdrop on them. She hears Snowie tell Moonie and Cutie how she seduces men and does so many unethical things.

Snowie says, "Lady, she's more erotic than any paramour on Earth. She's such a slut she can't sleep any night without a man next to her. Any sexual acts other women can't perform, she can perform well. She poisoned her husband to death before she came here. She wants to eat me alive now. She's mesmerized Master so much he always finds fault with me."

Moonie says, "With all due respect, you should make the pancakes and send his maid off nicely when he sent her to get them. Why did you scold her for no good reason?"

Snowie responds, "You think I scolded her for no good reason? She was already insubordinate when she served you in the past, and you didn't say anything when I hit her with the spine of my cleaver at that time. After I lost to her today, she'll be prouder of herself!"

Jadie comes over and says, "Goldie is outside."

Goldie stares at Snowie as soon as she enters the room, and says, "Even if I'd murdered my husband, it wasn't up to you to stop Master from marrying me and claim I encroach on your territory. Concerning Plumie, she wasn't my dowry maid. If you're really upset, you can recall her to serve Lady Call, and it'll spare me the trouble of getting involved in your dispute. Do you think I murdered my late husband to marry another man? This problem is easy to solve. I'll ask him to sign a dismissal document when he returns, and I'll be gone."

Moonie says, "I don't know the story behind all these issues. Why don't you call a truce?"

Snowie says, "Lady, see how she has diarrhea of the mouth! Nobody can argue with her. She spreads rumors in front of Master, then denies everything in no time. Based on what she said, except Lady Call, all other concubines should be kicked out, and she'll be the only one left."

Moonie sits there, falls silent, and lets both concubines fight it out verbally.

Snowie scolds, "Goldie, you call me a slave? You're the real slave!"

Moonie asks Jadie to drag Snowie to the kitchen when the argument almost escalates to a fistfight.

Goldie returns to her bedroom, removes her makeup, lets her hair hang loose, and cries so much her eyes are swollen like peaches as she lies in her bed.

Westgate has 4 oz of pearls in his pocket when he returns from the temple in the evening. He looks at Goldie as he enters her bedroom and asks, "What happened?"

Goldie cries buckets, asks Westgate for a dismissal document, and says, "I married you not because of your money, so why did she bully me like that? She kept saying I murdered my late husband. I'd better not having a maid to serve me, or else she'll scold me no end. She thinks my maid is a waste of space."

Westgate is so upset he rushes to the kitchen, drags Snowie by the hair, and beats her a few times with a club.

Moonie comes over, holds onto Westgate's hand, and says, "Snowie, it's just a tempest in a teapot! Don't upset Master!"

Westgate says, "Snowie the hussy! I heard with my own ears how you scolded her maid, and you still want to mess Goldie up. You'd better behave yourself!"

After beating up Snowie, Westgate returns to Goldie's bedroom. He takes out the 4 oz of pearls he just bought from the temple and lets Goldie string them up to wear.

Goldie is overjoyed to have Westgate fight on her behalf. They love each other even more. She sets up a table in the garden on another day to wine and dine Moonie, Towie, and Westgate.

Westgate has organized a club of ten friends who meet once a month to drink tea and wine.

Member #2 is Badger Yep 应伯爵, a prodigal son who has squandered his entire family's fortune and becomes a brown-noser who latches onto other rich kids in brothels.

Member #3 is Ceder Thank 谢希大, of noble descent. He is an orphan since his youth, and he is an idler and gambler who is good at football.

Member #4 is Remnant Bless 祝日念.

Member #5 is Gotcha Heir 孙寡嘴, about 50 years old. He earns commissions in brothels by hooking up young men with prostitutes.

Member #6 is Dangler Call 吴典恩. He used to be the geomancer of the town but was dismissed because of a misdemeanor. He helps people get bails in the town hall and therefore makes friends with Westgate.

Member #7 is Leisure Cloud 云离守, the brother of a brigadier general.

Member #8 is Seizure Oft 常时节.

Member #9 is Eunuch Bloom's nephew Jesse Bloom.

Member #10 is Leech White 白来创.

The ten members including Westgate, let Westgate be the leader of the club because he has money to spend.

When it is Jesse Bloom's turn to throw a party at his mansion right next door of Westgate's mansion, he uses imperial utensils of large trays and bowls to serve sumptuous food.

Everyone has arrived except Westgate who is busy, and they reserve a seat for him. He later arrives, followed by four valets, and everyone gets up to greet him. After he takes the seat of honor, a songbird and two courtesans, unbelievably beautiful and artistic, sing with pipa and zither. They come over and bow down to Westgate after their impressive performance. He then orders his valet Deon to take out of his briefcase three envelopes stuffed with coins, and the three performers receive the tips thankfully. He then asks, "Jesse, who's this songbird? She sings so well!"

Before Jesse can reply, Badger says, "Tycoon's too busy to remember minor things. The one who played zither is Jesse's sweetheart Silvie Call 吴银儿 from the alley behind the brothel. The one who played lute is Lovelie Red 朱爱爱, the daughter of

Hairy Red 朱毛头. The one who played pipa is Olie 桂姐, a daughter of Mama Plum and the younger sister of Osmie Plum 李桂卿 whose paternal aunt is your concubine. How could you not recognize her?"

Westgate replies bemusedly, "I haven't seen her for six years, and she has matured so beautifully!"

Olie serves wine seductively when it is time to drink wine.

Westgate asks, "What do your mom and your sister Osmie do at home? Why don't they come to my mansion to see your aunt?"

Olie replies, "My mom had a stroke last year and she's still paralyzed in one leg and needs people to support her to walk. My sister Osmie has been hired by an out-of-towner for half a year and seldom comes home. My household depends on me to sing every day to entertain a few old clients, which is very tiring. I'd like to visit my aunt in your mansion, but I never have the time. Master, why haven't you visited our place for so long? Why not let my aunt visit my mother?"

Impressed by Olie who is so friendly and speaks so fluently, Westgate begins to be attracted to her. He says, "I'll bring along two good friends to escort you home today. What's your take on that?"

"Master, no kidding! How can a nobleman like you be willing to set foot on my insignificant doormat?"

"I'm not kidding." Westgate then takes out of his pocket a face towel and a box of tea and gives them to Olie.

Olie says, "Let's send my valet home to prepare for your visit."

Westgate says, "We'll wait until the party ends before we leave."

Westgate asks Badger Yep and Ceder Thank to join him in escorting Olie back to her brothel when the party ends.

When Olie's palanquin arrives at her brothel, Osmie comes out to receive them into the hall. After they greet each other, they invite Olie's mother to come out.

A bawd soon comes out with a cane, and half of her body is paralyzed. She greets Westgate and exclaims, "My goodness! What a pleasant surprise to see my noble brother-in-law!"

[Since the bawd is the sister of Cutie Plum, a concubine of Westgate, she considers Westgate her brother-in-law. —Ed.]

Westgate says, "Please excuse me for not having the time to visit you."

The bawd asks, "What are the names of these two gentlemen?"

Westgate replies, "They're my good friends Badger Yep and Ceder Thank. We met Olie at the party held in the Bloom mansion today, and we escorted her home. Let's have some drinks."

The bawd offers the three guests the seats of honor and serves them tea. A servant soon sets up a table, lights the lamps, and puts dishes and wine cups on the table.

Olie puts on makeup and comes out to keep Westgate company. She and her sister Osmie sing a duet while everyone is enjoying his drink.

Westgate says, "Osmie, since my two friends are here today, and I've heard Olie's good in singing southern tunes, why not sing a piece to accompany my two friends' drinks?"

Badger says, "We peons are more than happy to listen to your impressive performance."

Olie sits there, just smiles, and does not move. As it so happens, Westgate wants to hook up with Olie, and he makes the request. However, the girls in the brothel are smart enough to detect Westgate's amorous intentions, and they know how to play hard to get.

Osmie says on behalf of Olie, "Olie has been pampered at home so much she's too shy to perform without any incentives."

Westgate then orders his valet Deon to take a 5-oz silver nugget out of his bag. He puts it on the table, and says, "This is a minor gift for Olie to buy cosmetics. I'll give her several expensive clothes next time."

Olie gets up thankfully and orders a maid to put the silver away. She pulls up a chair and sings *Flying on Clouds* so melodiously Westgate keeps praising her.

Westgate asks Deon to bring the horse home so that he can spend the night in Olie's room. He is in love with her, and encouraged by Badger Yep and Ceder Thank, he sends his valet home the next day to get 50 oz of silver and four suits of satin dresses to please her.

Cutie Plum is glad to know Westgate is in love with her niece. She quickly gets an ingot of silver, hands it over to Deon to pay for the expense of making new clothes and three days of singing and banquets. Badger Yep and Ceder Thank also invite Gotcha Heir, Remnant Bless, and Seizure Oft to join in the fun.

Chapter 12. Goldie Rinse Seduces a Valet

Westgate loves Olie so much he does not return home for half a month. Olie's family hides his clothes and hat so that he cannot leave when Moonie dispatches a valet with a horse to Olie's brothel to bring him back. His spouses at home remain idle, which is fine for most of them except Goldie, not yet 30 years old, whose lust cannot be suppressed. She and Towie put on makeup every day and wait at the gate until evening. She cannot go to sleep when she returns to her room at night because she has no companion.

When Towie married into the mansion, she brought along a 16-year-old handsome and smart valet named Xylo who has reached puberty. Westgate assigned him to live in a small side room near the gate to take care of the garden. Goldie and Towie often sit together in the garden's pavilion in the daytime to do needlework or play chess. He serves both concubines eagerly, and whenever he sees Westgate return home, he promptly reports to them. Goldie likes him and often asks him to come to her room and offers him wine to drink. After seeing each other for so many days, they become attracted to each other.

Westgate's birthday on August 28 is just around the corner. Since Westgate is in love with the prostitutes in the brothel and forgets to come home, Goldie asks his valet Deon to take a horse to the brothel to pick up Westgate. She also secretly gives a letter to Deon and says, "Give this letter to your master when nobody watches you and say Goldie invites him to return home early."

Deon obediently trots to the Plum's brothel where he sees Badger Yep, Ceder Thank, Remnant Bless, Gotcha Heir, and Seizure Oft accompanying Westgate, cuddling the girls, and enjoying their drinks.

Westgate sees Deon arrive and asks, "Why are you here? Any problems at home?"

Deon replies, "No problem at home."

Westgate says, "Ask Jason to take care of all the accounts. I'll work on the ledger with him when I return home."

Deon says, "Jason has collected a lot of money, waiting for Master to return home to do the accounting."

Westgate asks, "Have you brought the dress for Olie?"

Deon replies, "It's here." He takes out of the baggage an outfit consisting of a red blouse and a blue skirt and hands it over to Olie.

Olie and Osmie thank Westgate and accept it. They quickly order their servant to treat Deon to lunch.

Deon comes back after lunch to serve Westgate, and he whispers, "Madam Rinse asked me to deliver a letter to invite Master to return home early."

Olie sees the letter. Thinking the letter was sent from a prostitute of another brothel, she snatches it, opens it, and sees several lines of words. She hands it over to Remnant Bless and asks him to read it out:

Day and night, I've been thinking about my beloved one who still has not returned. I'll die of depression for his sake, and it's a pity my embroidered blanket will be left alone! The lamp will burn out when the woman is asleep, while the moon can be seen through the half-open window. My lover has a heart of steel, so how can I endure this pitiful night?

In response to the letter, Olie leaves the banquet, goes to her room, lies on the bed, and sleeps facing away from the door.

Since Olie is upset, Westgate tears the letter into pieces and kicks Deon twice in front of everyone. He invites Olie twice but she does not come back. He then anxiously goes to the bedroom, carries her out, and says, "Deon, bring the horse home. As for the slut at home who sent you here, I'll beat her to death when I return home."

Deon then returns home in tears.

Westgate says, "Don't be upset, Olie. This letter was sent by my fifth spouse who has some issues to discuss with me. There's nothing to it."

Remnant Bless, sitting nearby, teases, "Don't let him fool you, Olie! Goldie Rinse is a whore he's just met at the other brothel. She is so gorgeous. Don't let him go to see her."

Westgate slaps Remnant laughingly and exclaims, "Oh you devil, you're killing me! No sooner had Goldie given me a tough time than you added fuel to the fire!"

Osmie says, "Master, since Goldie belongs to the other brothel, she should just mind her own business. You haven't been here for too long, and she already wants you to abandon us."

Badger Yep says, “Well said! Don’t go home, Tycoon! Don’t be upset, Olie! Anyone upset from now on will be fined 2 oz of silver to treat others to dinner.”

The revelers fool around, play games as they drink, and very soon, they calm down Olie who is cuddled by Westgate.

Badger recites a poem about tea to praise the superb quality of the tea being served.

Ceder says cheerfully, “Everyone must either recite a poem or tell a joke, to entertain Olie.”

It is Ceder’s turn to tell a joke, and he says, “There once was a mason who worked in the yard. Since the granny didn’t treat him well enough, he secretly blocked the drainpipe with a brick. The entire yard was full of water after a downpour. The granny nervously looked for him, treated him to dinner, gave him 0.1 oz of silver, and then asked him to drain the water. After being wined and dined, he secretly went to the drainpipe, removed the brick, and the water was drained quickly. The granny then asked the mason, ‘What problem was that?’ The mason replied, ‘The drainage is like your guests, you’d better spend money on them to make things work!’ ”

Realizing the joke makes fun of Olie’s family, Olie responds, “I also have a joke for you. Once upon a time, Bishop Heir threw a party and asked his tiger to invite the guests. The tiger ate every one of the guests on their way to the party. When none of the guests arrived in the evening, the bishop asked, ‘Why don’t I see any of the guests you’ve invited?’ The tiger replied, “Master, to be honest with you, I specialize in eating party crashers.’ ”

Since the joke makes fun of the uninvited guests, Badger Yep responds, “I shouldn’t be eating you out of house and home. It’s my turn to be the host.” He then pulls a cheap 0.1 oz hair clip from his hair. Ceder Thank takes out a pair of 0.095 oz golden scrunchies, Remnant Bless takes out of his pocket an old face towel worth 200 coins, Gotcha Heir removes his sash worth two bottles of wine. Seizure Oft, with nothing to offer, borrows 0.1 oz of silver from Westgate. Their valuables are all given to Osmie to treat Westgate and Olie to dinner. Osmie then asks the valet to buy crabs, pork, and chicken. Olie spends her own money to buy a few more dishes.

When the chefs in the kitchen finish the cooking, the dishes and bowls are put on the table. Everyone eats voraciously as soon as Olie says ‘Help yourself.’ The dishes are all cleaned up by the starving men as if they were raised by wolves and there is no tomorrow. They fight so hard for the food they break two chairs. Westgate and Olie hardly have a few bites.

Meanwhile, Moonie is sitting with Towie and Goldie when Deon brings the horse home and sees her.

Moonie asks, "Have you brought Master home?"

Deon replies tearfully, "Master scolded me and kicked me back here! He said anyone who sends for him will be scolded by him when he returns home.'

Moonie says, "It's so unreasonable! If he didn't want to return, so be it. Why kicked the valet? How could that vixen change his heart so much?"

Towie asks, "In addition to scolding the valet, why did he scold us also?"

Goldie says, "A prostitute never loves any men. As the saying goes, 'A boatload of gold and silver cannot satisfy a brothel.' " She scolds Westgate's new lover without knowing someone overhears her complaint.

It so happened when Deon came back from the brothel, Cutie Plum came to the window to eavesdrop on Goldie. She is very offended when Goldie keeps scolding her niece Olie is a slut in front of Moonie, so she is not on good terms with Goldie anymore.

Goldie returns to her room, and time crawls like a snail when Westgate is not home. She sends away her two maids, then walks to the garden and invites Xylo over to have a drink with her. When the valet is drunk, she closes the door, takes off her clothes, and does what comes naturally. She then invites the valet to her room every night and sends him away before dawn. She pulls out two silver hair clips from her hair and lets him wear them. She also removes a brocade purse she carries on her skirt and ties it in his underpants.

Unfortunately, the valet has a big mouth, and he often drinks and plays with other valets on the street. As the saying goes, "Three may keep a secret, if two of them are dead." Snowie and Cutie hear about Goldie's affair one day and say, "That slut talks the talk but doesn't walk the walk! She even has an affair with a valet!" They both go and report the affair to Moonie.

Moonie does not believe them and says, "I know you don't get along with Goldie, but you'll offend Towie by accusing her valet."

Goldie later forgets to lock the kitchen door when she makes love to the valet in her room. Her maid Chrysie who goes to answer the call of nature sees them in action and tells Jadie about it the next day. Jadie then tells Snowie.

Westgate returns home from the brothel for his birthday party on August 27. Snowie and Cutie go to Moonie again and say, "Even her maid told on her. It shows we're not falsely accusing her. If you don't tell Master about it, we'll tell him. Sparing this slut is like sparing a scorpion!"

Moonie says, "He's coming home for his birthday party. If you don't listen to me and tell him about it, and if anything goes wrong, I won't be responsible."

Both concubines do not listen to Moonie, and they report Goldie's affair with a valet to Westgate. Westgate is furious. He goes to the hall and summons Xylo.

Someone has already reported to Goldie about the summons. Goldie nervously orders Plumie to ask Xylo to come to her room first, and she says, "Don't say anything!" She takes back the hair clips she has put on Xylo's head. However, she is so nervous she forgets to take back the brocade purse.

When Xylo arrives at the hall, he falls to his knees while several valets are holding bats and waiting for instructions.

Westgate asks, "Will you confess your crime, slave?"

Xylo is too afraid to reply.

Westgate orders his valets, "Take off his hat and remove his hair clips. Let me look at them." When he does not see the silver hair clips, he asks, "Where are the silver hair clips you wear?"

"I don't have any silver hair clips."

"You still want to fool me! Take off his clothes and spank him!"

Two valets are holding Xylo while the third valet strips him. When they take off his pants, they see a brocade purse hanging from his sash.

Westgate sees the purse and immediately says, "Bring it over for me to inspect!" He recognizes it comes from Goldie's skirt and asks in fury, "Where did it come from? Honestly tell me who gave it to you?"

The valet finally has enough courage to reply, "I picked it up when I swept the garden one day. Nobody gave it to me."

Westgate says angrily, "Tie him up and beat him!"

Xylo is spanked 30 times and is beaten almost to a pulp. Westgate then orders, "Lebron, shave his head, kick him out, and never let him set foot in my mansion again."

Xylo bows down and leaves the mansion in tears.

The news of Xylo's spanking and dismissal sends shivers down Goldie's spine. Her heart misses a beat when Westgate enters the room. She submissively helps Westgate take off his clothes, but he slaps her so hard she falls onto the floor.

Westgate orders, "Plumie, lock the front and back doors. Don't let anyone enter!" He sits in a chair under the flower trellis in the yard, holds a horsewhip in his hand, and shouts, "Take off your clothes and kneel, slut!"

Knowing she is in the wrong, Goldie takes off her clothes, drops her head, and dares not say a word.

Westgate asks, "You can't lie anymore, slut! I've just questioned him, and he confessed everything. Honestly tell me how many trysts you had with him when I wasn't home."

Goldie replies tearfully, "My goodness! Don't falsely accuse me! I've been with Towie doing needlework ever since you left home two weeks ago. I closed the doors in the evening before I slept. I dare not go out this corner gate to do any other things. If you don't believe me, just ask Plumie. There isn't anything in here she doesn't know." She then calls, "Plumie, come here and speak to Master."

Westgate scolds, "Someone said you've given your two hair clips to the valet, slut! Why don't you admit it?"

"Don't falsely accuse me! Some unethical slut must've seen you come to my room frequently and was so upset she made up the story. The hair clips you've given me are all here. Why don't you count them? Why would I give that slave anything for no good reason?"

"I don't care about the hair clips." Westgate then takes out the purse he took from Xylo, and says, "This belongs to you. How could it be inside that valet's clothes? How can you deny it?" He then lashes Goldie with the horsewhip.

The beating is so painful Goldie replies tearfully, "Master, spare your slave! I did needlework with Towie in the garden one day when you weren't home. Since it wasn't tied securely, it fell to the ground when I walked by the fence. I couldn't find it afterward. I didn't know the slave had picked it up. I never gave it to him."

Her explanation fits well with what Xylo fabricated while being questioned in the hall. Westgate's heart softens as he looks at Goldie's naked body like a delicate pretty flower. He then asks Plumie to come over. He cuddles Plumie and asks, "Did this slut have an affair with the valet? If you tell me to spare this slut, I'll spare her."

While sitting on Westgate's lap, Plumie replies seductively, "Master, you're so unreasonable! You've always been infatuated with Madam Rinse, so how could she be willing to sleep with Xylo? It's all because others are jealous of her and spread this rumor. You should be careful not to let them ruin your reputation by spreading this rumor to the outside world!"

Westgate is at a loss for words, and he drops the horsewhip. He asks Goldie to stand up and put on her clothes. He then asks Chrysie to serve dinner in the room.

Goldie fills up a cup with wine and offers it to Westgate on her knees.

Westgate says, "I spare you today. If I'm not home, you'd better close your door, don't think about anything else. Otherwise, I won't spare you if I discover any secret affairs!"

Goldie says, "I understand all your instructions." She then bows down four times before she sits down and drinks with Westgate. While they are drinking, a valet suddenly knocks on the door and says, "Master, Uncle Kyle Call 吴大舅, Uncle Deuce Call 吴二舅, Jason, your daughter, your son-in-law, and your other relatives are all here offering you birthday presents."

Westgate leaves Goldie behind, spruces himself up, and greets his guests. His club members like Badger Yep, Ceder Thank, all have presents for him. Olie Plum from the brothel also asks her valet to deliver a present.

Towie hears that Goldie has been beaten up. When Westgate is not in Goldie's room, she visits Goldie behind Cutie's and Snowie's back. Goldie is sleeping in bed when she asks, "What happened, Goldie? Tell me about it."

Goldie replies tearfully, "They accused me of seducing a man, Towie, and I was beaten up. Those two sluts now have a vendetta against me!"

Towie says, "Even if they find fault with you, my valet shouldn't be kicked out. Don't worry. Master will listen to me. If he comes to my room, I'll put in a good word for you."

Goldie says, "Thanks for your kindness!" She then asks Plumie to serve tea.

Towie returns to her room after a while.

Since Mrs. Kyle Call 吴大妗子, Moonie's sister-in-law, is in Moonie's room in the evening, Westgate spends the night in Towie's room.

Towie says, "Goldie didn't have an affair. Her argument with Cutie and Snowie caused my valet to become the scapegoat. Don't make unjustified accusations against her. It's so unfair to blame Goldie. If she had an affair, why wasn't Lady Call the first to complain?"

"I asked Plumie, and she gave me the same answer."

"Goldie doesn't feel well in her room. Why don't you go and see her?"

"I know. I'll go and see her tomorrow."

Westgate's birthday is the next day. Protector Fringe, Prosecutor Fab 夏提刑, Instructor Pull 张团练, Kyle Call, and many official guests come to his birthday party. He hires Olie Plum and two songbirds to sing for an entire day.

Cutie's niece Olie arrives, and Cutie leads Olie to pay her respects to Moonie and have tea in Moonie's room. Goldie feigns sickness and refuses to come when Cutie sends a maid to invite Goldie twice.

Moonie gives Olie a jacket, a face towel, and other floral ornaments before Olie takes off in the evening. Olie goes to the garden corner and says, "I want to see Goldie."

Goldie orders Plumie to shut her gate tight as a drum when she knows Olie is coming. She barricades herself and says, "I won't open the door!" Olie is embarrassed as she leaves.

Westgate goes to Goldie's room in the evening. Goldie receives him without grooming herself. She takes off his clothes, serves him tea, and prepares hot water to wash his feet. She serves him tenderly and tries her best to satisfy him in bed. She then says, "Do you know who in this family really loves you, darling? The other ones are all superficially nice to you. I'm the only one who knows your heart. The other concubines are so upset they spread rumors against me when they see you love me so much and come to my room so frequently. You're dumb enough to fall into their traps and hurt your sweetheart. I belong to you forever. Even if you beat me to death, I'll still die in your mansion. The valet you beat up used to work for Towie, and she agreed with me the whores in the brothel will hurt your health. The singers there only want money. Why would they care about you? I didn't expect the other two concubines who eavesdropped on me worked together to hurt me. I need you to administer justice."

Goldie's words are so convincing they make love fervently again.

Westgate has the horses ready to go with his valets Deon and Peon to the brothel the next day.

Olie is putting on makeup to get ready to receive clients when Westgate arrives. She quickly enters her room, washes off her makeup, takes off her hair clips and bracelets, and lies in bed.

Westgate sits for a while without any girls keeping him company. Olie's mother is the only one who comes out to greet him and asks, "Brother-in-law, why haven't you come for several days?"

"It's all because I spent time at home preparing for my birthday party."

"My daughter bothered you too much that day."

"Why didn't her elder sister Osmie visit me?"

"That's because her client who has hired her hasn't released her."

A young whore is serving Westgate tea and keeps him company, and Westgate asks, "Why don't I see Olie?"

The bawd replies, "She's so childish, Brother-in-law! Somehow, she was upset when she returned home that day. She just went to sleep and hasn't come out of her room up to now. You're too cold-hearted not to come to see her!"

Westgate asks, "Really? I didn't know anything about it." He then asks, "Which room is she in? I'll go and see her."

The bawd replies, "She's in the bedroom in the back." She quickly asks a maid to open the portiere.

Westgate enters Olie's room and sees her lying inside a blanket with hair hanging loose and facing away from him. She does not move although she knows Westgate is next to her.

"What went wrong when you were in my mansion?"

Olie does not reply.

"Please tell me who upset you?"

"It's Goldie! If you have such a great concubine who knows how to satisfy her clients, why did you bother to visit me? Although I was born in a brothel, I'm higher class than those cheap concubines out there! I went to your mansion that day to celebrate your birthday, not for anything else. Lady Call was so nice to me and gave me beautiful clothes. I wanted to pay Goldie my respects when I knew she's your fifth spouse, but she didn't come out. She asked her maid to shut her door on me when my aunt and I wanted to say goodbye to her."

"She wasn't in a good mood that day. Otherwise, how could she not come out to see you? I also want to beat up that slut who's made waves several times to hurt others."

"Shameless sweetheart, go ahead and beat her up!"

"I've used my whip to tame my concubines and maids., and I even cut off their hair."

"You can say whatever you want, but where's the proof? I dare you to go home and cut a bunch of her hair and show it to me to prove you're the best woman tamer in town."

Before Westgate rides his horse home the next evening, Olie says, "I'm waiting for the good news. Don't bother to see me when you go home and can't get what you've promised me!"

Westgate is drunk while being provoked by the challenge, so the first place he visits is Goldie's room when he returns home.

Goldie serves Westgate tenderly when he is drunk. Since he does not want to eat or drink anything, she asks Plumie to make the bed, lock the door, and leave the room.

Westgate sits on the bed and asks Goldie to take off his boots. He does not sleep afterward but orders Goldie to take off her clothes and drop to her knees.

Not knowing what is going on, Goldie breaks out in a cold sweat. She kneels and says tearfully, "Master, if you tell me what's going on, I'll die with no regrets. Don't put me on edge day and night. No matter how hard I try, I just can't figure out what's on your mind. How can I endure your cutting me with a blunt knife?"

Westgate says, "You'd better watch out if you don't take off your clothes, slut!" He then calls, "Plumie, give me the horsewhip on the back of the door!"

Plumie does not enter the room. After being called a few more times, she slowly opens the door and enters the room. She sees Goldie kneeling in front of the bed, and she walks over to the table to fill up the lamp with oil. She does not respond when Westgate calls her.

Goldie exclaims, "Sister Plumie, come to my rescue! He wants to beat me up!"

Westgate says, "Don't listen to Goldie. Just give me the horsewhip so I can lash her."

Plumie responds, "Master, don't you feel ashamed? What has Goldie done wrong? Do you believe the other sluts who stirred up a tempest in a teapot? You want to find fault with Madam Rinse who loves you wholeheartedly, while you love the other one who's a thorn in your side." She closes the door and goes to the other room.

Westgate then says laughingly, "Goldie, I won't beat you up. Come over here. I want to get something from you. Will you give it to me?"

Goldie asks, "My entire body belongs to you, darling! There isn't anything you want I won't give you. What object do you have in your mind?"

"I want a bunch of hair from your head."

"I can let you burn any part of my body, darling! But don't cut my hair. You scare me to death. For the 26 years of my life, I've never cut my hair to earn a living. Moreover, I've lost a few strands of hair lately. Please take pity on me!"

"You want to pacify me, but you don't listen to me."

"If I don't listen to you, whom should I listen to?" She then asks, "Please tell me honestly why you need my hair."

"I need your hair to weave a net."

"If you want to weave a net, I'll give it to you. But don't give it to any sluts who think they can use it to overpower me."

"I won't give it to anyone else. I'd like to weave your hair to make a net."

"If you want to weave my hair, I'll cut it for you." Goldie then splits apart her hair, and Westgate uses a pair of scissors to cut a large chunk of hair from the top of her head, wraps it in paper, and puts it in his waist bag.

Goldie then falls onto Westgate's chest, and says tearfully, "I listen to you all the time, so you shouldn't forget about me. No matter whom you also fall in love with, just don't abandon me." She then spends an exciting night with Westgate.

Goldie serves Westgate breakfast the next day and sees him off at the gate. Westgate then gallops right to the brothel.

Olie asks, "Where's her hair you've cut?"

"I have it here." Westgate then takes the wrapped paper out of his waist bag and hands it over to Olie.

Olie unwraps the paper and sees a bunch of good, oily, and black hair.

Westgate says, "After you finish looking at the hair, return it to me. It wasn't easy for me to cut it yesterday. I had to pretend to be angry before she let me cut this bunch. I fooled her into believing I wanted to weave a net. I then came right here for you to look at it, to show you I keep my promise."

"What's so special about her hair to make you so uptight. I'll return it to you when you go home. If you were so afraid of her, you shouldn't cut it."

"How could I be afraid of her? I just didn't express myself properly."

Olie asks Osmie to drink with Westgate while she goes to the back of the brothel where she ties Goldie's hair under her shoe so that she can step on it every day. She manages to keep Westgate in her brothel and stop him from returning home for a few days.

Ever since Goldie cut her hair, she feels quite upset and stays in her room every day. Since she has lost her appetite, Moonie asks a valet to send for Hag Slay 刘婆, the witch doctor who frequently visits the mansion.

Hag Slay says, "Madam Rinse, you have some dark energy locked in your heart and therefore have a headache, feel dizzy, and lose your appetite." She then takes two dozes of black pills out of her medicine bag, and says, "Take it with ginger soup at night." She also says, "I'll ask my husband tomorrow to check you up, to see if you'll encounter any disasters this year."

"Is your husband a fortuneteller?"

"Although he's blind, he's an expert in three techniques. Firstly, he can perform fortunetelling. Secondly, he can perform acupuncture. Thirdly, he can perform 'about-face', a technique that's hard to describe."

"What do you mean by 'about-face'?"

"Suppose a father doesn't get along with his son, or an elder brother is at odds with his younger brother, or a wife fights against her husband's concubines, if they hire him, he'll stabilize the situation with his lucky charm, then give them holy water to drink. The father and son will get along in less than three days, the brothers will be on good terms, and the wife and concubines won't fight each other. Anyone whose business is failing, or whose harvest is not bountiful, can have their situation turned around by hiring him, for he can lead people in a prosperous direction and pray to the polar stars.

"There was a woman who came from a poor family. Since she had sticky fingers, after she got married, she secretly took some stuff to enrich her mother. Her husband beat her up when he discovered the theft.

"The woman then hired my husband to perform an 'about-face'. He wrote two talismans he burned to ashes and put the ashes in the bottom of their water barrel. The entire family drank from the barrel, and amazingly, they could no longer detect the woman stealing anything even with eyes wide open. He also put a lucky charm under the pillow so her husband who slept on the pillow no longer hit her."

Goldie pays attention to Hag Slay's story and asks her maid to serve Hag Slay tea and desserts. She spends 0.3 oz of silver on the medication and spends 0.5 oz of silver to buy josh paper to be burnt by Blind Slay 刘瞎 who will be invited to visit her the next day.

Hag Slay indeed leads Blind Slay to Westgate's mansion early the next morning. Westgate is still in the brothel and has not returned.

The valet guarding the gate asks, "Blind man, where are you going?"

Hag Slay replies "He'll visit Madam Rinse to burn joss paper today."

The valet says, "You may lead him in, but watch out for the dog."

Hag Slay then leads Blind Slay straight to Goldie's building.

Goldie takes half a day to come out. Blind Slay pays her his respects and sits down. Goldie tells him the day and hour of her birth and her horoscope. Blind Slay then computes with his fingers and says, "Your date and time of birth indicate two husbands will succumb to you."

Goldie says, "One husband has already succumbed to me."

Blind Slay says, "Your horoscope indicates you have too much water that dominates too little soil. For a man, dominance means getting a powerful position. For a woman, dominance means murdering her husband. Your horoscope also indicates your master loves you because you're clever and adaptive. And another thing, you'll encounter a disaster this year when rats disturb you. Although your two nemeses cannot hurt you, they make your master quarrel with you, and it can be annoying."

Goldie then says, "Mister, I'd like you to perform an 'about-face' for me. Here's an oz of silver for you to buy tea. I don't need anything special except to drive the annoying people away so Master will love me." She enters her room, takes out two pieces of jewelry, and gives them to Blind Slay who puts them in his pocket.

Blind Slay then says, "To perform an 'about-face', get a piece of willow board, and carve on it the figures of a man and a woman. Write on the figures their respective birth date and time. Tie them up with 7 x 7 = 49 strands of red thread. As for the male figure, use a piece of red gauze to cover its eyes. Stuff its heart with artemisia, nail its hands with needles, use adhesive to glue its feet. Secretly put the willow board under the pillow. Also, use red ink to write a talisman you'll burn, and secretly put the ashes in his tea. After your master drinks the tea and sleeps on the pillow, you'll see the effect in less than three days."

Goldie asks, "Mister, may I ask how these four techniques work?"

Blind Slay replies, "For your information, the red gauze that covers the eyes will make your husband think you're as beautiful as Beauty West 西施. The artemisia stuffed in the heart will make him love you. The needles that nail the hands will stop him from beating you up and will even make him kneel before you. The adhesive that glues the feet will stop him from going to undesirable places."

Goldie is overjoyed to hear the explanation.

Blind Slay then burns joss paper for Goldie.

Hag Slay brings the holy water and lucky charm for Goldie the next day. They follow the instruction, burn the talisman into ashes for her to put into the tea.

Goldie waits for Westgate to return home so that she can ask Plumie to serve him the spiked tea. She hopes the special pillow he sleeps on will make him love her more than ever.

Chapter 13. Vasie Plum Has a Tryst with Westgate

Westgate goes to Moonie's room on July 14, and Moonie says, "The Bloom family's valet delivered an invitation card to invite you for a drink, but you weren't here."

Westgate looks at the invitation card that reads "I will be at Silvie Call's house this noon and hope you can join me. Cheers!" He then spruces himself up, orders two valets to follow him, and rides a thoroughbred to the Bloom mansion.

Unexpectedly, Jesse Bloom is not home. His wife Vasie Plum, dressed in beautiful summer clothes, stands at the inner gate with a handheld fan in her hand. Westgate is in such a rush he bumps into her as soon as he enters through the gate.

Westgate is aware of Vasie for a long time, but since he has seen her only once, he couldn't admire her in detail until they are face to face. She is short, has a fair complexion, a pumpkin-seed-shaped face, and curvy eyebrows. His spirit is on Cloud Nine when he bows deeply to her. She greets him back, stands behind the gate, and orders Stitchie to serve Westgate.

"Tycoon, please sit for a while. My husband has just gone out for some minor business and will be back soon."

After another maid serves tea, Vasie asks, "Where will he invite Tycoon for a drink today? Please persuade him to come home earlier because he'll bring along the two valets, leaving these two maids and me alone at home."

Westgate replies, "Lady, I couldn't agree more. He should take care of his household. I'll follow your instruction and won't lose track of him."

Jesse Bloom returns home while they are talking, and Vasie returns to her room. He greets Westgate and says, "Thanks for your visit. I went out earlier because of an issue. Sorry for not welcoming you sooner." After they sit down, he orders, "Serve tea and ask Vasie to prepare a meal. I'll leave with Tycoon Westgate to celebrate Silvie Call's birthday after the meal."

Westgate says, "Why didn't you tell me about it earlier, comrade?" He then orders, "Deon, quickly go home and get a gift envelope of 0.5 oz of silver."

Jesse says, "Sorry for causing you so much trouble."

The servants serve them dishes of chicken, beef, and pancakes, and goblets of wine. After Deon brings back a gift envelope, they ride their horses to Bawd Call's brothel to celebrate Silvie Call's birthday. They are followed by Westgate's valets

Deon and Peon, and Jesse's valets Taffy and Tassy 天喜. When they arrive there, they enjoy the music and dance until 7 p.m.

Westgate later escorts the intoxicated Jesse home, as requested by Vasie. The valets open the gate and help Jesse sit in the lounge. Vasie and her maid then hold a lamp and help Jesse enter the bedroom.

Westgate, having performed his duty, is ready to leave when Vasie comes out and says thankfully, "My husband drank too much. I'm so thankful you escort him home for my sake. Please don't laugh at us."

Westgate quickly bows and says, "No problem. After you gave me the instructions, I made sure he went there and returned here in one piece. How could I not fully follow your order? I want to make sure you won't worry, otherwise, it'll show I'm incompetent in performing my duty. When he was in the brothel, he was tied up by those whores, and I had to force him to leave. As he went past Happy-Star Brothel 乐星堂, he wanted to visit Scentie Stern 郑愛香, the courtesan who looks as beautiful as Bodhisattva Compassion, but I stopped him right away and said, 'Comrade, return home. Come here another day. Your wife at home worries about you.' He then headed straight home. Otherwise, if he stayed at Stern's brothel, he wouldn't be here tonight. Lady, to tell you the truth, he's too foolish. Since you're so young, and he has such a large estate, how could he abandon everything and not stay home?"

Vasie says, "Tycoon, I couldn't have said it better. I have all kinds of ailments because he's been fooling outside and wouldn't listen to other people's advice. Please persuade him for my sake to come home early whenever you see him in a brothel, and I'll repay your kindness."

Westgate is a smart playboy. As an expert in exploiting all kinds of situations, he detects Vasie is willing to be seduced, and he responds smilingly, "Lady, you're too courteous. You scratch my back, and I'll scratch yours. I'm determined to edify my comrade, so don't worry."

Vasie thanks Westgate again and asks her maid to serve Westgate fruit tea in an engraved cup with a silver spoon.

Westgate finishes the drink and says, "Lady, I have to take off, take care!" He then heads home.

Westgate's plan to seduce Vasie is by having the gang of Badger Yep and Ceder Thank hang out in the brothel with Jesse to make Jesse sleep elsewhere overnight. He gets out of his mansion and sees Vasie standing at the gate with her two maids. He clears his throat, walks east for a while, then walks west for a while. He sometimes stands at the gate and peeps inside to look at Vasie's shadow. Vasie goes inside when she sees him coming. He then goes further inside and peeps around. They are obviously ogling each other.

Westgate is standing at the gate one day when Vasie asks her maid Stitchie to invite him over. He then asks purposely, "Why do you invite me, Sister? Is your master home?"

Stitchie replies, "My master is not home. Lady would like to ask Tycoon a question."

Westgate couldn't be happier to enter and sit in the lounge.

Vasie comes out after a while and says thankfully, "Tycoon, you were so helpful last time, and I thank you from the bottom of my heart. My husband went out yesterday and hasn't returned yet. Have you seen him?"

Westgate replies, "He went with three or four friends to Stern's brothel for a drink yesterday. I left because I had to resolve a minor issue. I didn't go there today, so I don't know if he's still there. If I were there, I'd surely urge him to come home so you wouldn't worry."

Vasie says, "You took the words right out of my mouth. He never listens to me. He always sleeps with other women outside and neglects his home."

Westgate says, "Except for this problem, my comrade is a loyal and kind man." Afraid that Jesse may come home at any time, he takes leave of Vasie.

Vasie earnestly asks Westgate to go to the brothel the next day to persuade Jesse to return home, and says, "I thank you in advance!"

Westgate says, "Since Comrade and I are very good friends, there's no need to thank me." He then returns home.

Jesse Bloom returns home from the brothel the next day, and Vasie complains no end, "You enjoy wine and women outside. Luckily our neighbor Westgate took care of you several times by escorting you home. You should buy a present to thank him."

Jesse quickly buys a present of four boxes of food and one keg of wine and orders his valet Taffy to deliver them to Westgate's mansion.

Westgate receives the present and tips the valet.

Moonie then asks, "Why did the Bloom mansion send you this present?"

Westgate replies, "Comrade Bloom invited me to the birthday party of Silvie Call in the brothel yesterday. Since he was drunk, I escorted him back to his mansion. I've often persuaded him not to spend the nights in the brothel. His wife, thankful for my help, must've asked him to buy this present for me."

Moonie listens to the righteous explanation and sneers, "My, oh, my, why don't you first take care of yourself? This is a case of the pot calling the kettle black. You seldom stay home but just molest other women outside, and to think you're righteous enough to convince others to take the virtuous path!" She then asks, "Do you think you deserve to accept this present?" She continues, "Who signed the name on the card? If it was signed by his wife, I'll write a card to invite her over. It's about time she visited us! If the card was signed by Jesse, it's up to you to invite him, and I don't care."

"It was signed by Jesse. I'll invite him over tomorrow."

Westgate indeed invites Jesse over for dinner the next day.

Jesse returns home after an entire day of entertainment, and Vasie says, "Make sure you return the favor. You sent him a present, he then treated you to dinner, so we should treat him to dinner some other day."

Time flies like an arrow. During Double-Ninth Festival, Jesse makes use of the festive environment to hire two songbirds and invites Westgate over to enjoy chrysanthemums. He also invites Badger Yep, Ceder Thank, Remnant Bless, and Gotcha Heir to join in the fun.

Westgate gets up to take a leak outside when it is time to light the lamps. Vasie is unexpectedly standing outside peeking at him, and he sees her.

Vasie then goes to the door at the west corner and secretly sends her maid Stitchie to approach Westgate in the darkness.

Stitchie whispers, "Master, Lady asks you not to get drunk and return home early. She'll then send her husband to the brothel so she can speak to you privately."

Westgate is thrilled. After taking a leak, he returns to the banquet table, secretly dumps all the wine passed to him, and pretends to be drunk.

Vasie keeps walking outside the portiere and peeking inside at around 7 p.m. She sees Westgate sitting there and pretending to snooze. Badger Yep and Ceder Thank are glued to their chairs and enjoy their meals and drinks like there is no tomorrow. After Remnant Bless and Gotcha Heir are gone, those two loafers remain stationary.

Westgate wants to leave, but Jesse holds onto him and says, "It's my turn to return the favor today. Comrade, why don't you stay?"

Westgate replies, "I'm drunk and can't eat anymore." He pretends to stagger and orders his two valets to support him as he returns home.

Badger Yep says, "I don't know why he got drunk so easily today. Since my host has spent so much money on this banquet with two courtesans to entertain us, we'd better eat and drink as much as we can before we leave."

Vasie keeps cursing at those party crashers as she listens to the conversation behind the portiere. She secretly sends the valet Tassy to ask Jesse to come in and says, "If you want to keep eating and drinking with those revelers, continue your party in the brothel. They're wasting my lamp oil at night. I can't stand them!"

Jesse says, "If you send me to the brothel at this late hour, don't blame me if I can't return home tonight."

Vasie says, "Go ahead, I won't blame you."

Jesse couldn't be happier to get the approval. He says, "Comrades, let's go to the brothel."

Badger asks, "Did Lady Plum approve it? Don't fool me! You should ask her again before we leave."

Jesse replies, "She just approved it and allowed me to return tomorrow."

Ceder says, "Come on! Badger is such a nagging nanny. Comrade already got the go-ahead."

They also bring along the two songbirds and the two valets Taffy and Tassy and arrive at Silvie's brothel in the back alley at 9 p.m. Silvie is already asleep when they knock on the door. She quickly gets up, lights the lamps, and receives them.

Badger says, "Jesse treated us to dinner to enjoy chrysanthemums today. He invited us here again before we finished our drinks. If you have drinks, bring them out for us to enjoy."

Meanwhile, Westgate pretends to be drunk and returns home. He goes to Goldie's room, takes off his coat, and goes to the front garden to wait for Vasie's invitation. After some time, he hears the other mansion close its gate. He later sees the maid Springie 迎春 climb over the wall in the darkness. She meows like a cat and gives Westgate the high sign.

Westgate pulls up a chair, steps on it, and secretly climbs over the wall. The other side already has a ladder set up for him to climb down.

After sending Jesse off, Vasie takes off her headdress and stands in the corridor. She is overjoyed to see Westgate arrive. She receives him in her room with dinner already set up by lamplight. Springie fills the cups with wine from a bottle while Vasie bows deeply to Westgate and says, "Tycoon, I'm so thankful for your help. The banquet you treated my husband last time made me owe you further, so I set up this small dinner to repay your kindness. Unfortunately, the two shameless gluttons just sat there and wouldn't leave until I sent them to the brothel."

Westgate asks, "Will Jesse return home?"

Vasie replies, "I've told him to spend the night there, and the two valets went with him. No one else is here except these two maids and Mrs. Trot 冯妈妈, the gatekeeper who's been my nanny since my youth. The front and back gates have all been closed."

Westgate then happily sits shoulder to shoulder and drinks with Vasie. Springie serves wine while Stitchie serves dishes of delicious food. The maids remove the dining table and lock the door after the meal so that the couple can make love in the bed.

It turns out Vasie's mansion is so modern its windows all have two layers. The outer layer is the actual window, while the inner layer is the screen. After Vasie sent away her two maids, people outside cannot see what is going on in the room by lamplight when the windows are closed.

Springie is a 17-year-old maid who has reached puberty and knows something about sex. When she sees the master and lady are getting on like a house on fire, she secretly uses her hair clip to pop out the outer window, peeps through the inner screen window, and what she sees by lamplight through the gauze bed curtain are two people in action. One is thrusting, while the other is receiving. One is raising his flagpole, while the other is shaking her bottom. One is cawing like a swallow, while the other is chirping like a nightingale. One is in the state of total ecstasy, while the other is like a butterfly or honeybee totally in love with the pollen. The battle in the bed goes on like tidal waves. One has attractive breasts, while the other's silver rod makes her eyebrows roll up. Springie the spectator peeps from the outside while they are in orgasm and enjoys it no end as she listens to the conversation.

Westgate asks, "How old are you?"

Vasie replies, "I was born in the year of the goat. I'm 23 years old." She then asks, "How old is your wife?"

"She's 26 years old, born in the year of the dragon."

"She's three years older than me. I'll buy a present and visit her tomorrow, but I'm afraid to be too close to her."

"My wife is good-tempered. Otherwise, how could she allow me to have so many concubines?"

"Does your wife know you've come here? If she asks you, how will you answer her?"

"My first four spouses all live in the four suites of the living quarters located at the back of my mansion, except my fifth spouse Goldie Rinse who lives alone in the building in the garden located at the front of my mansion. She dares not interfere in my affairs."

"How old is Goldie?"

"She's the same age as my wife."

"Sounds good to me. If she doesn't look down on me, I'll bow down to her as my elder sister. Bring a sample of your wife's and Goldie's shoes tomorrow. I'll sew two pairs of shoes and bring them over to express my love for them." She pulls out two golden hair clips from her hair, gives them to Westgate, and says, "Don't let Jesse see them when you're in the brothel."

"That's for sure." They continue to make love until 5 a.m. when roosters crow and the eastern sky brightens. Fearing Jesse may come home, Westgate gets up and spruces himself up.

Vasie says, "You can climb over the wall as before."

They agree on a secret signal such that when Jesse is not home, her maid will stand near the wall and give a cough or drop a tile. If the coast is clear, her maid will then go up the wall and call Westgate who will use a chair to climb over to the other side.

They are in love despite being separated by a wall, and how can the neighbors know what is going on when love is made without going through the main gate?

Westgate climbs over the wall to come back to Goldie's room at dawn. Goldie, still lying in bed, complains, "Nobody knew where you were yesterday. You should let me know you wouldn't stay here for the night."

Westgate says, "Comrade Bloom sent a valet to invite me to the brothel to have a midnight drink. I managed to escape and return home."

Although Goldie believes Westgate, she is quite doubtful. One day when she and Towie sit in the garden's pavilion after dinner to do needlework, she happens to see a tile thrown over the wall. Towie, with her head lowered to sew a shoe's sole, does not see the tile. Goldie looks around and vaguely sees a face disappear behind the wall. She quickly pushes Towie, points at the wall, and asks, "Did you see the maid who works for our neighbor, the Bloom mansion? She was looking at the flowers over the wall. She disappeared when she saw us."

Westgate enters Goldie's room when he returns from a banquet in the evening. After he hangs up his coat, he tells her he does not want to have food or tea. He just strolls in the garden.

Goldie secretly watches Westgate for a while and sees the maid, whom she saw before, appearing above the wall. Westgate then leaps over the wall from a chair.

Westgate is having fun with Vasie on the other side while Goldie returns to her room, tossing and turning throughout the night.

Goldie lies in bed and ignores Westgate when she sees him push open her door at dawn.

Westgate sits at the bedside, feeling somewhat guilty.

Goldie jumps up, sits on the bed, twists Westgate's ear, and scolds, "Disloyal thief! Where did you go last night? You upset me for the whole night! So, you did that kind of business while I was bored to death! You'd better tell me how many times you've visited our neighbor, the slut of the Bloom mansion. If you tell me, then I'll let you off easy. Otherwise, as soon as you go over there tomorrow, I'll scream here so a heartless jerk like you won't know where to put himself! You ask your valets to take her husband to the brothel to spend the nights there so you can have his wife here. There ain't no such thing as a free lunch! No wonder a few days ago, I was doing needlework in the garden with Towie when I saw the maid of the Bloom mansion sticking her head above the wall in broad daylight, and it was, in fact, that slut's grim reaper dispatched to grim-reap you! You converted that cuckold's mansion into a brothel!"

The accusation disturbs Westgate so much he falls to his knees and responds wryly, "Keep quiet, you and your big mouth! To tell you the truth, she has asked about Moonie's and your age, and she'll borrow a sample of your shoes to make a pair of shoes for each of you, and she'll bow down to each of you as her elder sister. She's willing to be the younger sister."

"I couldn't care less whether she'd treat me as her elder sister. She takes away another person's husband and offers a small gift in return. You can't pull the wool over my eyes." She pulls down his pants while she is speaking, looks at his limp dick, which still has the cock ring on, and asks, "Honestly tell me how many times you made love to that slut last night."

"Several times, but only one orgasm."

"I dare you to take an oath on what you just said. How could one orgasm make your schlong as soft as your snot, like a guy who has suffered a stroke? You'd better behave like a man!" She then pulls off his cock ring and scolds, "Mobster! I had so much trouble finding it, and it turned out you secretly brought it along to screw that slut"

"You're so annoying, slut! She's told me several times she'll come over to bow down to you tomorrow and make a pair of shoes for you. She sent her maid to get Lady Call's shoe sample yesterday. She asked me to give you a pair of longevity hair clips today." He then takes off his hat, pulls off the hair clips, and hands them over to Goldie.

Goldie holds the hair clips in her hands and looks at them. They were made of exceptionally elegant imported material, with the word 'Longevity' engraved on them. They were made for the emperor and were taken out of the imperial court. She then says, "I won't complain now. I'll be your spotter here when you go over there so you can sleep with her to your heart's content. How about that?"

Westgate cuddles Goldie joyfully and says, "It couldn't be better, honey! You're worth your salt. I'll use my own money to buy a new dress for you tomorrow."

"Don't sweet talk me. For me to help you out, you'd better agree to three conditions."

"I'll agree to any conditions."

"Condition one: You're not allowed to go to the brothel. Condition two: You'll always listen to me. Condition three: After you go over there to sleep with her, you'll tell me all the pillow talk you have with her without missing a single word."

"I have no problem with your conditions."

Westgate henceforth provides a report whenever he goes to the other mansion to sleep. Some of the reports are:

Her skin is as white as snow. Her body is as soft as cotton. She is good at making love. She is a gourmet. Inside her bed curtains are boxes of candy and fruit. They play cards while they drink...

Westgate brings along a scroll one day, hands it over to Goldie, and says, "These pictures came from the mansion of the eunuch uncle of her husband. Let's light both lamps to look at them.

Goldie opens the scroll and looks at 24 pornographic pictures drawn by the imperial artists, with amazing details. She is so mesmerized by them she refuses to hand the scroll back to Westgate. She hands it to Plumie and says, "Store them in my chest so I can enjoy them every night."

Westgate says, "After you finish looking at the scroll for two days, return it to me. I borrowed it from her and I must return it to her."

"How did her stuff come to my room? I didn't take it from her. Even if she beat me, she couldn't get it back."

"You didn't ask her for it. I was the one who borrowed it from her. Just don't fool around." Westgate then tries to snatch the scroll back.

"If you try to snatch it back, I may end up tearing it into pieces, and then nobody can enjoy looking at it."

"It's up to you. If you return it to her, she has more precious stuff I can show you tomorrow."

"Only your mother would think you're smart enough to fool people this way. You'd better bring the more precious stuff here before I give you back this scroll."

They chat for a while until night when Goldie lights incense and the silver lamps in the room. She opens the scroll and looks at the drawings with Westgate. They imitate the postures drawn in the scroll to make love, while Westgate sleeps on the pillow with the voodoo board constructed per Blind Slay's instructions, with strange consequences.

Chapter 14. Vasie Celebrates Goldie's Birthday

One day when Mrs. Kyle Call comes to visit Moonie, Moonie feels quite gloomy and invites her to stay for two days. Deon, holding a suitcase, comes over while they are chatting and says, "Master has come home."

Mrs. Kyle Call quickly goes to Cutie's room. Westgate enters the room, takes off his coat, and does not bother to drink the tea served by Jadie.

Moonie notices Westgate look worried, and she asks, "You came back from your club meeting quite earlier today."

Westgate says, "Seizure Oft was the host today. Since he didn't have space in his house to throw a party, he invited me to visit Ever-Blessed Monastery 永福寺. Comrade Bloom later invited Badger Yep, me, and four more comrades to have drinks at Scentie's brothel. We were having fun when several officers suddenly came in and arrested Comrade Bloom without any explanations. We were all scared. I then went to Olie Plum's brothel to hide for half a day while asking people to find out the news. It so happened the clan members of Eunuch Bloom, viz. Bloom I, Bloom III, and Bloom IV are fighting to get their shares of the inheritance, and they submitted a complaint to the prefecture hall of the capital. The complaint was filed, and a warrant was issued to this town's police to arrest the defendant. I then felt relieved enough to come home."

Moonie says, "I'm not surprised! You go out with those people every day, thinking you have the leadership qualities and forget about your home. If you fly with the crows, you get shot with the crows. Why wait until someone beats you to a pulp before you repent? Why don't you listen to the good advice of your wife at home? When the sluts in the brothels say something, you prick up your donkey ears and listen to them. My words go in one ear and out the other, while their words are like quotes from the Scriptures!"

Westgate says laughingly, "Who dare beat me to a pulp?"

Moonie says, "A wimp like you can only toot his own horn at home. You just chicken out when push comes to shove in the outside world."

While they are talking, Deon comes over and says, "Lady Plum next door dispatched Taffy here to invite Master over to talk."

Moonie says, "Someone may drag your name through the mud tomorrow."

Westgate says, "Visiting a neighbor shouldn't matter. I'm going over there to hear what she has to say."

Westgate then walks to Jesse Bloom's mansion, and Vasie asks her valet to invite Westgate to the back room.

Vasie puts on casual clothes as she comes out of her room. She begs Westgate on her knees, "Tycoon, I need your help. Since my husband didn't listen to good advice, he neglected the important home affairs. He just listened to the outsiders and seldom stayed home. Someone stabbed him in the back today, and stuff happened. It was not until now that he told the valet the problem and asked me to find someone to come to his rescue. I'm a woman who is like a crab without legs, so where can I find anyone to help him? I was so mad at him for a while, I thought he deserved to be beaten to a pulp in the capital. But then it'd be a pity his late uncle's reputation would be ruined. I have no choice but to ask you to help him get out of prison. For my sake, please find someone who can protect him from being beaten up."

As soon as Vasie bows down, Westgate says, "Lady, please get up. I still don't know what kind of lawsuit he got involved in. I was drinking at Stern's brothel when I saw several officers come and take him to the capital."

Vasie says, "It's a long story. My husband's late uncle Eunuch Bloom has a cousin who has three sons named Jewel Bloom 花子由, Jigar Bloom 花子光, and Jehan Bloom 花子华. My husband is more closely related to Eunuch Bloom because his father is Eunuch Bloom's brother. Eunuch Bloom had saved a lot of money, and when he came back from Wide-East 广东 and saw my husband acted like a prodigal son, he asked me to take care of all his properties because he knew I could be trusted. When Eunuch Bloom died last year, Jewel, Jigar, and Jehan inherited the stoves and kitchen sinks but not a single coin.

"When I told Jessie his cousins should inherit some money, he couldn't care less. He just fooled around outside every day and got arrested today." She cries buckets after she finishes telling the story.

Westgate says, "Lady, don't worry. I at first thought it was a major problem. It turns out to be just a matter of splitting the inheritance, which is a minor issue. Since you asked me for help, my comrade's problem is my problem. I'll be in charge no matter what."

"Tycoon, I'm glad you're willing to help. How much money do I need to bribe the officials?"

"You don't need to spend much. I know Prefect Sheen Birch 杨时 of the capital is a student of Preceptor Weed. Commander Jeer Birch 杨戬 is the in-law of my in-law. Since Preceptor Weed and Commander Jeer Birch are both important officials of the imperial court, how can Prefect Sheen Birch not listen to them? There aren't any major problems we can't resolve. We should send a present to Preceptor Weed now. Commander Birch, my relative, doesn't need to be bribed."

Vasie goes to her room, opens her chest, takes out 60 ingots worth 3000 oz of silver, and asks Westgate to take them to bribe the officials.

Westgate says, "Half of them is enough. Why spend so much?"

Vasie says, "You may keep the extra silver. Behind my bed are four golden chests of python-pelt jackets, jade belts, hat rings, sashes, and other valuables and antiques you can help me hide in your mansion. I'll take them when I need them. If I don't plan but just trust Jesse, I'll live miserably in the future. My two fists can't fight against the six hands of his cousins who all want to snatch these treasures. If they stab me in the back, I'll have nothing left."

"What'll happen when Comrade Bloom returns and asks for these treasures?"

"These were all given to me for safekeeping by Eunuch Bloom when he was alive. Jesse knows nothing about them. You may keep them for me."

"Since you say so, I'll go home now and ask my servants to put them away." He then goes straight home and consults Moonie.

Moonie says, "The silver can be put in lunch boxes for our valets to bring them here. As for the treasure chests, if we move them through the main gate, they may get our neighbors' attention. To keep things secret, we'll move them at night over the wall that separates our two mansions."

Westgate is pleased with Moonie's plan. He orders his four servants, Leroy, Deon, Lesing, and Peon, to use lunch boxes to first carry home the 3000 oz of silver. Vasie and her two maids, Springie and Stitchie, set up tables and chairs to lift the chests over the wall at night. Moonie, Goldie, and Plumie use ladders to receive them at Westgate's side. The top of the wall is covered with rugs to protect the chests. Everything is delivered to Moonie's room.

The neighbors do not know Westgate has received so much jewelry, gold, and silver. Westgate wraps the present at night and asks his Show mansion's in-law to send a letter to the capital. The messenger who arrives in the capital delivers the letter to Commander Jeer Birch who then asks Preceptor Weed to write a letter to Prefect Sheen Birch.

Sheen Birch is a laureate from Notch-West 陕西. Although he is a righteous official, since Preceptor Weed was his former teacher and Commander Jeer Birch is an important officer of the imperial court, how can he not listen to them?

Westgate also sends an overnight express letter to Jesse Bloom that reads "They have all been bribed. When the prefect asks about the inheritance, just say you have spent all the cash and only the real estate is left behind."

The day Prefect Birch starts a court session, various officials arrive. Jesse and the plaintiffs all kneel in court. Jesse is questioned about the inheritance, and he responds, "After my old uncle died, the cash was spent in the temple for his funeral. Only two mansions and one farm are left. The other things like the stoves and kitchen sinks have all been taken by the clan members."

Prefect Birch says, "Your uncle's properties have no traceable records, and it was a case of easy come, easy go. Since no cash is left, I'll assign an official in Clearstream Town to sell the two mansions and the farm of Eunuch Bloom, and the money from the sale will then be split by Jewel Bloom and his two brothers."

When Jewel and his two brothers insist on auditing Jesse's bank account, Prefect Birch retorts, "You deserve to be spanked! Why didn't you promptly submit any complaints when Eunuch Bloom died? You now come to disturb the court after such a long time to waste my paper and ink!"

Jesse does not receive any punishment. A document is sent to Clearstream Town to appraise Eunuch Bloom's real estate.

Lebron rushes back to report the court's decision to his master Westgate who is glad that Prefect Birch listened to the preceptor and the commander and released Jesse from prison.

Vasie invites Westgate to discuss the matter, and says, "Since I'll soon be your concubine, spend a few oz of silver to buy Jesse's mansion."

Westgate returns home and consults Moonie who then says, "Let the officials appraise Jesse's mansion, but don't purchase it, or else Jesse will be suspicious of you."

When Jesse returns home a few days later, Clearstream Town assigns Counselor Tune 乐县丞 to appraise Jesse's properties. The large mansion in Safejoy Square 安慶坊 worth 700 oz of silver is sold to Royalty Rex. The farm outside the South Gate worth 655 oz of silver is sold to Protector Sill Fringe 守备周秀. However, nobody dares buy the smaller mansion worth 540 oz of silver because it is located right next to Westgate's mansion. Jesse sends an agent to sell it to Westgate, but Westgate pretends he does not have enough money, while the town hall urgently wants to report all three transactions back to the capital.

Vasie anxiously instructs Mrs. Trot to tell Westgate, "Please take 540 oz from the silver she's deposited in your mansion to buy it."

Westgate then agrees to do so, and the three properties are sold with Jesse's signatures. The town hall then sends back a document with 1,895 oz of silver to be split among the three second nephews of Eunuch Bloom.

The lawsuit virtually took Jesse to the cleaners. The two mansions and the farm are gone, and the two chests that have 3000 oz of silver have disappeared. He anxiously asks Vasie to question Westgate how the silver has been used to bribe the officials. He asks, "How much is left now? We need some money to buy a house to live in."

Jesse ends up being scolded by Vasie for several days, "Stupid is as stupid does! You ignored the important business matters, slept with the prostitutes outside, never stayed home, and therefore were ensnared by others and ended up in jail. You sent a messenger to ask me to find someone to help you. I'm a woman who never goes outside, so what could I do, whom did I know, and where could I find help? What could you reap when you never sowed anything in the past? What straw could a drowning man like you clutch at? Luckily, our neighbor Westgate was nice enough to send his servant to the capital to take care of you when you were in dire straits. No sooner had the lawsuit been taken care of than you asked me for money. I still have your letter with your signature that asked me to spare no expense to bribe the officials to save your life. Without your authorization, how could I spend any coins to bribe anyone? You think I could rob the bank?"

Jesse says, "I know I've sent that letter to you, but I was hoping we still have some money left to buy a house to continue our livelihood and live on a shoestring afterward."

Vasie says, "A dummy like you who doesn't know arithmetic would think 1,000 is the same as 10,000. How much could your 3000 oz of silver accomplish? Do you think Preceptor Weed and Commander Birch have small appetites? You were lucky I could bribe them so you got off scot-free without being spanked even once! No sooner had you been released from jail than you complained at home. Westgate is neither your underling nor your relative, so why did you expect him to come to your rescue and be willing to spend his own money to go to the capital to bribe the powers that be? You'd better invite him for dinner to thank him instead of hitting him with a broom and telling him he owes you money!"

Jesse remains silent after being scolded.

Westgate sends Deon to deliver a present to Jesse the next day to reduce Jesse's anxiety.

Jesse plans to host a banquet with entertainment provided by two courtesans. He wants to invite Westgate over to express his gratitude and have a chance to ask if there is any of his money left.

Westgate intends to give Jesse several hundred oz of silver to buy a house to live in, but Vasie secretly dispatches Mrs. Trot to tell him, "Don't attend Jesse's banquet. Just give him a balance sheet that shows all his money has been spent."

Westgate hides in the brothel when Jesse dispatches a valet to invite him over, and his servant says, "Tycoon's not home." Jesse is upset, but all he can do is stamp his foot. He later manages to come up with 250 oz of silver to buy a house on Lion Street. Right after he moves into that house, he catches the flu and cannot get out of bed since the first week of December. Vasie at first hires Doctor Wild to see Jesse. She later lets Jesse's illness drag on to save money, and Jesse kicks the bucket on December 20, at the age of 24.

Jesse's valet Tassy embezzled 5 oz of silver and disappeared while Jesse was sick.

As soon as Jesse meets his maker, Vasie asks Mrs. Trot to invite and consult Westgate. They buy a coffin and bury him in a cemetery. Jewel Bloom, Jigar Bloom, and Jehan Bloom all attend the funeral. Westgate asks Moonie to host a banquet that day in memory of Jesse.

After Vasie rides a palanquin home, she sets up an altar in her room. Although she is supposed to be in mourning, she only thinks of Westgate. After Jesse died, there is more traffic between the two families. To celebrate Goldie's birthday on February 9, she puts on a white coat, blue skirt, white headdress, and pearl necklace. Mrs. Trot carries the baggage, Taffy follows the palanquin, and when they arrive at Westgate's mansion, she first bows down four times to Moonie and says, "My late husband's burial made you work too hard, and I also thank you for your great gift!" She then invites Cutie Plum and Towie Prime over and greets them.

Someone introduces Goldie to Vasie: "This is the fifth spouse." Vasie is ready to bow down, and says, "Sister, your slave greets you!" Goldie refuses to be treated as Vasie's superior, so they finally bow to each other on equal status. Goldie then thanks Vasie for the birthday gift.

Mrs. Kyle Call and Granny Rinse also come to see Vasie.

Vasie wants to pay her respects to Westgate, but Moonie says, "He has gone to the Temple of Emperor-Deva Jade 玉皇大帝." They then sit down and have tea. Vasie later sees Snowie Heir, less well dressed than the others, approaching her. She gets up and asks, "Who is she? Please introduce me to her?"

Moonie replies, "She is his concubine." Vasie wants to bow down, but Moonie says, "Don't be too courteous, just bow to each other on equal status."

Vasie then greets Snowie.

Moonie goes to her room, changes her clothes, and asks her maids to set up a table to serve tea. The maids soon put dishes of hot food and bottles of wine on the table.

Mrs. Kyle Call, Granny Rinse, and Vasie take their seats. Moonie and Cutie take the top seats, Towie and Goldie then sit at the side. Since Snowie needs to take care of the kitchen, she does not sit for too long.

Moonie personally gives everyone a toast and notices Vasie is a drinker. She also orders Cutie to give everyone a toast, and teases, "Vasie has moved farther away from us, so she's forgotten about us. She's so cold-hearted she seldom comes to see us."

Towie then says, "Were it not for Goldie's birthday, Vasie wouldn't come!"

Vasie responds, "Dear Moonie and Towie, you love me so much I'm always more than eager to visit you. I'm still observing the mourning period, and I don't have enough people to take care of my house. This is the fifth week of his passing. I've forced myself to come today because I worry Goldie would be mad at me if I didn't come." She then asks, "When is Lady Call's birthday?"

Moonie replies, "It's too early!"

Goldie says, "Lady Call's birthday is on September 15th. Vasie, you'd better come that day."

Vasie says, "You bet."

Towie says, "Vasie, since you're here with so many of us today, you don't need to go home."

Vasie says, "I'd like to chat with every sister. To tell you the truth, ever since I moved there after my husband died, nobody else is there. The wall at the back of my house is next to Royalty High 乔皇亲's garden which is so empty! There are always some vixens throwing bricks and stealing tiles to scare me at night. I used to have two valets. The older valet has run away, leaving the younger valet Taffy to guard the front gate. The back half of my house is empty. Luckily, Mrs. Trot is my old servant. She often comes to do laundry for me and makes shoes with my maid."

Moonie asks, "How old is Mrs. Trot? She's such a trustworthy nanny who never raises her voice!"

Vasie replies, "She's 56 years old, born in the year of the dog. She doesn't have any sons or daughters and depends on matchmaking to earn her living. I ask her to take care of my clothes, and after my husband died, I often ask her to be my companion. She slept with my maid last night."

Goldie responds quickly, "That's it. Now you have Mrs. Trot at home to take care of your house, you should stay here overnight. Since Jesse is no more, nobody else is in charge!"

Towie says, "Listen to me, Vasie. Ask Mrs. Trot to cancel the palanquin's return trip."

Vasie smiles and remains silent.

Granny Rinse gets up first and leaves after a few rounds of drinks, and Goldie follows her mother to her room.

When Vasie says she has enough wine, Cutie responds, "You drank when Lady Call and Towie gave you a toast, but you didn't drink when I gave you a toast. Aren't you biased?" She then offers Vasie a big cup of wine.

Vasie says, "Dear Cutie, I really can't drink anymore, and I'm not pretending."

Moonie says, "You may rest after you finish this cup, Vasie."

Vasie then receives the cup, puts it in front of her, and speaks to others.

Towie sees Plumie standing nearby, and asks, "What is Goldie doing in her room, Plumie? Go and invite Granny Rinse here and say Lady Call wants to invite her to drink with Vasie."

Plumie returns shortly afterward and says, "Granny Rinse is resting because of her arthritis. Madam Rinse will come after she finishes putting on makeup."

Moonie says, "I've never seen a host like Goldie who abandons her guest and goes back to her room. The sisters here don't just go away to put on makeup. She's quite childish."

Goldie comes back while Moonie is speaking. She has changed into a new dress and new jewelry like Towie and has a longevity hair clip on her hair.

Towie looks at Goldie and teases, "Today is your birthday, Goldie. How dare you abandon your guests and hide in your room! It's your turn to give Vasie a toast."

Vasie says, "Towie has already given me a toast. I've had enough."

Goldie says, "Towie's toast doesn't count. Here's a cup from me." She then fills a big cup with wine and gives it to Vasie.

Vasie just puts the cup on the table and does not drink.

Moonie is coming out of her room with Mrs. Kyle Call. She sees Goldie keeping Vasie company, and asks, "Why doesn't Granny Rinse keep Vasie company?"

Goldie replies, "My mom has arthritis, and is resting in my room."

Goldie is wearing the longevity hair clips, and Moonie asks, "Vasie, you've given Goldie a pair of longevity hair clips. Where were they made? They're so nice. Every one of us should get a pair tomorrow."

Vasie replies, "I still have a few pairs. I'll offer a pair for every sister tomorrow. These were made inside the palace and brought out by my late uncle-in-law. The outside world doesn't have this model."

Moonie says, "I was just kidding. There are so many sisters here. How can you give one to each of them?"

They keep drinking and laughing until sunset when Mrs. Trot, a little bit drunk while helping Snowie serve wine, comes out and says, "Vasie, it's time to ride the palanquin home."

Moonie says, "Vasie is not going home. Ask Mrs. Trot to send the palanquin home."

Vasie says, "There's nobody home. I'll visit everyone another day."

Towie says, "Vasie is so stubborn and looks down on us. Even if she doesn't send away the palanquin, Master will still keep Vasie here when he returns."

Vasie has no choice but to give her house key to Mrs. Trot and says, "Since the sisters all want to keep me here, to show my respects, send away the palanquin and let it pick me up tomorrow. You and the valet should take good care of the house." She then whispers, "Ask Springie to use the key to open the trunk under my bed and take out four pairs of golden longevity hair clips. You bring them along so I can give them to the four spouses of Westgate tomorrow."

Mrs. Trot understands the instructions and takes leave of Moonie.

Moonie says, "Have some drinks before you leave."

Mrs. Trot says, "I already had food and wine when I was in the kitchen. I'll come early tomorrow." She then leaves thankfully.

Moonie invites Vasie to her room to have a cup of tea with Mrs. Kyle Call. Westgate suddenly returns with his valet Deon, and Vasie quickly gets up to greet him. Moonie asks Flutie to hang up Westgate's coat.

Westgate says, "Today's club meeting was at the Temple of Emperor-Deva Jade. It was my turn to treat everyone, and since I also spent time doing all kinds of bookkeeping with the priest over there, I came back late after lunch." He then says, "I hope Vasie won't go back home today."

Towie says, "She didn't want to stay, and it took us a lot of effort to force her to stay."

Vasie explains, "I worried nobody would be home."

Westgate says, "Don't worry. The police have been patrolling the streets diligently these past two days. If anything goes wrong, Protector Fringe will respond as soon as I notify him." He then asks, "Why is Vasie sitting so lonely here? Have a drink."

Towie replies, "Every one of us tried to give her a toast, but she didn't drink."

Westgate says, "You were not persuasive enough, let me try." He then orders the maids to set up a dining table in the room, and the dishes contain the delicious food reserved for him.

Mrs. Kyle Call is smart enough not to interfere in their intimate dinner. She decides to go to Cutie's room.

Westgate takes the host's seat. The other four women, Vasie, Moonie, Towie, and Goldie, also sit down and start drinking from large cups instead of small cups.

Moonie becomes annoyed when she sees Westgate and Vasie constantly ogling each other. She goes to the other room to keep Mrs. Kyle Call company.

Vasie is so drunk at midnight she can hardly stand. She holds onto Goldie to go to the restroom.

Westgate staggers to Moonie's room and asks, "Where will Vasie sleep?"

Moonie replies, "She sleeps with the one whose birthday she came to celebrate."

Westgate asks, "Where will I sleep?"

Moonie replies, "It's up to you. You can sleep with her."

Westgate says laughingly, "That's inappropriate." He then says, "I'll sleep in your room."

Moonie says, "Enough with your nonsense! If you sleep here, where can Mrs. Kyle Call sleep?"

Westgate says, "So be it! I'll sleep in Towie's room." He then sleeps in Towie's room.

Goldie leads Vasie out of the restroom to her room where Vasie sleeps with Granny Rinse.

Vasie gets up in the morning and combs her hair in the mirror. Plumie brings her a bowl of water to wash her face. Since Plumie is cute, she feels Plumie is virtually at concubine status with Westgate, so she gives her a gold ornament.

Plumie quickly tells Goldie about the gift.

Goldie says thankfully, "Vasie, I appreciate the gift you awarded Plumie."

Vasie responds, "You're fortunate to have such a good maid."

Goldie asks Plumie to open the garden gate in the morning so that she can give her mother and Vasie a tour of the garden.

Westgate's mansion and Vasie's former mansion are separated by a wall. When Vasie sees a new door at the wall, she asks, "When did Master begin the remodeling?"

Goldie replies, "He hired a geomancer who told him to start the construction in March. The wall between this mansion and your former mansion will be removed to create a bigger garden with an artificial hill and a fenced enclosure in the front. There will be a new three-story building next to the three-story building where I'm living."

Vasie finds the renovation interesting. While they are talking, Moonie asks Jadie to invite them for tea, and they arrive at Moonie's room where Moonie, Cutie, and Towie are drinking tea with Mrs. Kyle Call.

Mrs. Trot arrives afterward, and they offer her a seat. She takes out of her pocket four pairs of golden longevity hair clips wrapped in an old face towel and hands them to Vasie.

Vasie first offers a pair to Moonie, then to Cutie, Towie, and Snowie, so that every spouse of Westgate gets a pair.

Moonie says, "We shouldn't have Vasie spend so much money on us."

Vasie says courteously, "Lady, these are nothing special. I hope you all enjoy them."

Moonie and the other women all gratefully bow to Vasie before they insert the hair clips into their hair.

Moonie says, "Vasie, I heard there's an exciting lantern market near your house. We'll visit your house when we go to watch lanterns."

Vasie says, "I'll respectfully invite everyone that day."

Goldie says, "I heard Vasie's birthday is on the 15th."

Moonie says, "Let's confirm this appointment. On Vasie's birthday, every one of us will go to celebrate it."

Vasie says cheerfully, "I'll be more than happy to receive you if you're willing to come to my snail-sized house."

After a good lunch and dinner, a palanquin arrives to pick up Vasie in the evening.

Vasie says goodbye to all the women and wants to say goodbye to Westgate.

Moonie says, "He got up and left home early to see the town counselor off."

Vasie then rides her palanquin and returns home.

Chapter 15. Westgate Visits a Brothel

Time goes by fast. February 15 is just around the corner. Westgate dispatches his valet Deon on the 14th to deliver a birthday present of four dishes, two plates of longevity peaches, one keg of wine, one plate of longevity noodles, and one golden-stitched silk dress. The greeting card reads, "From Lady Call of the Westgate Mansion".

Vasie asks Deon to come to her bedroom while she is grooming, and says, "I disturbed Lady Call last time. She spent money on my birthday gift again today."

Deon says, "Master and Lady Call both said this is an insignificant present for you to enjoy."

Vasie orders Springie to set up a small table outside to serve Deon four dishes. She gives Deon 0.2 oz of silver and a bright handkerchief before he leaves, and says, "When you return home, tell everyone I'll dispatch Mrs. Trot to deliver invitation cards so they'll all come here tomorrow."

After Deon leaves, Vasie puts five invitation cards in a big envelope and orders Mrs. Trot to deliver them to Moonie, Cutie, Towie, Goldie, and Snowie. She also has a secret invitation for Westgate to visit her at night.

Moonie leaves Snowie behind the next day to take care of the mansion. She and Cutie, Towie, and Goldie put on embroidered brocade dresses and travel on four palanquins, followed by the four valets, Lesing, Leon, Deon, and Pixel 画童. They arrive at Vasie's newly purchased house on Lion Street. Her house has three buildings. The front building is a tower with four rooms. The middle building behind the inner gate has two chambers, three guest rooms, and one closet. The back building adjacent to Royalty High's garden has three bedrooms and one kitchen.

Knowing her visitors have all come to watch lanterns, Vasie sets up tables and hangs some flowery lanterns on the top floor of the tower facing the street. The guests first have tea in the large back room. She sets up four tables in the guest room at noon to treat her guests to lunch, and they are entertained by the songbirds Dearie Boss 董娇儿 and Golden Fence 韩金钏. After drinking and chatting for the whole afternoon, she treats her guests to a banquet in the front tower. They then go to the top floor to watch lanterns. As they lean against the window to look at the lanterns on the street, they see some lanterns shaped like lotuses and hibiscuses, and some shaped like monkeys and elephants. Some are even shaped like crabs and dragons.

Moonie feels dizzy looking at so many colorful lanterns, so she returns to the dining table to drink with Cutie.

Goldie and Towie, together with the two songbirds, continue to lean against the window to look at the pedestrians on the street.

Some playboys on the street begin to gossip when they look up and see the beautiful women upstairs. One says they must be ladies from the duke's or marquis' mansions. Another says they must be from the brothels. One of them finally recognizes Goldie and talks about the murder of Dally Brawn and the exile of Sawn Brawn.

When Moonie sees people crowding downstairs and looking up, she asks Goldie and Towie to return to the banquet seats to continue the banquet and music.

Moonie sits for a while, then gets up and says, "I'm full. Cutie and I will leave first. Towie and Goldie may stay longer to chat with you. Westgate isn't home today. I'm worried when I have only the maids at home." She tips each songbird 0.2 oz of silver before she leaves.

Meanwhile, Westgate has lunch at home with Badger and Ceder before they go to the street to enjoy lanterns. Since he knows Moonie and his other concubines are all at Vasie's house for Vasie's birthday party, to avoid being seen by them, when they arrive at the east end of Lion Street, he does not go west but just turns around at the shop that sells gauze lanterns. He bumps into Gotcha and Remnant as soon as he makes a turn.

Remnant greets Westgate and says, "Long time no see!" But when he sees Badger and Ceder, he scolds, "You two jerks stroll around with Comrade Westgate without notifying us!"

Westgate says, "Comrade Bless, you blamed the wrong guys. I also just bumped into them on the street."

Remnant asks, "Where will you go after watching the lanterns?"

Westgate replies, "I'll go to a restaurant to have a few drinks with all of you. Since my spouses have all gone to another party, this is a good chance for me to treat all my comrades."

Remnant says, "Instead of going to a restaurant, why don't we visit Olie Plum? We should say hi to her during this big festival. Gotcha and I visited her yesterday, and she tearfully told us she couldn't even see your shadow for the past few weeks. I covered up for you by saying you were too busy. I'll go there with you while you're free."

Westgate has Vasie's evening invitation on his mind, so he declines the invitation and says, "I'm still quite busy and can't go there. I'll go tomorrow." However, he cannot resist being pushed and pulled by his four comrades, so they go together to the brothel.

Osmie, well dressed, is standing at the door when they arrive at the Plum brothel. She greets and leads the guests to the hall.

Remnant Bless says loudly, "Ask Mama to come out! It's not easy for us to invite Tycoon here today."

The bawd comes out with a cane before long, greets Westgate, and says, "I don't think I've slighted you. Why didn't you come to see my daughter? I guess you must've found a new girlfriend elsewhere—"

Remnant interrupts, "You're good at guessing. Tycoon now makes friends with a gorgeous whore, visits her every day, and has forgotten about Olie. Had we not bumped into him at the lantern display, he wouldn't have come. If you don't believe me, ask Gotcha Heir." He then points at Badger Yep.

Ceder says, "These three jerks are all bullshit artists."

The bawd says wryly, "Comrade Yep, why didn't you put in a good word for me before my brother-in-law? I'm not tooting my own horn when I say my Olie is good enough for a connoisseur like him."

Westgate takes 3 oz of silver out of his pocket, hands them to Osmie, and says, "I'll treat my friends for this major festival."

Osmie teases, "I won't accept it." She then hands the silver to the bawd.

The bawd says, "What happened? Does my brother-in-law think I can't afford to treat my guests to dinner during this major festival? The way he spends his money here makes other people think the workers in the brothel only love money."

Badger Yep comes over and says, "In my opinion, you ought to just take the money and quickly serve us some food and drinks."

The bawd says, "I don't think I should take it." She puts the silver in her pocket while she declines to take it. She then bows to Westgate and says, "Thanks for your generosity."

Badger Yep says, "Wait a minute, let me tell you a joke. There was a man who loved to visit brothels. He pretended to be a pauper one day just for fun. The bawd ignored him when she saw he wore tatters, and she didn't serve him tea for half a day. The man said, 'Mama, I'm hungry, do you have any rice for me to eat?' The bawd replied, 'I have no rice left.' The man said, 'Since there's no rice, bring me some water for me to wash my face.' The bawd said, 'I've run out of water.' The man then took out a 10-oz silver nugget, put it on the table, and asked the bawd to use it to buy rice and get water. The bawd was so shocked she stuttered dyslexically, 'I'll quickly let you eat the face and wash the rice...Wash the rice and eat the face.' "

Everyone laughs at the joke, and the bawd asks, "You've come here to tell such a stupid joke? It couldn't be true."

Badger Yep says, "Let me tell you something true. Tycoon is now hooked up with Silvie Call of the other brothel and doesn't want your Olie anymore. Had I not dragged him here, he wouldn't have come."

The bawd says, "I don't believe you. Not that I'm tooting my own horn, my Olie is so much better than Silvie. My family and my brother-in-law are relatives that can't be cut apart by the sharpest knife. He's a connoisseur who surely knows which girl is the most beautiful." She then brings out four armchairs for Badger, Ceder, Remnant, and Gotcha to sit on, while Westgate takes the seat of honor.

After some time, Olie comes out in exquisite attire. She greets everyone, serves delicious melon tea, and then sits down with Osmie to entertain the guests.

Two peddlers stick their heads through the portiere just when the valet cleans up the table. They then enter the room, fall to their knees, offer melons, and say, "This is to show our filial piety to Master during the major festival!"

Westgate recognizes one peddler named Chuck Hence 于春 and asks, "How many of you are here?"

Chuck replies, "Mensa Cut 段绵纱 is outside waiting for me."

Mensa Cut then enters the room, sees Badger, and quickly bows down.

Westgate gets up, takes their melons, opens his wallet, and throws an oz of silver onto the floor.

Chuck takes the silver. He and the other peddlers all bow down and say, "Master, thanks for your gift." They then run outside.

Osmie and Olie sing a song with zither and pipa when the banquet starts. Three football players come in with a box of roast goose and two bottles of wine during the singing. They say, "We express our filial piety to Tycoon for this major festival."

Westgate recognizes the players, and they are Baldy White 白秃子, Idle Pull 张闲, and Muslim Net 罗回子. He says, "Just wait for me outside. I'll play football after a few drinks." He then offers the football players four dishes of food and a bottle of wine. When he goes out of the room, he kicks the football for a while, then asks Olie to join him to play against two of the football players. The spectators flatter the players by applauding all the good kicking and scoring attempts and ignoring all the bad ones. To get more gratuities from Westgate, one football player exclaims, "Olie is such a great football player! The way she kicks the ball sideways, nobody can ever block her. She'll soon be the champion of all the brothels."

Olie then plays two more rounds of football until she is sweating and panting. She then takes out her handheld fan and holds Westgate's hand as she watches Osmie, Ceder Thank, and Idle Pull kick the ball while Baldy White and Muslim Net stand on the sidelines to help pick up the ball when it is kicked out of bounds.

Westgate is watching everyone playing backgammon, football, and drinking wine in the yard when Deon arrives on horseback and whispers, "Lady Call and Madam Cutie Plum have returned home. Mrs. Bloom asked me to invite Master to her place." Westgate then asks Deon to lead the horse out the back gate. He stops drinking, goes with Olie to her room, sits for a while, and pretends to take a leak to sneak out to the back gate. Before he can ride his horse, Badger orders a valet to drag him back. He then explains he has a problem at home and refuses to stay. He asks Deon to give the football players 1.5 oz of silver to send them away. Badger and his comrades continue to enjoy themselves until 9 p.m.

Chapter 16. Vasie Plum, the Restive Widow

Westgate leaves the brothel followed by Deon, and they head straight for Lion Street where they dismount outside Vasie's house. When he sees the gate tightly shut, he knows the female guests have all returned home. He orders Deon to ask Mrs. Trot to open the gate.

Westgate enters the hall and sees Vasie in a nice dress leaning near the curtain cracking melon seeds by candlelight.

Vasie comes over to receive Westgate and says smilingly, "If you arrived earlier, you could see Towie and Goldie. They just went home on their palanquins. Lady Call went home earlier today, and she said you weren't home. Where did you go?"

"I went with Badger and Ceder to watch lanterns this morning and went past your gate. I accidentally bumped into two friends who dragged me to the brothel where I stayed for some time until my valet went to look for me. I pretended I need to go to the restroom and escaped through the back door to come to see you."

"Tycoon, thanks for the expensive gift. Your wife didn't want to stay for too long. She said nobody was home, and I felt bad." Vasie then serves tasty food and wine, lights all the lanterns in the hall, and lowers the curtains. She offers Westgate a cup of wine, then bows down and says tearfully, "I have no relatives after my husband passed away. The drink I just offered you is to have you decide whether you'll accept me. If you don't think I'm ugly, I'm willing to make your bed, become an additional member of your spouses, and die with no regrets. What are your views regarding this point?"

Westgate holds the cup of wine and replies smilingly, "Please get up. The love you expressed will be in my mind forever. I'll take care of everything after you observe the mourning period. Let's have a drink for your birthday today." He finishes the cup of wine Vasie offered him, then fills the cup with wine and offers it back to Vasie.

Mrs. Trot is doing the cooking in the kitchen. She soon serves noodles.

Westgate asks, "Which two songbirds performed the singing today?"

Vasie replies, "Dearie Boss and Golden Fence were here today. I asked them to escort Towie and Goldie home so they could get more tips."

The two maids Springie and Stitchie are serving Westgate and Vasie food and wine when Deon comes in, falls to his knees, and bows down to congratulate Vasie's birthday.

Vasie quickly gets up, bows back, and orders, "Springie, ask Mrs. Trot to serve Deon noodles, desserts, and a bottle of wine."

Westgate says, "Deon, bring the horse home after your meal."

Vasie says, "If Lady Call asks you questions, don't say your master's here."

"I know. I'll just say Master is spending the night in the brothel, and I'll bring him home tomorrow."

Westgate nods and Vasie says cheerfully, "He's such a nice kid. He knows how to cover up for you!" She orders Springie to give Deon 0.2 oz of silver to buy melon seeds for the festival and says, "Lend me one of your shoes tomorrow so I can use it as a template to make a pair of good shoes for you."

Deon quickly bows down and says, "I dare not accept such a kind gesture." He then goes to another room for dinner and leads the horse out the gate before Mrs. Trot closes it.

Vasie plays guessing games with Westgate for a while, followed by a game of dominoes by lamplight using a set of 32 ivory tiles. She orders Springie to light candles in the bedroom.

After Jesse Bloom passed away, Vasie lets Westgate sleep with her maids Springie and Stitchie, so she does not hide her affair from them. She asks that the bed be made and candy and wine be available near the bed. As she sits next to Westgate and rubs her naked shoulder against his shoulder, she looks at the domino tiles and asks, "When will you remodel your mansion?"

Westgate replies, "I'll wait until March to start the construction. I'll demolish the wall that separates your former mansion from my mansion so I'll have a bigger garden with an artificial hill and an additional three-story building."

Vasie says, "I've hidden several tea chests behind my bed. They contain 40 lb of incense, 200 lb of wax, two cans of mercury, and 80 lb of ground pepper. You can move them out for me tomorrow and sell them to subsidize your home remodeling. If you don't mind I'm not pretty, please tell your wife I'm willing to be her subordinate to work for her as a concubine of any rank. I don't want to lose you, darling!" She bursts into tears as she says those words.

Westgate quickly uses his handkerchief to wipe away her tears and says, "Let's wait while you observe the mourning period and my mansion is being expanded. Otherwise, you have no place to live when I marry you."

Vasie says, "Since you're willing to marry me, make sure the building I'll live in will look like Goldie's building. I like Goldie who looks so cute. Towie is also very nice to me. They dress as if they were born from the same mother. The only problem is Lady Call who glanced at me with no emotion."

Westgate says, "My wife from the Call family is easygoing. Otherwise, how could she allow me to have so many concubines? I'll construct an identical three-story building for you, with two corner gates for entrance and exit. Is that OK with you?"

Vasie replies, "It couldn't be better, darling!" They then make love with abandon until 4 a.m. before they sleep, and they can hardly get up the next morning for breakfast served by Springie. She eats half a bowl of porridge with Westgate and then drinks wine with him again.

Deon, who has brought along a horse for Westgate, soon knocks on the gate. Westgate then speaks to him through the window.

Deon says, "Three visitors from Four-Streams 四川 and Wide-East are sitting in our lounge discussing many transactions with Jason and they want 100 oz of silver as a down payment. The rest of the payment can be made in the middle of September. Lady Call dispatched me to invite Master home to take care of it."

Westgate asks, "Did you say I'm here?"

Deon replies, "I just said Master is in Olie's brothel."

Westgate says, "You're so dumb! Ask Jason to send them off. Why invite me?"

Deon replies, "The visitors refused to sign the contract with Jason. They want to sign the contract with Master."

Vasie says, "Master, since Lady Call dispatched him to invite you, it must be an important business transaction. If you don't go, won't she blame me?"

Westgate says, "Those cunning merchants won't come to my mansion to sell their stuff unless they have excess inventory to dispose of, and I can exploit them by delaying the payment by three to six months. If I pay them too early, they'd think they're smart cookies. My store is the only one that sells merchandise in bulk quantities in this entire Clearstream Town. I don't worry they can't wait for me."

Vasie says, "The customer is always right in the business world. In my humble opinion, since we're going to see each other for years on end, you should first take care of them."

Westgate follows Vasie's advice. He takes his time to groom himself and put on his headscarf and coat. After he arrives home, he goes to his store where four salesmen are already waiting for him to finish their business transactions. He signs the contracts, sends the salesmen off, and walks to Goldie's room.

Goldie asks, "Where did you go yesterday? You'd better tell me the truth or else I'll make a scene."

Westgate replies, "I strolled on the street with my comrades to watch lanterns while you were at Vasie's birthday party. We then went to the brothel for a drink and spent a night there until my valet fetched me and I came home today."

Goldie says, "I knew the valet fetched you, and you think I could be fooled into believing you were in the brothel. Come on, cheater! And you still want to fool me. That slut sent us off yesterday, then secretly invited you to satisfy her for the whole night before she let you go. Deon is such a jerk. He covers up for you all the time. He said one thing to Lady Call, then said another thing to me. When Deon brought the horse home, Lady Call asked, 'Why didn't Master come home? Which family invited him for a drink?' And he replied, 'He watched lanterns with Mr. Yep and the other comrades, they then went to Olie Plum's brothel for a drink, and he asked me to pick him up tomorrow morning.' But when I later asked him, he just smiled and didn't answer. I then forced him to answer, and he replied, 'Master is in Lady Plum's house on Lion Street.' This jerk knew I couldn't be fooled. You've been teaching him how to lie!"

Westgate says wryly, "I never taught him how to lie." Knowing he cannot fool Goldie, he says, "Vasie invited me for a drink last night and said you're all on friendly terms with her. She then said to me tearfully she doesn't have enough servants in her house, and the back half of her house is so empty she's fearful at night. She wants me to marry her and asked me when I'll remodel my mansion. She still has some wax and incense worth several hundred oz of silver, and she asked me to sell them and use the money to subsidize and expedite the construction of the new building in my mansion for her to live in. She wants to live near you but is not sure if you're willing to have her as your sister."

Goldie says, “Since I feel so lonely living in this empty garden, I’m more than happy to have a companion. Anyway, you’re like a harbor that doesn’t have enough boats to moor. If nobody rejected me when I came here, why should I reject her? Do you think I have the clout to make any objections? But I don’t think your other spouses are as easygoing as me. You’d better inform Lady Call.”

Westgate says, “Be that as it may, Vasie is still observing the mourning period.”

An object slides out of Westgate’s pocket while Goldie is taking off his white silk coat. She holds it in her hand, looks at it for a while, and cannot figure out what it is. She then asks, “What’s this thingamajig? It’s so heavy!”

“This ding-a-ling made in Burma is worth at least 5 oz of silver.”

“How do you use this whatchamacallit?”

“First heat it in the stove. You’ll be on Cloud Nine when I use it during copulation.”

“Did you use it with Vasie?”

Westgate then tells Goldie how much he enjoyed the previous night. As he describes his experience in graphic detail, Goldie is aroused and wants to make love to him in the daytime. They close the door, take off their clothes, and have a blast in bed.

Westgate meets a sales agent one day. He sells the incense and wax stored in the tea trunks behind Vasie’s bed and gets 380 oz of silver. Vasie keeps 180 oz of silver as pocket money and gives the rest to Westgate to subsidize the construction of the new building. The geomancer has selected March 8 as the day to begin the building construction. He gives 500 oz of silver to steward Lejon and custodian Ditcher Lithe 贲地传 to oversee the roofing, carpentry, and masonry work.

Ditcher is a young and slick jack-of-all-trades. He used to be the aide of the imperial eunuch but was kicked out because of disorderly conduct. He was a part-time laborer at first. He worked in a mansion as a servant later and married the nanny who eloped with him. When he worked as an agent in a clothing store, Westgate appreciated his talent and employed him as a drugstore salesman. He is involved in many business activities nowadays.

Ditcher and Lejon supervise the tradesmen to start the construction. They first demolish the old mansion of Jesse Bloom, break down the wall, and build the foundation. It will take some time to build the fenced enclosure, artificial hill, and various pavilions and terraces.

Time flies like an arrow. Westgate has been looking at the construction of the new garden for over a month. Vasie invites Westgate over in the first week of April, which is near the 100th day of Jesse Bloom's passing, to discuss the removal of Jesse's altar.

Vasie says, "You should sell the house I'm now living in. If you can't sell it, ask someone to maintain it. Please marry me into your mansion so I don't feel so lonely here day and night. I can feel the vixen and ghosts in this deserted place. Tell Lady Call to take pity on me when you go home. I can be your concubine of any rank to serve you and make your bed with no complaints." Her tears stream down her face as she says those words.

Westgate says, "Don't worry. I've relayed your message to Goldie. When you finish observing the mourning period, the construction of your building will also be finished, and you can be married into my mansion."

Vasie says, "Sounds good to me. Since you want to marry me, just construct a slipshod building for me as soon as possible. Once I move into your mansion, I can die with no regrets. Time crawls like a snail here."

Westgate says, "I understand."

Vasie says, "If my building can't be constructed too fast, another alternative is to let me live on the upper floor of Goldie's building as soon as Jesse's altar is removed, and I'll move to my new building later. You should go home and speak to Goldie, and I'll wait for your answer. April 10th is the 100th day of Jesse's passing when I'll say prayers and remove his altar."

Westgate tells Goldie everything the next day, and Goldie, eager to please Westgate, has no objection and says, "Go ahead. The early bird catches the worm."

Westgate asks for Moonie's opinion on Vasie's desire to marry into the mansion.

Moonie responds, "Don't marry her. Firstly, she is still observing the mourning period. Secondly, you were her husband's friend. Thirdly, you've been involved in her financial affairs; not only have you bought her mansion, but you've also hidden and sold her valuables. Your accountant will tell you, 'Don't commingle assets.' I've heard Jesse's cousin Jewel Bloom is a very nasty guy. If anything leaks out, you'll stir up a hornet's nest. I'm giving you my honest opinion. It's up to you whether you follow my advice."

Westgate is at a loss for words. He goes to the lounge, sits on the couch, and is on the horns of a dilemma. He thinks for quite a while and unable to come up with a satisfactory answer to tell Vasie, he goes to Goldie's room again.

Goldie asks, "What did Lady Call say when you went to her room?"

Westgate relays what Moonie said, and Goldie says, "Lady Call disagrees with you because, from her point of view, you've eaten Jesse out of house and home, and want to marry his wife while claiming to be his best buddy. However, I have a different point of view: I couldn't care less about my friend unless he's a high official."

Westgate says, "Be that as it may, I'm afraid Jewel Bloom will find fault with Vasie, and he'll be the spoiler if he finds out Vasie is still observing the mourning period. I just don't have any satisfactory answers for Vasie."

Goldie says, "Psst. Just make up a story when you see her. Tell her after you talked to me, I reminded you my rooms upstairs have been converted to storage rooms for the herbs of your drugstore, so there's no space to store her luggage and furniture. Furthermore, tell her the construction of her building is 70% complete, and you'll rush the workers to paint and decorate it. Everything can be done smoothly by the time she finishes observing the mourning period. That'll be much better than squeezing into my rooms upstairs where the smell of the herbs will smother her. I'm sure she'll agree with you."

Westgate is pleased with Goldie's advice, and he heads straight for Vasie's house.

Vasie asks, "What did you say when you went home?"

Westgate replies, "It'd be better to wait for your building to be painted and decorated. Goldie's rooms upstairs have been used to store my herbs and are too messy for your baggage and furniture to fit in. Jesse's cousin may object because you're still observing the mourning period, which can be a major problem. How should we handle it?"

Vasie replies, "He can't mess with me. Not to mention the court has already decided the amount of his inheritance and nothing more, per the traditional rule, a girl's first marriage is decided by her parents, and her second marriage is decided by herself. No man can ever control what his former sister-in-law may do. If he dares flatulate, I'll make an example of him. Don't worry, Tycoon. He wouldn't touch me with a ten-foot pole." She then asks, "Concerning the new building, when will it be ready?"

Westgate replies, "I've told the workers to expedite the construction of your three-story building. It'll be painted in early June."

Vasie says, "Push them harder, darling! I'll wait for them to finish the work."

The maid then serves drinks, and Westgate spends the night with Vasie. He then visits her every three to five days.

Time goes by fast, and the expansion of Westgate's mansion has been going on for two months already. The construction of the three-story building is almost complete, except the fenced enclosure is not yet ready. Vasie throws a party during Dragon-Boat Festival and invites Westgate over. They eat glutinous-rice dumplings while deciding on the wedding date. They select June 15 as the day to invite monks to say prayers and remove Jesse's altar. Vasie will be married into Westgate's mansion afterward.

The day to invite the monks is also the birthday of Badger Yep. Westgate puts 0.3 oz of silver in an envelope as birthday cash for Badger, and he gives Deon 5 oz of silver in the morning to buy chicken, goose, and duck to throw a birthday party. He also orders his valets Peon and Pixel to go to Badger's house in the afternoon. The comrades who attend the party consist of Ceder Thank, Remnant Bless, Gotcha Heir, Dangler Call, Leisure Cloud, Seizure Oft, Leech White, and the new member Ditcher Lithe. Every member of the club is present. They also hire two minstrels to sing.

Westgate recognizes one minstrel as Silvie Call's brother Wade Call 吴惠. The other one he cannot recognizes then says, "I'm Scentie Stern's elder brother Funk Stern 郑奉."

Deon brings along a horse to pick up Westgate in the evening. He goes to the banquet table and whispers, "She wants Master to leave early." He leaves when Westgate winks at him.

Badger stops Deon and exclaims, "You'd better tell me the truth, puppy, or else I'll twist your ear. How many birthdays does your Papa Yep have in a year? You now bring a horse to take your master away in broad daylight, so where are you going? Which concubine in your mansion dispatched you here? If you don't tell me, I won't help you find a wife for a century."

Deon replies, "I wasn't dispatched by anyone. I worry Master may want to go home at this late hour, so I bring his horse here to wait for him."

Unable to persuade Deon to tell the truth, Badger says, "Since you won't tell me, if I find out the reason tomorrow, I won't let you off easy." He then pours a cup of wine and picks out half of a dessert dish for Deon.

Westgate emerges from the restroom after some time and asks Deon to go to a quiet place. He then asks, "Who went to the Bloom mansion today?"

Deon replies, "Jigar Bloom has gone to the countryside, Jehan Bloom has an eye ailment, so they didn't come. Only Jewel Bloom and his wife came and had a vegetarian meal. Jewel Bloom left first, and Vasie gave his wife 10 oz of silver and two suits of clothes before she left. She then bowed down to Vasie."

Westgate asks, "Did Jewel Bloom have any objections?

Deon replies, "He had no objection, but just said after Vasie marries into your mansion, he'll visit you."

Westgate asks, "He really said that?"

Deon replies, "I dare not tell lies."

Westgate asks joyfully, "Is the religious service over?"

Deon replies, "The altar was removed before the monks left. Lady Plum said Master should visit her early."

Westgate says, "I understand. Take care of the horse outside."

Deon goes outside. He does not know Badger Yep has eavesdropped on him in the corridor. His heart misses a beat when Badger shouts at him.

Badger complains, "I overheard what you didn't tell me, puppy. So, your master is involved in monkey business yet again!"

Westgate exclaims, "Don't publicize it, doggy!"

Badger says, "I'll only announce it to our club members, and nobody else." He then goes to the banquet table, tells everyone what he just heard, holds onto Westgate, and says, "How could you hide this important problem from us, comrade? If Jewel Bloom has any objections, just tell us, and we'll confront him, and he'd better yield to us, or else he'll get big bumps on his head from us. Just tell us your problem, and we'll solve it for you. That's what friends are for! We'll go through fire and water and die for you with no regrets for your sake. We trust you with all our hearts, yet you hide things from us."

Ceder says, "Senior Comrade, if you don't tell us the truth, I'll spill the beans to Olie Plum and Silvie Call tomorrow, and then you don't know where to put yourself."

Westgate responds laughingly, "For your information, the wedding has been arranged."

Badger says, "It ain't over till the fat lady sings!"

Ceder says, "I'll celebrate your wedding, but make sure you hire four male and female singers to entertain me when you invite me to your banquet."

Westgate says, "It goes without saying. I'll invite every comrade."

Remnant says, "Instead of celebrating his wedding in the future, why don't we celebrate it now?"

Badger hands out the goblets, Ceder holds the wine bottle, and Remnant holds a dish, while the other comrades take turns bowing down and giving a toast to Westgate. They also ask the two minstrels to play and sing wedding songs while they make Westgate drink four cups of wine.

Remnant says, "Don't forget about Funk Stern and Wade Call when you invite us to your wedding, comrade."

Funk Stern says, "I'll be there early."

Since it is getting dark, Westgate eats a few more dishes and is eager to leave. Badger tries to detain him, but Ceder says, "Let him go, Comrade Yep. Otherwise, his fiancée will be mad at you."

Westgate rides his horse to Lion Street.

Vasie has already taken off her mourning headdress and changed into a stunning outfit. The hall is brightly lit with candles, and they are ready to enjoy a sumptuous dinner.

After Westgate sits in an armchair, the maid opens a bottle of wine. Vasie gives him a toast, bows down four times, and says, "My late husband's altar was removed today. I'm so glad Tycoon is willing to accept me."

Westgate also gets up when Vasie gets up. He gives her a toast, sits down, and then asks, "Did the Bloom couple say anything today?"

Vasie replies, "After we had a vegetarian lunch, I invited him to my room and mentioned my marriage to Tycoon. He had no objection at all and said he'll ask his wife to visit our mansion in the next three days. I gave them 10 oz of silver and two sets of clothes, and they were overjoyed. They thanked me again before they left."

Westgate says, “If that’s how they behave, I’ll let them visit my mansion. But if they misbehave, I won’t spare them.”

The food served by Mrs. Trot includes a dish of scallion mutton cooked by Vasie.

Vasie says smilingly, “Master, when you were drinking at Yep’s house, I waited for quite a while, and since I was afraid you might get drunk, I asked Deon to invite you here early. Did anyone over there discover anything?”

“Badger found out my wedding and then joked around with my other comrades who then congratulated me and forced me to have a few drinks. He tried to stop me from sneaking out. Another comrade then convinced him to let me leave.”

“He was nice enough to let you leave.”

Westgate kisses Vasie who looks so cute when she is drunk.

Vasie cuddles Westgate and says, “You should marry me as soon as possible, darling! It’s so inconvenient for you to come here. Don’t leave me here yearning for you day and night.”

Chapter 17. Affected by Jeer Birch's Impeachment

Protector Fringe throws a birthday party on June 20. Westgate prepares a birthday present, spruces himself up, and rides a large white horse followed by four valets to attend the party. The attendees consist of Prosecutor Fab, Instructor Pull, Colonel Thorn 荊千戶, Colonel Greet 贺千戶, and other military officers. They are entertained by a band and an opera troupe, with four singers giving everyone a toast.

Deon brings the horse home. When he takes the horse to the party in the evening to pick up Westgate, he bumps into Mrs. Trot at the west street corner. He then asks, "Granny, where are you going?"

Mrs. Trot replies, "Lady Plum dispatched me to invite your master to her house because Silversmith Gaze 顾银匠 delivered the wedding ring in a jewelry box today. She wants your master to look at it, and she also wants to speak to him."

Deon says, "Master is at Protector Fringe's party today. I'm now picking him up. You may return. I'll tell him when I arrive there."

Mrs. Trot says, "Please tell him Lady Plum is waiting for him."

When Deon arrives at Protector Fringe's mansion, the officers are busily enjoying the party. He goes to Westgate's table and says, "I was bringing your horse here when I bumped into Mrs. Trot at the street corner. She was dispatched by Lady Plum to tell you Silversmith Gaze has delivered the wedding ring. Lady Plum wants you to look at it, and she wants to speak to you."

Westgate picks up some food for Deon to eat. He is ready to leave when Protector Fringe stops him and gives him a goblet of wine. He then says, "Thanks for your kindness. I'll finish this goblet of wine and then take care of some minor business." He guzzles down the wine, takes leave of Protector Fringe, and heads for Vasie's house. After Vasie receives him, he orders Deon to take his horse home and pick him up the next day.

Vasie asks Springie to take the wedding ring out of the jewelry box for Westgate to inspect. The ring looks beautiful and its gold has a fiery finish. The engagement is on June 24, and the wedding is on July 4. She joyfully has dinner with Westgate.

They go to the bedroom after dinner, take off their clothes, sit shoulder to shoulder, and begin to chat and make love.

Westgate is drunk as he asks teasingly, "Did you serve Jesse well when he was alive?"

Vasie replies, "I didn't bother to sleep with him because he lived the life of a zombie. Since he spent his days in the brothels, I wouldn't touch him with a ten-foot pole when he came home. We slept apart when his eunuch uncle was alive. When he misbehaved, I reported him to his uncle who beat him up with no mercy. So how could he possibly be compared with you? You're the only man I think about day and night."

Someone bangs on the gate while they are talking. Mrs. Trot opens the gate and the visitor is Deon.

Westgate says, "I ordered him to pick me up tomorrow. Why is he here at night?" He then orders Deon to enter the bedroom.

Deon anxiously approaches the door of the bedroom, but since Westgate is sleeping with Vasie, he dares not enter the room. He stays outside the portiere and announces, "Master, your daughter and her husband have both moved into your mansion, and they've brought along bag and baggage. Lady Call dispatched me to invite you back home for discussion."

Westgate thinks hesitantly, "There must be a reason to call me at this late hour. I'd better go home and speak to her." He quickly gets up. Vasie helps him put on his clothes and offers him a cup of wine before he gallops home. The hall is brightly lit with lamps, and his daughter and son-in-law have all arrived, with trunks and bags piled up in the hall. He asks in shock, "Why are you here?"

Jimmy Show, his son-in-law, bows down and replies tearfully, "Commander Jeer Birch was recently indicted by the inspector, and there was an edict to imprison him. His students, relatives, and staff members will all be exiled to prison camps. Staff Shane Birch 杨干办, who managed to escape from his mansion, notified my father of this shocking news last night.

"My father was so scared he asked me and Lassie to bring our belongings here for temporary storage, and we'll hide here for a while. He then fled to the capital to live in his sister's house to await more news. We'll return the favor when things become normal again."

Westgate asks, "Do you have your father's letter?"

Jimmy replies, "I have his letter here." He takes a letter out of his pocket and gives it to Westgate who then reads it.

The letter explains since Minister of War Full Rex 王黼 had not defended the northern territory against the Manchurian invaders, Commander Birch was also sent to jail, and Commander Birch's relatives will be exiled. Therefore, Jimmy's father wants Jimmy and Westgate's daughter to hide in Westgate's mansion for the time being, and he pays Westgate 500 oz of silver for their living expenses, while he goes to the capital to stay at his brother-in-law Salem Pull 张世廉's house to ride out the storm.

Westgate reads the letter and nervously asks Moonie to treat his daughter and his son-in-law to dinner. He orders his servants to clean up the three rooms of the chamber to the east of the front lounge for the couple to live, while the couple's extra baggage will be stored in Moonie's room.

Jimmy takes out 500 oz of silver and gives them to Westgate to pay for his living expenses.

Westgate gives Custodian Call 5 oz of silver to go to the town hall to make a copy of the document sent from the capital.

Westgate later gets a copy of the document from the capital. He then knows Minister of War Full Rex has been impeached for losing Song dynasty territories to the Manchurian invaders, and Commander Birch and Preceptor Weed were also responsible for the loss. Although the emperor lets Preceptor Weed continue to work in the imperial court, Minister Rex and Commander Birch will be executed. The relatives of Commander Birch, including his in-law Honk Show, will be exiled.

The information scares the living daylights out of Westgate. He quickly packs up enough gold, silver, and jewelry, summons his servants Lebron and Leroy to his room, and orders, "Hire a carriage and head for the capital tonight to get more information. You don't need to find Honk Show, my in-law. Based on the information you obtain over there, bribe the appropriate officials and then return quickly to report to me." He then gives 20 oz of silver for the travel expenses of his two servants who leave at 5 a.m.

Unable to sleep at night, Westgate orders Lejon and Ditcher the next morning to stop the construction of the garden and lay off the workers for a while. His servants dare not go outside, and the gate will not be open for any visitors. He only walks inside his mansion like an ant on a hot pan. His plan to marry Vasie has already gone out the window.

Moonie, seeing Westgate staying in his room so worriedly, says, "The Show family, our in-law, has a problem over there, and they reap what they sow. Why are you so worried?"

Westgate replies, "It's one thing to have my daughter and my son-in-law move into my mansion and bother me. It's another thing to have my neighbors—mostly jealous or angry with me—to have a chance now to add fuel to the fire to expose my flaws and take me down."

Meanwhile, Vasie waits for two days and does not see anything happening. She dispatches Mrs. Trot twice to Westgate's mansion, but the gate is shut so tight not even Hercules can barge through. After waiting for half a day, Mrs. Trot does not see a single person coming out. Vasie dispatches Mrs. Trot to deliver the wedding ring on the 24th and invite Westgate over to chat, but nobody answers the door at Westgate's mansion.

Mrs. Trot then goes and stands under the eaves of the house across the street. Deon later comes out to feed his horse. He sees her and asks, "Why are you here, Mrs. Trot?"

Mrs. Trot replies, "Lady Plum asked me to deliver the wedding ring. Why is this mansion so quiet? Please ask your master to come over to chat with her."

Deon says, "Master has been busy these few days. You should bring home the wedding ring. I'll tell Master about it after I finish feeding my horse and come back."

Mrs. Trot says, "Dear Deon, I'll wait here while you take the wedding ring inside and speak to your master. Otherwise Lady Plum will be mad at me."

Deon ties his horse and walks into the mansion. He comes out after some time and says, "I talked to Master, and he took the wedding ring. He wants you to tell Lady Plum he'll go to her house and speak to her a few days later."

Mrs. Trot relays the message to Vasie who waits a few more days again, but she still does not hear any news in July.

Since Westgate does not show up, Vasie gradually loses her appetite and becomes depressed. While tossing and turning, someone knocks on the door, and it seems Westgate has arrived. She receives him joyfully, and they hold hands as they walk into her room and speak to each other intimately. But Westgate suddenly disappears at dawn when the rooster crows. Vasie is devastated and loses her mind. The commotion causes Mrs. Trot to anxiously come into the room to see her, and she says, "Westgate has just left. Have you closed the gate?"

Mrs. Trot replies, "You've been thinking about him so much you now hallucinate. I didn't see Tycoon, not even his shadow!"

A vixen keeps transforming itself into a human to disturb Vasie in her dreams every night.

Vasie loses her appetite that causes her weight loss, and she cannot get out of bed. Mrs. Trot recommends Vasie to see Zuke Grass 蒋竹山, whose booth is at the street corner, so that he may cure her illness.

Zuke Grass has not yet reached his thirties, is very short and skinny, and is like a snake in the grass. He takes Vasie's pulse and is impressed by her beauty when he gives her a diagnosis. "The problem with your inch pulse is caused by your sex drive. Your mood fluctuates between coldness and heat when your negative energy counters your positive energy, and it is caused by your disappointment of not accomplishing your goal, not by malaria or the flu. You feel tired in the daytime and befriend ghosts in the nighttime. If your illness is not cured soon, you'll be paralyzed. What a pity!"

Vasie asks, "Sir, please prescribe a good medication for me, and I'll reward you."

Zuke says, "If you take my medication, you'll recover." He then prescribes a medication to help Vasie sleep well at night.

Vasie gradually regains her appetite and mobility. She makes a full recovery a few days later and asks Mrs. Trot to invite Zuke Grass over for dinner to thank him. Zuke has coveted Vasie ever since he laid his eyes on her, so he spruces himself up upon receiving the dinner invitation.

Vasie puts on a beautiful dress and receives Zuke Grass in the hall. She invites him into her room after dinner, and her maid Stitchie brings out a tray containing 33 oz of silver.

Zuke looks at the 3 oz of silver and says, "It's my duty to cure your illness. I dare not accept so much compensation."

Vasie says, "This isn't much. Please accept it."

Zuke glances at Vasie and admires her beauty as he finally accepts the silver. He tries to woo her and asks, "May I ask Lady her age?"

"I've squandered 24 years of my life."

"How could a lady, so young and grown up in the luxury of the boudoir, be afflicted with depression?"

"My house has been so empty ever since my husband passed away. How could a lonely woman like me who worries so much not be depressed?"

"When did your husband pass away?"

"It's been eight months since my husband succumbed to the flu last December."

"Who prescribed him the medication?"

"Mister Wild who resides on the main street."

"You mean Ghastly Wild 胡鬼嘴 who lives in Eunuch Slay 刘太监's house on East Street? He didn't graduate from the medical school I attended, He couldn't know how to take your husband's pulse. Why did you hire him?"

"He was recommended by my neighbors. I wouldn't blame him. It was just my husband's sad twist of fate."

"Do you have children, lady?"

"I don't have any."

"Lady, it's a pity for you to remain a childless widow at such a youthful age. Why don't you look for other opportunities? How can you not be sick when you live a gloomy life?"

"I'll get married soon."

"Lady, may I ask you whom you'll marry?"

"He's the tycoon who owns the drugstore next to the town hall."

"Oh no! Lady, why would you marry him? I've been hired by his family several times, so I know what he's really like. He's a lobbyist in the town hall, a loan shark, and a human trafficker. He has five spouses at home, not to mention the maids he's ravished. He beats any woman who doesn't satisfy him. As the champion of wife-beating, he's against women's liberation. Luckily, you told me his name. Otherwise, if you marry into his mansion, it'll be like a moth to a flame. It'll be too late for regrets when you're caught between the devil and the deep blue sea. He's been hiding in his mansion lately because of his in-law's exile, and he abandoned his home remodeling. The town hall is ready to arrest him per the document dispatched from the capital. His new building under construction will be confiscated before you know it. Why would you be willing to marry him for no good reason?"

Vasie is at a loss for words, especially since most of her properties have already been transferred to Westgate's mansion. She thinks for a while, and secretly stamps her foot as she thinks, "I kept inviting him over, but he never showed up because he's in trouble." Impressed by Zuke's eloquence and modesty, she continues to think, "I may as well marry this man! But I don't know if he's already married." She then asks, "Sir, I'm so grateful you helped me see the light at the end of the tunnel. I'll marry another man you recommend."

Zuke seizes the opportunity and asks, "May I know what kind of man you have in mind? I'll find one for you."

Vasie replies, "I don't care about his status. I prefer someone like you."

Zuke, happy as a flea in a doghouse, drops to his knees and says, "Lady, I've been a widower for some time and have no children. If you take pity on me and marry me, it'd be a dream come true! And I'll never forget your kindness!"

Vasie holds Zuke's hand and says delightedly, "Please get up. May I know how long you've been a widower? How old are you? If you want to marry me, you should follow the tradition of hiring a matchmaker."

Zuke falls to his knees again and pleads, "I'm 29 years old, born on February 27th at 6 a.m. My wife unfortunately died last year. I come from a poor family. Since your promise is as good as gold, why do we need a matchmaker to speak on our behalf?"

Vasie replies cheerfully, "Although you have no money, I have Mrs. Trot here. You can have her as the matchmaker to save you money. I'll select an auspicious day and time to have you married into my house. Is that OK with you?"

Zuke immediately bows down and says, "Lady, you're giving me a new lease of life. I couldn't be more fortunate!"

They then give each other a toast in the room for their engagement. After Zuke leaves in the evening, Vasie says, "Mrs. Trot, the way things are going, I can't tell whether Westgate can survive the current fiasco. Since I don't have anyone here to help me, if I get dragged into his fiasco, I may even lose my life. The best alternative for me to survive is to have this man married into my house. Why not?"

Vasie dispatches Mrs. Trot the next day to tell Zuke July 18 will be the wedding date. She gives Zuke 300 oz of silver three days later to open a drugstore next to her house.

Zuke then has the money to buy a donkey to ride back and forth on the street instead of walking to his patients' houses as he did in the past.

Chapter 18. Lebron Goes to the capital

Meanwhile, to bribe the powers that be, Lebron and Leroy travel day and night to arrive in the capital where they enter Longevity Gate 万寿门 and rest in an inn. When they walk on the street the next day, they hear people gossiping, and the latest news is about Minister of War Full Rex who has been sentenced and will be executed in autumn. Commander Birch, whose relatives have not all been arrested, will be sentenced that day.

Lebron and Leroy bring along the present and quickly arrive at Preceptor Weed's mansion. Since they have been there twice in the past, they know the roads very well. They stand below the arch of Dragon Virtue Street to await news from the mansion. A man in azure attire soon comes out nervously and heads east.

Lebron recognizes the man as Staff Birch, the confidante of Commander Birch. He wants to stop and question Staff Birch, but since Westgate has not instructed him to contact that man, he lets that man pass by.

After some time, Lebron and Leroy go to the gatekeeper of the mansion and say respectfully, "We'd like to know if Preceptor Weed is home."

The gatekeeper responds, "He's not home. He's still discussing various matters in the imperial court. Why do you ask?"

Lebron replies, "In that case, I'd like to see Butler Plume 翟管家."

The gatekeeper says, "Butler Plume is also not home. He followed Preceptor out."

Lebron says, "Wait a minute. I have a present for you." He then takes an oz of silver out of his pocket and gives it to the gatekeeper.

The gatekeeper receives the silver and asks, "Do you want to see Preceptor or Minister? Twain Plume 翟谦 is the butler who works for Preceptor. Arn Tall 高安 is the steward who works for Minister. They have different duties. Since Preceptor hasn't returned from the imperial court, only Minister is home. What issue would you like to report? Let me invite Steward Tall over."

Lebron trumps up his status and says, "I work in Commander Birch's mansion, and I have an urgent matter to report."

The gatekeeper then quickly enters the mansion.

When Arn Tall comes out after some time, Lebron bows, hands over 10 oz of silver, and says, "I'm a relative of Commander Birch. I was supposed to come here with Staff Birch to receive a message from Preceptor. I came here late because I spent too much time at breakfast. Staff Birch must've arrived early to see Preceptor before I could catch up with him."

Arn Tall receives the present and says, "Staff Birch has just left, and Preceptor hasn't returned yet from the imperial court. Just wait a while for me, and I'll bring you to see Minister." He then leads Lebron to a second hall and lets Lebron wait there while he continues to go through another inner door to see Yo Weed 蔡攸, Jinx Weed 蔡京's son, who is another trusted lord of the emperor and the Minister of Rites.

Lebron waits outside the door until Arn Tall summons him into the second hall where he kneels.

Yo Weed, sitting behind a red portiere, asks, "Where do you come from?"

Lebron replies respectfully, "I'm the servant of Honk Show, Commander Birch's in-law. I was supposed to come with Staff Birch of our mansion to see Preceptor. I didn't expect Staff Birch to come here first, and I arrived late." He then takes a letter out of his pocket and hands it over.

Since the letter mentions a bribe of 500 barrels of rice, Yo Weed says, "Lebron, Preceptor has been keeping a low profile because of the current fiasco. All the imperial court proceedings, including yesterday's sentencing of the guilty officials, are handled by Right Chancellor Plum. Although Commander Birch has been sentenced, his associates are still under investigation. You should go to Chancellor Plum's mansion to obtain more information."

Lebron bows down and says, "I don't know where Chancellor Plum's mansion is. I hope Minister will take pity on me for the sake of Commander Birch."

Yo Weed says, "Ask about Right Chancellor Banyan 李邦彦 Plum when you go to the tower over the north slope by Superman Bridge 天漢桥, and everyone can tell you where he is. Anyway, I'll dispatch a deputy to go with you." He then writes a letter and dispatches Steward Arn Tall to go with Lebron to see Chancellor Plum.

Arn Tall leaves the mansion with Lebron, and with Leroy carrying the present, they make a turn at Dragon-Virtue Street and head straight for Banyan Plum's mansion near Superman Bridge.

Meanwhile, Banyan Plum gets out of an adjourned imperial court session and rides a palanquin home. He is sitting in the hall when the gatekeeper reports, "Minister Weed has dispatched his steward here." Banyan first summons Arn Tall who later leads Lebron and Leroy into the hall. Lebron and Leroy are kneeling while Arn Tall hands him the letter from Yo Weed. Lebron offers Banyan a present, and Banyan says, "Since you're from the Birch mansion and Minister Weed has put in a good word for you, I shouldn't accept this present. Furthermore, His Majesty had a change of heart yesterday and decided not to punish Commander Birch. However, the reports written by the inspector about Commander Birch's subordinates and relatives were so incriminating even those at the bottom of the pecking order couldn't be ignored." He then orders his aide to bring over the list of names. The ones who will be severely punished are:

Full Rex's clerk Sink Boss 董升, servant Liam Rex 王廉, and deputy officer Yule Blond 黄玉.

Jeer Birch's clerk Hood Grey 卢虎, staff member Shane Birch 杨盛, aides Zoe Fence 韩宗仁 and Honda Pass 赵弘道, deputy officer Chuck Slay 刘成, and relatives Honk Show, Chic Westgate, and Sid Wild 胡四.

These underlings are all scoundrels who bribe local officials to hurt citizens. They are cruel, and they must all be exiled or executed for the countless crimes they have committed.

Lebron is so nervous to see the list he bows down repeatedly and says, "I'm Chic Westgate's servant. I hope Your Highness can kindly spare my master's life."

Arn Tall also kneels and pleads on Westgate's behalf.

Banyan looks at the 500 oz of silver bribed by Lebron just to change one name on the blacklist, which is a piece of cake for him. He then asks his aides to bring over a small table, places the list on it, and changes the name Chic Westgate to Chic West. He accepts the bribe and writes a reply letter to Minister Weed.

Lebron takes leave of Steward Tall, returns to the inn, packs up, and pays the bill. He rushes back to Clearstream Town to see Westgate and describe all the transactions he has conducted in the capital.

Westgate heaves a sigh of relief and says, "Moonie, I was smart enough to bribe the officials as fast as I could!" After two days, he no longer closes his mansion, and the construction of his new garden resumes as he gradually walks more and more around the neighborhood.

One day, Deon is riding his horse along Lion Street when he notices a new drugstore, fully stocked with herbs and drugs, next to Vasie's house. It is quite crowded with many customers. He returns to the mansion and reports to Westgate. Since he does not know Vasie has married Zuke, he just says, "Lady Plum has opened a drugstore with a new business partner."

Westgate does not totally believe Deon.

One day while Westgate is riding his horse on the street, he bumps into Badger Yep and Ceder Thank who then dismount and greet him.

Badger exclaims, "Long time no see, comrade! We've visited your mansion several times, but we dare not call you when we saw the gate tightly shut. It's been so boring these past few days without you. What have you been doing inside your mansion? Have you married your new girlfriend yet? Why haven't you invited us to your wedding?"

Westgate replies, "It's a long story. I got involved in my in-law Honk Show's fiasco, and it took me many days to resolve his problem. That's why my wedding has been postponed."

Badger says, "We didn't know you were in a jam, comrade. Since we've bumped into you today, how can we let you walk away? Why don't you go to Silvie Call's brothel to have a few drinks with us to relieve your stress?" Without waiting for Westgate's response, he and Ceder drag Westgate off to the brothel, accompanied by Deon and Peon.

After spending a day drinking in Silvie Call's brothel, Westgate emerges tipsy from the brothel in the evening. As he rides back home, at the east street corner, he bumps into Mrs. Trot walking hurriedly from the south. He reins in his horse and asks, "Where are you going?"

Mrs. Trot replies, "Lady Plum asked me to go to the monastery to make an offering of incense to the late master. I'm rushing back home now."

Westgate asks drunkenly, "How's Vasie doing at home? I'll speak to her tomorrow."

Mrs. Trot replies, "Why bother asking how she's doing? The wedding banquet she'd prepared for you was eaten by another guy."

"Did she marry someone else?"

"She asked me to deliver the wedding ring to you, but your gate was shut every time I went to your mansion. She had asked you to marry her, but you ignored her. After she married someone else, what can you complain about?"

"Who married her?"

Mrs. Trot then describes how Vasie was possessed by a vixen at midnight and almost died, how Zuke Grass was hired to cure Vasie's depression, how Vasie and Zuke tied the knot afterward, and how Vasie spent 300 oz of silver to help Zuke open a drugstore. While she is telling the story from the beginning to the end, Westgate repeatedly kicks at the stirrup and bellows, "Oh blood and thunder! I wouldn't mind if she married someone else, but she married that midget turtle? What's so special about him?"

Fuming with rage, Westgate gallops back home. As he passes through the inner gate, he sees Moonie, Towie, Goldie, and Lassie jumping ropes in the courtyard. They all return to their rooms when they see Westgate, except Goldie who leans casually against a pillar. Westgate shouts in his drunken rage, "Why are you sluts making so much noise? Why jump-rope for no good reason?" He then kicks Goldie twice, and instead of walking to Moonie's room to take off his clothes, he goes to his studio in the west chamber, orders his servant to make his bed, and sleeps there. He hits his maids and scolds his valets to vent his frustration.

As Westgate's spouses fearfully huddle together without knowing what is going on, Moonie scolds, "Goldie, when you saw him stumble around in a drunken stupor, you should've gone back to your room right away. Why did you laugh so casually in front of him? You annoyed him so much he berated every locust, ant, and grasshopper in his path!"

Towie says, "I could tolerate how he called his spouses slut, but how could he call Lassie a slut? He's so messed up!"

Goldie says, "I'm the easiest to be bullied in this family. He only kicked me when there were three spouses around. What happened to the one who deserved to be kicked?"

Moonie retorts, "So you want him to kick me too? If you didn't deserve it, who deserved it? He chose his concubines in bad taste! I originally wasn't planning to comment on this matter, but I changed my mind when you began talking nonsense."

Since Moonie is annoyed, Goldie tries to explain herself, "Lady, you misunderstood me. Someone somewhere must've annoyed him for some reason and he later substituted me for that person and kicked me as soon as he saw me."

Towie says, "Lady, let's ask the valet in which house Master had a drink today. He was fine when he went out in the morning. Why did he return home in such a bad mood?"

They summon Deon for questioning, and Moonie scolds, "Listen up, you jerk! If you don't tell us the truth, I'll ask the other footmen and valets to hang you up from a hook and have both you and Peon spanked ten times.

Deon responds, "Lady, please don't spank me. Let me tell you the truth. Master and Mr. Yep had a drink in the Call brothel today. Master later bumped into Mrs. Trot at the corner of East Street. Mrs. Trot then told him Lady Plum, who didn't have the patience to wait for Master, married Doctor Grass of Main Street. Master was extremely upset afterward."

Moonie says, "So it was that unabashed slut who married another guy, causing Master to vent his anger at home!"

Deon says, "Lady Plum didn't marry out of her house. It was Doctor Grass who married into her house. She then gave him money to open a drugstore. Master at first didn't believe me when I told him about it."

Towie says, "As a matter of fact, her late husband passed away not too long ago, so she shouldn't have gotten married while observing the mourning period."

Moonie asks, "Why do you care whether she is still observing the mourning period? She's not the only one who rushed to marry again while observing the mourning period. The slut had already been sleeping with her lover all the time, so why did you expect her to be chaste?"

Dear reader, Moonie's statement hit a raw nerve. Towie and Goldie, who had both remarried while observing their mourning periods, return shamefully to their rooms.

Meanwhile, Westgate sleeps in the front chamber at night. He works on the ledger the next day with his son-in-law Jimmy and the custodian Ditcher. He assigns Lejon to guard the main gate.

Lassie spends her time with Moonie and the others in the living quarters in the daytime, and she returns to the front chamber to rest in the evening.

Jimmy supervises the work in the garden every day and dares not enter the central hall without being summoned. His meals are all brought to him from the kitchen by the valets, so Westgate's concubines have not met him yet.

One day, Westgate attends a farewell party for Colonel Greet. During his absence, Jimmy works hard supervising the workers. While chatting with Towie and Cutie, Moonie thinks Jimmy should be treated to dinner as a reward for his challenging work, and she says, "Master said I was too nosy when I tried to help Jimmy. But I feel bad not helping Jimmy. He's been getting up early and sleeping late to work diligently in our mansion. Are you interested in making him feel appreciated?"

Towie replies, "Lady, you oversee this household. If you don't take care of him, who will?"

Moonie then orders the kitchen to prepare good dishes at noon to treat Jimmy to lunch.

Jimmy lets Ditcher supervise the construction work, and he heads straight to the living quarters. He pays his respects to Moonie before he sits down. Jadie serves him tea and then places food and wine on the table.

Moonie says, "You work hard every day to supervise the construction, and that's why we've invited you over here to sit down and relax. Your father-in-law isn't home today, so we're free to treat you to lunch to reward you for your diligence."

Jimmy says, "I'm so glad you appreciate my work. You shouldn't worry about having to reward me though."

Moonie eats for a while and then orders, "Jadie, invite Lassie to sit here."

Jadie says, "Lassie is playing dominoes right now. She'll come over later."

They hear dominoes in the room, and Jimmy asks, "Who's playing dominoes?"

Moonie replies, "Lassie and the maid Flutie are playing dominoes."

Jimmy says, "See how disrespectful she is? She doesn't come when you call her over, but just continues playing in the room."

Lassie presently comes out, sits opposite her husband, and has a drink.

Moonie asks, "Does your husband know how to play dominoes?"

Lassie replies, "He knows a little bit."

Moonie then considers Jimmy a modest son-in-law. She has no idea not only is Jimmy a good dominoes player, but he is also an expert in poetry, backgammon, chess, crossword puzzles, and many other things.

Moonie says, "Since you know how to play dominoes, why don't we go inside and watch the game?"

Jimmy replies, "Lady and Lassie may watch it, but it's not appropriate for me to do so."

Moonie says, "You're my close relative. What is there to worry about?"

Towie is lying on a red blanket on the bed, watching the game. When she sees Jimmy enter the room, she wants to leave.

Moonie says, "Lassie's husband isn't an outsider. You should greet each other." She then says, "Jimmy, she's the third spouse."

Jimmy quickly bows politely, and Towie bows back to him. Moonie, Towie, and Lassie then play dominoes while Jimmy watches from the side.

Goldie opens the portiere and enters the room during the game. She says laughingly, "I was wondering who's here. Now I see it's just Lassie's husband."

Jimmy turns around and is shocked to see Goldie, his lover in his past life, who will be reunited with him. And he is mesmerized.

Moonie says, "She's the fifth spouse. Please greet her, Jimmy."

Jimmy quickly takes a deep bow, and Goldie returns the greeting.

Moonie says, "Come over here, Goldie. The fledgling is defeating the old crow."

Goldie walks over, and with one hand holding the bedpost and the other hand holding a fan made of white gauze, she gives Moonie hints on how to win the dominoes game.

Everyone is excitedly involved in the game when Deon suddenly comes in with a suitcase and says, "Master has returned home."

Moonie quickly urges Jadie to escort Jimmy out the corner gate.

Westgate enters through the main gate. He then goes around the front garden to inspect the work in progress before he goes to Goldie's room. Goldie promptly receives him, takes off his coat, and says, "You saw him off earlier today and now you've returned home early."

Westgate says, "Colonel Greet of the Bureau of Prosecution has just been promoted to chief of New Peace Fortress 新平寨. His friends at the bureau all saw him off in the countryside. I felt obligated to go when they sent me an invitation card."

Goldie says, "I'll ask the maid to serve you wine."

The table is soon full of wine, fruit, and other types of food. Westgate eats and drinks while he talks about the construction of the fenced enclosure in the garden that will soon be completed. He also talks about inviting his relatives and friends for the grand opening and hosting a banquet for them.

Plumie lights the lamp in the evening and leaves the room while Westgate and Goldie go to bed.

Since Westgate got up early, he feels tired, falls asleep after a few drinks, and snores like thunder.

Goldie is unable to fall asleep due to the stifling heat during the night of August 20. She suddenly hears the buzzing of mosquitoes, so she gets up naked, picks up a candle, and attempts to set the mosquitoes near her bed on fire. She then turns around and sees Westgate still sound asleep. Unable to immediately shake him awake, she puts down the candlestick and continues to shake him until he wakes up.

Westgate scolds, "Just go back to sleep, slut! Why are you fooling around here?"

Westgate suddenly remembers something after a while. He asks Plumie to come in and stand next to the bed to serve him wine.

Goldie scolds, "You filthy pervert! When did you acquire the habit of ordering a maid to watch us while we're making love?"

Westgate replies, "Let me tell you something. Vasie and I often did it in the past. She asked her maid Springie to bring over a bottle and serve wine next to her bed. It was so much fun."

Goldie says, "There you go again! Who cares about Vasie? Why even mention that slut's name? She didn't have the patience to wait for you and rushed to marry another guy. While the three of us were jump-roping in the yard, you used me as a punching bag and kicked me when you came home drunk. I then ended up arguing with another person. I'm so easy to be bullied."

"With whom did you argue?"

"Lady Call was very rude to me when you came to the yard that day. She said I shouldn't talk back in front of her and you chose your concubines in bad taste. I'm thinking by not acting like a brown-noser, I ended up having you annoyed at me."

"I wasn't annoyed at you. Comrade Yep dragged me to Silvie Call's brothel for a drink and I later bumped into Mrs. Trot on the road. After she told me the story, I was so mad I blew my top. Vasie has married, of all people, Doctor Grass the thievish midget turtle. Why didn't Jewel Bloom just bite off his pecker? What's so special about him? Not only did she marry him into her house, but she also gave him money to open a drugstore right before my very eyes!"

"And you have the nerve to mention it! What did I tell you last time? The early bird catches the worm. Instead of listening to me, you tried to get Lady Call's permission. Whom can you blame when you shut the stable door after the horse has bolted?"

Goldie's words make Westgate's face turn red, and he snaps, "I let that slut slip through my fingers because I listened to Moonie. I won't communicate with Moonie from now on."

Westgate is so mad at Moonie he no longer speaks to her when he sees her.

Moonie lets Westgate sleep in any concubine's room and does not ask him why he returns late or leaves early. She ignores him when he comes to her room to take things, and just asks her maid to respond to him.

Meanwhile, Goldie feels victorious to have Westgate on her side whenever she argues with Moonie. She dresses herself up and hopes to further seduce Westgate.

Remembering how smart and handsome Jimmy was on the day she first met him, Goldie tries to hook up with him, but she is afraid of Westgate, so she dares not make a move. She dispatches her maid to invite Jimmy over for tea when Westgate is not home, and they sometimes play chess.

When the construction of the fenced enclosure is complete, Westgate's relatives and friends send fruit and gift baskets to congratulate him, and he rewards the construction workers and the other laborers. He treats his guests to lunch in the main lounge until they leave in the afternoon, and then retires to his bedroom to sleep.

Goldie is playing pipa on her bed when Jimmy comes over to her room and asks her for a cup of tea. She asks, "Haven't you eaten enough in the main lounge? Why come over to my room to ask for a cup of tea?"

Jimmy replies, "To tell you the truth, I've been working so hard since midnight I didn't have time to eat anything."

"Where's your father-in-law?"

"He's sleeping in the living quarters."

"Since you haven't eaten anything, I'll ask Plumie to serve you a steamed fruitcake."

There are four dessert dishes on the table before long. Since Goldie is playing the pipa, Jimmy asks, "What musical piece are you playing? Why don't you sing a song for me?"

"My dear Jimmy, I'm not your lover, so how can I sing for you? I'm going to tell on you when your father-in-law comes back."

Jimmy drops to his knees and pleads slyly, "Please take pity on me. I dare not misbehave again."

Goldie stands up and giggles. The young man grows closer to Goldie every day. He often has tea or lunch with her to chat with her.

Moonie treats Jimmy as if he were a son and is completely unaware of his treachery.

Chapter 19. Westgate Punishes Zuke Grass

Prosecutor Fab throws a birthday party during the first week of September in the manor he has just purchased, and he hires four singers and a band to provide entertainment. Westgate spruces himself up at 10 a.m. and rides his horse out, with four valets tailing behind.

Moonie throws a party at home for Cutie, Towie, Snowie, Goldie, and Lassie. She opens the new garden gate to enjoy the view of the flowers, trees, pavilions, and towers inside. The garden has an artificial hill with a real creek. It has places for people to enjoy throughout all the seasons. They can take in the fresh aroma of cypress at Swallow Trip Hall in the spring or view the brilliant lotuses at Creekside Lodge in the summer, or gaze at frosty yellow chrysanthemums from Stacked Emerald Tower in autumn or admire snow-covered white plums from Tryst Den in the winter.

Moonie goes to Cloudy Pavilion 卧雲亭, the garden's tallest pavilion, to play chess with Towie and Cutie. Goldie, Lassie, and Snowie ascend a floral tower, and from their vantage point at the top of the tower, they take in the view of the peonies, begonias, multiflora roses, costuses, bamboos, and pines. Lunch is ready before long. Moonie takes the host's seat and Cutie sits opposite her. Towie, Snowie, Goldie, and Lassie sit in rank order beside Moonie.

Moonie says, "I forgot to invite Jimmy." She then says, "to Jadie, go to the front chamber to invite my son-in-law over."

Jimmy soon arrives and sits next to Lassie. Moonie continues to play chess with Cutie and Lassie after several drinks. Snowie and Towie ascend the tower to enjoy the scenery. Goldie is the only one hanging around the foot of the hill by the lotus pond, and she catches butterflies with a white gauzed fan to entertain herself. She does not know Jimmy is watching her from behind.

Jimmy says, "You don't know how to catch butterflies, Goldie. Let me catch one for you. This butterfly flies up and down in such an unpredictable manner. Don't let it get away."

Goldie turns around, glances at Jimmy, and scolds, "Do you want to die, bozo?"

Jimmy approaches Goldie smilingly and hugs and kisses her. He falls when Goldie pushes him. Little do they know Towie is watching them from the floral tower.

Towie calls, "Come over here, Goldie. I have something to tell you."

Goldie then leaves Jimmy behind and ascends the tower.

After Goldie is gone, Jimmy sadly returns to his room.

Meanwhile, Westgate leaves Prosecutor Fab's manor when the birthday party is over. He trots through South Red-Light District where the rogues all know him. Among them is one named Snake-in-Grass Wart Rash 鲁华, and another named Rat-on-Street Shunt Pull 张胜. They are the good-for-nothings Westgate has helped out in the past. When he sees the two of them panhandling, he reins in his horse to speak to them.

The two rogues quickly come over and ask respectfully, "Tycoon, where are you going at this late hour?"

Westgate replies, "Today is Prosecutor's birthday. He invited me to his party at his manor outside the city. I'd like you to work on an assignment for me."

Wart says, "Tycoon, you've helped us so frequently in the past we're willing to go through fire and water for your sake."

"Since you're willing to help me out, come to my mansion tomorrow and I'll give you instructions."

"Why wait until tomorrow? Please tell us what the problem is."

Westgate tells both rogues how Zuke Grass has taken Vasie Plum away from him, and he whispers, "I need you to avenge this injustice." He then takes 4 oz of silver out of his pocket and says, "Here, use this to buy yourself some drinks. I'll reward you again when you finish the job."

Wart refuses to accept the money and says, "Master, you've already done so many favors for me! If you ask us to go to the East Ocean to yank the horn off an old dragon, or to Mount Grand 华山 in the west to extract the teeth of a fierce tiger, we will do it. This small task is a piece of cake. We don't need the silver."

"If you don't accept the silver, I won't ask you to work on it." He then asks Deon to keep the silver and seems ready to take off.

Shunt stops the horse and says, "Wart, if you don't accept Master's payment, he'll think you're declining the assignment." He receives the silver, kneels to the ground, bows, and says,

"Master, just go back home. Your problem will be completely resolved within two days." He then adds, "I hope in the future you'll help me get a job at the Bureau of Prosecution. Will that be OK?"

Westgate replies, "It shouldn't be difficult."

Dear reader, Westgate later recommends Shunt Pull to work as an aide in Protector Fringe's mansion. You will hear about Shunt Pull again near the end of this novel.

The two rogues take off with the silver and spend it.

Westgate rides back home in the evening. Moonie and the others all go back to their rooms when they see him. Goldie is the only one staying behind the garden fence to clear the picnic table. Westgate does not go to the living quarters but heads straight for the garden. He sees Goldie clearing the picnic table in the pavilion, and asks, "What did you do when I wasn't here?"

Goldie replies smilingly, "Lassie and I opened the garden gate to take in the view. How could I know you'd return so early?"

Westgate says, "Prosecutor Fab was nice enough to hire four singers and four actors to perform at his party today. He only invited five guests, but I worried the return trip might take too long and therefore returned home so promptly."

Goldie takes off Westgate's coat and says, "There's no wine here. Should I ask the maid to serve you wine?"

Westgate orders, "Plumie, clear all the dishes from the table except these two little bowls of fruit and bring over a bottle of wine for me." He is aroused as he sits in a chair and admires Goldie's beautiful dress and accessories. He cuddles and kisses her. Kissing and drinking simultaneously, they loudly smooch away as Plumie serves them wine.

Goldie sits on Westgate's lap, orally transfers the wine in her mouth to Westgate's mouth, then picks up a lotus seed from the table and attempts to hand-feed Westgate.

Westgate says, "Why should I eat this kind of stuff?"

Goldie replies, "You're lucky to eat delicious things delivered by me, darling!" She also places a shelled walnut in her mouth and orally transfers it to his mouth.

After fooling around for a while, Westgate says slyly, "I have something funny to tell you to make you laugh your head off. Doctor Grass, the fellow who has opened a drugstore, will have a fruit store on his face tomorrow."

"You're a devil in disguise. Who knows what crime you'll commit tomorrow!" She then asks, "Is he Doctor Grass who often makes house calls to cure our sick ones? He looks like a modest and polite man who lowers his head whenever he sees us. He looks so pitiful. Why would you mess up someone like him?"

"Appearances can be deceiving. He stares at your pretty little feet when he lowers his head."

"I can't believe he stares at the feet of other people's wives!"

"There's more to his appearance than meets the eye. A neighbor once hired Zuke who had just bought a fish.

"Zuke said, 'Let me bring my fish home before I pay you a visit.'

"The neighbor said, 'I've got an emergency at home, please come over right now.'

"Zuke then followed the neighbor, and when he entered the patient's room, he saw a beautiful sick lady lying in bed. He suddenly remembered his fish while he was taking her pulse. He then hung the fish on the bedpost and asked worriedly, 'Lady, do you have a pussycat down there?'

"It so happened her husband overheard the word pussy. Not surprisingly, he came over and beat the pants off Zuke.

"Not only was Zuke not paid for his services, but his clothes were also torn into pieces before he could escape with his tail between his legs."

Goldie exclaims, "What a pity! It's hard to believe a nerdy guy like him would behave so badly."

"You can't judge a book by its cover. He's a wolf in sheep's clothing."

They continue to tell jokes for a while. When they finish their drinks, the maid clears the picnic table, and they retire to their bedroom.

Let's flash back to two months earlier when Zuke married into Vasie's house:

Zuke gives Vasie dildos, cock rings, vibrators, beads, and magic wands to please her. Little does he know Westgate has been satisfying her with rough sex, not with toys.

Vasie is thoroughly disgusted by Zuke's seemingly impotent behavior, and she uses a rock to smash all his sex toys to smithereens. She scolds, "Your schlong is like a limp eel, and you have the nerve to tease me with all those toys! I used to think you had a nice piece of meat, but it's just like inedible melted wax. You son of a turtle!"

After being scolded in no uncertain terms, Zuke does not know where to put himself. He's been given the boot by midnight and is forced to sleep in his drugstore outside Vasie's house.

Vasie has only Westgate on her mind from then on and forbids Zuke from entering her room. She gradually takes back the money she has invested in Zuke's drugstore.

One day Zuke is sitting dejectedly at the counter of his store when he sees two drunkards stagger in, sit on the bench, and stare at him.

The first drunkard asks, "Do you sell dog manure?"

Zuke replies politely, "Don't tease me. Some stores sell cow manure, but where can you possibly buy dog manure?"

The drunkard replies, "If you don't have dog manure, I'll buy radish powder instead. I'd like to buy 2 oz of it."

Zuke says, "I have only radish slices in my store, and they come from Persia. There's no radish powder."

The other drunkard says, "Don't bother to ask him. He just opened his store a few days ago, so how could he have these two types of drugs? Let's go to Tycoon Westgate's store to buy them."

The first drunkard says, "Let's talk serious business now, Comrade Grass. No more screwing around! You borrowed 30 oz of silver from Comrade Rash when your wife died three years ago, and you owe a lot more now when you include interest. We want you to pay back the loan today. Since you just recently opened this store, we didn't want to be too mean and hurt your feelings right away, so we first chewed the fat for a while when we walked in through your door. But business is business. You'd better pay off your loan."

Zuke stares at them and responds fearfully, "But I didn't borrow any money from him."

The second drunkard asks, "Why would I ask you to pay back the money you didn't borrow? A guilty conscience needs no accuser. Enough with your nonsense!"

Zuke replies, "I know neither your surname nor your first name. How can you ask me for money if I don't even know you?"

The drunkard says, "Comrade Grass, you're mistaken. Neither a borrower nor a lender be, for loan oft loses both itself and friend. Don't forget when you desperately rang bells on the street in the past to sell drugs, it was Comrade Rash who lent you a helping hand, and that was how you got to where you are to-day!"

The other drunkard says, "My name is Wart Rash and I'm going to say once more: You borrowed 30 oz of silver for your wife's funeral. Now, including interest, you must pay me back a total of 48 oz you owe me."

Zuke says nervously, "When did I borrow your money? Even if I borrowed your money, there's got to be a witness."

Shunt Pull says, "I was the witness." He then whips out a document and flashes it in Zuke's face.

Zuke is too upset to keep his cool. He scolds, "Go climb a tree. Don't monkey around with me and throw a monkey wrench into my business?"

Wart Rash angrily punches at Zuke whose nose then bends sideways, and the drugs in the cabinet are scattered onto the street.

Zuke shouts, "How dare you rob my merchandise, thief!" He calls Taffy for help, but after Wart kicks Taffy away, nobody dares come to his rescue.

Shunt lifts Zuke over the counter, blocks Wart's fist, and says, "Comrade Rash, since you've been waiting for such a long time, just give him two more days to get the money. Comrade Grass, what's your take on that?"

Zuke asks, "When did I borrow his money? Even if I did borrow his money, it should be negotiated in a civilized manner. How could he behave like a savage?"

Shunt replies, "You've made your bed, now lie in it. There ain't no such thing as a free lunch. If you behave yourself, I'll ask Comrade Rash to charge you a little bit less interest to make it easier for you to pay him back his money. Why do you think by acting up, he'll let you off easy?"

Zuke replies, "I've heard enough of his nonsense! I'll sue him in court and see who owes whom!"

Shunt exclaims, "There you go again!"

Wart unexpectedly punches Zuke again.

The punch sends Zuke right into a ditch. With his hair hanging loose and his clothes all soiled, he cries foul at the top of his lungs. The headman then comes over and binds him with a rope.

When Vasie hears a commotion in the store, she goes to the portiere, looks outside, and watches the headman tying up and dragging Zuke away. She is so upset she orders Mrs. Trot to take down the drugstore banners and bring back the merchandise, but a lot of herbs and drugs have already been snatched up by the pedestrians. After she shuts down the store, she sits in her house.

Someone has already reported the incident to Westgate who immediately orders his servant to notify the prosecutor to punish the defendant in court the next morning.

Prosecutor Fab begins the court session when the defendant is brought to court the next morning. He looks at the complaint, and asks, "Are you Zuke Grass? Why did you borrow money from him and then insult him? That's despicable!"

Zuke replies, "I don't know this man, and I've never borrowed any money from him. When I tried to reason with him, he kicked and punched me and stole my merchandise."

Prosecutor Fab then orders Wart Rash to come over and asks, "What's your statement?"

Wart Rash replies, "He borrowed money from me for his wife's funeral, but he still hasn't paid me back after three years. When I heard he'd married into another family and started a big business, I asked him to pay me back the money, but he insulted me and accused me of stealing his merchandise. I have the paper that documented the money he's borrowed, and Shunt Pull was the witness. Your Highness, please look at it." He then takes the document out of his pocket and hands it over to Prosecutor Fab who reads it:

Borrower Zuke Grass is a doctor in this town. He has borrowed 30 oz of silver from Wart Rash because he has no money for his wife's funeral, and Shunt Pull is the witness. The monthly interest rate is 3%, and the total amount will be paid the next year. The lender may liquidate the borrower's belongings to ensure the payment.

After reading the document, the prosecutor bangs his fist on the table and says angrily, "Holy mackerel! He still denies it even with this document and witness! And with his super-nerdy and wimpy look, he's got to be guilty!" He then orders, "Use extra-large bats to spank him hard!"

Four officers come over before Zuke can say anything. They push him onto the ground and spank him 30 times, beating his buttocks to a bloody pulp.

The court then dispatches two officers to bring Zuke home to get 30 oz of silver to pay Wart Rash. If he fails to pay the money, he will be brought back to jail. He staggers back home and begs Vasie tearfully for money to pay Wart Rash.

Vasie spits in Zuke's face and scolds, "You shameless turtle! Have you ever earned any money for me? And you're asking me for money instead! If I'd known you're a deadbeat, I wouldn't have married you, you impotent turtle!"

An officer outside who hears Vasie berating Zuke then shouts, "Since Zuke has no money to pay, don't waste our time here. Let's bring him back to jail."

Zuke comes out to pacify the officers and then re-enters Vasie's house and pleads, "Please consider this a 30-oz silver donation to the temple for your good karma. Otherwise, they'll bring me back to court and spank my bloody, pulpy butt, and I'll meet my maker!"

Vasie has no choice but to give Zuke 30 oz of silver so that he can return to court to pay Wart Rash.

After being awarded 30 oz of silver, Wart and Shunt report back to Westgate who then treats them to dinner. They give a detailed account of what transpired, and he says delightedly, "I'm so glad you could help me get my revenge." He refuses to accept the 30 oz of silver Wart tries to hand over to him and says, "Use this money to buy some drinks for yourselves. This is my payment for a job well done. I may need you again in the future."

The two rogues accept the payment, leave the mansion, and spend the money.

Meanwhile, Zuke pays the money, leaves the court, and returns home. However, there is no way Vasie would let him live in her house anymore. She says, "You're not allowed to live here. I'll just treat the 30-oz silver as payment for medical treatment. You'd better move out fast. Fish and guests stink after three days."

Knowing he can no longer stay in Vasie's house, Zuke endures the pain in his spanked buttocks and leaves tearfully. Vasie keeps the herbs and drugs she has invested in the drugstore, and she allows Zuke to keep his original old medicine bag. To shoo Zuke out of the house, Vasie asks Mrs. Trot to splash a bucket of cold water on him.

After sending Zuke away, Vasie keeps thinking about Westgate. She is very remorseful when she hears Westgate has ridden out the storm of his in-law's fiasco. She waits every day for Westgate to visit her.

One day when Deon is riding around town, he trots past Vasie's gate and notices it is closed and her drugstore has apparently closed its doors for good. He returns home and reports what he saw to Westgate.

Westgate says, "I guess that midget turtle was spanked so severely he needs to recuperate at home. It'll probably be half a month before he comes out to reopen his store." He then ceases to think about the matter.

Time passes by and before long, it is September 15, which is Moonie's birthday, and many guests are seated in the hall. Since Westgate does not communicate with Moonie anymore, he visits Olie's brothel, and orders, "Deon, bring the horse home and pick me up in the evening." He invites Badger Yep and Ceder Thank to be his companions. Osmie is also at the brothel, and the two sisters work together to entertain the three clients.

Soon it is evening, and Westgate is answering the call of nature in the back of the building when Deon brings the horse along to pick him up. He asks, "Deon, are there any problems at home?"

Deon replies, "No problems at home. The guests in the lounge have all left, and the tables have been cleared. Lady Call has invited Mrs. Kyle Call over for a chat.

"Mrs. Trot was dispatched by Lady Plum of Lion Street to deliver a birthday present of four trays of fruit, two trays of longevity noodles, one roll of cloth, and one pair of hand-made shoes to Lady Call who then tipped her 0.1 oz of silver, told her Master wasn't home, and didn't invite her to join the party."

Westgate looks at Deon's red face and asks, "Where did you have a drink?"

Deon replies, "Lady Plum asked Mrs. Trot to invite me for a drink just a while ago. I told her I don't drink, but she forced me to have two drinks, and my face became red. She was so remorseful about what she did to you she cried buckets before me. I've told you before about her remorse, but you didn't believe me. When Zuke came out of the Bureau of Prosecution that day, she kicked him out of her house. She deeply regrets how she's treated you, and she still wants to marry you. The emotional wounds have caused her to lose some weight, and she begged me to invite you over and asked me to relay a message back to her."

Westgate says, "The slut still wants to bother me after she married another man! Anyway, I don't have the time to visit her. Just tell her to select a good day to get a palanquin to carry her over to my mansion."

Deon says, "Since she's waiting for me to relay back your words, I'll ask Peon and Pixel to wait for you here."

Westgate says, "I understand. You may leave now."

Deon leaves the brothel and heads straight for Vasie's house.

Vasie is thrilled to hear the good news from Deon, and says, "What a nice brother you are! I'm so glad you put in a good word for me to help me accomplish this task." She then goes to the kitchen and personally prepares various dishes to treat Deon to dinner and says, "I don't have enough servants here. Please come tomorrow and help Taffy supervise the workers to move my furniture over to your mansion." She hires four porters to move her belongings over the next four days.

Westgate does not inform Moonie of the situation and just piles Vasie's belongings into the newly built floral tower.

Westgate dispatches a large palanquin on September 20. It is decorated with a roll of satin and four pairs of lanterns, and it is escorted by Deon, Peon, Pixel, and Lesing, to carry Vasie into his mansion in the afternoon. Vasie asks Mrs. Trot and Taffy to take care of her house before she boards the palanquin.

Westgate does not go to Vasie's house. He stays in his new garden to await Vasie's arrival.

Vasie waits for quite a while when she arrives at Westgate's mansion, but nobody comes out to receive her. Towie goes to Moonie's room and says, "Sister, you're in charge of this mansion. Now Vasie is at the gate, if you don't welcome her, won't Master blame you? Master is sitting in the garden while Vasie's palanquin is at the gate. Without anyone going out, how can she come in?"

Moonie is too upset to go out to receive Vasie, but she fears not doing so may anger Westgate. After some hesitation, she decides to go out and receive Vasie.

Vasie heads straight for the new building with a precious vase in her hands. The two maids, Springie and Stitchie, have already set up her room properly, waiting for Westgate to enter in the evening. However, Westgate is still too upset to enter her room.

Moonie invites Vasie to her room the next day and establishes her as the sixth spouse of Westgate.

Vasie meets the relatives and friends during a three-day banquet, but Westgate just does not go to her room.

On the first night, Westgate goes to bed in Goldie's room, and Goldie says, "Vasie is your new spouse, and on her first night here, you're leaving her by herself in her room?"

Westgate replies, "That slut still needs to be tamed. I'll let her hang in there for two days before I go to her room."

After the banquet ends on the third day, Westgate still does not go to Vasie's room but just sleeps in Towie's room.

Since Westgate has not yet entered her room despite her third night at his mansion, Vasie sends her two maids out. Feeling completely distraught, she weeps uncontrollably, stands on her bed, and hangs herself with a stocking.

A maid notices the lamp in the room has burnt out. As she goes back to replenish the candle, she suddenly sees Vasie hanging from the bed, and she is frightened out of her wits. She runs out and cries, "Plumie, Madam Plum has hanged herself!"

Goldie rushes to Vasie's room and sees Vasie, dressed in red clothes, hanging from the bed. She and Plumie cut the noose loose to save Vasie.

They perform chest compressions on Vasie until she regains consciousness and coughs up some saliva. Goldie then orders Plumie to fetch Westgate.

Meanwhile, Westgate is drinking in Towie's room and is not ready to sleep yet. Towie says, "Master, you married her into this mansion but haven't gone into her room for three days. Won't she feel bad? I'm really bothered by this. Why don't you spend tonight with her?"

Westgate replies, "I'll wait three days before I visit her. That slut thinks the grass is always greener on the other side of the fence. The more I think about it, the more pissed off I get. Since I've been so close to you ever since your husband passed away, I always tell you what's on my mind. What irritates me is the way she let Doctor Grass marry into her house to make me feel I'm no match for him! And now she thinks she can come back to me just like that?"

"You have a point. She shouldn't upset you."

They suddenly hear people banging on the inner gate while they are chatting. Towie orders Orchie to find out what is happening. Orchie later comes back and exclaims, "Madam Plum hanged herself in her room!"

Towie says anxiously, "Master, I asked you to visit her, but you didn't listen to me. We now have this problem!" She then picks up a lantern and goes to Vasie's room. Moonie and Cutie also go to Vasie's room when they hear about the incident, and they see Goldie lending Vasie some support. Towie asks, "Have you fed her some ginger soup, Goldie?"

Goldie replies, "I fed her some after I rescued her from the stocking wrapped around her neck."

Vasie makes choking noises in her throat for a while before she begins to sob. Moonie and the others feel relieved when they can hear her cry. After comforting her, they return to their rooms to rest. It is not until the next day at noon that she drinks some porridge.

Westgate says, "Don't be fooled by that slut who feigns death to scare us. I won't let her off easy. I'll go to her room this evening and personally watch her hang herself before I believe it. Otherwise, I'll give her a good beating. That thievish slut takes me for granted!"

They all worry for Vasie when they hear him talk tough.

Westgate takes a horsewhip and goes to Vasie's room in the evening. Towie and Goldie order Plumie to close the door and not let anyone in. They all stand silently outside in a corner to eavesdrop on the drama.

Meanwhile, Westgate enters the room. Vasie, lying prostrate in bed and crying, does not get up and he is not pleased. He first sends the two maids out. He then sits in a chair, points at her, and scolds, "Slut, if you felt guilty, why did you come to my house? Why hang yourself instead of staying with that midget turtle? Who invited you here? I haven't buried you yet, so why are you crying like a baby? I've never seen anyone hang herself before. I'd like to watch you hang yourself today." He then tosses a rope in front of Vasie and asks her to hang herself.

Vasie remembers Zuke Grass saying Westgate is a wife-beating champion and the nemesis of women's liberation. She ponders what kind of bad karma she had in her past life makes her jump out of the frying pan into the fire. She is so distressed she cries even more despondently.

Westgate angrily orders her to get out of bed, take off her clothes, and kneel. When she refuses to do so, he drags her onto the floor and whips her twice. She then fearfully takes off her clothes and kneels on the floor. He sits down and says, "I told you to wait for a while because I had problems at home. Why did you hurriedly marry Doctor Grass instead of obeying me? I wouldn't mind if you'd married someone else, but what's so special about that midget turtle? You married him into your house, and even gave him money to open a drugstore to take away my business!"

"I know it's too late for regrets. I've been hallucinating because you didn't come to see me. Royalty High's garden is behind my house, and a vixen frequently transformed herself into your clone at midnight to suck out my energy and disappeared when the rooster crowed at dawn. If you don't believe me, you can ask Mrs. Trot and my two maids to verify this fact. Mrs. Trot invited Doctor Grass to see me by the time I was almost sucked to death, and I fell for his con game. He told me you'd gone to the capital because you had problems at home, and that left me with no choice but to accept him. I didn't know he's a deadbeat who should've been sent to the guillotine? After the creditors came and beat him up at his door, he was brought to court. I then wasted a few oz of silver and kicked him out right away."

Westgate asks, "Why did you ask him to submit a complaint accusing me of taking your properties and then have the nerve to come to my mansion recently?"

Vasie replies, "I never did that. I'd die a thousand deaths first!"

Westgate says, "Even if you sued me, I wouldn't be scared. The way you used your money to swap husbands pissed me off. To tell you the truth, the two fellows who beat up that doctor were my henchmen who played a con game on him to bring him to his knees. They can also easily hang you out to dry."

Vasie says, "I know you have a bag of tricks. Please take pity on me. I'd rather die than continue to stay in my former house, which is like no man's land."

After letting off some steam, Westgate asks, "Let me ask you something, you little slut. How do I compare with Doctor Grass?"

"How can he be compared with you? You're above the 33rd level of the Sky, and he's below the 99th level of the Underworld. You're an eloquent gentleman who fights for justice, has deep pockets, wears the best clothes, and is like the lord of the world. The delicacies you consume from your cornucopia are precious items he could never possibly see even if he could live for several hundred years. You're the only medication to cure my illness. Your Midas touch makes me think of nobody else but you—all day and all night."

Westgate is overjoyed by the flattery. He puts down his whip and helps Vasie up. After she puts on her clothes, he cuddles her and says, "I couldn't have said it better myself, honey! That guy is indeed a piece of crap."

Chapter 20. Vasie With Westgate's Spouses

Meanwhile, Goldie and Towie stand at the corner door, awaiting news of what has transpired between Westgate and Vasie. Since the door is closed, Goldie pulls Towie over, and they both peer through a crack in the door. They can see the lamp in the room but cannot hear the conversation inside.

Goldie whispers, "We're not like Plumie who has the ears of a fox."

Plumie then goes to the window and eavesdrops for a while. When she comes back, Goldie softly asks her about what has happened inside the room, and she replies, "Master ordered her to take off her clothes and kneel. When she refused to take off her clothes, he lashed her twice with his horsewhip."

Goldie asks, "After he lashed her, did she take off her clothes?"

Plumie replies, "When she saw Master in fury, she quickly took off her clothes and knelt on the floor. Master is now asking her some questions."

Towie, fearing Westgate may hear them, whispers, "Let's go over there." She then tugs on Goldie's arm, and they head over to the west corner door.

On September 20, the moon has just risen in the sky. Goldie cracks melon seeds as she chats with Towie. Plumie is the only maid who has been assigned by Westgate to serve him, so they wait for Plumie to come out to tell them more news.

Goldie says, "Towie, before he sleeps with her, he first gives her a few lashes. He's such a heartless man. He takes advantage of her and squeezes money out of her because she's a widow. He knows how to tame a woman by first beating her up. I've been very careful in serving him and still couldn't avoid shedding quite a few tears! Since you've been here for quite a while, you should know his character!"

While they are chatting, they hear the door crack open when Plumie comes out and goes to the kitchen.

Plumie does not expect Goldie to call in the dark, "Where are you going, dummy?"

Plumie smiles and continues to walk on.

Goldie says, "Come over here, dummy! Why run away when I want to ask you a question?"

Plumie then stays put and replies, "She cried and talked a lot with Master. Master was satisfied with her explanation and helped her up. He ordered her to put on her clothes and asked me to set up a table. I'm now going to the kitchen to get some wine."

Goldie exclaims, "He's such a bullshit artist! It was blood and thunder when he entered her room, but then he was all mouth and no trousers afterward! I'm not surprised. Go ahead and get his wine. By the way, that room should be serviced by Sprintie and Stitchie. Why do you substitute them?"

Plumie replies, "Master selected me, and I had no choice but to obey him!" She chuckles as she runs away.

Goldie says, "My maid is slow as molasses whenever I ask her to do some work. But when there's a chance to brownnose him, she runs as fast as her legs can carry her! He already has two other maids assigned to work in that room. Plumie has no business replacing them!"

Towie says, "Same here! My maid Orchie drags her feet whenever I ask her to do needlework. But she takes off like a bat from hell whenever Master asks her to do some monkey business!"

Flutie suddenly comes out from behind them while Towie is speaking, and says, "I've come to pick you up."

Towie exclaims, "You scared me, bitch!" She then asks, "Does Lady Call know you've come here?"

Flutie replies, "I waited until she went to sleep before I came here to look around. I just saw Plumie go to the kitchen to get some wine and fruit." She then asks, "What happened when Master went to Madam Plum's room?"

Goldie replies, "It's an interesting case of chickens coming home to roost."

Flutie then asks Towie to elaborate, and Towie gives her a detailed account of what has transpired.

Flutie asks, "Did he order her to take off her clothes and lash her five times with the horsewhip?"

Towie replies, "Master lashed her because she refused to kneel."

Flutie asks, "Was she lashed with or without clothes on? How could her delicate skin withstand the lashes?"

Towie replies smirkingly, "Don't worry your pretty little head about it!"

During their conversation, Plumie brings back a bottle of wine and Jadie carries over a box of desserts. As these two maids head straight for Vasie's room, Goldie says, "After you deliver this stuff, ask their own maids to serve them. I still need you to serve me!"

Plumie walks smilingly into the room with Jadie. They put down the wine bottle and desserts and then come out. The maids then answer Towie's and Goldie's questions, and the four of them leave.

Springie and Stitchie stay behind to serve Westgate and Vasie who express their love for each other and spend the whole night together.

Vasie gets up the next morning and combs her hair in front of the mirror. Springie brings over four vegetable dishes, a plate of braised pigeon, a plate of biscuits, ham, fish, and two bowls of rice. Vasie drinks half a cup of wine with Westgate and says, "Springie, bring me the silver bottle of wine left over from yesterday." She drinks two more cups of wine, grooms herself, and then opens a trunk of valuables for Westgate to look at. She shows him the 100 western pearls she has brought from Regent Beam's mansion. She also takes out the late eunuch's gold-plated hat ornament, and it weighs 0.48 oz on the scale. She wants Westgate to ask a silversmith to make a pair of earrings out of it. She also takes out a 9 oz golden hairclip and asks, "Does Lady Call have this kind of hair clip?"

"She has two or three silver hairclips, but not this kind."

"I don't want to wear this. Please take it to the silversmith to smash it and make an ornament with nine phoenixes such that each phoenix has a pearl in its mouth. As for the remaining gold, make a Bodhisattva hairclip as the one Lady Call wears."

Westgate takes the jewelry, combs his hair, puts on his coat, and is just about to go out when Vasie says, "Since nobody is living in my house over there, you should take care of it. Assign a servant to guard it so my valet Taffy can come here to serve me. I worry Mrs. Trot is too old to stay alone over there."

"I understand your concerns." Westgate puts the two pieces of jewelry in his pocket and goes out. When he gets to the east corner door, he unexpectedly bumps into Goldie who asks, "Where are you going? I bump into you as soon as I come out!"

Westgate replies, "I have some business to take care of."

Goldie says, "Come over here, bozo! Why are you in such a rush? I have something to tell you."

Westgate listens to her earnest request and follows her into her room. Feeling something heavy in his pocket, she asks, "What's in your pocket? Take it out for me to see."

"It's my silver."

Goldie does not believe Westgate. She puts her hand inside his pocket, finds a golden hairclip, and says, "This is her hairclip. Where are you taking it?"

"She asked me to take it to a silversmith, smash it, and make two ornaments out of it."

"How much does this hairclip weigh? What do you want to make out of it?"

"This hairclip weighs 9 oz. She wants it to be made into a nine-phoenix ornament and a Bodhisattva hairclip like the one Moonie wears."

"The nine-phoenix ornament can't weigh more than 3.5 oz of gold. And I estimate the hairclip Lady Call wears is worth 1.6 oz. You'd better make the same nine-phoenix ornament for me with the leftover gold."

"But the new ornaments have to be solidly constructed."

"Even if they are solidly constructed, there should still be 2 or 3 oz of gold left over."

"You never miss a chance to take advantage of others!"

"You'd better remember what I said or else I'll nag you to death."

Westgate puts the hairclip back in his pocket. He chuckles and is ready to leave when Goldie says teasingly, "Your con game was successful!"

"What con game are you talking about?"

"The way you lashed her and wanted her to hang herself yesterday was nothing but sound and fury to me, but it was enough to make her offer you this golden hairclip today to pacify you. You're such a snake oil salesman!"

"Enough with your nonsense, slut!" Westgate then leaves.

Meanwhile, Moonie is chatting with Towie and Cutie in her room when they suddenly hear Peon calling for Leroy who has disappeared. Moonie opens the portiere and asks, "Why are you looking for him?"

Peon replies, "Master is urgently waiting for Leroy."

Moonie says, "I've dispatched him to work on an assignment."

It so happens Moonie sent Leroy to Nun Rex's 王姑子 convent in the morning to deliver alms of incense, oil, and rice.

Peon says, "I'll report to Master that Lady has dispatched him to work on another assignment."

Moonie scolds, “Go ahead and tell on me if you want to, punk!”

Peon is too frightened to say a word as he goes outside.

While the other concubines are around, Moonie says, “If I open my mouth, he says I’m nosy. But if I shut up, his mistakes worry me. After dragging the woman here, he should sell her house. Why should he waste his time taking care of it? Since Mrs. Trot’s already in that house, just send an unmarried valet to sleep there. Does he think that house has legs and can run away? Why ask Leroy and his wife to go there? Leroy’s wife is prone to illness, and if she falls ill there, who’ll take care of whom?”

Towie replies, “Lady, I’ll put in my two cents’ worth. Although you don’t get along with Master, the valets have no choice but to act as his running dogs. It may look stupid for Master to be fooling around these past two days, but in my humble opinion, why not let him off easy?”

Moonie says, “Funny you should ask. I never quarreled with him. Since he threw a fit for no good reason, he shouldn’t expect me to apologize. Behind my back, he says I’m not virtuous. But how unvirtuous am I? It wasn’t until he acquired five concubines in this mansion that he discovered I’m not virtuous enough! As the saying goes, ‘Advice most needed is least heeded.’ It was for his own good when I first stopped him from marrying this latest concubine. The way he ate Jesse Bloom out of house and home and spouse, no official can ever cover up for him, not to mention Vasie was still observing the mourning period when he wanted to marry her, and he took me for a fool. Instead of staying at home, he goes to various brothels every day, and all he does is sweet-talk every woman he encounters. So how can an honest woman like me argue with him? Old habits die hard, and good medicine tastes bitter. Since I still have my three meals a day, I might as well be a grass widow here. I couldn’t care less about what he’s doing.”

Moonie’s tirade makes Towie and the others feel uneasy.

Vasie, beautifully dressed, comes into Moonie’s room soon afterward to offer tea to everyone. She is accompanied by Springie holding a silver vase and Stitchie holding a tea box.

Moonie asks Jadie to pull up a chair for Vasie. Snowie joins them later on. Goldie, the talkative concubine, is the first one to say after tea, “Come over and pay Lady Call your respects, Vasie. To tell you the truth, Lady and Master haven’t been getting along because of you, and I just spent some time to put in a good word for you. You should throw a party to help Lady and Master call a truce next time."

Vasie says, "Thanks for giving me the heads-up." She then walks gracefully in front of Moonie and bows down four times.

Moonie says, "Goldie was just kidding you, Vasie!" She then says, "Goldie, I've already taken an oath I wouldn't touch him with a ten-foot pole for the next 100 years."

No one dares bring up that topic from then on.

Goldie sees Vasie's golden hair clip shaped like insects and says, "Vasie, you shouldn't use this insect-shaped hairclip that doesn't hold your hair too well. Why don't you use one like the Bodhisattva hairclip Lady Call wears? It has solid branches."

Vasie replies, "I've asked a silversmith to make a similar one."

After Vasie returns to her room, Westgate visits her and tells her he has asked Silversmith Gaze to work on the ornaments.

Vasie says, "I already have Mrs. Trot to take care of my house. You may ask your valets to take turns living there. Since Lady Call said Leroy's wife is prone to illness, you shouldn't send Leroy over there."

Westgate says, "I didn't know that." He then summons Peon and says, "You and Taffy take turns every other day to live in the house on Lion Street."

Westgate throws a post-wedding party on the 25th and hires four songbirds and some actors to provide entertainment. Jewel Bloom and Kyle Call sit at the first table, Deuce Call and In-law Sink 沈姨夫 sit at the second table, Badger Yep and Ceder Thank sit at the third table, Remnant Bless and Gotcha Heir sit at the fourth table, Seizure Oft and Dangler Call sit at the fifth table, and Leisure Cloud and Leech White sit at the sixth table. Westgate sits at the main table, and seated at his sides are Jason Aide, Ditcher Lithe, and Son-in-law Jimmy Show. Olie Plum, Silvie Call, Dearie Boss, and Golden Fence arrive in palanquins at noon and sit in Moonie's room.

The guests are invited into the newly-built fenced enclosure for tea. After everyone has arrived, the banquet begins in the main lounge. Mick Plum 李铭 and Wade Call, the two minstrels, are the first to sing and play instruments, followed by the four songbirds.

Badger, sitting at the banquet table, starts speaking: "For today's banquet, may I ask the bride to come out and pay her respects to the seniors. Although I'm insignificant, Jewel Bloom, Kyle Call, Deuce Call, and In-law Sink are the seniors here."

Westgate says, "My concubine is ugly and should be exempt from paying her respects to you."

Ceder says, "With all due respect, comrade, if it were not for the sake of your concubine, why would we come here? Not to mention the presence of Comrade Jewel Bloom who was your friend and is now your relative. She shouldn't be so shy as to hide from us."

Westgate says, "Enough with your nonsense!" However, unable to withstand the pressure, he orders Deon to go to the living quarters to invite Vasie over.

Deon returns later and says, "She says she's not coming."

Badger says, "You bone-chewing puppy, you didn't go to the living quarters at all! And you try to fool me. If you don't swear you're telling the truth, I'll go there to fetch her myself."

"I dare not fool you. You can go there and ask her yourself."

"You think I dare not go there? This garden is so breathtakingly beautiful. I might as well stroll along and drag all the concubines out."

"The bulldog in our house is ferocious. It can bite something off your lower body."

Badger ostentatiously leaves the banquet table, playfully kicks Deon twice, and says with a smile, "You know how to hurt my feelings, puppy! You'd better make her come here or else I'll spank you 20 times."

The guests and the four songbirds all burst out into laughter.

Deon stays put and glances at Westgate.

Westgate has no choice but to ask Deon to come over and say, "Tell Vasie to dress up and come out."

Deon goes to the living quarters, and a while later he invites Westgate to come for Vasie who has Goldie and Towie help spruce her up. The four songbirds play their instruments as they escort Vasie to the lounge covered with rugs.

Vasie, dressed elegantly, walks like a moon fairy who has just left the moon palace. They all get up and greet her as she pays them her respects.

Meanwhile, Towie, Goldie, and Cutie accompany Moonie to the area behind the partition of the lounge to listen to people chatting in the banquet. As they listen to songs such as *Perfect Couple* and *Happily Ever After*, Goldie says, "Lady, a concubine shouldn't sing these kinds of songs. If she and Westgate are a perfect couple, where do you fit in this mansion?"

Although Moonie is easygoing, it is hard not to be annoyed by Goldie's comments, especially since Badger, Ceder, and the other sycophants are so eager to praise Vasie and say, "You're the most beautiful girl on Earth! The other girls are no match for you! You're so virtuous, gentle, and graceful I can never find another girl like you in this world! I can die with no regrets after seeing you only once today!"

Since the four songbirds know Vasie is rich, they all flatter her no end.

Moonie returns to her room gloomily. She does not bother to look at Deon and Peon carrying a present of coins and satin rolls, but just scolds, "Take the present somewhere else, jerks! Why bring it to my room?"

Deon replies, "Master ordered us to deliver the present here."

Moonie then orders Flutie to put the present on her bed.

Kyle Call, having eaten enough at the banquet table, goes to Moonie's room. Moonie quickly bows to her brother.

Kyle says, "Your sister-in-law visited you yesterday and when she returned home, she told me you and my brother-in-law don't talk to each other anymore. I was planning to visit you, and unexpectedly, my brother-in-law invited me here today. When it comes to relationships, it's easier to pull down than to build up. Dumb guys are afraid of their wives, while virtuous women are afraid of their husbands. A woman is expected to be obedient and virtuous. Sister shouldn't interfere with his actions from now on. Why not express your virtue?"

Moonie says, "My virtue upsets him. Now he has a rich concubine, he looks down on his wife, who comes from a poor official family as if I were his late wife. Don't worry about him. No matter how he treats me, I can still stand on my own feet." She cries after expressing her feelings.

Vasie gives each songbird a gold-threaded face towel and 0.5 oz of silver when the guests leave in the evening, and they all go home happily. Westgate stays in Vasie's room for many nights. The other concubines do not mind as much as Goldie.

Goldie is so jealous she spreads rumors against Vasie when she is with Moonie and spreads rumors against Moonie when she is with Vasie.

Vasie is unaware of Goldie's deception and continues to treat Goldie as her sister.

After Vasie married into Westgate's family, Westgate's assets increased tremendously with several successful business transactions, and his mansion is now fully renovated. His barns are full and he has a big herd of horses and donkeys and many more servants. Taffy, the valet Vasie brought over, is renamed Xylo. Westgate also acquires two new valets: one is named Leon 来安, and the other is named Chessy 棋童. He selects four maids, viz. Goldie's Plumie, Moonie's Flutie, Vasie's Springie, and Towie's Orchie, dressed in the same uniform, to practice musical instruments and singing in the west chamber of the front lounge under the musical direction of Cutie's brother, Mick Plum. Plumie learns pipa, Flutie learns zither, Springie learns fiddle, and Orchie learns spike fiddle. Mick Plum's monthly salary is 5 oz of silver with free meals.

Westgate invests 2000 oz of silver in a pawn shop. He assigns Ditcher to manage the ledgers and inventories. He also assigns Jason to supervise the drugstore and appraise the items in the pawnshop. Herbs and drugs are stored on the top floor of Goldie's building. Shelves are built on the top floor of Vasie's building to store pawned items of the pawnshop. Son-in-law Jimmy has the keys to those top-floor rooms to retrieve items. There are many monetary transactions taking place every day.

Jimmy gets up early and sleeps late every day. He carries the keys and works with the employees to take care of the cashiers and records everything clearly in the ledger. Westgate is very impressed by him and one day while they are eating at the same table in the front lounge, he says, "Son-in-law, your father should be proud of you for being such a good businessman, and you're someone I can depend on. As the saying goes, 'The son-in-law is as good as your son if you don't have a son.' After I pass away in the future, you and my daughter will inherit my property."

Jimmy says, "Unfortunately, the imperial court ruled against my family, and it caused me to be far from my parents. I'm so grateful my father-in-law can make good use of me even though I won't be able to fully return the favor. Since I'm young, I hope you can forgive the many mistakes I've made. How can I expect any more than what I deserve?"

Westgate is very pleased with Jimmy who is so eloquent and smart, so he delegates many major and minor household tasks to Jimmy who becomes the communications and hospitality director. He has no idea Jimmy is a wolf in sheep's clothing.

Time goes by fast. One day during the last week of December, Westgate attends a party of his friend Seizure Oft. The party ends early, and it begins to snow heavily just when Badger Yep, Ceder Thank, Remnant Bless, and Westgate get out of Seizure Oft's house.

Badger says, "You haven't seen Olie in a long time, comrade. Since it's snowing now, instead of going home, we should visit her."

Remnant says, "Badger has a point. You've been paying her a monthly fee of 20 oz of silver. You give her too much free time when you don't visit her."

The three comrades manage to persuade Westgate to go to the brothel on East Street. It is almost evening when they arrive at Olie's place. The maid is sweeping the floor and the lamps have been lit. The bawd and Osmie come out to greet them, and then invite them to sit in four armchairs.

The bawd says, "When Olie visited your mansion, Madam Plum gave her a face towel and tips. She's very thankful."

Westgate says, "I couldn't socialize with her that day. I let her leave when the guests left."

The maid puts food and wine on the table while they are drinking tea.

Westgate asks, "Why don't I see Olie?"

The bawd replies, "Olie has been waiting for Tycoon, but Tycoon hasn't shown up for quite some time. Today's her aunt's birthday, so she rode a palanquin to attend the party."

Dear reader, in this world, the ones who value money the most are priests, monks, and whores, and they are more interested in communicating with the rich than with the poor. The truth is, Olie did not go to celebrate her aunt's birthday. Since Westgate has not shown up lately, she has received a new client named Satchel Mann 丁双桥, the son of a silk clothing merchant of Sailshire 杭州. Satchel has just sold 1000 oz worth of silk, and his father does not know he is spending his time in a brothel. He has given the brothel 10 oz of silver and two suits made of Sailshire silk to sleep with Olie for two nights. Satchel is drinking with Olie in her room when Westgate unexpectedly arrives, so the bawd asks Olie to take Satchel to a quiet room in the third building at the back of the brothel.

Westgate believes the bawd and says, "Since Olie is not home, let's have a drink here. I'll wait for her."

To entertain Westgate, the bawd serves a lot of food and Osmie sings several songs. While they are having fun, Westgate needs to go to the back building to take a leak, and it so happens he hears people laughing in the east side room. He goes over there, peeks through the window, and sees Olie drinking with a young man in the room. He angrily storms back to the front building, kicks down the table, and breaks all the plates and cups. He then orders his four valets, Peon, Deon, Pixel, and Xylo, to smash the windows and tear down the portieres of Plum brothel. Badger, Ceder, and Remnant cannot stop the rampage.

Westgate vows he will find Olie and her new boyfriend and tie them up.

Satchel is a timid man. When he hears the commotion outside, he hides under the bed and pleads, "Save my life, Olie!"

Olie says, "Psst! My mom can take care of this. Do not go out no matter what."

When the bawd sees Westgate act up, she walks calmly with a cane towards him.

Westgate shouts, "You're so unfair, bawd! You let her dump her old flame and switch to a new lover. I've spent at least 1000 oz of gold in your brothel, and all I get in return is fake love."

The bawd responds, "Tycoon, business is business. Since you haven't shown up for quite some time, I had to receive a new client for Olie, the breadwinner. You're acting up for no good reason. Think about it. She's neither your wife nor your concubine."

Westgate is so enraged by the bawd's refutation he almost beats her up. Luckily, Badger, Ceder, and Remnant manage to drag him away in time. After the rampage, he finds his way back home through the blizzard, vowing never to set foot in that brothel again.

Before our reader proceeds to the appendix section, we would like to clarify that this is only 1 of the 6 formats of our *Plum Blossoms in a Golden Vase* translation. Among our 6 formats are large print ones for readers with slightly impaired vision, and unabridged ones for advanced study:

Paperback	5 volumes	
Large print	5 volumes	
Kindle ebook	5 volumes	
Abridged paperback	1 volume	most popular
Abridged large print	1 volume	
Abridged Kindle ebook	1 volume	

You may also be interested in our other translations:

Journey to the Western Sky 西游记
Red Tower Dream 红楼梦
Marsh Warrior Legend 水浒传
Three Kingdom Epic 三国演义
Scholarly Journal 儒林外史
Journey of the Lamer 老残游记

Please visit our website www.TranslatedClassics.com which will direct you to the exact Amazon.com webpages where you can learn more about, or buy, any of our translated novels.

Appendix 1-A. Glossary

The words abbey, monastery, monk, priest, etc. may seem too mundane to be listed in a glossary, but there are two dominant religions in China, so some of these words refer to the Taoist clergy while other words refer to the Buddhist clergy. This glossary also tries to explain the differences between God, heaven, and hell of many Western religions and the deva, Bodhisattva, Sky, and Underworld Prisons of many Eastern religions. In the political sector, the difference between a chancellor and a minister, and a prefect and an inspector, can be confusing, and in the academic sector, there are scholars, savants, laureates, and littérateurs who need to be differentiated from one another. This glossary is also an attempt to point out many mistranslations made over the years by other translators who may not fully comprehend the Chinese historical or mythological differences between words such as alce vs unicorn, rocket vs cannon, continents vs archipelagic islands, etc.

abbey 观: A large Taoist temple.
abbot 长老: A senior monk who oversees a monastery.
acolyte 道童: A young Taoist student.
alce 麒麟: A mythical fiery creature with a lion's body and is considered the king of beasts. The Chinese alce has a dragonish head while the Western alce has an aquiline head. It has often been mistranslated as a unicorn, but a unicorn resembles a horse, and we all know the lion, not the horse, is the king of beasts.
altar boy 小道童: A Taoist boy.
apprentice 沙弥: A young Buddhist disciple.
arhat 罗汉: An enlightened Buddhist of lower rank than a Bodhisattva.
bishop 真人: A high-ranking celestial priest.
Bodhisattva Compassion 观音菩萨: One of the Four Great Bodhisattvas who saves people from suffering and disasters. She lives on an island in the South Sea.
Bodhisattva Defender 韦驮菩萨: The bodhisattva who defends Buddhism.
Bodhisattva Land 地藏菩萨: One of the Four Great Bodhisattvas. The Ten Underworld Kings report to him. He lives in Aqua-Cloud Palace 翠云宫.
Bodhisattva Meditation 普贤菩萨: One of the Four Great Bodhisattvas. He lives on Mount Lofty 峨眉山.

Bodhisattva Wisdom 文殊菩萨: One of the Four Great Bodhisattvas. He lives on Mount Five-Terrace 五台山.
bodhisattva 菩萨: A compassionate enlightened Buddhist.
Buddha Kindness 弥勒笑佛: A smiling, potbellied buddha whose statue can often be seen in Buddhist temples.
Buddha Lantern 燃灯古佛: An ancient buddha who has been in existence for many kalpas.
Buddha Light 阿弥陀佛. A buddha often invoked in Buddhists' greetings and prayers because he helps people get reborn in the Western Paradise of his Pure Land 净土.
Buddha Medicine 药师琉璃佛: A buddha who lives in a crystal world.
Buddha Supreme 如来佛祖: A buddha known as Shakyamuni 释迦牟尼佛 or Siddhartha Gautama who preached Buddhism on Earth 2,500 years ago.
buddha 佛: An enlightened Buddhist with great wisdom.
bunch of coins 弔钱/贯钱: A thousand coins, each with a hole in its center, tied together and worth about 0.4 oz of silver.
butler 总管: The top servant of a mansion.
Capital Done 成都: The capital of the Western State 西蜀 of the Eastern Han dynasty.
Capital East 东都/洛阳: The capital of the Eastern Han dynasty.
Capital North 北京/北平/燕京: Known as Beijing but mistransliterated as Peking in the old days, it is the capital of the People's Republic of China and many ancient dynasties.
Capital South 南京/金陵/秣陵/建业: The capital of the Eastern State 东吴 of the Eastern Han dynasty.
Capital West 西京/长安/西安/京兆: The capital of the Western Han dynasty.
Cardinal Primordial 元始天尊: Trinity's first cardinal. He lives on the 35th level of the Sky.
Cardinal Spiritual 灵宝道君: Trinity's second Cardinal. He lives on the 34th level of the Sky.
Cardinal Ultimate 太上老君: Trinity's third cardinal. He lives on the 33rd level of the Sky. Also known as Laozi 老子, he preached Taoism on Earth 2,500 years ago.
cardinal: The highest celestial priest. There are three of them, collectively known as Trinity, and they live in Outer Space.
Central Plains 中原: The area of River-South 河南, southern River-North 河北, southern Mount-West 山西, and western Mount-East 山东.

chancellor 丞相: One of the three highest officials who report to the king or emperor.
city 城: A fortified subdivision of a prefecture or a shire where the prefect or sheriff resides. Like the European castle, it is surrounded by high walls and a moat and there are gates on its four sides for citizens to enter or exit the city via drawbridges.
commissioner 撫臺: A high official who governs a region.
concubine 妾: The secondary wife of a nobleman, the tertiary wife of a prince, or the quaternary wife of a king. A concubine in a mansion is considered a servant of the lady or senior lady and her duty is to bear children for the master.
consort 妃: The primary wife of a prince or the secondary wife of a king or emperor.
daytime hours: Authors of classic Chinese novels often divided a day into 12 time intervals. We convert the 6 daytime intervals (branches) to a.m. and p.m. to simplify the reading:

辰时	7 a.m. to 9 a.m.
巳时	9 a.m. to 11 a.m.
午时	11 a.m. to 1 p.m.
未时	1 p.m. to 3 p.m.
申时	3 p.m. to 5 p.m.
酉时	5 p.m. to 7 p.m.

demon 妖魔: An evil being on Earth different from a devil in the Underworld. A demon consumes humans and is usually evolved from a more primitive evil creature, but can also be a transformation of a former inhabitant of the Sky.
detention center 廂鋪: A building in a village where a suspect is detained overnight before being sent to the town hall.
deva 神: A Taoist deity who may reside on Earth, in the Underworld, or the Sky. He is different from the god of Western religions because he does not possess the power of creation.
devil 鬼: An evil being in the Underworld who tortures the sinners. A victim possessed by a devil requires exorcism to recover. The most well-known devils are Grim Reaper 勾死人, Ox-Head Devil 牛头鬼, and Horse-Face Devil 马面鬼.
Diamond Guard 金刚: One of the 8 guards at the outer and inner gates of Buddha Supreme's Thunderous Monastery.
disciple 徒弟: A Buddhist student.
Double Ninth Festival 重阳节: A festival on the 9th day of the 9th lunar month in which people hike on mountains and drink chrysanthemum wine to ward off danger.

dowry maid 陪房: A maid brought to a mansion by the lady when the lady marries into the mansion.
Dragon Boat Festival 端午节: A festival on the 5th day of the 5th lunar month when people consume glutinous rice dumplings and watch dragon-boat races to commemorate their ancestors' faithfulness to their country.
dragon 龙: A mythical creature that can fly in the sky, swim in the water, and transform itself into a human. The dragon kings of the four oceans are simply referred to as Dragon East, Dragon South, Dragon West, and Dragon North.
Emperor-Deva Jade 玉皇大帝: The deva who oversees all creatures on Earth, in the Sky and Underworld, except Trinity and the enlightened Buddhists not under his jurisdiction.
five elements 五行: Metal, wood, water, fire, and soil.
footman 仆人: A male servant who works under a steward.
friar 行者: A traveling Buddhist monk.
gauze hat 纱帽: A hat worn by an official
glaive 朴刀: A saber attached to a pole. If the blade is wide and heavy, then it is known as a crescent-moon glaive 偃月刀.
goblin 小妖: An evil creature that works for a demon.
governor 督: An official who governs a province.
grand lady 太君: The wife of the grand master of a mansion.
headman 保正: An honorable citizen who helps the mayor maintain law and order in a village or hamlet.
housekeeper 女仆人: A female servant who works under a stewardess.
ingot 元宝: a 50-oz piece of gold or silver.
inspector 刺史/巡按: An official dispatched by the Emperor to assess the performance of local officials.
jail: A building in a town where a suspect is detained for 60 days before sentencing by the shire or prefecture hall.
junior lady 少奶奶: The wife of the junior master.
junior maiden 小姐: The unmarried daughter of the master.
junior master 少爷: The son of the master of a mansion.
King-Deva Hades 阎罗王: The most well-known king-deva of the Ten Underworld King-Devas.
lady: The primary wife 奶奶 of a nobleman, the secondary wife 嫔 of a prince, or the tertiary wife 贵人 of a king.
land deva 土地: The deva in charge of a neighborhood.
Lantern Festival 元宵节: A lantern-filled festival on the 15th night of the first lunar month.
laureate 进士: A savant who has passed the imperial exam.

littérateur 学士: A laureate appointed by the emperor to work in Quill Woods Academy.
Long-River South 江南: The area of southern River-Wake 江苏, southern Safe-Badge 安徽, northern River-West 江西, and northern Bent-River 浙江.
lunar month: A month of the Chinese lunar calendar, which is 3 to 5 weeks behind the Gregorian calendar. To simplify our novels, a phrase such as "the 30th day of the 11th lunar month" is translated as "December 30".
maiden 姑娘: An unmarried daughter of the senior master.
maid 丫头: An unmarried young female servant.
Manchuria 满洲: A region in Northeast Asia. After the Manchurians expelled the Mongolian invaders from their territories, they invaded China and called themselves Jin 金人.
master 爷: The father of the junior masters and junior maidens of a mansion. A Buddhist monk is also addressed as a master.
mayor 知县: An official who governs a town.
Memorial Day 清明节: The 15th day after the spring equinox when people sweep the tombs of their ancestors and fly kites shaped like animals.
Mid-Autumn Festival 中秋节: A festival on the 15th day of the 8th lunar month when people eat mooncakes filled with sweet bean paste to enjoy the full moon.
monastery 寺: A large Buddhist temple.
Mongolia 蒙古: A country in East Asia. After the Mongolians conquered the Huns 匈奴 and the Manchurians 满洲, the merged country was called Liao 辽.
monk 僧: A Buddhist preacher.
mountain deva 山神: The deva in charge of a mountain.
multiverse: A collection of many universes. Buddha Light oversees a western universe while Buddha Medicine oversees an eastern universe. Buddha Supreme is aware of 3,000 multiverses. In *Marsh Warrior Legend*, Just-So-Rash 鲁智深 entered a wormhole and experienced time dilation in another universe.
nighttime hours 更: Authors of classic Chinese novels often divided a day into 10 time intervals. We convert the 5 nighttime intervals (watches) to a.m. and p.m. to simplify the reading.

1st watch	一更	7:12 p.m.
2nd watch	二更	9:36 p.m.
3rd watch	半夜三更	12:00 a.m. midnight
4th watch	四更	2:24 a.m.
5th watch	五更	4:48 a.m.

novice 小沙弥: A Buddhist boy or girl apprentice.
nugget 锭: a 5-oz piece of gold or silver.
piety savant 孝廉: A scholar who obtains the savant title without taking the prefecture exam because his filial piety 孝 and virtue 廉 have impressed the local officials.
prefecture 府: A division of a province.
prefecture 府: A division of a province.
prefect 太守/知府: An official who governs a prefecture.
priest 道士: A preacher of Taoism.
prime minister 尚书: One of the three highest officials who report to the king or emperor. The Minister of Personnel 吏部尚书/太仆, Minister of Revenue 戶部尚书/司徒, Minister of Rites 礼部尚书/太常, Minister of War 兵部尚书/大司马, Minister of Justice 刑部尚书/司寇, and Minister of Works 工部尚书/司空 all report to him.
proctor 僧官: An official monk appointed by the imperial court to disciplines the clergy of a large monastery.
protector 守备: A major general assigned to a garrison to protect the local citizens.
province 省: A principal division of China.
Queen-Mother Deva 王母娘娘: The highest-level female deva in the Sky.
Quill Woods Academy 翰林院: Ancient China's Institute for Advanced Study.
region: An area that consists of one or more provinces.
rocket 火箭炮: A firecracker with a stick attached to its side to create sparks and loud noises when shot into midair. It should not be translated as cannon 大炮 in classic Chinese novels because the cannon was not used until the Ming dynasty.
savant 举人: A scholar who has passed the prefecture exam.
scholar 秀才: A student who has passed the town exam.
secretariat general 中书: One of the three highest officials who report to the king or emperor.
senior lady 太太: The wife of the senior master of a mansion.
senior master 老爷: The father of the masters and maidens of a mansion.
sheriff 州尹: An official who governs a shire.
shire 州: A division of a prefecture. It is equivalent to the county of a Western country.
shrine 祠: A small temple that is usually a room with an altar.
Sky 天: When the word Sky is capitalized, it refers to the 36 levels of the Sky inhabited by devas. This deva Sky is different from

the regular atmospheric sky. It is also different from the heaven 天堂 of Western religions because the privilege of living in the Sky is neither guaranteed nor permanent. Any inhabitant of the Sky who commits sins will be demoted to Earth, as experienced by Porcine 猪八戒 and Sandy 沙僧 in *Journey to the Western Sky*.
social deva 社令: A deva who oversees various societies.
Spring Festival 春节: Also known as Lunar New Year, people celebrate this festival by greeting each other and letting off firecrackers. Two auspicious mythical creatures participate in the celebration in the form of dragon dance and alce dance. By the way, lion dance is a mistranslation of alce dance because the lion is neither mythical nor auspicious.
sprite 夜叉: Also known as Yaksa, it is an ugly spirit who patrols an ocean or river for the dragon king. A nasty woman may also be called a sprite.
square headscarf 方巾: A headscarf worn by a scholar.
steward 管事: A senior servant who works under a butler.
string of coins 串钱: A hundred coins, each with a hole in its center, tied together and worth about 0.04 oz of silver.
town deva 城隍: A deva who oversees the land devas in his town.
Trinity 三清: The three Taoist cardinals who live in Outer Space 太虚, the space beyond the 32 Skies.
Underworld Prison 地狱: The 18 prisons of the Underworld are not translated as hell because unlike in many Western religions, any punishment received there is not eternal. Those who have committed crimes, no matter how serious, will eventually be released and born again in one of the six realms.
valedictorian 状元: A laureate who receives the highest score on the imperial exam.
Valentine's Day 七夕节: The 7th day of the 7th lunar month when people celebrate the one-day reunion of the star-crossed celestial cowboy and seamstress who can cross a temporary celestial bridge created by a flock of magpies.
valet 小厮: A young male servant.

Appendix 1-B. Table of Diminutive Names

Diminutive	Original	Full Name
Chrysie	Autumn Chrysanthemum	
Cutie	Cute Girl	Plum, Cutie
Flutie	Jade Flute	
Golden	Gold Band	Fence, Golden
Goldie	Golden Lotus	Rinse, Goldie
Jadie	Small Jade	
Lassie	Elder Sister	Westgate, Lassie
Lovelie	Love Girl	Red, Lovelie
Moonie	Moon Lady	Call, Moonie
Olie	Oleaceae Girl	Plum, Olie
Orchie	Orchid Fragrance	
Osmie	Osmanthus Girl	Plum, Osmie
Phoenie	Little Phoenix	
Pixel	Picture Boy	
Plumie	Spring Plum	
Scentie	Lovely Scent	Stern, Scentie
Silvie	Silver Girl	Call, Silvie
Snowie	Snow Beauty	Heir, Snowie
Springie	Welcome Spring	
Stitchie	Stitch Spring	
Towie	Marble Tower	Prime, Towie
Vasie	Vase Girl	Plum, Vasie
Xylo	Xylophone Boy	

Appendix 1-C. Table of Full Names

English/Pinyin	Chinese	Role
Aide, Jason Fu Zi-Xin	傅自新	Clerk of Westgate drugstore
Bag, Ms. Bao Shi	包氏	Courtesan
Barrette Yi Zhang-Qing	一丈青	Wife of Lejon
Beam, Regent Liang Zhong-Shu	梁中書	Regent of Famed City
Birch, Aunt Yang Guliang	杨姑娘	Aunt of Salsa Birch
Birch, Jeer Yang Jian	杨戬 提督	Commander
Birch, Salsa Yang Zong-Xi	杨宗锡	Late husband of Towie Prime
Birch, Salvo Yang Zong-Bao	杨宗保	Younger brother of Salsa Birch
Birch, Shane Yang Sheng	杨盛 干办	Staff of Jeer Birch
Birch, Sheen Yang Shi	杨时	Prefect of Capital-East
Bless, Remnant Zhu Ri-Nian	祝日念	4th member of Westgate Club
Bloom, Eunuch Hua	花太监	Uncle of Jesse Bloom
Bloom, Jehan Hua Zi-Hua	花子华	Nephew #4 of Eunuch Bloom
Bloom, Jesse Hua Zi-Xu	花子虛	9th member of Westgate club
Bloom, Jewel Hua Zi-You	花子由	Nephew #1 of Eunuch Bloom
Bloom, Jigar Hua Zi-Guang	花子光	Nephew #3 of EunuchBloom
Boss, Dearie Dong Jiao'er	董娇儿	Songbird
Brawn, Dally Wu Dalang	武大郎	Pancake peddler
Brawn, Eva Wu Ying'er	武迎儿	Daughter of Dally Brawn

Brawn, Sawn Wu Song	武松	Younger brother of Dally Brawn
Bright, Dior Zhuo Diu-Er	卓丢儿	3rd Concubine of Chic Westgate
Bull, Ms. Niu Shi	牛氏	Courtesan
Call, Colonel Wu Qian-Hu	吴千户	Father-in-law of Chic Westgate
Call, Dangler Wu Dian-En	吴典恩	6th member of Westgate Club
Call, Deuce, Mrs. Wu Er Jin Zi	吴二妗子	2nd sister-in-law of Moonie
Call, Deuce Wu Er-Jiu	吴二舅	2nd brother of Moonie
Call, Kyle, Mrs. Wu Da Jin Zi	吴大妗子	1st sister-in-law of Moonie
Call, Kyle Wu Kai	吴铠 大舅	1st brother of Moonie
Call, Moonie Wu Yue-Niang	吴月娘	Wife of Westgate
Call, Silvie Wu Yin'er	吴银儿	Prostitute
Call, Wade Wu Hui	吴惠	Brother of Silvie Call
Cash, Lou Qian Lau	钱劳	Deputy of Clearstream Town
Chessy Qi Tong	棋童	Valet of Westgate
Chrysie Qiu Ju	秋菊	Maid of Goldie
Cloud, Leisure Yun Li-Shou	云离守	7th member of Westgate Club
Cut, Mensa Duan Mian-Sha	段绵纱	Peddler
Deon Dai An	玳安	Valet of Westgate
Emperor Badge Hui Zong	宋徽宗 1082—1135	Emperor 8 of Song dynasty
Fab, Gorge Xia Gong-Ji	夏恭基	Penal officer of Clearstream Town

Fab, Louis Xia Long-Xi	夏龙溪 提刑	Prosecutor
Fame, Holly Hua, He-Lu	华荷禄	Registrar of Clearstream Town
Fence, Golden Han Jin-Chuan	韩金钏	Songbird
Flutie Yu Xiao	玉箫	Maid of Lady Call
Fringe, Sill Zhou Xiu	周秀 守备	Protector
Grace, Elon Yao Er-Lang	姚二郎	Neighbor of Dally Brawn
Grass, Zuke Jiang Zhu-Shan	蒋竹山	Doctor
Greet, Colonel He Qian-Hu	贺千戶	Colonel
Guess, Jibble Bu Zhi-Dao	卜志道	Former member of Westgate Club
Heir, Gotcha Sun Gua-Zui	孙寡嘴	5th member of Westgate Club
Heir, Snowie Sun Xue-Er	孙雪娥	4th spouse of Westgate
Heir, Walter Sun Wai-Tou	孙歪頭	Husband of Aunt Birch
Hence, Chuck Yu Chun	于春	Peddler
High, Royalty Qiao Huang-Qin	乔皇亲	Relative of the emperor
High, Yorky Qiao Yunge	乔郓哥	Lad of Sunvale Town
Jadie Xiao Yu	小玉	Maid of Lady Call
Lebron Lai-Bau	来保	Servant of Westgate
Lejon Lai-Zhao	来昭	Steward of Westgate
Leon Lai An	来安	Valet of Westgate
Leroy Lai-Wang	来旺	Servant of Westgate

Lesing Lai Xing	来兴	Servant of Westgate
Lithe, Ditcher Ben Di Chuan	贲地传	Custodian of Westgate
Mann, Satchel Ding Shuang-Qiao	丁双桥	Silk merchant
Mine, Lady Yu Shi	余氏	Wife of Honcho Pull
Oft, Seizure Chang Shi-Jie	常时节	8th member of Westgate Club
Orchie Lan Xiang	兰香	Maid of Towie
Peon Ping an	平安	Valet of Westgate
Phoenie Xiao Luan	小鸾	Maid of Towie
Pixel Hua Tong	画童	Valet of Westgate
Plum, Banyan Li Bang-Yan	李邦彦	Right Chancellor
Plum, Bawd Li Mama	李妈妈	Mother of Olie Plum
Plum, Cutie Li Jiao Er	李娇儿	2nd spouse of Westgate
Plum, Data Li Da-Tian	李达天	Mayor of Clearstream Town
Plum, Gossip Li Wai Chuan	李外传	Cop of Clearstream Town
Plum, Mick Li Ming	李铭	Minstrel
Plum, Olie Li Gui-Jie	李桂姐	Prostitute
Plum, Osmie Li Gui-Qing	李桂卿	Prostitute
Plum, Quake Li Kui	李逵 黑旋风	Black-Cyclone 22nd Star
Plum, Vasie Li Ping'er	李瓶儿	Wife of Jesse Bloom
Plume, Twain Zhai Qian	翟谦	Butler of Preceptor Weed

Plumie Chun Mei	春梅	Maid of Goldie Rinse
Prime, Towie Meng Yu-Lou	孟玉楼	3rd spouse of Westgate
Pull, Honcho Zhang Dahu	张大戶	Millionaire
Pull, Idle Zhang Xian	张闲	Idler
Pull, Instructor Zhang Tuan-Lian	张团练	Maternal uncle of Jimmy Show
Pull, Salem Zhang Shi-Lian	张世廉	Brother-in-law of Honk Show
Pull, Shunt Zhang Sheng	张胜	Rogue
Pull, Sid Zhang Si	张四	Maternal uncle of Salvo Birch
Quest, Jupe He Jiu	何九	Coroner of Sunvale Town
Rash, Wart Lu Hua	鲁华	Rogue
Red, Hairy Zhu Mao-Tou	朱毛头	Father of Lovelie Red
Red, Lovelie Zhu Ai-Ai	朱爱爱	Prostitute
Red, Marshal Zhu Mian	朱勔 1075—1126	Imperial Marshal
Reed, Mrs. Xue Sao	薛嫂	Florist
Rex, Charles Wang Chao	王潮	Son of Mrs. Rex
Rex, Full Wang Fu	王黼 1079—1126	Minister of War
Rex, Mrs. Wang Po	王婆	Teahouse owner
Rex, Luan Wang Luan	王鸾	Restaurateur
Rex, Pacifier Wang Jao-Xuan	王招宣	Pacifier
Rex, Royalty Wang Huang-Qin	王皇亲	Relative of the emperor

Rinse, Goldie Pan Jinlian	潘金莲	Wife of Dally Brawn
Rinse, Mrs. Pan Mama	潘妈妈	Mother of Goldie Rinse
Rinse, Tailor Pan Cai	潘裁	Father of Goldie Rinse
Script, Mrs. Wen Shao	文嫂	Matchmaker of Show mansion
Show, Honk Chen Hong	陈洪	Father of Jimmy Show
Show, Jimmy Chen Jing-Ji	陈经济	Son-in-law of Westgate
Show, Lady Chen Shi	陈氏	Late wife of Westgate
Show, Venture Chen Wen-Zhao	陈文昭 府尹	Prefect of Eastpeaceshire
Sink, In-law Shen	沈姨夫	Brother-in-law Of Towie
Slay, Hag Liu Po-Zi	刘婆	Witch doctor
Springie Ying Chun	迎春	Maid of Vasie Plum
Stern, Funk Zheng Feng	郑奉	Elder brother of Scentie Stern
Stern, Scentie Zheng Ai-Xiang	郑爱香	Prostitute
Still, Luten Shang Liu-Tang	尚柳塘 推官	Magistrate
Still, Lance Shang Liang-Quan	尚两泉 举人	Savant
Stitchie Xiu Chun	绣春	Junior maid of Vasie
Stroll, Eunuch Xu Gong Gong	徐公公	Landlord of Aunt Birch
Stroll, Sam Xu San	徐三	Peddler
Taffy Tian Fu	天福	Valet of Vasie
Tall, Arn Gao An	高安	Steward of Yo Weed
Tassy	天喜	Valet of

Tian Xi		Jesse Bloom
Thank, Ceder Xie Xi-Da	谢希大	3rd member of Westgate club
Thorn, John Jing Zhong	荆忠 千戶	Colonel
Trot, Mrs. Feng Mama	冯妈妈	Old nanny of Vasie
Tune, Howard Yue He-An	乐和安	Counselor of Clearstream Town
Weed, Jinx Cai Jing	蔡京 1047 - 1126	Preceptor
Weed, Yo Cai You	蔡攸	Son of Jinx Weed
Westgate, Chic Ximen Qing	西门庆	Tycoon
Westgate, Lassie Ximen Da-Jie	西门大姐	Daughter of Chic Westgate
White, Leech Bai Lai- Chuang	白来创	10th member of Westgate Club
White, Quartzie Bai Yulian	白玉莲	Maid of Honcho Pull
Wild, Elder Hu Lao Ren	胡老人	Doctor
Xylo Qin Tong	琴童	Valet of Towie
Yep, Badger Ying Bo-Jue	应伯爵	2nd member of Westgate Club
Yep, Boss Ying Da Ge	应大哥	Elder brother of Badger Yep

Appendix 1-D. The Title of the Novel

The title of this novel, *Plum Blossoms in a Golden Vase* contains the names of the three most seductive female characters. The word *Plum* refers to Plumie Hulk. The word *Golden* refers to Goldie Rinse. The word *Vase* refers to Vasie Plum.

The accurate translation of the word *Plum* for Plumie Hulk's first name is *Prunus salicina*, and the accurate translation of the word *Plum* for Vasie Plum's surname is *Prunus mume.* These two different flowering plants are often translated into the single English word *Plum*, which is quite confusing.

Appendix 1-E. Academia

One thing special about the Chinese feudal system is that students from any family background (noblemen or peasants) can take exams to become government official and make his family prosperous. Students who pass the basic exam are called pre-scholars 童生. The basic exam consists of two parts. Part I is administered by the town and part II is administered by the prefecture. The prefecture has test centers for the pre-scholars to take the exam to become scholars 秀才. The scholars can later become pre-savants 监生 and take a more advanced exam to become savants 举人. The savants who pass the highest-level exams in the capital are called laureates 进士. Unlike other countries that give college diplomas and high school certificates to hundreds of thousands of youths, few youths in feudal China could pass the exams. Firstly, in the agricultural society, only the brilliant young kids can stay at school while the not-so-brilliant ones must work on the farms. Secondly, the exams only take place once or twice every three years. Thirdly, the exams are extremely difficult. There are seven levels of academic achievements:

Pre-scholar	童生	
Scholar	秀才	See Note 1
Pre-savant	监生,贡生,荫生	See Note 2
Savant	举人,孝廉	See Note 3
Pre-laureate	贡士	
Laureate	进士	See Note 4
Littérateur	学士	

Note 1: There are three grades of scholars. A grade-A scholar gets free food (grain) from the government and is therefore eponymously known as a "Granary Scholar 廪生". Any pre-scholar who wants to take the scholar exam must be endorsed by a granary scholar. A grade-B scholar is known as an "Additional Scholar 增生". A grade-C scholar is known as an "Auxiliary Scholar 附生".

Note 2: A pre-savant can be a "Hereditary Pre-savant 荫生" based on hereditary entitlement, or a "Commended Pre-savant 贡生" recommended by local officials or paid by sponsors, or a "Lycée Pre-savant 监生" of National Lycée 国子监.

Note 3: A person can become a savant based on the recommendations of local officials because of his filial piety 孝 and virtue 廉 and he is known as "Piety Savant 孝廉".

Note 4: The laureates consist of three grades 三甲.

1. The grade-A summa cum laude 赐进士及第 consists of the top three laureates, viz. Valedictorian 状元, Salutatorian 榜眼, and Laurelian 探花. The laurelian collects laurels from the imperial garden for the graduation ceremony.
2. The grade-B magna cum laude 赐进士出身 consists of dozens of laureates.
3. The grade-C cum laude 赐同进士出身 consists of dozens of laureates.

A valedictorian who has also obtained the highest score 解元 in his savant exam and the highest score 会元 in his pre-laureate exam is known as a Triple Crown 三元.

Some top laureates who prefer to remain in academia may be appointed littérateurs 学士 by the emperor to continue to study or work at the graduate school. They have the important tasks of translating foreign languages, compiling dictionaries, encyclopedias, anthologies, and history books. There is only one graduate school in feudal China. That institute for advanced studies is known as Quill Woods Academy 翰林院.

Other laureates or savants who prefer to work outside the imperial court may get the following appointments based on their family connections and job openings. The official ranks are listed in descending order, and the mayor at rank 9 is the lowest.

Commissioner 撫臺 of a region **道**
Governor 督 of a province 省
Prefect **太守/知府** of a prefecture 府
Sheriff 州尹 of a shire 州
Warden 郡守 of a ward 郡
Mayor 知县 of a town 县

Appendix 1-F. Surnames

The Chinese *Hundred Family Surnames* contains 444 single-character surnames, but the Pinyin system can transcribe only 135 of them uniquely, while the others all have duplicates. For instance, there are 12 Yu, 11 Ji, 8 Yan, and so on, which can confuse readers where the surname-based clan system is emphasized. The surnames 尤, 何, and 佘 transcribed as You, He, and She respectively in Pinyin look like second-person and third-person pronouns to the English readers. Therefore, we translate single-character surnames to unique single-syllable English words and double-character surnames to unique double-syllable English words thus:

Chinese	Pinyin	Translation	Better Translation
赵	Zhao	Pass	
钱	Qian	Cash	
孙	Sun	Heir	Grandchild
李	Li	Plum	Prunus salicina
周	Zhou	Fringe	Surrounding
吴	Wu	Call	Shout
郑	Zheng	Stern	
王	Wang	Rex	
冯	Feng	Trot	
陈	Chen	Show	
褚	Chu	Rose	Broussonetia
卫	Wei	Fend	
蒋	Jiang	Grass	
沈	Shen	Sink	
韩	Han	Fence	
杨	Yang	Birch	Poplar
朱	Zhu	Red	
秦	Qin	Chin	Transcription
尤	You	Sole	Especially
许	Xu	Let	
何	He	Quest	Question
吕	Lu	Note	Musical note
施	Shi	Grant	
张	Zhang	Pull	
孔	Kong	Pore	
曹	Cao	Sarge	Officer
严	Yan	Strict	
华	Hua	Fame	

金	Jin	Gold	
魏	Wei	Arch	Palace gateway
陶	Tao	Clay	
姜	Jiang	Root	Ginger
戚	Qi	Sad	
谢	Xie	Thank	
邹	Zou	Hay	Hayville
喻	Yu	Tell	
柏	Bo	Shrub	Cypress
水	Shui	Wet	Water
窦	Dou	Hole	
章	Zhang	Part	Chapter
云	Yun	Cloud	
苏	Su	Wake	
潘	Pan	Rinse	
葛	Ge	Bean	
奚	Xi	Yet	
范	Fan	Mould	Model
彭	Peng	Drum	Drumville
郎	Lang	Gent	
鲁	Lu	Rash	
韦	Wei	Hide	Leather
昌	Chang	Good	
马	Ma	Mare	
苗	Miao	Sprout	
凤	Feng	Joy	Phoenix
花	Hua	Bloom	
方	Fang	Square	
俞	Yu	More	
任	Ren	Trust	
袁	Yuan	Robe	
柳	Liu	Branch	Willow
酆	Feng	Ripe	Ripeville
鲍	Bao	Shell	Abalone
史	Shi	Scribe	
唐	Tang	Vain	
费	Fei	Fee	
廉	Lian	Just	Honest
岑	Cen	Steep	
薛	Xue	Reed	
雷	Lei	Thor	Thunder
贺	He	Greet	Congratulate
倪	Ni	Frail	
汤	Tang	Broth	

滕	Teng	Prance	
殷	Yin	Rich	
罗	Luo	Net	
毕	Bi	End	
郝	Hao	Bare	Bareville
邬	Wu	Pitch	Pitch-dark
安	An	Safe	
常	Chang	Oft	
乐	Yue	Tune	Music
于	Yu	Hence	At
时	Shi	Time	
傅	Fu	Aide	
皮	Pi	Skin	
卞	Bian	Haste	
齐	Qi	Flush	Level
康	Kang	Health	
伍	Wu	Cinque	Five in French
余	Yu	Mine	Me
元	Yuan	Head	
卜	Bu	Guess	Fortune telling
顾	Gu	Gaze	
孟	Meng	Prime	First
平	Ping	Flat	
黄	Huang	Blond	Yellow
和	He	Mild	Harmonious
穆	Mu	Truce	Peaceful
萧	Xiao	Mourn	
尹	Yin	Rule	
姚	Yao	Grace	Elegant
邵	Shao	Hail	Hailville
湛	Zhan	Deep	
汪	Wang	Vast	
祁	Qi	Pray	
毛	Mao	Fur	
禹	Yu	Flood	Flood-Control King
狄	Di	Rough	Northern barbarian
米	Mi	Rice	
贝	Bei	Conch	
明	Ming	Light	Bright
臧	Zang	Right	
計	Ji	Plan	
伏	Fu	Crouch	
成	Cheng	Done	
戴	Dai	Wear	

谈	Tan	Talk	
宋	Song	Song	Transcription
茅	Mao	Thatch	
庞	Pang	Hulk	
熊	Xiong	Bear	
纪	Ji	Mark	Record
舒	Shu	Ease	
屈	Qu	Bend	
項	Xiang	Neck	
祝	Zhu	Bless	
董	Dong	Boss	
梁	Liang	Beam	
杜	Du	Halt	
阮	Ruan	Lute	
蓝	Lan	Blue	
闵	Min	Grief	Pity
席	Xi	Mat	
季	Ji	Last	
麻	Ma	Hemp	
強	Qiang	Strong	
贾	Jia	Trade	
路	Lu	Road	
娄	Lou	Dress	
危	Wei	Risk	
江	Jiang	Stream	River
童	Tong	Child	
颜	Yan	Face	
郭	Guo	Wall	
梅	Mei	Prune	Prunus mume
盛	Sheng	Much	Abundant
林	Lin	Woods	
刁	Diao	Sly	
钟	Zhong	Cup	
徐	Xu	Stroll	Slow
邱	Qiu	Mound	
骆	Luo	Roan	White roan
高	Gao	Tall	
夏	Xia	Fab	
蔡	Cai	Weed	
田	Tian	Field	
樊	Fan	Rail	Railing
胡	Hu	Wild	Barbarian
凌	Ling	Pure	
霍	Huo	Brisk	

虞	Yu	Fret	
万	Wan	Chron	Ten thousand
支	Zhi	Pay	
柯	Ke	Hilt	
昝	Zan	Own	Myself
管	Guan	Pipe	
卢	Lu	Grey	Black
莫	Mo	Nope	Don’t
经	Jing	Thru	
房	Fang	Room	
裘	Qiu	Coat	
缪	Miao	Wrap	
干	Gan	Dry	
解	Xie	Loose	
应	Ying	Yep	Response
宗	Zong	Clan	
丁	Ding	Mann	Man
宣	Xuan	Say	Declare
贲	Ben	Lithe	
邓	Deng	Rise	Riseville
郁	Yu	Fine	
单	Shan	Lone	
杭	Hang	Sail	
洪	Hong	Huge	
包	Bao	Bag	
诸	Zhu	Rife	
左	Zuo	Left	
石	Shi	Stone	
崔	Cui	Loft	
吉	Ji	Nice	
钮	Niu	Knob	
龚	Gong	Gift	
程	Cheng	Trip	
嵇	Ji	Check	Inspect
邢	Xing	Shape	
滑	Hua	Slip	
裴	Pei	Gown	
陆	Lu	Land	
荣	Rong	Luxe	
翁	Weng	Aged	Elder
荀	Xun	Plant	
羊	Yang	Goat	
於	Yu	Whencen	
惠	Hui	Kind	Benefit

甄	Zhen	Grade	
麴	Qu	Yeast	
家	Jia	Home	
封	Feng	Seal	
芮	Rui	Small	
羿	Yi	Shoot	Legendary archer
儲	Chu	Save	
靳	Jin	Strap	Horse strap
汲	Ji	Drink	
邴	Bing	Glad	
糜	Mi	Mash	
松	Song	Pine	
井	Jing	Well	
段	Duan	Cut	
富	Fu	Wealth	
巫	Wu	Witch	
乌	Wu	Black	
焦	Jiao	Burn	
巴	Ba	Hope	
弓	Gong	Bow	
牧	Mu	Tend	Shepherd
隗	Wei	Grand	
山	Shan	Hill	
谷	Gu	Vale	
车	Che	Car	
侯	Hou	Earl	Marquis
宓	Mi	Mute	
蓬	Peng	Fluff	
全	Quan	All	
郗	Chi	Rare	Rareville
班	Ban	Class	
仰	Yang	Look	Look up
秋	Qiu	Fall	Autumn
仲	Zhong	Mid	
伊	Yi	Ye	
宫	Gong	Shrine	Palace
宁	Ning	Calm	
仇	Qiu	Foe	
栾	Luan	Ledge	
暴	Bao	Force	Violent
甘	Gan	Sweet	
钭	Dou	Flask	Flagon
厉	Li	Whet	
戎	Ron	Brute	Western Barbarian

祖	Zu	Fore	Forefather
武	Wu	Brawn	
符	Fu	Charm	
刘	Liu	Slay	
景	Jing	View	
詹	Zhan	Chat	
束	Shu	Bind	
龙	Long	Saur	Dragon
叶	Ye	Leaf	
幸	Xing	Luck	
司	Si	Steer	Control
韶	Shao	Fair	Beautiful
郜	Gao	Sue	Sueville
黎	Li	Dark	
蓟	Ji	Bur	Thistle
薄	Bo	Thin	
印	Yin	Print	
宿	Su	Lodge	
白	Bai	White	
怀	Huai	Chest	
蒲	Pu	Palm	Calamus
邰	Tai	Stage	Stageville
從	Cong	Since	
鄂	E	Shock	
索	Suo	Rope	
咸	Xian	Salt	Salty
籍	Ji	List	Register
赖	Lai	Lean	Rely
卓	Zhuo	Bright	
蔺	Lin	Rush	Juncus effusus
屠	Tu	Snuff	Slaughter
蒙	Meng	Cloak	Cover
池	Chi	Pond	
乔	Qiao	High	
阴	Yin	Shade	
郁	Yu	Dense	
胥	Xu	Clerk	
能	Neng	Can	Able
蒼	Cang	Green	Blue
双	Shuang	Dual	
闻	Wen	Hear	
莘	Shen	Long	
党	Dang	Gang	Party
翟	Zhai	Plume	Pheasant

譚	Tan	Speak	
貢	Gong	Gift	
劳	Lao	Toil	
逄	Pang	Pang	Transcription
姬	Ji	Mate	Consort
申	Shen	Speech	Report
扶	Fu	Hold	Help
堵	Du	Stop	
冉	Ran	Drift	
宰	Zai	Reign	
郦	Li	Beau	Beauville
雍	Yong	Blend	Harmonious
郤	Xi	Crack	
璩	Qu	Ring	Jade ring
桑	Sang	Silk	Silkworm's mulberry
桂	Gui	Oz	Osmanthus
濮	Pu	Serf	Serf River
牛	Niu	Bull	
寿	Shou	Life	Lifespan
通	Tong	Same	Common
边	Bian	Edge	
扈	Hu	Pal	Retinue
燕	Yan	Swift	Swallow
冀	Ji	Wish	
郏	Jia	Wedge	Wedgeville
浦	Pu	Shore	
尚	Shang	Still	
农	Nong	Farm	
溫	Wen	Warm	
别	Bie	Next	Other
庄	Zhuang	Ville	
晏	Yan	Late	
柴	Chai	Splint	Firewood
瞿	Qu	Spear	Pole weapon
阎	Yan	Gate	
充	Chong	Fill	
慕	Mu	Zeal	Admire
连	Lian	Join	
茹	Ru	Eat	
習	Xi	Learn	
宦	Huan	Geld	
艾	Ai	Herb	Mugwort
魚	Yu	Fish	
容	Ron	Form	Appearance

向	Xiang	Via	Toward
古	Gu	Old	
易	Yi	Change	
慎	Shen	Care	Careful
戈	Ge	Lance	
廖	Liao	Void	
庾	Yu	Store	Storehouse
终	Zhong	Thus	Final
暨	Ji	Reach	
居	Ju	Live	
衡	Heng	Weigh	
步	Bu	Pace	
都	Du	Whole	
耿	Geng	Shine	
满	Man	Full	
弘	Hong	Big	
匡	Kuang	Scrub	Revise
国	Guo	State	Country
文	Wen	Script	
寇	Kou	Rob	
广	Guang	Wide	
禄	Lu	Worth	Opulence
阙	Que	Hall	Palace hallway
东	Dong	East	
欧	Ou	Hit	
殳	Shu	Knife	Weapon
沃	Wo	Plush	Fertile
利	Li	Sharp	
蔚	Yu	Thick	
越	Yue	Cross	
夔	Kui	Beast	Monster
隆	Long	Lots	
师	Shi	Teach	
鞏	Gong	Firm	
厍	She	Town	
聂	Nie	Hush	Whisper
晁	Chao	Dawn	
勾	Gou	Hook	
敖	Ao	Play	
融	Rong	Melt	
冷	Leng	Cold	
訾	Zi	Smear	Slander
辛	Xin	Sour	Bitter
阚	Kan	Stare	

那	Na	That	
简	Jian	Terse	
饶	Rao	Heaps	Plenty
空	Kong	Zilch	Empty
曾	Zeng	Past	Great-grandparent
毋	Wu	Naught	Don’t
沙	Sha	Sand	
乜	Nie	Squint	
养	Yang	Rear	
鞠	Ju	Raise	
須	Xu	Ought	
丰	Feng	Lush	
巢	Chao	Nest	
关	Guan	Close	
蒯	Kuai	Sedge	
相	Xiang	Lord	
查	Zha	Seek	
后	Hou	Queen	
荊	Jing	Thorn	
红	Hong	Rouge	
游	You	Swim	
竺	Zhu	Zen	Buddhism
权	Quan	Might	Power
逯	Lu	Leave	AWOL
蓋	Ge	Lid	
益	Yi	Earn	
桓	Huan	Tree	Sapindus mukurossi
公	Gong	Duke	
万俟	Moqi	Ever	Forever
司马	Sima	Marshall	Minister of War
上官	Shangguan	Highlord	
欧阳	Ouyang	Solar	
夏侯	Xiahou	Summer	Summer marquis
诸葛	Zhuge	Legume	
闻人	Wenren	Renown	
东方	Dongfang	Eastern	
赫连	Helian	Glitter	
皇甫	Huangfu	Royal	
尉迟	Yuchi	Warlord	
公羊	Gongyang	Billy	Billy goat
澹台	Tantai	Tender	
公冶	Gongye	Foundry	
宗政	Zongzheng	Proper	
濮阳	Puyang	Servesun	

淳于	Chunyu	Lucid	
单于	Chanyu	Hunschief	Huns chief
太叔	Taishu	Grandunc	Granduncle
申屠	Shentu	Butcher	
公孙	Gongsun	Noble	Duke's grandchild
仲孙	Zhongsun	Middle	Middle grandchild
轩辕	Xuanyuan	Chariot	
令狐	Linghu	Vulpine	
钟离	Zhongli	Goblet	
宇文	Yuwen	Culture	
长孙	Zhangsun	Descent	First descendant
慕容	Murong	Marvel	
鲜于	Xianyu	Refresh	
闾丘	Luqiu	Highland	
司徒	Situ	Treasure	Minister of Revenue
司空	Sikong	Labor	Minister of Works
亓官	Qiguan	Major	
司寇	Sikou	Justice	Minister of Justice
仉	Zhang	John	Transcription
督	Du	Run	Supervise
子车	Ziju	Carriage	
颛孙	Zhuansun	Honor	Honorable grand-child
端木	Duanmu	Lumber	
巫马	Wuma	Equine	
公西	Gongxi	Dukewest	
漆雕	Qidiao	Lacquer	
乐正	Yuezheng	Tonal	
壤驷	Rangsi	Stable	
公良	Gongliang	Elder	
拓拔	Tuoba	Expand	
夹谷	Jiagu	Valley	
宰父	Zaifu	Leader	
谷粱	Guliang	Barley	
晋	Jin	Plus	Increase
楚	Chu	Clear	
闫	Yan	Out	Gate
法	Fa	Law	
汝	Ru	Thou	
鄢	Yan	How	Howville
涂	Tu	Path	
钦	Qin	Laud	Admire
段干	Duangan	Cutter	
百里	Baili	Yonder	Hundred miles

东郭	Dongguo	Eastwall	
南门	Nanmen	Southgate	
呼延	Huyan	Holler	
归	Gui	Back	Return
海	Hai	Sea	
羊舌	Yangshe	Goattongue	
微生	Weisheng	Microbe	
岳	Yue	Mount	
帅	Shuai	Chief	
缑	Gou	Cord	
亢	Kang	Proud	
況	Kuang	Too	Furthermore
後	Hou	Hind	Behind
有	You	Have	
琴	Qin	String	String instrument
梁丘	Liangqiu	Beamhill	
左丘	Zuoqiu	Lefthill	
东门	Dongmen	Eastgate	
西门	Ximen	Westgate	
商	Shang	Biz	
牟	Mou	Make	
佘	She	Shea	Transcription
佴	Nai	Help	
伯	Bo	Count	
赏	Shang	Tips	Reward
南宫	Nangong	Palace	South Palace
墨	Mo	Ink	
哈	Ha	Ha	
谯	Qiao	Blame	
笪	Da	Rug	Bamboo mat
年	Nian	Year	
爱	Ai	Love	
阳	Yang	Sun	
佟	Tong	Tong	Transcription
第五	Diwu	Penta	
言	Yan	Word	
福	Fu	Bliss	

Made in the USA
Monee, IL
08 June 2022